ISBN: 9798362493356

Editing and Cover Design by C.L. Book Services; Jordan Loft.

Nothing held back.

CRY ABOUT IT

AN ENEMIES TO LOVERS ROMANCE

MAGGIE GATES

1

VAUGHAN

My coffee tasted like brewed cigarettes and industrial cleaner. Not that the gas station I'd gotten it from had ever seen so much as a wet wipe...

The cup that had kept me awake through the final haul from Little Rock to Maren went cold before I ever crossed the Arkansas-Texas border.

The sleek sedan's leather interior was nearly soundproof. It had cost a pretty penny, but it was worth it to have a shield from sixteen hours of road noise and tractor-trailer horns.

Leaving Chicago and driving through the night to the cow town where I had spent the first eighteen years of my life hadn't been in my plan this week.

Tamara, my assistant, was appalled when I told her to clear my schedule for the next seventy-two hours. Hopefully, that would be all I needed to fix the mess back in Maren.

I dropped one hand from the steering wheel and unbuckled my belt, relieving the pang that resonated from my bloated stomach.

The expired honey bun I pulled from an I-30 rest stop was already screwing with my digestive system. No fucking way was I going to pull over and take a shit in the middle of the night at a run-down truck stop bathroom. I'd have to burn my suit.

Then again, it probably needed to be burned either way. I'd been wearing it since yesterday morning.

When my stepmother got through to my office with news about my old man, I swiped my arm across my desk, shoveled all the necessities into a bag, and grabbed my keys. Tamara ran to my apartment and loaded up a suitcase with half of my closet inside. It was overkill, but it was her job to make sure I was prepared.

That was fourteen hours ago.

I had been planning on burning the midnight oil at the office. I was in the process of onboarding a slew of new investment clients. All that changed when Faith called and told Tamara that my dad had fallen from a combine and broken his back.

The oldies station that had carried me through most of the drive crackled as I edged the outskirts of Smith County.

Two hours to go.

Thoughts of Maren, Texas echoed through my mind. Latent memories of my blue and gold football jersey. The way rays of sunlight danced through the mist as it crept over the horizon. The way soil caked my boots after a walk through the fields to get out of the chaos in the big house. The smell of diesel, the growl of farm equipment, and the prattle of livestock.

Those were the good memories I held on to when the miles between Chicago and Maren seemed to be in the millions.

Luckily, I didn't have to replay them often. I was happy

with my life. Happy with what I had made of it, anyway. At the ripe old age of eighteen, I left home and never looked back. I loved my father and, in my own way, the family he had tacked on to the two of us. He never expected me to stay, and he told me as much at my high school graduation.

I guess it could have been worse.

Without warning, an RV hauling a coupe crossed the middle line. Its obnoxious halogen headlights stared into my soul.

"Oh, shit." I jerked the steering wheel, and slammed my palm into the horn. "Wake up or get off the road, jackass!"

I didn't feel like becoming a cross on the side of the highway just because the driver didn't have the sense to call it a night. Then again, I probably should have grabbed at least a cat nap between Illinois and Texas.

I could push through two more hours of mind-numbing radio drivel.

Then what? You get to see your father in a hospital bed. You get to fix the dumpster fire they should have told you about when the match was struck—not when the blaze was already out of control.

I had an inkling that things weren't good the last time my father called. I remember the sound of his worn voice as he asked me to pray for the farm. But he didn't tell me it was *this bad.*

I wasn't a praying man. To be honest, neither was my father. But it didn't matter. Growing up, we bowed our heads at each meal and begged for rain.

That was the one reliable thing in my life—a prayer for rain.

It was the constant when my father, my mother, and I would gather around the kitchen table for dinner. It was the constant when my mom got sick—my father begging for rain to keep the crops alive.

Crops made money. Money kept food on the table. It paid the medical bills when Mom, in her twenties, went to the hospital and didn't come home.

No amount of praying could have saved her.

We still prayed for rain even when I didn't want to. Even when it was just my dad and me at the table.

When my dad met Ms. Faith, she prayed too. I think her prayers were stronger than ours because we got rain—great Texas gully washers that drenched the fields.

The prayers continued when Dad got remarried. Ryman, Cash, and baby Bristol came along, and they were taught to pray, too.

But I stopped.

Prayers didn't bring the rain. Preparing the fields did.

The sun was beginning to peek over the skyline as I passed a sign for a beaver-themed gas station that was as big as a superstore. I glanced at the gas tank and decided to press on.

The sooner I got to the farm, the sooner I could get back to my life.

Maren, Texas hadn't changed much in the eighteen years I had been gone. At this point in my life, I had lived away from my hometown as long as I had lived in it.

The old Texaco station, now called Jay's Gas-N-Go, had a sign flaunting two-for-one breakfast tacos. The *Welcome to Maren* sign still bragged about the high school football team being state champions back in 2003.

And the roads still sucked.

I swerved around a pothole large enough to swallow my BMW and hit the gas, leaving the single stoplight and water tower in the dust.

The Thompson Farm was situated on the western side of the outskirts of Maren. Fifteen minutes separated the town from over six hundred acres of grain sorghum, soybeans, wheat, and winter grasses for cattle feed. Silos rose in the distance, unencumbered by the flat landscape as they sliced into the sky.

A shuddering *kerthunk* beneath my car shocked me out of the daze.

My body went numb, and my heart leaped into my throat. I had zoned out and couldn't remember the last quarter mile.

I yanked on the steering wheel, trying to get away from whatever was disemboweling my vehicle. With each metal-on-metal *thunk* I cursed the airlines that were grounded because of storms in the Midwest.

I should have waited for a fucking flight.

My tire caught the soft shoulder of the road, and I nearly vomited my heart straight out of my mouth. The car tipped to the side and landed in the ditch with a sickening crunch.

I lurched forward and flopped toward the steering column, but I managed to catch myself before I smacked my head against the wheel.

To add insult to injury, the check engine light had the audacity to ding.

Motherfucker.

The sputter of a truck engine well past its prime clamored through the pre-dawn air. I could hear the screech of old brakes from a quarter of a mile away.

Spewing a chorus composed of every profanity I could think of, I shucked off my suit jacket and opened the door. The grassy ditch was damp with dew and covered the bottom of my Oxfords with mud. *At least I hoped it was mud...*

The pickup that sounded like a rolling bucket of bolts drew closer, headlights flashing through the mist.

It had been a minute since I'd popped the hood on a vehicle, but it couldn't have changed that much in eighteen years. Right?

Wrong.

The minute I punched the button and lifted the hood, I knew I was fucked. The luxury car that had carried me a thousand miles south wasn't the standard collection of parts my old man had taught me to fix up. It was all computers and European engineering.

It was like teaching a child the alphabet and then handing them a book in Mandarin.

The racket from the beater truck grew before coming to a screeching halt on the side of the road. The driver-side window lowered in jerky fashion at the behest of a hand crank inside.

A pretty brunette poked her head out. "Need a hand? I've got a chain in the back. I can get you outta that ditch in a jiff."

I opened my mouth to respond, but she was already out of the truck, dropping the tailgate. The beams from my headlights illuminated her backside. Her legs, tanned dark from hours in the sun, were accented with the smallest pair of denim shorts I'd ever seen. The hem of her tank top rode up, exposing a swatch of skin around her middle that was the same color as her legs.

Her skimpy outfit probably wasn't purposely risqué— though it did have my cock thickening in my slacks. Summer in Texas demanded a less-is-more approach. The sun wasn't even up yet, and I was already sweating through my shirt.

"New in town or just passing through?" she asked as she

tossed a tow chain over her shoulder and turned, pointing to the open hood. "I can take a look and see what the damage is. I'm pretty good with—"

I put my hand out to stop her. "I appreciate it, but no thanks. I'll call for a tow."

"I know what I'm doing." The woman slapped her hand on the side of the rusted pick-up. "I've kept this ol' girl running for over a decade. When I got her, she was already older than I was."

The beater truck looked like she had pulled it out of the depths of a landfill.

"No thanks," I hissed through gritted teeth.

She made a move for the engine block. "Hank won't be on the road with his rig for at least another hour. I'd hate for you to be stuck out here in the heat."

I pinched the bridge of my nose as a migraine formed behind my skull, courtesy of sleep deprivation and this nuisance. I tamped down the Chicagoan in me, gritting my teeth instead of biting her head off. "I do not need nor want your help. Kindly, move along."

"Seriously?" Her pale pink lips pursed in a thin line. "I'm trying to do you a solid. I'll just be a sec. Might not be that—"

"This is a luxury vehicle," I snapped. "It needs to go to a dealership where someone trained to do more than duct tape a muffler back on can repair it."

Her eyes hit me like a blue spark of electricity. They were the same color as the pale-washed denim covering her ass. Long waves of hair brushed the small of her back. It was only a few shades darker than her skin.

She was all warm tones except for those eyes.

Blue was a rare color in the plant and animal kingdom.

It was usually a way for predators to be warned that the pretty shade was chock full of toxins and poison.

Beautiful, but deadly.

A scar ran from her hairline, slicing across her temple toward her eye. The silvery skin slashed through her eyebrow. It made her slightly imperfect, turning an already exquisite face into something that was endlessly fascinating and utterly breathtaking.

Sweet as sugar and as condescending as an old biddy in the front pew at a church, she said, "I'm not the one who landed that fancy piece of shit in a ditch with its tail in the air like a whore on her hands and knees."

I snapped. "Seriously, lady? I've had a shitty night, and I don't need some GED-wielding country bumpkin fucking up my car any more than it already has been. So, why don't you just move along and go do whatever you were on your way to do?"

She stood stock-still for a moment, taking me in. It was fucking unnerving, is what it was—like she was an executioner about to decide my fate.

"Closest dealership is two hours away in Austin. Or Hank can take it a mile down the road to Willard's. Make sure you have them check your undercarriage," she said flatly as every hint of friendliness leached from her tone.

Images of prostate exams flashed in my delirious mind.

I slammed the hood shut. "I will have him do no such thing."

She didn't laugh. Just turned and tossed the heavy chain back in the bed of her truck and slammed the tailgate. "The undercarriage of your *car*." She pointed a few feet down the road. "You hit an armadillo. It's like running over a cannonball."

I opened my mouth, but she cut me off.

"But like you said, you don't need advice from a—how did you put it?" She popped her hand up on her hip. "A 'GED-wielding country bumpkin?'" She flashed a pageant queen smile—nauseatingly cloying and dripping in venom. "You're not from around here, are you?"

"Drove in from Chicago, and I'm running on a serious sleep deficit. Now, feel free to be on your way. I don't need your intrusive hospitality."

Her sweet-as-sugar tone turned to salt. "I'll do you a solid and let Hank know you need a tow. What's your name?"

If she could get me in with the tow truck driver without me having to talk to him while he—presumably—spat dip into an empty soda bottle, I'd take it.

"Vaughan," I said, cuffing the sleeves of my dress shirt to get a little more air to my skin. The heat was stifling, and the sun wasn't even up yet. "Vaughan Thompson."

For a split second, her eyes went wide. She probably knew my last name because of the farm. The surprise washed away from her features, replaced by a wicked grin.

"Well, bless your heart. I'll let him know right where to find you."

And that was the moment I knew that I had really fucked up.

2

JOELLE

"Dude, seriously?" I rolled over and chucked a pillow at my bedmate. "Your breath reeks."

Bean lifted an eyebrow and let out a blustering huff.

I choked on the cloud of canine morning breath and threw back the covers. That pissed him off. Bean was nothing if not a cover hog.

A warbled tone blared from the alarm clock perched on a stack of worn paperbacks that served as my nightstand. It swayed and teetered precariously as I smacked the snooze button.

"Hate to break it to you, big man, but I don't think these treats are doing a damn thing for you." I grabbed his bag of overpriced dog biscuits that claimed to eradicate bad breath. *Crock of shit.*

But they made my man happy.

Bean's stubby tail thumped on the wood floor of the cabin. I tossed a treat in the air and watched as he snarfed it down in one swallow.

"Wanna ride into town with me?" I asked as I measured out a scoop of kibble and dropped it into Bean's dish.

He huffed and retreated to the bed while I filled his water dish.

"You gonna go to work today?" I asked, annoyed at how much of a leech my dog was. *Lazy ass.*

I washed my hands and rummaged through the pile of clothes I really needed to get around to folding. The mountain of clean but unfolded clothes had been there for damn near six months. Another week in the pile wouldn't hurt.

When I looked back over my shoulder, Bean was almost back to dreamland. "At least put your work clothes on."

Bean let out a low whine as he lifted his muscular frame off my bed and trotted over to his doggie bed. With the gentleness of a baby bunny, he trapped a bow tie in his mouth and brought it to me.

"Feeling purple today, huh?" I yanked open the velcro closure on the band of the eggplant-colored paisley bow tie and fastened it around his massive neck. I scratched behind his ear and kissed his silver suede snout. "Stay excellent. I'll be back in a few. Do your business and be ready to leave for work by the time I get back. Getting out of the house will make you feel better."

Bean yelped and pointed his nose toward the dish of dry kibble, then looked longingly at the door.

"Fine," I huffed as I grabbed my boots, tipping them upside down to make sure no tarantulas or scorpions had made my shoes their home for the night. "I'll grab you breakfast, too." I gave the boots an extra thorough shake before sliding my socked feet in them.

Bean found his stuffed armadillo wrapped in the sheets and brought it between his paws.

"Spoiled brat," I muttered as I snatched my keys and headed out to the truck.

The farm was quiet. It always was at this hour. Dim lights glowed in the distance as the big house slowly came to life. Ms. Faith had probably gotten up an hour ago to fix breakfast to fuel all those Thompsons.

I jammed the key into the ignition. The engine sputtered for a moment before rolling to life. My cash bag, full from riding at the saloon last night, was wedged under the visor. No one dared trespass onto the farm. If, by some act of God, they had the ovaries to do so, everyone knew better than to mess with me.

I made the ride into town in silence, letting the rumble of the tires on cracked asphalt wake me up. I loved driving through town before the rest of Maren woke up. It was like surveying my kingdom.

My single stoplight and a water tower kingdom.

A dark ball scampered across the blacktop, hauling ass down the road. I swerved into the empty left lane. I had no desire to put new tires on my truck if I hit that nine-banded menace.

The armadillo disappeared into the distance, but I slowed up to give him a little more space. Breakfast tacos at Jay's would still be there, even if I was a few minutes later than usual.

Jay wouldn't dare run out before I swung by.

Oncoming headlights caught my attention. The only people out this early were me, Hank, Jay, and a few of the farmhands who worked the land surrounding the town. All of us drove vehicles that were bigger than the tin can rolling toward me.

I watched the shadow of the armadillo in the beams of

headlights. The driver hit it head-on. The animal's plated shell beat the undercarriage of the car to death. The car swerved, caught the shoulder, and tipped headfirst into the ditch.

"Well, shit." I slammed my foot onto the gas. The engine kicked, sending me down the road. I didn't bother with my emergency flashers as I skidded to a stop.

The driver was out of the car and seemed fine—if fine meant sexy as hell.

"Need a hand?" I called out as I rolled the window down, backing in so that I could haul him out of his rather large situation. "I've got a chain in the back. I can get you out of that ditch in a jiff."

I jumped out and dropped the tailgate, stealing a moment to let out a breath.

Holy shit.

He was hot. Not just good-looking and muscular—he was refined. I rarely found city boys attractive, but this one was a different breed. Miles tall, with dark hair, sharp brown eyes, and a jawline that could cut steel. His dress shirt was still tucked into his pants, highlighting the contrast between his broad shoulders and narrow waist. The only thing that marred his otherwise flawless appearance were the bags under his eyes.

"New in town or just passing through?" I asked as I tossed a tow chain over my shoulder and turned. "I can take a look and see what the damage is. I'm pretty good with—"

He held his palm up, as if I was a dog he could command to sit and stay.

"I appreciate it, but no thanks. I'll call for a tow."

"I know what I'm doing," I said, barely managing to tamp down the eye roll I so badly wanted to give him. "I've kept this ol' girl running for over a decade, and when I got her she was already older than I was."

He waved his hand dismissively. "No thanks."

Asshole, I thought to myself. "Hank won't be on the road with his rig for at least another hour. I'd hate for you to be stuck out here in the heat."

He pinched the bridge of his nose. "I do not need nor want your help. Kindly, move along."

"Seriously?" I wanted to clock that man-sized queef in the head and knock some sense into him. "I'm trying to do you a solid. I'll just be a sec. Might not be that—"

"This is a luxury vehicle," he snapped. "It needs to go to a dealership where someone trained to do more than duct tape a muffler back on can repair it."

A slow, nefarious smile drew across my lips. Dripping with placating sarcasm, I said, "I'm not the one who landed that fancy piece of shit in a ditch with its tail in the air like a whore on her hands and knees."

"Seriously, lady?" he snapped. "I've had a shitty night, and I don't need some GED-wielding country bumpkin fucking up my car any more than it already has been. So, why don't you just move along and go do whatever you were on your way to do?"

This bag of ass had some nerve.

I steeled my expression and barely withheld a 'bless your heart.' "Closest dealership is two hours away in Austin. Or Hank can take it a mile down the road to Willard's. Make sure you have them check your undercarriage," I said without a grain of amusement.

He looked a little green around the gills. "I will have him do no such thing."

I tossed the tow chain back into the truck bed. "The undercarriage of your *car*." I pointed down the road and narrowly avoided punching him square in the face. "You hit an armadillo. It's like running over a cannonball." A huff of air escaped my flaring nostrils like a pissed-off bull ready to storm out of a chute. "But like you said, you don't need advice from a—how did you put it?" I cocked my hip and looked him up and down. "A *GED-wielding country bumpkin?*"

The way he swallowed nervously gave me the serotonin boost I needed.

"You're not from around here, are you?"

"Drove in from Chicago, and I'm running on a serious sleep deficit," he said. "Now, feel free to be on your way. I don't need your intrusive hospitality."

Okay, so that was how it was going to be.

I tried. I really did. If he had only crossed me once, I would've given him a pass because he was a tired out-of-towner. But he crossed me twice. I wanted to nail his ass with a railroad spike and wait for a train to squish him like an ant on a sidewalk.

He was going to rue the day he decided to run his fucking mouth around me.

"I'll do you a solid and let Hank know you need a tow. What's your name?"

"Vaughan," he said, cuffing the sleeves of his dress shirt. "Vaughan Thompson."

I was too enamored by his corded forearms that I almost missed his name. My eyes widened.

The surprise quickly washed away, and I grinned. *So, this was the long-lost Thompson brother.*

"Well, bless your heart," I said with a barely disguised laugh. "I'll let him know right where to find you."

The sheer horror in his eyes as I hopped back in my truck was fucking delightful.

I left him and his expensive pile of mangled metal in the ditch and didn't feel the least bit bad about it. I knew his daddy, and I knew he raised the other Thompson boys to behave better than that. Especially to a lady.

I didn't act like one, so I wasn't sure if I counted in that demographic or not. But he didn't know that.

Still, it was never too late to teach an old dog some new tricks. Or at least the consequences of being a rude motherfucker.

I pulled under the buzzing fluorescent lights of Jay's Gas-N-Go and cut the engine. The bells on the door chimed as I strolled in. The gurgle of warm coffee, the sizzle of bacon on the flat top, and hearty laughter greeted me.

"Mornin,' JoJo," Jay called from behind the counter where he shimmied between scrambling eggs, flipping pancakes, crispifying bacon, and mixing ingredients for a fresh batch of pico de gallo. "You want your usual?"

"Two for me, one for Bean," I hollered and made a beeline for the coffee machine.

"You got it, sweetheart," he said as he swung his ball cap backward and threw more fixings on the grill.

Hank Jackson stood by the percolator, stirring a cavity's worth of sugar into his coffee. "Morning, JoJo."

"Morning," I said as a couple of old-timers sauntered in and dropped their breakfast orders off with Jay. "Did you see the BMW on the side of the road on your way in?"

Hank snickered. "No. But I have a feeling you did if you're telling me about it."

"Well," I said, carefully circumventing the driver's name. I didn't want Hank to pity Vaughan Thompson because of what happened to his daddy. "The driver hit an armadillo and landed in the ditch. I stopped to help, and he made it known that he needs a bit of an attitude adjustment."

Hank's wry chuckle rumbled across the shoebox gas station. "So, you're saying I should take my time going to pull him out?"

I patted the front of his shirt. "You're gettin' up there in age. Don't stress yourself out today. Take your time, you know? City folks are in too much of a hurry these days."

He grinned. "Want me to call Willard's and have him give the newcomer the royal treatment?"

I dumped an acceptable gallon of coffee into the largest cup Jay had and slammed a lid on it. "Oh, I wouldn't want to put you out."

Hank snickered beneath his gray handlebar mustache. "That interloper must have really pissed in your sweet tea."

"You know me," I said as I snagged the bag of breakfast tacos from Jay and settled my tab for the food, coffee, and the mountain of ice I was going to grab for my cooler on my way out. "I'm just out here protecting the Maren way of life. Do unto others—"

"Until they piss you off. Then match that energy and teach the son'a'bitch a lesson," Jay finished for me.

I noted his knowledge of my personal life motto with a finger gun. "And this is why I love y'all."

Hank snickered. "You don't love us. You just know er'body around these parts fears you."

People fear what can't be killed.

"You flying today?" Jay asked as he counted out my change.

I nodded. "The Thompsons need a load of fertilizer dropped on the milo fields."

Jay handed me a second grease-soaked to-go bag. "Then take another. The brisket was lookin' real sexy when I pulled it from the smoker this morning. Thick bark, a clean smoke ring, and pink and juicy as a desperate pussy. Can't have you covering six hundred acres on an empty stomach."

Six hundred and forty, but who was counting? I took the bag and gave him a grateful nod. "Much appreciated."

"Don't thank me," Jay clipped. "Good cows make good brisket. Good cows need good feed. Good feed comes from good farming. You're doing a public service, JoJo."

I offered Jay and Hank a salute before heading out the door to fill the cooler in the back of my truck with ice.

It was the way of life in Maren. Everyone did their part to keep food on store shelves and on plates. Dry seasons were a death sentence. Rainy seasons were equally hellish if it was too much. Hurricanes destroyed crops or forced farmers to harvest early.

And I didn't even want to think about developers.

They were a pestilence of the worst kind.

As the thought crossed my mind, I spotted a mangled yard sign poking out of a trash can beside the gas pumps. It was an anti-Vulkon sign that read *Save Our Farms*. There was a circle with a slash through it printed over the word *quarry*.

I grabbed it out of the trash can and flattened it before shoving it back in the grass on the side of the road.

I inhaled one of the breakfast tacos that was filled with fluffy scrambled eggs, chorizo, guacamole, pico de gallo, and a sprinkle of cotija. I'd give Bean his, then throw the other two in my insulated bag for later. The brisket taco had 'lunch' written all over it.

By the time I returned to the cabin, the Thompson boys were out in full force. Even Bristol was tromping around in the dirt, loading up an ATV for a day in the fields.

I honked the horn as my old truck bumped and bobbled over the divots in the dirt. I cranked down the window, stuck my head out, and wolf-whistled at Bristol. "Hey, babe!"

Bristol's dark hair whipped around, and she grinned. "Morning, JoJo!"

Cash Thompson, Bristol's older brother, was standing beside her, loading up bags of seed. They were probably planting the tilled fields on the far side of the property today. Once they got the seed in, I'd fly over with my Ag Cat, and make that dirt the most fertile soil in all of Texas.

"I thought you came by to tell me you're finally gonna marry me," Cash shouted.

"Keep dreaming, hot stuff!" I hollered with a cackle as I lumbered back toward my cabin.

Cash, still baby-faced at twenty-four, loved when I ribbed him about taking me out on a date. We could joke about it because I was too old for him and everyone knew I didn't date.

Didn't want to. Didn't have time to. Didn't need to.

Bean waited for me at the cabin door when I pulled up. I skipped up the three creaky stairs to the wood-slat porch and unwrapped his breakfast.

"Good boy," I cooed and scratched behind his good ear while he chowed.

When he finished, Bean grabbed his stuffed armadillo and lumbered over, passing me in the doorway and wandering out to the truck.

I quickly used the bathroom and packed my plane bag. Stopping to help that jackass left me pressed for time. I needed to get in the air.

I smiled at the thought of him stranded on the side of the road in the blazing sun. By the time he realized his tow wasn't coming anytime soon, word would have spread across town that Mareners weren't supposed to help him.

Hopefully, by then, his family would be too far out in the fields for any cell reception. A nice ten-mile walk to the farm would give him the necessary time to reflect on his horrible personality.

The grin stayed on my face all the way to the hangar that housed my sunshine yellow crop-dusting plane.

Just call me Karma, Vaughan Thompson. Because I can be a real bitch.

3

VAUGHAN

*F*uck *that bitch. And fuck her stupid truck. And fuck her for distracting me from the evil lurking behind that breathtaking face and her tight little ass.*

Actually, that last one isn't a bad idea.

The thought of punishing her for the tow truck stunt by bending her over and—

Shit. My cock strained against the front of my sweat-soaked slacks. I slowed my steps and swiped at my forehead.

One would think that walking ten miles in hundred-degree heat would have restricted the blood flow to my dick. Apparently, that wasn't the case. Delirium was the only explanation as to why I was getting a fucking hard-on as I passed through the front gate. The old metal sign that read *Thompson Family Farm* still hung between thick log posts.

I was drenched. My phone probably needed to go into a bag of rice from all the sweat surrounding it. Hell, I'd probably need to double up on meals to put back on the weight I had sweated off.

It wasn't just the tow truck not showing up for six hours. It was that the fucking gas station had a closed sign hanging from it in the middle of the fucking day. It was the fact that no one in my family was answering their goddamn phones.

I guess I understood that Cash and Ryman wouldn't be too keen on taking my calls. I barely spoke to them.

But I at least expected Bristol or Ms. Faith to pick up. My stepmom was the one who had called and told me to come down to this hellhole. Then again, Ms. Faith was probably at the hospital with my dad, so I couldn't really blame her for being otherwise occupied. But I could blame the bitch who turned an entire town against me.

So help me, if I ever see that woman again, I'll—

The rumble of a utility vehicle ripped across the plain. "Vaughan?" a feminine voice shouted.

My head whipped around like a porcelain doll in need of an exorcism. "Bristol?"

My half-sister's eyes were wide as she slowed the Gator to a stop. "Holy shit. What happened to you?"

I stopped stumbling like a drunk and looked down at my dirt-caked dress shoes. They were Italian leather—or at least they used to be. Now they were ninety percent clay, cow shit, and road dust.

The edges of my pant legs were frayed and torn. I had stripped out of my suit jacket and dress shirt, leaving me in my white undershirt, stained yellow with sweat. I could barely see through the salty sting dripping from my brow. My hair was a wet blanket plastered to my scalp.

"Oh, God..." Bristol wrinkled her nose and reared back. "You smell ... *ripe*."

I needed to keep walking, or I'd drop dead on the dirt driveway. Sighing, I said, "I'd give you a hug, but—"

Bristol laughed. "Don't pretend like you were ever a hugger." She hooked her thumb over her shoulder, pointing to the back. "Come on. Get in."

"I can't sit up front with you?" It took a mountain of effort to get my feet moving again. Slowly, I loped to the back of the UTV.

She snickered. "Fuck no. I need your smelly ass downwind."

The breeze whipping around me as Bristol gunned it toward the big house felt like heaven. After being awake for almost forty-eight hours and unintentionally walking a near half-marathon, I was dead on my feet.

But I still had work to do.

The faster I did it, the faster I could hop on a plane back to Chicago. After the day I'd had, I didn't give two shits about my car. They could scrap it for all I cared. All I wanted was to fix whatever mess the farm was in and get out of this fucking town.

I hopped off the back of the Gator and lumbered toward the front door of the big house. The solid cedar posts that bracketed sections of the wraparound porch still looked the same. The old rocking chairs that had been there for at least thirty years were still the same, though they now sported all-weather pillows in a crisp apple red. An old church pew had been added to one side. It was bracketed by lush ferns. Just above it was the five-pointed metal star. They were all over the property—a sign of good luck for farmers.

"Ay!" Bristol shouted from where she parked the ATV. "Don't you even think about setting foot in the house in your state. Momma will tan your hide."

I looked down at the putrid used-to-be-suit clinging to my body. *Crap.*

"There's a hose hooked up to the spigot." Bristol pointed to the outbuilding closest to the house. It was where Ms. Faith kept her gardening tools. "Clean yourself off first." Her sharp tongue turned soft. "Daddy's gonna be alright.

Momma called not too long ago. He came out of surgery just fine. We're all heading over there to see him when the boys get in from the fields. I just came up to start heating up dinner. It's Momma's shepherd's pie."

I held my tongue, resisting the urge to remind Bristol that her mother wasn't mine. But Ms. Faith had always been good to me, so I kept my mouth shut.

When I didn't say anything, Bristol turned and went into the big house, careful to take her boots off before stepping through the door.

I dragged my tired ass to the gardening shed and found the hose coiled on the side. The first splash of water was boiling hot. I yelped and turned the spray on to the begonias Ms. Faith had planted on the perimeter, waiting for the hose to cool off.

I kicked off my shoes and socks and stripped out of my undershirt. No one was around, so I unfastened my belt and dropped my slacks. I'd need a proper shower with a bulk bottle of soap, pronto. But this would stave off the stank.

I picked up the hose and held it over my head, letting the water rain down on my shoulders and chest.

Fuck, that was good. Sweet water, laced with the tang of vinyl and rubber from the hose, ran in rivulets down my skin. The grime pooled in the grass around my feet. My boxer briefs would need to be burned.

Hopefully, Ryman would be cool with me stealing a set of clothes. No amount of dry cleaning could make these functional again.

That reminded me...

My hastily packed suitcase was still in the trunk of my wrecked car. *Fucking armadillos.* I'd have to run into town tomorrow and get it from Willard's. Chances were, the mechanic was in the same place it had been since I was knee-high to a grasshopper.

Great. I hadn't even been here for twenty-four hours and I was already reverting back to saying shit like that.

Walking through Maren was a mind-fuck. On the one hand, it was exactly as it had been when I left eighteen years ago. On the other hand, it was completely different. There were new businesses, though they looked old from the lack of health inspections and general maintenance. The original businesses looked even worse.

Maren was the size of a postage stamp. If I could steal a farm truck tomorrow, I'd find a proper mechanic for my car in the time it took me to say, "Fuck that petty bitch."

A low rumble echoed across the plains. Probably Ryman or Cash, or one of the other farm hands coming up to the house. I cut the water and grabbed my clothes. I could sneak in the back and jog up the stairs, evading Bristol in the kitchen.

I righted myself, tucked my clothes under my arm, and wrapped the hose back around the hook. The low shrubs shook, and I felt vibrations pulsing through the ground. I had been through a few earthquakes during my years living in Texas, but they never felt like this. I looked around, waiting to see Bristol pop her head out the door to see what the hell was going on.

But she never did. She stood at the kitchen window, busy at the sink, working without a care in the world.

The rolling thunder came closer, but I didn't see anything. Even the horses in the stable seemed unbothered, and they were temperamental princesses.

Without warning, a blast of power whooshed overhead. A streak of yellow flashed above me like lightning. A tornado of dust kicked up from the ground, coating my freshly washed body with an even layer of dirt.

"Fuck!" I bellowed as I pitched my clothes at the side of the shed. All I wanted was a fucking break! Was that too damn much to ask?

The wings of the crop-dusting plane rocked back and forth as if the pilot was waving.

Fuck. That. Shit. I lifted my hand and flipped the bird to the pilot. Petty, sure. But after the last forty-eight hours, I felt absolved of any sins I committed in the name of petty.

I stomped up the porch steps, not giving two shits about tracking filth through the house. I'd pay for a cleaning crew to pick up each individual speck of dirt off the floors until they were sparkling.

I slipped into the hallway bathroom that Ryman and Cash shared. I was in a foul mood, but I didn't want to sully Bristol's bathroom or the one connected to my dad and Faith's room.

The water was ice cold as I stood under the showerhead and washed dirt off for the second time today. Muddy puddles pooled in the tub, slowly turning from murky brown to dingy beige. When the water ran clear, I cut the shower off. I dried my body and ran my hand through my hair. Instead of raiding one of the boys' drawers, I wrapped the towel around my waist and slipped into my room—the one that looked like a time capsule.

My high school football trophies were stacked on the shelf above the bed. Picture frames filled with memories of my childhood cluttered the top of the dresser. The bedspread was neatly made.

Ms. Faith had probably washed it and put fresh sheets on it. Something about that tugged at my heart, but I was too tired to give the notion any consideration.

I opened the dresser and found a small stack of undershirts and a pair of jeans. I peeked at the tag. They were a little small, but they'd do until tomorrow. If my memory served, I had been about that size in my college years.

I had put on a little bulk after hitting thirty. I chalked that up to laying off the ramen noodles and leaning into my protein shake and gym routine. I cooked a little, but didn't have time to make it a habit. So, I paid people to cook for me.

I didn't indulge much. Most of my colleagues paid out the nose for country club memberships and drivers on call. I didn't give a shit about playing overpriced golf or having someone chauffeur me around. I preferred to keep my wealth liquid or in aggressive investments.

That approach had paid off.

I squeezed into a pair of jeans and found a cotton button-up to throw over an undershirt. The mirror in front of me was a dirty liar. The boy I used to be stared back at me.

"Vaughan?" Bristol called as she stomped up the stairs.

I sat on the edge of the bed and pulled on a pair of socks. If I needed to leave the house, I could borrow a pair of my dad's boots. We wore the same size, and it wasn't like he'd be needing them anytime soon.

"In here."

She poked her head in and, for the first time since I had gotten back, I took her in.

Bristol wasn't the kid she had been the last time I visited. She looked more like a woman now. I could still remember the day she was born. My dad and Faith hadn't bothered with finding out the gender—convinced that it was yet another Thompson boy.

But man, did Bristol surprise us all. After my dad remarried and my half-brothers were born, I kept a cautious distance to Faith and her children. I had vivid memories of my mom. I was young when she died, but I was old enough to miss her. I remembered how good she was with me and my dad. How much she loved us and the farm.

It probably would have been different if I had been a baby when she died. Having those memories of her always put distance between me and the rest of my family. That, and the fact that I was a good deal older than my half-siblings. But the day my dad had walked me into Faith's hospital room and I saw Bristol crying her head off in that bassinet, she had me wrapped around her finger.

Not much had changed.

"You want me to fix you a plate before the Neanderthals get up from the fields?" Bristol asked.

I adjusted the sock seam that ran across my toes. "I'm good. Probably just gonna make a pot of coffee and go through dad's office to see what needs to be done."

A look of disappointment crossed her face, but I didn't let the pang inside deter me.

Bristol looked at her feet, her dark hair falling like a curtain. "You don't want to come with us to the hospital?"

"Nah. Three's company, four's a crowd."

I may have been gone for over a decade, only visiting here and there, but I knew my dad. Knew what he would want.

I didn't know how much had been divulged to Bristol, Cash, and Ryman about the financial state of the farm, so I kept my mouth shut. Hell, for all they knew, I was just around to make sure things didn't fall through the cracks while my dad was laid up.

I'd see where everything stood here while the house was empty, then visit my dad tomorrow when I had a plan of action together. Once I put a clear step-by-step process for financial recovery in motion, I'd pack up and be gone.

I piddled around in the kitchen while Bristol finished heating the dinner Ms. Faith had prepared, sipping my coffee and letting it energize me for the task ahead. Bristol chatted about her college classes and some guy who she was dating. I made a mental note to grill Ryman and Cash on who the fucker was.

I made myself scarce when Bristol's brothers came up from the fields. Once the house was silent and the growl of Ryman's diesel truck faded in the distance, I walked down to the main floor and opened the door to dad's office.

Fuck.

Mountain was an understatement. Files had been pushed into a mound on the desk. Stray invoices—some payable, some receivable—were scattered about the small room.

A desktop computer from the era of Macintosh—not Mac—sat covered in dust. Dad had never been a tech guy.

Sticky notes were plastered to nearly every hard surface.

Feed delivered to the Grundy Ranch 4/15

Paid Bubba in copper pipe for four days' labor.

Call Tim Hooper.

Pay Jo for extra fertilizer.

Hobbs Ranch wants Tuesday delivery.

I scrubbed my palms down my face, muttering under my breath. This wasn't just a mess. It was a goddamn shit show. *So much for seventy-two hours.*

There had been a dry season two years ago that first put them in the red. After that, it was little things piling on top of one another. Equipment needing to be repaired or replaced. Gas prices going up. Rising labor costs.

And the nail in the coffin: after several rough years,

cattle ranchers were throwing in the towel and selling their land to Vulkon Incorporated.

The Thompsons had been farming grain for generations. Those ranchers were our buyers. No ranchers meant no grain sales. No grain sales meant no money for food on the table. But no cattle ranchers *also* meant no food on the table.

Most people didn't realize how delicate the farm-to-table cycle really was. When one domino started to fall, they all did.

4

VAUGHAN

Alarm clocks started blaring across the big house. Ryman was up first, stomping around as he got dressed for work. Cash was soon to follow. Bristol —the most considerate of the bunch—gave me another fifteen minutes of snoozed foghorns before she finally smacked her alarm hard enough to get it to shut up for good.

The sun hadn't even begun to peek over the horizon when the walls started shaking. At first, I thought the sensation was a side effect of sleep deprivation, but then it got worse. So much worse.

What sounded like a jet turbine thundered overhead, shaking the house like it was a baby rattle.

"Good morning, Thompsons!" a voice crackled over the house's PA system.

I didn't know if I was more shocked that it still worked after thirty years or that someone had hijacked the frequency for some apparent prank.

"This is your captain speaking," the voice continued. "If

you're not already up and at 'em, you've got ninety seconds to do so. Second pass is coming in fast and low."

I rolled over in the full-size bed. My feet hung off the end, but I didn't care. All I wanted was five more minutes.

I had almost drifted back into the land of blissful unconsciousness when that fucking menace zipped over the house again. It was twice as low and three times as fast. The rumble echoed across the plains, rattled the windows, and set off the farm animals like a barnyard fire alarm.

Fuck my life.

I rolled and peeled open a bleary eye. A string of colorful profanities scrolled through my mind like stock exchange listings on a Monday morning. It had only been four hours since I had gone to sleep after combing through every scrap of paper in my dad's office and organizing them based on priority and clarity.

I had no idea what the fuck to do about decades-old invoices that said things like *hangar deal is good.* What the hell was the hangar deal, and who was it with?

I didn't know what I was supposed to do with a faded receipt with *outstanding balance paid in goats* scrawled across the bottom. *Goats are not legal tender, dammit!*

Dad should've hired a business manager thirty years ago, but he insisted that he had it covered. Ms. Faith did her best to help, but the old man was stubborn and wanted things done *his way.*

The rumble of diesel engines and the growl of farm machinery bellowed from outside. I rolled to my back and stared at the ceiling. What I wouldn't give for the soothing ambiance of car horns in traffic and Chicago PD sirens.

I needed my coffee with a double shot, I needed clothes from this decade, and I needed to murder a crop duster pilot.

Unfortunately, there would be no hand-crafted espresso beverage. I had to settle for room-temperature Folgers in the kitchen coffee pot. And it probably wasn't even brand-name Folgers. It was most likely generic H-E-B coffee dumped into an old Folgers tin.

I trudged down the stairs in search of caffeine anyway.

"Shit," A deep voice said, startled.

I looked up from the mug I was pouring and saw Ryman cutting through the first floor. His eyes were wide, like he had just spotted an intruder.

Ryman was the spitting image of his mom. Like Ms. Faith, he had blonde hair and blue eyes.

"Uh, hey," he said. "Didn't know you were up."

"Couldn't sleep," I muttered. I was an early riser, but not *this much* of an early riser.

"Dad asked about you when we went to the hospital." He grabbed a set of keys hanging on the hook by the door.

I set the coffee pot back beneath the machine and downed the tepid mug in one gulp. "I'm going to visit him today. Needed to see what the situation here was before I talked to him."

Ryman's eyes flicked to dad's closed office door. "It's bad, isn't it?"

I was eight years his senior, but Ryman had the shrewd judgment of a seasoned farmer. From what I gathered, he had slowly been taking over the day-to-day operations from our dad.

I kept my poker face locked on tight. "It's definitely not good."

"He's not gonna take the Vulkon offer, you know," Ryman said as he yanked the door open.

That was the unfortunate truth I discovered when I was sifting through the mess last night. *Err, this morning.*

I had found the scapegoat papers in the trash. There was an out. A solution that provided not just financial recovery, but profit.

Vulkon Incorporated had made an offer to buy the land. The numbers were obscene and quite lucrative.

"Figured as much," I clipped. It was exactly why I needed to talk to my father.

Ryman tossed me the keys in his hand. "You can borrow the ol' F-150 while yours is in the shop." A cocky smirk drew up on his mouth. "Thought you knew better than to go head to head with an armadill'a. City life's made you soft."

I flipped him the bird as he jogged out of the house and hauled ass into his truck. The engine faded into the distance, and silence settled over the house.

I drained the rest of the coffee pot into my mug and knocked it back. What I really wanted was an iced Americano with a few shots of espresso. Unfortunately, the chances of finding a cup of coffee that wasn't made at a place that also sold gas and questionable hot dogs were slim to none.

The F-150 Ryman gave me the keys for cranked up on the third try. The air conditioning rattled like a tin can full of loose change. *As long as I didn't have to walk into town.* The blisters on my feet were practically craters after walking ten miles in leather Oxfords.

City life hadn't made me soft. My half-siblings wouldn't last a day in Chicago. They were big fish in a small pond. I was a shark in the ocean.

There was a reason that sharks didn't do well when they were put in a fish tank.

I made a quick stop at Willard's—a rundown, backwoods mechanic with a spray-painted sign. The owner was completely unhelpful in letting me know when my car would be repaired and, for that, I blamed the blue-eyed menace.

At least I had been able to change into a mostly fresh suit and had the rest of my luggage in the passenger's seat of the truck.

I bounced and bobbed out of town, heading thirty minutes south to the hospital.

The radio was stuck on a country station where a front porch crooner whined about his dog. Nothing like kicking off the morning with some depression.

I pulled into the hospital lot and eased into a space toward the back.

The sharp odor of rubbing alcohol and despair greeted me when I entered the building. "George Thompson," I said to the man behind the front desk.

His fingers flew across his keyboard. "West wing, Room 383." Without peeling his eyes off the riveting game of solitaire on the other half of his screen, he pointed down the hall. "Elevator's that way."

I used the thirty-second ride to scroll through my emails. I had lost an entire day of work yesterday, and Tamara was sending me thinly veiled threats about getting my ass back to the office. I flagged a few emails that I needed to respond to personally and left the rest to her.

Sometimes I didn't know who was more high maintenance: my assistant or my ex-wife.

Just the thought of Meredith had a shudder running down my spine. If I never saw that woman again, it would be too soon.

The elevator doors peeled back, and I strode into the hallway. The door to Room 383 was open, and I could see Ms. Faith sitting in a bedside chair. I pocketed my phone and tapped a knuckle on the door.

"Vaughan!" she said as she dropped the book she was reading on the floor and jumped out of the vinyl chair. Before I even made it inside, she had her arms around me in a hug.

Ms. Faith hadn't changed a bit since the last time I saw her. Her hair was still warm blonde streaked with silver, though it was a little more silver now. Eyes still blue. Expression still warm. She was still soft around the middle. And, as much as I never wanted to admit it, she gave the best hugs.

Memories flickered through my mind.

My dad was a gruff farmer—even more so after we lost my mom. The strong, silent type. But more than once in my adolescence, Ms. Faith had given me space to grieve. And when I needed it, she would give me one of those maternal hugs. I never cried in front of my father, but Ms. Faith's arms were a safe, quiet place to get the anger and heartbreak out of my system. She had never been put off by my standoff-ishness.

"I'm so glad you made it in after that terrible time you had yesterday. I'm just happy we get to see you, even if I wished it was under better circumstances."

I offered a polite nod. "Good to see you, Ms. Faith."

Her lips twitched in a sort of sad smile. But, like always, she never said anything about my insistence on not calling her 'mom.'

When my dad started dating her way back when, he had introduced her as Ms. Faith. And, in my eight-year-old mind, that's what she always would be. A kind presence. Someone good for my dad. The mother of my half-siblings.

But she wasn't mine.

"Vaughan," my father said with the kind of rasp that came from exhaustion and annoyance. He hated sitting still.

Being laid up and in pain wasn't doing a damn thing for his mood. "Heard you got yourself into a bind yesterday."

I had done no such thing. It was an armadillo and the wicked bitch of the south.

There was no way to be completely sure that the woman who had stopped on her way into town had turned the entire population against me, but I was relatively certain.

But those eyes... I dreamed about them in my sleep. They were bright like bluebonnets blooming in April.

I shook my head to rid my mind of the premonition and focused on my dad. His face and skin was tanned and weathered from decades spent in the fields. It was an uncomfortable contrast to the crisp, sterile hospital bedding and fluorescent lights. His age was showing.

"How'd the surgery go?"

"Just fine," he harrumphed as he raised the tethered remote and clicked through the stations on the TV that was mounted in the corner.

"The nurses had him up and walking this morning," Ms. Faith said proudly as she lowered into the chair again and picked up her book. It was a romance novel with a shirtless man on the front, written by an author named Whitney West.

She thumbed through the dog-eared pages and found her place again. "They said it'll be a few months and a lot of rehab before he can get back to work, but things are looking good. We're praying for discharge papers today." Her chipper smile was warped and weary around the edges. The lines around her eyes drooped in a tired fashion.

I was a straight shooter. Always had been. I preferred to be all business all the time. It kept things simple. I knew where I fit into that equation. Home life was complicated, and I could never figure out my place in all of it.

But numbers... I understood numbers. And if I didn't understand what they were doing, it was usually only a matter of time before I had those figures working for me, instead of the other way around.

"Let's talk about the farm," I said, easing into the seat beside the hospital bed.

"Ry and Cash've got it covered. Might bring on another farm hand to help out until I can get back on a tractor."

"You don't have the money to bring on another set of hands," I clipped.

My dad's face turned to stone. "What are you talkin' about?"

Ms. Faith stared at her book, though I could tell from the way she looked blankly at the page that she wasn't actually reading.

"I've been going through the finances. You've been in the red for three years now. You've got missed payments on the mortgage and a loan that's about to default. Half of the equipment needs to be replaced or needs repairs that you don't have the capital to cover." I rested my elbows on my knees. It wasn't a posture I would ever use with a client, but I needed my dad to know that I wasn't coming at him. I was going to get him out of this mess, come hell or high water. "I'm working on a plan of action to consolidate your debt and find new income or distribution avenues, but if it doesn't work, I think you should consider the Vulkon—"

"No," he bellowed. "And I should wash your mouth out with soap for having the gall to even suggest that."

It was the reaction I expected, but it didn't make the frustration any less annoying. I could be a stubborn asshole. My divorce papers were proof of that. But the man sitting across from me was the one who gave me that stubbornness.

"You can come in this room and visit because you're my

son and I love you," he clipped. "But if you *ever* utter that horse shit around me about sellin' our land, I'll—"

"*George*," Ms. Faith said in a gentle warning. "Vaughan's just trying to help."

"Then what in the tarnation is he doing, talking about that comp'ny, comin' in and buying up all the farms for what—rocks?"

Faith's warm presence turned chilly as her eyes narrowed on him. "Vaughan is here to help because *I* asked him to come." She closed her book. "I know things haven't been easy the last few seasons. Whether you want to admit it or not, we need a fresh perspective to get the farm back on track before we have no other option *but* to sell to Vulkon."

And that was that. Ms. Faith may have looked sweet, but inside, she could be as prickly as barbed wire. It took that kind of backbone to survive raising Ryman, Cash, and Bristol. *And me.*

Dad glared at her, but we all knew he didn't mean any harm by it. He was frustrated, and being saddled to a hospital bed didn't help.

Then again, it would just make the situation worse if he racked up more medical bills by jumping up on a combine and getting hurt again as soon as he was discharged.

Someone was going to have to keep him on a short leash, and I had a feeling that someone was going to be me.

"What do you need from me?" he grumbled as he stabbed the power button on the TV remote.

I tapped the screen on my phone and opened my photo gallery. There were so many receipts, sticky notes, and scraps of paper that were used in lieu of invoices that I had resorted to taking photos of each one to run by him.

"Let's start with this one." I zoomed in on the photo. "What's the hangar deal?"

A smile crept up the corner of his mouth. "Jo flies the Ag Cat that's older than Methuselah. I paid to have it fixed up and, in return, my fields are cared for at-cost." He pointed a calloused finger at my phone. "I'm coming out on top with that deal. All I pay for is fuel and supply. No labor cost."

I'd be the judge of that. "Where can I find Joe? I need a word with him."

It sounded like Ms. Faith laughed, but when I looked up, her nose was buried in that Whitney West book.

My old man looked equally amused. "Oh, just drive out to the old hangar that's toward the back of the east fields. You remember where it is, right?"

I nodded. That hangar and the cabin close to it used to be a graveyard for old farm equipment, machinery, and tools.

He chuckled, a dry laugh that had him reaching for the styrofoam cup of water. I beat him to it, adjusting the straw for his ease. "Jo'll be out there 'round five o' clock. Go have your talk, then come and have family dinner at the big house."

I would have preferred to eat while I worked through the rest of the farm's books, but the look in his eye told me that I didn't have a choice in the matter.

I rose to my feet and smoothed out my slacks. "I'll see you back at the big house."

The hours passed quickly since I wasn't looking at the clock. By the time five rolled around, I had given myself four papercuts, cursed my dad's accounting skills, and digitized most of the files I could get my hands on.

Time to go have a word with Joe.

I didn't bother with my suit jacket. It was too fucking hot.

I hopped in the truck and followed the dirt path out to the eastern side of the back forty. A metal shelter cropped up in the distance as dust billowed around my tires. Peeking out of the hangar doors was a bright yellow biplane. I pulled up next to an oddly familiar rusted blue Ford and cut the engine.

"Hello?" I called out over the racket of honky-tonk radio trash.

No reply.

I dipped in the hangar. "Hello?" I bellowed again before nearly choking on my tongue.

Ho-ly shit.

Sweat glimmered like diamonds on bare skin that had been tanned to a deep bronze from hours in the sun. The woman's back was arched. A pair of shredded denim shorts clung to her ass like a second skin. Her white sports bra was soaked through. The curve in her spine was the sexiest curve I'd ever seen.

Legs taut with muscle teased me. Her calves were bowed back, ankles wide as she bent at the waist and wielded a socket wrench to tighten a bolt on the plane's landing gear. Hair the color of dark chocolate was pulled up in a wild tail. Long strands streaked her neck and shoulders.

That heart-shaped ass rocked back and forth to the beat of the music. I watched for a moment as her hands, covered in grease, methodically twisted and tightened each bolt and nut. Satisfied with her work, she straightened and slipped the wrench into the back pocket of those obscene shorts.

I cleared my throat and rapped my knuckles on the side of the plane to catch her attention.

She turned, pale blue eyes slicing me like a razor blade. That scar...

It was her.

For a millisecond, I let my stony façade drop and I hissed, "*You.*"

5

JOELLE

Sweat trickled down my spine. It was a scorcher today. I had just landed and gotten the plane back in the hangar when an alert went off about the landing gear. I went through a quick check and deduced that it was simply a loose bolt on the aft brace.

Trace Adkins blared over the old boombox I kept out here. If I could just get the bolt tightened a little more, I'd be done for the day. A cold bath out on the porch sounded like heaven before dinner.

A faint tapping caught my attention and I peered out of the corner of my eye.

Tall, handsome, and hella uptight stood behind me, checking out my ass. The lust in his eyes cued me into the fact that he either hadn't recognized me yet or didn't have enough blood left in his brain to care. I swayed my ass just to tease him before pocketing the socket wrench and turning around.

He paled. *A miracle since he was sunburnt from his walk of shame through town.* "You—"

I smirked and grabbed the grease rag I had tucked in my

front pocket. "I was wondering when I'd see your ornery ass again."

Chuckling under my breath, I pitched the rag into the pile I kept by the hangar entrance. I'd wash them out before calling it a day.

"Heard you decided to take the scenic route out to the farm. Did'ya have a nice little walk?"

"You're a fucking evil mastermind," he spat, pointing a finger in my face. If he wasn't careful, I'd snap that finger clean off and shove it up his ass.

A carefree laugh escaped my mouth. "I'm not an evil mastermind. I'm just a petty bitch."

"I could have died in a ditch on the side of the road!" he shouted. "It was triple digits all day, and you somehow managed to turn an entire town against me. I couldn't even get a fucking bottle of water!"

Drama queen much? I snorted and strode over to the pegboard wall of tools. "Maybe you should take that as a lesson that words have consequences around these parts. You mess with the bull, you get the horns. Thought you would have learned that growing up here."

The shock on his face was palpable. It was always fun to be the smartest one in the room. For the other person to realize that you knew more about them than they knew about you.

Vaughan's sharp features pinched together like a puckering asshole. "You're a sadistic cunt," he hissed.

I laughed. *So, there was a little fire under all those suits.* City boys were always fun to break. Name calling would have been more effective if it didn't turn me on. I liked a little degradation, but he didn't need to know that.

"You know, you should really see a chiropractor. Having your head up your ass can't be good for your back, old man."

Vaughan pinched the bridge of his nose as if he was trying to ward off a headache. I preferred to think of myself as a human aneurysm.

I wouldn't annoy him. I'd kill him.

"I'm here to talk to Joe," Vaughan snapped in utter irritation. "Where is he?"

He?

Oh, I was going to enjoy this.

"What'cha need?" I asked as I grabbed my flight log and double-checked the day's entries.

Vaughan rested his hands on his hips.

My god, he had huge hands. Ryman and Cash were handsome in a small-town farm boy kind of way, but Vaughan wasn't just handsome.

He was sin.

Dark stubble covered his cheeks and jaw. His sleeves were cuffed at the elbows, showing off thick forearms with just the right amount of hair to be masculine without looking like Sasquatch. His dress pants sat just above his hips, tapering in at the base of his narrow waist. His fancy suit vest was painted on his muscular chest.

I kind of hated him for being so attractive.

Vaughan's dark eyes narrowed as if he was contemplating just how dense I was. "To talk to Joe," he said slowly, as if he was explaining simple directions to a toddler.

"I heard you the first time, city boy," I clipped. "What do you need to talk about?"

"I don't need to have a damn word with you, Lady MacBeth."

"Well," I said as I closed the log book and chucked it back into the cockpit, then checked the clock on the wall. It was quitting time. "Jo's off for the day."

He opened his mouth to argue with me, but it was cut off

by the sound of a cell phone. He dug the device out of his pocket and swiped the screen. "Thompson," he answered.

I waited, crossing my arms and listening as he talked to a man on the other end of the line. Terms like "return on investment" and "client acquisition" were tossed around.

Bristol had given me the gossip when she called me from the big house yesterday. Her big brother had come in from Chicago to give their dad some advice on the farm's finances.

I didn't want the Thompsons to lose the farm. Hell, they *couldn't* lose the farm. It was my livelihood. My home. I had been trying to take steps to secure my stake in the land.

With the arrival of the long-lost Thompson brother—or as I liked to call him, the object of my disaffection—I needed to start making those steps happen before I lost everything, too.

Vaughan was still talking rather loudly, his deep voice echoing throughout the old hangar. Taking a phone call in the middle of a conversation was obnoxious and downright rude, but two could play that game.

I cut the radio, pulled my phone out of my back pocket, found the perfect song, and turned the volume all the way up. The acoustics in the metal building were *magnificent.* Def Leppard's "Pour Some Sugar On Me" blared through the space.

Vaughan's attention snapped to me, his eyes blazing with fire.

"Hey there, handsome!" I yelled in my most seductive voice, making sure whoever was on the other end could hear. "Welcome to Climax Gentlemen's Club. You look like you need to loosen up. My name is Candie—with an 'i.e.'" I giggled. "Let's get you in a VIP room, and I'll get Cinnamon. I promise the two of us will show you a good time."

I could hear the confusion from the man on the other end of his call. Vaughan balled his fists, trying to keep a lid on his temper.

"Oh, you don't have to be shy, Mr. Thompson," I said with a giggle, craning forward to pitch my voice toward his phone.

"Mr. Devers, let me give you a call back," Vaughan clipped, glaring at me. "I'm dealing with a... situation at the moment."

"That's right, sexy. I know it's annoying, but we do have a no phone policy since this is a *strip club*!" I tried to keep up the seductive stripper voice, but I finished in a laugh.

Vaughan's hand shackled my wrist. His grip was tight and unforgiving as he took measured steps forward, forcing me to walk backward. "No, sir. It's just—" he cut his eyes to me "—someone playing a ridiculous prank. I would never abuse my remote work ability like that."

I clapped my free hand over my mouth to muffle my laugh.

He pocketed his phone and slammed my wrist into the fuselage over my head. "You're a petulant little brat." He towered over me, hot breath laced with mint swirling between us. "Stop fucking with me just because you don't have anything better to do. Get this through your head: I'm done with you and your games."

Vaughan's chest pressed against mine. I had to tip my head back, resting it against the metal side of the plane so I could meet his eye line. He took another half-step forward, sandwiching my body between his and the plane.

My breasts strained against my sports bra. *Shit.* My nipples poked at the spandex, tiny points exposing the fact that this position wasn't exactly a turn-off.

"Then let this be a lesson to you," I said between labored

breaths. "Don't cross me. I'll seduce your dad, become your new step-mom, and whip your ass."

"Tell Joe to come see me at the big house," Vaughan said as he dropped my wrist and took a staggering step back. His predatory eyes never left me. "You can handle passing on a message, can't you?"

Vaughan looked me up and down, brazenly assessing my appearance. I had shucked out of the button-up I'd put on this morning, opting to work on the plane in my bra and shorts. The stationary box fan I had perched in the corner didn't do anything to combat the heat that built up in the hangar. I wasn't the kind of woman who *glowed* or *got misty*.

I was downright soaked with sweat.

With purposeful strides, he turned and made a beeline for the bay doors. "And get a fucking hobby," he called over his shoulder.

Oh, I had found a hobby alright.

———

"JoJo," George said as he tried to lean up in his recliner. "Good to see you, kiddo."

"Don't get up on my account," I said as I leaned in and gave Mr. Thompson a gentle hug. "You need rest. I was worried about you. I'm glad you're home."

"Listen to JoJo," Ms. Faith said as she and Cash set the table. "No bending, twisting, or lifting. Your rear end stays in that chair."

I couldn't imagine going from being a daily go-getter— up before the sun, working the land—to a bedridden hermit. I'd lose my damn mind.

I tucked my hair behind my ear. "You're going stir crazy, aren't you?"

George cut his eyes to his wife, then sighed. "Yeah."

"Well," I said, perching my ass on the arm of the couch that was catty-cornered to his recliner. "You can always come on a flight with me. All I do is sit."

"No!" Faith and Cash said in unison.

Faith pointed a finger at me. "Don't go putting ideas in his head, Jo. He doesn't need to be climbing into that bucket of bolts you fly around in."

George chuckled.

I grinned. "Or you could come to the Silver Spur to watch me bullride."

"No!" Ryman shouted in a panic as soon as he stepped into the living room of the big house. "Dear God, no."

Cash joined us in the living room. "I love you, Dad, but if the toe of your boot ever enters the saloon, I will have to enter witness protection." He glanced at me and winked.

"Why is Cash entering witness protection?" Bristol asked as she thundered down the stairs. The girl was a buck-o-five soaking wet, but she stomped around like an elephant.

"Jo invited him to the Silver Spur for bull riding," Ryman said with a shudder.

"Ooh! I wanna go!" Bristol squealed.

"*No!*" Faith, George, Cash, and Ryman shouted simultaneously.

Bristol pouted.

"Sorry, Bris." I threw my arms out and shook my tits. "Gotta be twenty-one or older to see these babies."

She smirked. "I didn't say *I* wanted to watch *you* do topless bull riding. I want to try it!"

"Fuckin' hell, I'm gonna hurl," Cash said. His gait was fast as he hurried to the bathroom. He did look a little clammy.

Ryman crossed his arms, assuming the role of Bristol's

fraternal bodyguard. "I do not want to hear the words 'topless bull riding' come out of your mouth *ever* again."

"I'm eighteen," Bristol argued. "I can become a stripper if I want to, and you can't do a damn thing about it."

Ryman glared at his sister.

I looked at Bristol and stage-whispered, "Imagine what he'd do if he knew you've had *sex* before."

"Jesus Christ," George muttered as he looked toward the heavens and closed his eyes. "What is wrong with this family?"

Bristol grinned and tossed her arm around my shoulder. "You're like the missing Thompson sibling. There should have been four of us growing up."

"There *were* four of us here growing up," a deep voice rumbled from the staircase. Vaughan's long legs ate up the distance as he strode down the steps. "Not my fault I was away at college when you were born."

The lighthearted mood in the room shifted when Vaughan's slick dress shoes hit the landing. He was one giant joy vacuum, sucking every ounce of happiness out of each room he entered.

"Hey, sweetie," Ms. Faith said as she smiled warmly at Vaughan. How anyone could have affection for that human storm cloud was beyond me. "You met Jo earlier, right?" She motioned toward me. "Joelle, this my s—" she paused "—this is Bristol's oldest brother, Vaughan."

I'd have to ask Ryman if there were still security cameras on the main floor of the big house, because the look on Vaughan's face was priceless. I wanted to print it out and frame it.

Vaughan clenched his teeth. "*Jo?*"

"The one and only," I said with a grin.

His nostrils flared with heavy breaths of anger and

annoyance. "Jo." He tested the name again. "Jo, as in *the Joe I came to see this afternoon*?"

I eased off the couch and turned to face him. "Maybe next time you'll mind your manners and I will be a little more forthcoming."

His face was as cold as a polar bear's balls as he stared me down.

"Are you trying to look intimidating or are you constipated?" I asked. "I can't tell. But if you need some stool softener—"

Bristol giggled, while Cash and Ryman shared mischievous grins.

There was a slight twitch beneath Vaughan's eye. A chink in his armor.

I took pity on him and extended my hand. "Joelle Reed. Agricultural aviator and tenant of the cabin on the quarter acre next to the hangar."

"Tenant?"

"Jo's been renting the ol' cabin out there for going on ten years," George said. "Didn't I tell you to talk to her about the hangar deal?"

"Well, *Joelle*," he said calmly. His smile was that of a jungle cat baring its teeth. "It's a pleasure to finally meet you."

I opened my mouth, but he cut me off.

"You told me not to cross you," he continued, "but I'd be very careful about crossing *me* considering I'm now your landlord."

The oven timer sounded, slicing through the tension. "And on that note," Ms. Faith said, clapping her hands together. "Let's eat."

At the behest of Ms. Faith and Mr. George, I attended family dinner with the Thompsons at least once a week. I usually tried to get out of them. I hated feeling like the stray animal they sometimes let inside.

Given that it was George's first day out of the hospital after his back surgery, it was a dinner I couldn't miss. Usually I sat across from Ryman, but now he was squished between Vaughan and Ms. Faith. I had never been seated across from a scowling rectum of a man before.

"Are you flying tomorrow?" Bristol asked as she scraped her fork across her plate.

"Bright and early," I said.

Vaughan glared at me between bites.

"More like dark and early," Cash joked.

"Early bird gets the worm," George said.

"Remember that time we were in the north field and Jo flew over and dropped seed for ryegrass?" Ryman said with a grin.

"It was like getting hit by a thousand BBs!" Cash howled.

I laughed. "That's what you get for not looking at the schedule I sent!"

Vaughan scowled.

I turned to Bristol. "Why do you ask? Wanna come up with me? We can squeeze in the cockpit."

She shook her head. "I'm driving to Waco to explore the campus and figure out where my classes are before the semester starts. Figured I'd see if you wanted to come with me."

Bristol was starting her first semester at Baylor and was all too excited to finally be a college student.

"Can't tomorrow, but the next time it rains, I'm all yours." I nudged her shoulder as I slid another bite in my mouth.

I cleaned my plate and chatted with George while everyone finished up. Ms. Faith offered dessert and coffee, but I declined on the premise that I had an early morning. I wanted to get out of there as fast as I could.

Being in the big house, pretending like I was a part of the Thompson's big, happy family made my stomach turn. They were good to me, but they weren't mine to have.

Vaughan never stopped frowning as he watched me hug his parents goodbye and fist-bump his siblings. It made me wonder if his jaw was so chiseled from the muscles it took to be perpetually miserable.

6

JOELLE

"You know, purple is really your color," I said as I held Bean's paw and dabbed the nail polish brush on the tip of his claws. "It brings out the blue in your fur."

Bean gave a noncommittal grunt and turned his attention back to *Schitt's Creek* playing on my dinosaur of a laptop.

I hunched over and touched up a smear of polish on my big toe. I was thankful for the long summer days that gave me more daylight to be in the air, but it made for some exhausting days. Today was full of flying to a farm an hour north to spray fields with fertilizer, preparing for the midsummer planting that would turn into a fall harvest.

A knock at the door had Bean's good ear perking up. Apparently, whoever or whatever was on the other side wasn't cause for alarm because he let out a blustering huff and closed his eyes.

The person knocked again.

"Just a second!"

If it was Cash or Ryman, they would have given a

warning knock, then barged in. That meant it was probably Ms. Faith. She had a few more manners than the rest of the brood did.

I eased off my bed and waddled on my heels to the cabin door. So help me—if it was Vaughan and I messed up my manicure, I'd kill him.

I blew on my fingernails for a second before gingerly grabbing the door handle and twisting.

Bristol stormed in, looking like a bad omen as her dark hair flew around her. "Do you have wine?" She started yanking open cabinet doors and pawing through my dry goods.

Thanks to her long-lost brother, I was fresh out.

"Whoa, babe—" I grabbed her arm. "What the hell is going on? I thought you were going to Waco today?"

Her eyes were rimmed red. The puffiness of her cheeks gave away the fact that she had been crying.

My eyes narrowed. "Who is he? I'll kill him, then I'll call Ryman to help me dispose of the body."

I was already crossing the single room that served as a bedroom, kitchen, and living room, heading for my safe.

I could off the fucker with a single bullet, load the body into my Ag Cat, and fly out to dump it into the mountains just across the border. With any luck, a coyote or javelina would get a hold of the body and help start the decomposition process.

Dumping the bastard in the Gulf would have been way closer, but currents would bring the body back to shore. Besides—the Coast Guard was always crawling all over the place out there.

I'd have to stop and refuel a few times, but flying the Ag Cat would be less suspicious than my Cessna. Besides, with all the decontamination I had to do of the aircraft because of the chemicals that I sprayed, I could easily scrub away any DNA evidence.

"No!" Bristol shrieked. Tears were running down her cheeks. "Please, don't call them—I just..." She tossed her head back. "I just want to get drunk and forget it ever happened."

"First of all," I began. "I may let you steal the occasional glass of wine from my fridge, but you're only eighteen. I will not be held responsible for getting you wasted."

Bristol gave the trashcan a pointed look. At the very top was an empty wine bottle. I had downed it the night before when I left the big house after dinner. Either I gave myself a wine buzz, or I fingered my clit until I came to the mental replay of Vaughan pushing me up against the fuselage of my plane.

I chose the wine.

Bean, annoyed with the ruckus, darted off the bed and waddled to Bristol.

She knelt in front of my dog and squished his cheeks. "Please, you can't honestly tell me you never got drunk before you turned twenty-one."

"I did a lot of things before I turned twenty-one that I pray to God you *never* have to do," I snapped. Without thinking, I reached up and let my fingers graze the scar on my temple.

It wasn't often that I got tough with Bristol—or anyone for that matter. I was nearly twelve years older than her, which wasn't a lot in adult years, but the difference between being an adult at eighteen and at twenty-nine was about as polar as it got.

"Please, Jo?" She dropped to the floor and sat against the cabinets I had gotten from a charity shop and installed myself. "Can I crash here tonight?" Bristol scratched behind

Bean's ear. "I don't feel like going back to the house and getting grilled by everyone."

I was proud of those damn cabinets. Slowly, but surely, I had made something of my little one-room cabin. Sure, the roof still leaked like a colander, but that was only a problem when it rained.

I put my hands on my hips, debating whether to send one of the Thompsons a text. "What happened today?"

We settled on my bed with a bag of tortilla chips and a tub of salsa between us. Bean snuggled in with Bristol, offering some canine comfort.

"I loved him," she sniffled. "We were together for two years. He said he loved me. We were planning to go to Baylor together, but then he applied to UT." She dunked a chip into the salsa and shotgunned it. "At first Chad said it was his safety school, but when he got accepted to Baylor, he said he wasn't sure where he wanted to go."

I swallowed my bite and chased it with a swig of water. I *really* wanted a beer, but I was flying in just a few short hours. Being responsible *sucked.*

"Why the hell were you with a guy named Chad? Everyone knows that all Chads are assholes. Not their fault if their parents didn't read the naming rulebook. If you name your kid Chad, he'll grow up to be a bag of dicks."

Kind of like men named 'Vaughan.' But I didn't say that part out loud.

That made her crack a little bit of a smile. "He was kind of a dick sometimes."

I pointed a finger at her. "See?"

Bristol sighed and spooned with Bean, who didn't mind in the slightest. "A few months ago, he decided that he was going to go to UT. Which was fine—I mean, it's only an hour and a half away. He was supposed to meet me in Waco today. We were gonna have a lunch date and then explore Baylor together."

"And he didn't show?" I guessed, smoothing her hair away from her face.

"He was an hour late, but I waited. And then texted me and said that he didn't want to start college with "baggage" from high school."

That prick.

Part of me—a very small part—was glad he had dumped Bristol. For her sake, I didn't want her with a chuckle-fuck like that. The other part of me wanted Bristol to have her moment and eviscerate the little prick.

"Think of this as a good thing," I said. "He showed his true colors. Better to be single and happy than taken and miserable. You're getting a fresh start right before you meet a whole bunch of new people."

"I don't want to be single and happy or taken and miserable. I want to be taken and happy," she argued.

"Look at me," I said, tossing a chip in my mouth. "I'm gloriously single and happy. I work when I want. Go to bed when I want. I don't have to do someone else's laundry, and if I want to sit in the tub on the back porch and gorge myself on take-out, I can do so judgment-free. No one is leaving boxers on my floor. There are no pubes stuck to the toilet."

Bristol was quiet for quite a while. When Netflix got insecure and asked if we were still watching, I reluctantly queued up another episode.

"Boys aren't security blankets, Bristol." I snuggled in beside her, sandwiching the dog between us. "Yes, they can be cuddly, but after a while they get dull and smelly. You're not a kid. You're a badass woman and you can tackle life without dragging one around. Because eventually, it'll just weigh you down."

"I know," she said with a yawn. "And he was kind of awful in bed."

I snickered. "That's the spirit. We don't settle for weak orgasms or weak men."

Her eyelids were heavy as she rested her chin on top of Bean's head. My stolen pooch was the best bedmate. He was always down for a snuggle.

An engine rumbled in the distance, but it could have just been one of the boys coming or going. Given the time, I was surprised. It was pretty late—just after eleven. I didn't realize just how much time had passed since Bristol had dropped by for some commiseration.

The Thompsons, Bristol included, erred on the side of early to bed, early to rise. We all did. It was a way of life. Some of their equipment had floodlights for night harvests, but we had to take advantage of every second of sunlight from dawn until dusk.

"Thanks for letting me stay," she yawned. "You know how my brothers can be."

"Overprotective ogres?"

"And that's just Cash and Ryman. When Vaughan gets something in his head..." Her voice trailed off.

"Are y'all close?" I asked. "You and Hades?"

"He's not that bad."

"Tell that to the innocent armadillo he terminated like a video game obstacle."

Bristol snorted. "I guess we're close. He doesn't really spend much time around any of us, but I think he has a soft spot for me. It's probably just because I'm the baby of the family and the only girl." She rolled onto her back and closed her eyes. "He was eighteen when I was born. I have every birthday card and present he ever sent, but he wasn't around much. Ryman knows him the best out of all of us, I guess. He's always called my mom "Ms. Faith." It's kind of weird. I guess it's his way of reminding everyone that she's not his mom."

"Dick," I muttered under my breath.

"Did you know him before he moved?" she asked. "You're older than Ryman."

I was two years older than Ryman, but still six years younger than Vaughan.

I shook my head. "I heard his name thrown around, but I don't think we ever met. I would have been in middle school when he was in high school, and I had a lot going on back then. I didn't move onto the farm until well after he left town."

Light flashed across the front windows, illuminating the red gingham curtains I had hanging in front of the panes. Bristol's eyes widened as slow, heavy footsteps creaked across the porch.

Bean let out a low growl.

I put my finger to my lips, urging Bristol to be quiet. Like a ninja, I rolled out of the bed and dropped to the floor. I spun the combination on the safe. The only sound in the cabin was the click of the dial. I whipped open the door and grabbed my pistol. Bristol spotted the baseball bat under my bed and grabbed it, choking up on it like a slugger.

Plodding footsteps came closer. A man-shaped shadow rested against the window as if the intruder was trying to peer inside.

Everyone in town knew better than to trespass on farm property. Motion-activated trail cameras were all over the place, and farmers didn't hesitate to drag someone's ass to court for fucking with crops or livestock. That was, if they didn't get aerated with a few bullet holes first.

Whump, whump, whump! A fist pounded on the door,

nearly sending my soul through my skin. Bristol squeaked, and Bean lowered into attack position, his glittery magenta claws dazzling in the dim light.

My index finger rested snugly on the trigger guard of my gun. "This is private property!" I shouted. "The state of Texas allows for the use of deadly force to defend private property, so get your ass off my fucking porch!"

"Shut the fuck up, Discount Annie Oakley," a rather pissed-off voice bellowed from the porch.

Bristol's eyes widened.

Against my better judgment, I slid the barrel of my gun into the back waistband of my shorts and yanked open the door.

"And for the record, it's my family's property," Vaughan bellowed as he stormed in. "*Not yours.*"

I should have just shot him.

Vaughan was wearing those stupid office clothes he preferred. Suits and ties had no place on a farm. Hell, whenever George kicked the bucket, he'd probably be buried in a casket painted in John Deere green, wearing overalls and a flannel.

But there he was, all six-foot-something of pure, intolerable sexiness. I was starting to think that his scowl was what got me off.

Not a bad thing considering I couldn't stand the man.

His anger turned toward Bristol. "Where have you been?"

"Whoa," I said, snatching the bat out of Bristol's hands and poking him in the chest with it. "You don't get to come stomping into *my* house, yelling at *my* guests."

He looked at the trashcan and spotted the day-old wine bottle. "You are in so much fucking trouble, kid," he hissed at Bristol before turning to me. Dark eyes bored into me with barely restrained fury. "And *you.*" The venom dripping from his words nearly drowned all three of us. He pointed to the wine bottle. "What *the fuck* was going through your nonexistent brain when you decided to hide her here and get a teenager drunk? And neither of you bothered answering your phones!" He clenched one fist against his side and pressed the other to his mouth before turning to Bristol. "You were supposed to be home from Waco before dinner."

She paled. "I—"

"I don't want fucking excuses, Bristol," he snapped as he pulled out his phone and fired off a text. "I want you to apologize for nearly giving your mom a heart attack. And you'd better have some Oscar-worthy groveling ready for your brothers. Cash drove out to Waco to find the ditch you were murdered in. Ryman's been beating down every door in town while I combed through the entire fucking property in case you were out here somewhere."

The gall of this man.

I shoved him backward with the end of the bat. "Get out of my house before I crack your head open like a watermelon."

He looked clear over my head at Bristol. "Get in the truck."

"How dare you speak to her like—"

"It's fine, Jo," Bristol said quietly as she dabbed her eyes with the hem of her shirt. "I should have at least told them I was over here."

"You're an adult," I clipped. "You don't answer to your brothers."

"You stay out of this," Vaughan growled. "In the truck, Bris."

Steeling herself, Bristol said, "I think I'll walk back to the house." She glared at Vaughan. "If you find me dead on the dirt path, you can say *I told you so*."

He paused for a moment, as if contemplating her counteroffer. He slipped a small flashlight out of his pocket and offered it to her. "Call your brothers on your way back to the house."

I expected Vaughan to follow her out, but the fucker was a glutton for punishment.

The front door slammed shut, leaving the two of us in a standoff. Bean sided up to me, letting out a warning growl.

Vaughan looked down at the dog, completely unfazed that a pitbull was about to rip his face off.

Well, more like lick *him to death*. Bean's bark was menacing, but the bite was nonexistent.

But Vaughan didn't need to know that.

"Your dog is missing an ear. And why the hell does it have its nails painted?" he sneered.

"Because he looks fucking fabulous is why." I shouldered the bat and reached backward for my gun. "Now, leave or stay for a nine-millimeter attitude adjustment."

In the blink of an eye, Vaughan's hand whipped out. He snatched my pistol out of my hand, dropped the clip, yanked the slide back, and dumped the chambered round onto the floor. He tossed the ammo-free paperweight onto the bed as if he didn't have a care in the world.

But I still had a baseball bat, and I was the reigning county fair Whac-A-Mole champ.

"Not that it's any of your business, but I didn't give her so much as a sip of alcohol. Also, her fuck weasel of a boyfriend dumped her today in a really shitty way. Maybe keep that in mind the next time you open your mouth around her."

His head whipped around like a haunted house

mummy. "For some reason unbeknownst to me, Bristol idolizes you."

I gave him a sweet as sugar smile. "It's because I'm not a dick. You should try it sometime, you necrotic taint."

He laughed. It was a low bark of disbelief, but I guess that was as close to a laugh as a soulless automaton could get.

"I'm the dick?" Vaughan laughed again. "*I'm the fucking dick?*"

"Good to know that higher education worked wonders for your comprehension skills, Mr. Thompson. Yes, *you're* the dick."

"I'm the dick?" He stabbed the air between us with his finger. "Takes one to know one, you little brat. You're the one who had the tow truck driver fuck around all damn day before finally coming to get my car just because you got your precious little feelings hurt. Though I'm not completely certain, I'm pretty damn sure you're the one who has Willard's taking their sweet fucking time on the repairs. You nearly decapitated me with your goddamn plane after I had to walk ten motherfucking miles in the fucking heat."

"The fact that you think you're innocent in all of this is hysterical," I sassed.

He closed the space between us. "I would be very careful about how you speak to me if I were you," he said in a low, menacing rumble. "You know the old saying, don't you? Don't bite the hand that feeds you."

"I feed myself, thank you very much." I tipped my chin up, meeting his sharp gaze. "And as far as the roof over my head goes, I think your daddy and I are on pretty good terms."

A wicked smile curved at his mouth, like he was about to play a wild card that I didn't know he had. His tongue darted out, wetting his lips. "The land this dump is sitting on?" His grin grew wider. "It's not owned by my father. It's owned by the farm's LLC." He leaned in, his mouth coming dangerously close to mine. "Of which I am now a seventy-percent owner."

Shivers raced up and down my spine. The roots of my hair felt electrified, like I had stuck my finger in a light socket. Heat pooled low in my belly.

I tipped my head to the side, teasing him with my lips brushing against his.

Vaughan's spine stiffened, but he didn't move.

I smiled against his mouth. "Then you'll be a seventy-percent owner of the dirt I bury you with."

7

VAUGHAN

"You look like shit."

I peered up from my glass of whiskey as Ryman approached the high-top table I had commandeered as soon as I set foot in the Silver Spur.

The old saloon's exterior sported wood-paneled siding and neon signs that lured unsuspecting passersby with promises of cold beer.

There was a ten-foot-tall pin-up girl painted onto the side of the building. She was decked out in boots, spurs, and nothing else. Her painted hands barely covered the ballooning cartoon cleavage the artist had given her. A swish of light blue was all that covered her crotch. I assumed it was supposed to be an artistic interpretation of Daisy Dukes.

"Takes one to know one," I muttered before draining the glass.

Ryman caught the eye of the bartender and tipped his head. Apparently, they communicated telepathically because a pitcher of beer and two glasses appeared in front of us.

"First one's on the house for newcomers," the bartender said.

A strange tension that I couldn't quite put my finger on pulsed between him and Ryman.

Ryman tipped his head in appreciation. "Thanks, Ezra."

Without a word, Ezra headed back behind the bar.

"What was that about?"

For a second, Ryman glanced at Ezra, then focused all of his attention on pouring himself a beer.

Ah, I knew that look.

"You know what they say about hooking up with people in small towns," Ryman said.

I smirked. "That it's a terrible idea."

"Matched on an app and hit it off. Hooked up. Every time I bring up goin' out again, he shoots me down."

I peered over my shoulder and found Ezra studying me from across the bar. "Move on," I said. "People who like the chase get bored when the chase ends." I should know. That was my ex-wife to a T. She liked the wedding, but hated the marriage.

And that was that for the brotherly advice. We didn't do feelings. Didn't do heart-to-hearts. The two of us sat in silence, sipping on our drinks as a Garth Brooks tune I hadn't heard in damn near a decade played over the sound system. I never frequented the Silver Spur in my younger years. By the time I turned twenty-one, I was in Chicago, sipping overpriced cocktails and rubbing elbows with the who's-who of Midwestern finance.

But the Silver Spur Saloon was the party bar that everyone couldn't wait to go to as soon as they were of legal drinking age. The main draw was the mechanical bull in the middle of the bar. Well, that, and the fact that once a month the clothes came off for topless bull riding.

Another problem with small towns: everyone knew everyone. There was no sneaking in with a fake ID. Not when the bartenders and bouncers would call your parents and send your ass home.

The five o' clock crowd had yet to flood the place with paychecks in hand. Ryman had to come to town to pick up an order at the hardware store, and practically threatened to hog-tie me and drag me in for a drink himself if I didn't leave dad's office and see the sun.

Ryman's gaze turned to a pretty blonde woman bent over a pool table. He gave her a quick assessment, and I could see him formulating a plan to get her number before our pitcher was empty. The jeans she had painted on her legs were studded with rivets and jewels along the back pockets. Ryman was the *why date one-half of the population when you can date both* type.

"So," he said when all that was left in his glass was a thin film of foam. "What's the situation at the farm?"

What *wasn't* the situation at the farm? "I scheduled a meeting with the loan officer at the bank to go over options for the loan that's about to default, but I took care of some of the debt. For now, at least."

"As a majority owner," he muttered.

I knew what he was getting at. Ryman loved that land almost as much as my old man did. But love for a piece of dirt wouldn't do any good when bills had to be paid. I had the money to make the problem less volatile. Temporarily, at least.

"I didn't do it as some kind of hostile takeover. It looks good to the bank," I said, not put off by his prickly tone. "They see a new influx of cash and additional leadership. We're not out of the red yet. Not by a long shot, but it's a start."

The ability to move cash around without much trouble was all thanks to the lawyer who had drafted my prenup. I kept what was rightfully mine in the divorce, and didn't owe Meredith a cent in alimony.

Because fuck that bitch.

"What's next?" he asked.

I poured myself a beer. "Need to find new income. It's looking like it's going to be a good season. It'll be enough to keep everyone on the payroll and cover the cost of goods, but it's not going to put a dent into the debt."

"We could clear the land behind Jo's cabin," he offered. "There's another five acres behind the hangar. It'll be a pain in the ass, but if we could get the equipment in there to clear the land and get it plowed, we might have time for a late-season planting. Maybe rye or barley. Plenty of cattle ranches around that will buy dried forages from us for winter."

"As much as it would bring me joy to annoy the shit out of the queen of the underworld, another five acres of grain isn't going to help the bottom line. Especially when we'd have to spend more to clear the land than we'd make on the harvest."

"Solar?"

It was an option that I had researched but, like everything else, there were pitfalls. I swirled the warm beer in my glass. "I've thought about it. But we'd have the same problem. Either we have to clear more fields to have the panels installed, or give up fields we need for growing."

I knew he wasn't going to like the Band-Aid solution that I had, but we had to begin bringing in more revenue somewhere.

"I think to start, we have to raise our prices. Dad's still selling the harvest below market value."

"If we raise it, we'll lose our buyers. They'll go get their feed from another farm."

"Nothing drastic," I said, easing him into the idea. "Just enough to bring in a little extra while staying competitive. That, along with charging Jo for the hangar, cabin, and plane, and we might have a fighting chance until we can figure something else out."

Ryman sputtered on his beer. "Charging Jo?" He wiped the foam on his mouth with the back of his hand and shook his head. "No one's gonna go for that. Least of all, her."

"She lives on our land, she runs a business out of our hangar, and she's using a plane that Dad paid to have restored. Time for her to pay up."

He snickered. "That'll never fly with her."

That was the great thing about not giving a shit about her. I could slap an invoice to her door and not feel the least bit guilty. I had no loyalty to redneck Medusa.

Ryman shook his head. "Dad ain't gonna be on board with it either. They've had their deal for a long time. She takes care of the fields and all we do is pay for whatever she needs to spray or drop. Frankly, with what she charges other farms, I don't think we could afford her if we had to pay her. Especially when it comes to fuel. Flying low for crop maintenance burns a hell of a lot more than normal flights."

"I don't care."

"About your well-being," he said with a chuckle. "You keep coming at Jo like you have been, and she'll have your balls in a canning jar on her mantle before you can hand her an invoice."

I'd dare her to try.

Just the thought of that satanic pixie reaching in my pants had me shifting in my seat.

She was a brat. Her mouth wrote checks that her ass

likely couldn't cash. It took every ounce of self-control I possessed to stifle the part of me who wanted to take a stab at taming her ornery streak.

Or maybe I just wanted to stab her.

"Not a concern," I said as I reached into a communal bucket of peanuts and crushed a dusty shell in one hand. I popped the peanut in my mouth and imagined that it was Jo's head I was grinding between my molars.

"You two bring out the worst in each other." He grabbed a handful of peanuts out of the dingy aluminum bucket and cracked a grin. "Bristol told me about what happened at Jo's place."

I muttered something profane under my breath, cursing the she-devil and those pillowy lips of hers. If she ran out of lipstick, she'd probably slit my throat and use my blood to paint them instead.

Maybe Ryman had a point. A very, very small point.

"Bristol shouldn't be spending time around her. That woman is a bad influence."

His jaw flexed as he gritted his teeth. "*That woman's* been around more than you have. So, I'd say that when it comes to who gets an opinion on who Bris hangs out with, your opinion doesn't hold much weight."

It stung, but he wasn't wrong. I appreciated Ryman's ability to shoot straight and not apologize for it. Both of us acquired that trait from our father. Cash and Bristol tended to be the peacemakers. It was an odd balance that kept our motley crew from imploding.

"I'm surprised you don't remember Jo," Ryman mused as he watched the blonde move from the pool table to the dart board. He licked his lips, flagged down a bartender who wasn't Ezra, and sent the woman a drink. "She was around a little when you'd come back to visit."

I shrugged. "I was probably preoccupied with work or school. And she's quite a bit younger than me. Not like she would have been hanging around my friends."

He eyed me curiously for a moment before turning his attention to eye-fucking the blonde again. "Nah, Jo was all over the news back then." The bartender had brought the blonde another glass of whatever she had been drinking. She flashed him a bright smile and raised the glass in thanks.

I snorted. "For what? Robbing banks? Being both Bonnie and Clyde?"

Jo could have pulled it off with the dual personalities she kept neatly organized in her wardrobe. Sweet as sugar one minute, then sharp as a razor's edge the next.

"Testified in court against her daddy after he got caught wailing on her," Ryman said without a hint of emotion. "He nearly killed her, but she got him thrown in jail and convinced the court to emancipate her."

Jesus, Mary, and Joseph. I stared into the pale yellow of my beer and loathed the way my stomach turned. A faint memory from the other night floated through my mind. The scar that slashed across the side of her head. The way it cut through her brow, barely missing her eye.

The fact that she kept a loaded gun in the cabin.

She seemed competent, but I'd been able to take it from her too easily, and I was years out of practice with a firearm. Then again, the next time I tried that little stunt, she would probably shoot me before I made it through the door.

But emancipated at fifteen? Bristol was eighteen—a legal adult—and I couldn't imagine her being forced to fend for herself.

I choked down the bitter taste of guilt with another swig of beer. "How long has she lived on the property?"

Ryman tipped back in his chair, rocking on the back legs as he tried to recall the story. "Pretty sure Momma tried to convince her to move into the big house damn near a million times. I think they finally gave up on persuading her, and offered the cabin instead. I was only thirteen at the time, so Momma and Daddy tried to shield me from a lot of what had happened to her. I found out most of it when I got older."

"From Jo?"

He shook his head. "Nah. She doesn't talk about it. Pretends it never happened. I think she's happy thinking that one day she just woke up living in the cabin and everything before that was a dream."

I was a jackass of the worst degree because the first thing that popped into my mind was that I could use this against her.

How exactly, I wasn't quite sure yet. But I would. And I would make it brutal.

Everything she had done to fuck with me, I'd dish it back ten times worse. Like the old saying went: if you can't stand the heat, get out of the fucking kitchen.

If her dream was to forget the past, then I sure as hell wasn't about to let that happen.

"You're looking diabolical," Ryman said as he hopped up and adjusted his shirt, preparing to make a move on the blonde. "You must terrify the shit out of the wallets you manage money for."

I smirked, a wicked satisfaction flooding my bones. "Just gotta get back and start crunching some numbers."

8

JOELLE

The Thompson Farm looked like a postage stamp from the skies. Streaks of new growth dotted the otherwise brown fields.

It wouldn't stay that way for long. Soon, the pink seed the Thompson boys planted would sprout, and nearly every bit of brown would be covered. My favorite part of the growing season was when the milo plants flowered. It was like flying over fields of gold.

The handful of times I'd been to church and heard the preacher talk about streets of gold, I always imagined the milo fields. Heaven as far as the eye could see.

But heaven never lasted. Like clockwork, the sorghum would come to a head and gold flowers would tarnish into brown grain.

I spotted the farm truck Vaughan had been using since I had Willard sitting on his car for as long as he damn well pleased. *Lucifer was home.*

Instead of landing, I pulled up and gunned it. My hopper was empty and I had the fuel to spare. It had been a minute since I'd done any tricks over the house.

I figured George could use the entertainment since he was laid up after his surgery. From the looks of it, Ms. Faith had him stationed in a rocking chair on the front porch today.

Well, that or Cruella de Vaughan had kicked his dad out of the office so he could work.

George and Bristol thought the low passes I did around the property were fuckin' awesome. As a bonus, it would piss off his royal villain-ness.

More than anything, I wished I could have seen the look on Vaughan's face when I sandblasted his well-toned ass the day he got into town. When I saw him nearly naked and hosing off, I knew Lady Karma was opening doors for me left and right.

The metal ridges of the batten seam roof came into view as I pointed the nose of my Ag Cat at the house. George eased off the rocking chair and loped to the porch railing, craning his head out to watch. The altimeter dropped rapidly as I careened from five hundred feet to just under a hundred. The Thompson's farmhouse was forty-five feet tall at the highest peak of the pitched roof. I had *plenty* of room. It wasn't nearly as low as when I flew over fields. I was still above the power lines here.

I leveled out at seventy feet as I opened up the throttle, blasting over the house. I rocked my wings—a little wave to George as I headed back for the runway. I circled the small swatch of asphalt I used as my personal airstrip, tilting the yolk until I was lined up just right.

Most days I walked from my cabin to the hangar, but today I drove and locked up my truck in the hangar until I got back. I wasn't giving Vaughan easy access to my vehicle.

I didn't think he'd resort to cutting my brakes, but I wouldn't put it past him.

Especially because I had retaliated after his latest stunt.

But in my defense, Vaughan deserved every bit of hell coming his way.

I lowered the landing gear, feeling the shudder under my ass as it dropped, ready for touchdown.

The tires slid onto the asphalt with a buttery-soft landing. I slowed to a stop, just outside the hangar. I left just enough room so I could climb down, get my truck out, then ease my Ag Cat back inside. As soon as I dropped out of the cockpit and made the twelve-foot climb down to the ground, the heat hit me like a tractor trailer pancaking a squirrel on the highway.

I swapped my truck and the plane, situating my bright yellow baby in the hangar for some TLC before I called it a day. I donned a pair of plastic coveralls, a respirator, and red rubber boots for the post-flight plane spray down to wash away any lingering chemicals.

My back and hips ached from flying all day, and there was a kink in my neck that I couldn't quite loosen up. I had a standing invitation to dinner at the big house. But frankly, I didn't feel up to bickering with Vaughan, cutting up with the other Thompsons, or smiling for Ms. Faith and George.

I had leftover take-out on the verge of molding in my fridge. Finishing it off would be the responsible thing to do.

My boots squished through puddles of water as I trudged across the hangar, stripping off the coveralls and tossing them in the contaminated bin. I peeled off the respirator and hung it on the pegboard wall. Angry red lines streaked my cheeks and nose from the seal. I grabbed the back of my t-shirt and yanked it over my head. The shorts were last.

It didn't matter that I was walking around the hangar in

my underwear. Everyone knew what they'd see if they caught me in here after a flight.

Kind of a bummer that I hadn't completely stripped down when Vaughan came storming in the other day. I would have paid big money to see his reaction.

The thought of big money had me smirking to myself. I sprayed my clothes down with the hose, then dunked them in a five-gallon bucket to soak with a scoop of powdered detergent to neutralize the lingering chemicals before I laundered them tomorrow.

I grabbed my two-dollar flip-flops from the tool bench and slid them on. Another day in the books.

I strutted out to the truck in my skivvies—a modest black sports bra and boy shorts. I only made the mistake of wearing a thong once. Of course, that had been the day Cash showed up to ask me about my availability for spraying the fields with another pass of crop protectant. He had seen my boobs plenty, but apparently my ass was something to behold. The man nearly choked on his tongue.

The moment my rear end hit the driver's seat, exhaustion flooded my bones. Some General Tso's chicken and lo mein of questionable freshness was the only thing motivating me to get inside.

Bean was waiting patiently on the porch when my truck sputtered up to the cabin.

"Hey, buddy," I cooed as Bean dropped his head into my hands. I squashed his pudgy cheeks. "Who's my good boy?"

His response was a haughty snort. As if to say, "Me. *Obviously.*"

Bean's blue painted nails click-clacked against the wood-slat floor as we wandered inside. I gave his neck a good scruff as I yanked open the velcro that held his bow tie together. "How was your day?"

Bean yowled.

"Good, huh?"

"Mine was fine," I said as I drug my feet into the tiny kitchenette. "Got the Brenner farm sprayed. Did some aerial shots of the west fields for the Kleins. They're thinking of trying corn out there. Hate to tell 'em that the soil ain't right for it. They're gonna have to do a shit-ton of work to get that dirt to be worth a crap. Finished up the grain sorghum fields for Cash and Ry."

Bean harrumphed.

"I know, I know. Long day, but I gotta fatten up our bank account before growing season's over."

Agricultural aviation was feast or famine. During the season, it was a feast. But the winters brought little work. I tacked on additional services like aerial surveying and photography, on top of tending to the few winter grains that were grown. The days were long when the sunlight was short.

Maybe I'd ask Ezra if I could pick up a few bartending shifts this winter...

The microwave beeped, and I snagged the take-out box. Bean whimpered at the scent. "Sorry, dude. Vet said we have to cut down on the table food."

The pitiful eyes were brutal.

I cocked my hip. "You wanna go on a run or do you want the food you're allowed to have?"

He huffed and eyed his food bowl warily before starting the dejected walk to his dish.

"That's what I thought." I grabbed a beer out of the fridge and popped the top.

This was the part of the day I hated—when everything went still.

Everything got loud when I wasn't pulling quick maneuvers to dodge treelines and power lines while spraying fields at absurdly low altitudes. My mind went quiet when I was in the air. Just woman and machine, defying gravity.

I took another swig, letting the tang snap me out of my head. The sun was still high in the sky, baking everything around us. It was the perfect night for a soak.

I loaded up my arms with my food, drink, and some fancy bubble bath I had splurged on, and carried it to the back porch.

The cabin was more or less a large porch with a small room in the middle, but that was just fine for me. The back porch faced five acres of uncultivated land, which gave me some much-needed privacy. The galvanized stock tank I had set up under the back porch awning served as a makeshift hot tub. I yanked the garden hose around and dropped it down into the tank. The water sizzled and steamed as it splashed against steel that was hot enough to fry an egg. I dumped enough soap to turn the stock tank into a foam party, and dragged a rickety chair out of the cabin to hold my spoils.

I kicked my bra and underwear back into the cabin and peeked in on Bean who was happily parked in front of my laptop, catching up on his soaps.

The water was refreshing, the lo mein wasn't completely moldy, and the chicken was only a little dry. But the leftovers filled my stomach and I couldn't complain as I soaked my weary bones in the bubbly water.

The speakers on my old-as-dirt phone crackled as I queued up the Whitney West audiobook I had been hoarding for just the right occasion. My favorite narrator's low baritone began while I closed my eyes and sunk deep into the water.

H ER BREASTS HEAVED *as I trailed the tip of my finger along her exposed collarbone. Amelia trembled, her eyes heavy with desire as she tried to catch her breath. I loved seeing her quiver like the sparse leaves that still clung to the trees. Their effort to hold on was so valiant, even though a greater force would always win.*

For the leaves, it was the impending winter chill. For Amelia, it was me.

Her back pressed into the wall, and her eyes darted side-to-side, desperate for escape. She always looked like a deer ready to flee when we met like this—under the cover of darkness. The arousal that built from the spark of fear in our interludes was stronger than her fear of me.

"Are you going to obey me, pet?" My voice was a growl as I trailed my nose up the graceful column of her neck. "Are you going to do as you're told?"

Amelia tipped her head to the side, desperate to avoid my gaze. That wouldn't do.

I shackled her throat with my hand, squeezing the delicate points where her pulse thrummed in exhilarating fear.

She loved this.

She got off on it.

"Lorenzo," she whimpered as I began to pop the buttons that dotted the front of her shirt. A pretty little thing like her had no business being employed by a company that acted as a front for the Italian Mafia, even if she was just a secretary.

She especially had no business parading around in tight skirts that attracted my palm to her ass like a magnet.

She had absolutely no business wearing these button-up shirts that clung to her cleavage like a second skin. She kept every man in the building pent-up in a constant state of arousal.

They could look, but if anyone dared lay a finger on her, I'd chop off their hands.

On second thought, maybe I should start gouging out eyes for having the audacity to look at what belonged to me.

"Tell me, pet," I growled as I fingered the thin lace of her bra —lace that kept her nipples pebbled all day long. "Who does this body belong to?"

Ruby lips parted in desperation. She was rubbing her thighs together to ease the desire burning inside. "You."

I grabbed her blonde tresses, yanking her head backward. Amelia cried out; a pitiful sound that only served to thicken my cock. I didn't have to explain my actions. My little whore knew better than to speak to me like that.

"You, sir," she panted.

"Then raise your skirt and give me what is rightfully mine."

Amelia collapsed against the unforgiving stone wall, clawing at the hem of her simple black pencil skirt. She drew the tweed fabric up, letting it pool at her waist, just below her exposed breasts.

"Hands on your head."

Occasionally, my little brat was obedient. Amelia laced her fingers on top of her head. I arched an eyebrow, clicking my tongue and shaking my head as I took her in.

"Disobedient." *My knuckle trailed along the gusset of the thong she knew better than to wear.* "You'll be punished for wearing this."

A coy smile curved at the corner of her mouth. "Yes, sir."

"Naughty pet." *I grabbed the front of her thong and tugged it up, pinching the soft folds of her pussy between harsh lines of fabric. Amelia cried out—the very sound of her distress making my dick throb as it strained against the front of my trousers. I yanked again, punishing her for daring to cover her cunt.*

"When I'm through with you, you'll be begging me to let you come."

Amelia whimpered. "Sir—"

"Shut your fucking mouth." I grabbed her hair, shoving her down to her knees. I left her skirt pooled at her waist. "The only time I want those lips open is when you're taking my cock down your throat. The only time I want to hear you speak is when you say 'please' before you beg me to fill your mouth with my come. And that's if I'm feeling generous." I unzipped my trousers and let my cock spring free. I slapped her across the face with my dick like an insult. "I should make you lick my come off the floor like a cat lapping up milk." Her breath caught. My sweet girl liked the thought of—

"What the fuck is that?!"

I shrieked, rocketing out of the now-tepid water as a deep voice who was *not* Lorenzo Cortesi echoed from the porch.

Vaughan towered over me, hands on hips as a scowl graced his face.

I wondered if I could conjure my own morally gray Mafia man to gouge out Vaughan's eyes for daring to look at me. Then again, why hire someone to do what you can do yourself?

The fork I used to shovel my dinner in was still within reach.

It would be a disservice to rid the world of a pair of eyes as sexy and brooding as his, but I'd be doing the human population a favor. It all evened out in the end.

I sat up, streams of bathwater and bubbles running down my chest in rivulets as I made a move for the fork.

"Jesus—fuck—" Vaughan spun on the heels of his dress shoes, turning away from me.

"What?" I said, sitting up even straighter just to piss him off. "Don't tell me you've never seen boobs before."

Even with his back turned, his huff was as loud as a Clydesdale's. "You're naked in a water trough outside your house. What the fuck is wrong with you?"

"What I'm hearing is that I'm doing exactly what I want on my property and a trespasser happened to see my tits. You're welcome, by the way." I looked down, admiring my girls. "They're spectacular."

I swear on Bean's adorable little toenails, Vaughan growled.

Like...Whitney-West-hero-in-an-audiobook *growled*.

Still facing away from me, Vaughan lifted one finger in the air—surprisingly, it wasn't the middle one. "First, it's *my* property. Second, it's public nudity. What would you have done if it were Cash or Ryman—or if my dad came out here?"

I smirked. "You think they haven't seen my tits before? Baby, half the county's seen my tits. Even Ms. Faith has seen my tits."

He lifted his eyes to the heavens and muttered, "Take me now. Just fuckin' take me now."

I swirled a pointed toe in the water, moving all the bubbles strategically to the side of the tank. "Step into my office. What can I do for you, *Mr. Thompson*?"

Apparently, Vaughan was delusional and thought I had covered up because the shock was palpable when he turned.

"My cabin. My bathtub. My rules. If I want to be bare-ass naked on my porch, I am free to do so."

He didn't bother arguing semantics.

"Why the *fuck* did you write a check to my dad?" he hissed.

I batted my eyes innocently. "Whatever do you mean,

Mr. Thompson?" I was teasing him in my sarcastic falsetto and he was hating every minute of it. "I thought that's what you wanted when you pinned an itemized invoice to my door, covering the last fourteen years of my residence here."

The six-figure check I wrote would have bounced, but I knew it would never even make it to the bank, so I wrote it anyway.

And then personally handed it to George.

When he took the check from me and read the amount and memo, his face turned an unnatural shade of purple. I felt a little bad about it, given his accident, but there were always going to be casualties in war.

I explained that his son was intent on overriding our agreement and charging me fourteen years of back rent for the cabin, the plane, and the hangar.

But I knew his evisceration of Vaughan was better than any petty prank I could have played. Especially because it would nip this back rent nonsense in the bud once and for all.

George called me last night, apologized for Vaughan's chutzpah, and told me that he had shredded the check.

Much to Vaughan's very apparent dismay.

He leaned over the tub, bracing his hands on the metal edge. Muscled forearms flexed under cuffed shirtsleeves as he held up his weight. His posture nearly caged me in, but I didn't care.

Rather than fighting it, I leaned back, giving him a damn fine view. Like the moon eclipsing the sun at high noon, his eyes turned midnight black. My eyes lowered to the fly of his dress pants. The fabric was taut, the zipper bulging from the strain.

"Let me make one thing perfectly clear." His growl was accompanied by the slow grind of his molars. "You're done waking me up before the crack of fucking dawn with that bucket of bolts everyone thinks is a plane. You're done nearly crashing into the big house just to get a rise out of me. You're done with the petty bullshit. Acting like a brat and testing my patience will get you nowhere but my bad side."

The proximity of his hands to my body *really* made me want to test that threat.

I tipped my chin up. "Do you think you scare me?"

A near-feral smile drew across his mouth, flashing like lightning. "Trust me. I should scare you." He pushed away from the stock tank and dried his palms on his pants. "Better keep your claws in."

"Vaughan—" It was odd to utter his name. Usually I resorted to one of the childish monikers that floated through my head like a ticker tape.

He paused and looked over his shoulder.

"If you treat me like some sort of game, I'll show you how it's played."

A Cheshire grin spread across his lips. "Then I guess it's game on, tiger."

The unholy sight of his ass in those pants as he walked away had my body on a hair-trigger. Without even thinking, my fingers slid between my thighs and found my clit.

9

VAUGHAN

My back pressed against the side of Jo's cabin. I closed my eyes, blocking out every other sensory input. I listened to the gentle lap of the bathwater against the side of the stock tank.

Jo hadn't bothered turning on whatever she had been listening to after I had walked away. Instead of the narrator's gravel-filled timbre, I heard her soft intake of breath, then a whimpering exhale.

Fuck me. I groaned at the tent in my slacks. No way could I walk all the way back to the big house with an erection jabbing around in my boxers. I let out a long breath and thought about my ex-wife.

Immediate deflation.

I adjusted my flaccid dick and headed down the dirt path as Jo's redneck bathwater sloshed around. The wooden porch slats creaked. She must have been getting out. In desperate need to put some distance between us, I quickened my pace.

What the hell was wrong with me? I wasn't into women

like her—a brat whose only goal in life was to get a rise out of me. I was attracted to women who were driven. Women who were laser-focused on their goals like I was with mine.

Then again, maybe that's why things with Meredith went to hell in a handbasket.

Tiger. I tripped on a loose stone as I recalled what I had unintentionally called Jo.

But man ... it fit her.

Inside of every wildcat is a kitten. The sadistic side of me wanted to see just how far I could bend her until she broke. I wanted to see how far I could push her until that meek side of her peeked through all her bravado.

There was a skip in my step as I bounded up the stairs to the porch of the big house. Fragrant herbs and the tang of barbecue sauce filled the air. I kicked the dust off my Oxfords and stepped inside.

"Did'ya 'pologize?" my dad harrumphed from his recliner.

"No," I clipped. "Why would I apologize?"

His face turned beet red. "Because I told you to."

"You told me you needed help getting the farm's finances back on track. I'm not apologizing for doing the job." *And my actual job.* The ability to work remotely, keeping up with my clients' accounts and onboarding a few new ones while I was here, was a God-send.

Still, I was exhausted. I was nearing two and a half full-time jobs: my job as a financial adviser, my new job as the majority owner and CFO of the farm, and my job as Jo's worst nightmare.

The last one was quickly becoming my favorite.

"Not at the expense of treating family like shit," he glowered.

Ms. Faith craned her head in from the kitchen and

pointed a spoon at my dad. "No language like that in my house."

Fat chance of that. It hadn't stuck in the twenty-seven years that Ms. Faith had been with my dad. Both of us nearly choked on wry laughs.

"She isn't family," I countered. "She's a tenant. One who has been freeloading way too long."

That had my dad attempting to come up out of his chair. "She's been around more than you have."

"Proximity doesn't equal loyalty."

Ms. Faith popped in the doorway again. "George, so help me if you get out of that chair—"

"I'm sitting," he grumbled. "All I ever do is sit. Can't work. Can't ride on a goddamn tractor. Can't fuckin' walk around without a fuckin' walker."

Ms. Faith didn't bother scolding him for his language. Her expression softened, and all I saw was love. She had a way about her that was comforting. Though I rarely admitted it, she had been there for me after my mom died. And even though I never saw it, I supposed she had been there for my dad as well.

He sighed. "Can't even keep the damn farm afloat."

Forcing myself to tamp down the frustration with all of it, I let out a breath. "If the farm doesn't survive, she'll lose her business and her home, too. If the consequences affect her, she should have a say in helping find a solution."

Ms. Faith hummed in satisfaction as she sashayed back to the stove and stirred a bubbling sauce. "That's very magnanimous of you, Vaughan."

"That also means she has to be a part of the solution. And right now, that solution is income. She needs to pay up."

Before anyone could retort, Cash and Ryman barreled in, filthy from the fields.

"Supper ready?" Cash asked, breathless.

"In just a minute," Ms. Faith said. "Where's Bristol?"

"Here!" Bristol said as she slapped her palms against the doorframe. She was sweat-soaked and out of breath.

I raised an eyebrow. "What's wrong with you guys?"

"Whoever made it up here first, gets the other two's biscuits."

I shook my head in disbelief. No way were these three grown adults.

"Is Jo coming to eat tonight?" Bristol asked. Her admiration of Jo would have been adorable if the woman wasn't a human-sized black widow spider. *Pretty and dangerous.*

"No," I clipped.

Frankly, I didn't think I could handle seeing her again so soon.

Fuck. Those tits...

The way droplets of water clung to her tan skin...

The way I could make out the hidden treasure between her thighs...

Ryman and Cash looked at me curiously.

I blinked away the cloud of sex-starved lust. *Fuck her for getting under my skin like that.*

"Whatever," I grumbled and stormed out of the kitchen. I needed to find something much more diabolical to get her back. "I'll be in the office."

———

THE WATCH on my wrist was easily worth double the price of the jalopy of a truck that screeched to a halt in front of the

Maren Community Bank. I tipped my chin down, peering over the top of my sunglasses as I slid out of the driver's seat and smoothed down my suit.

Her royal nemesisness hopped out of the clunker. The rusted out truck gave a pitiful groan as she slammed the door and tucked a legal pad under her arm.

I stayed in the shadow of the tree I'd parked under, studying her for a moment. Wasn't that what Sun Tzu had said in *The Art of War*? To know your enemy.

Jo was decked out in something that she probably thought was professional. If 'thrift store professional' was a look, she was wearing it. I wouldn't have let the maintenance crew that worked for the firm be seen in such a walking travesty.

The pantsuit was boxy on her thin frame. It completely masked her cleavage. Hid her ass. Gave no definition to her trim waist or her toned legs. The white button-up shirt she wore beneath the God-awful blazer looked like it had been made for a middle school boy.

On top of that, she was wearing foam flip-flops.

She was a walking trainwreck.

Frankly, I had seen her not clothed just as much as I'd seen her dressed. *In the hangar in her bra and sorry excuse for shorts. On the back porch of the cabin in abso-fucking-lutely nothing.*

But the pantsuit... I hadn't expected that.

It was a hundred shades of dreadful gray. Her dark hair was left long and wavy. Two tendrils from either side of her head were pinned in the back, keeping it away from her face. She had put on a little makeup today. It wasn't much—the only reason I had even noticed was because she never wore makeup.

The effort didn't go unseen. It was like watching a little girl play dress-up with her mother's wardrobe, sliding into shoes that weren't meant for her.

Jo kicked off her flip-flops, toes dancing on the blistering asphalt as she reached into the bed of the truck and grabbed...

A pair of high heels.

They were nothing special. No red bottom. No killer spike. Just simple black pumps that still managed to make her wobble like a baby deer.

She was out of her element, and I fucking loved it.

My grin was lethal as I grabbed my leather portfolio—a monogrammed gift from Tamara last Christmas—and tucked it beneath my arm.

I crossed the bank parking lot on silent feet, a night-and-day difference to Jo's elephant stomps as she tried not to faceplant into the blacktop.

When she made a move for the door of the bank, I jumped in. My palm slapped against the metal pull handle, and I yanked it open.

Jo's head snapped, her neck cracking like a whip.

I smiled just to throw her off her game. "Morning, Maleficent."

The momentary surprise was replaced with utter disdain. "Morning, Skidmark."

A laugh caught in my throat. I quickly choked it back down and steeled my expression. "I thought it was too quiet on the farm this morning." I nearly ripped the door off the hinges, forcing her to accept the fact that I was going to hold it open and she was going to have to walk through it with her back to me. "No obnoxious flyovers. No sounds of terrified children. No evacuation sirens for the nuclear melt-down caused by you making breakfast in your cauldron."

There was a twitch of a smile at the corner of her mouth. I grinned.

"Don't get comfortable," she soothed as the bank's cool, recycled air conditioning swirled around us.

My sunglasses fogged. I pulled them off, opened my suit jacket, and slid them into the inside pocket.

When I looked back up, Jo was staring at me through the security mirror positioned above us.

"Well, good morning, Jo!" the teller behind the counter hollered. Much to my dismay, Jo's undivided attention moved from me to the teller.

She plastered on a fake-ass smile and pretended like she wasn't trying to play a part. Nerves buzzed off her shoulders like a bug light. But, to someone less observant, it didn't show.

Maybe it was because I had made her the target of my frustration since arriving back in Maren, but I had started to notice little things about Joelle Reed.

Things like the way her fingers twitched before she said something cutting. The way that her nostrils flared in a moment of frustration. She rarely let her temper get the best of her. Instead, she chose to harness the evil and funnel it into an eviscerating surgical strike rather than a mass explosion.

But the nerves were best masked by her hometown girl charm. She'd plaster on a smile, make a joke, and turn another Maren resident against me just by batting her eyelashes.

I fell in line behind her, waiting for the man who looked like he had one foot in the grave to finish up at the counter.

Jo shifted the legal pad, clutching it with both hands like a life preserver. When the old man shuffled off, glaring at me like I had just kicked a whole litter of puppies, Jo stepped up to the counter. Even in heels, she had to pop up onto her tiptoes to be a whole head higher than the granite top.

"Morning, Mary Beth," she said with a sweet-as-cotton-candy smile.

I hated cotton candy.

"Morning, JoJo." The teller reared back, taking her in. "Well, my goodness. Don't you look all grown up and pretty as a bluebonnet. What brings you in this morning? Deposits?"

Jo shook her head. "No, I'll swing in with those on Monday. I was actually hoping to talk to Bert about a loan. Is he in?"

Mary Beth's long, acrylic talons click-clacked across her computer keys. "Looks like he's got an appointment on the books in just a minute..." Her voice trailed off as she scanned the rest of the schedule, then looked over Jo's head to me. "But it's just with that Thompson boy." She looked at Jo. "Bert's on the phone right now, but I'll let him know you're here."

Jo grinned. "Thanks, Mary Beth."

"You know where the break room is, right?" Mary Beth asked as Jo moved away from the counter. When Jo nodded, she pointed a finger to a small side door. "There's fresh coffee and doughnuts. Go help yourself."

Jo practically skipped through the door that had *Employees Only* plastered on it while I stepped past the yellow line taped to the floor and came face-to-face with Mary Beth. I decided to leave my rancor at home and be... mildly pleasant.

"Good morning," I said as I buttoned my suit jacket. "I have an appointment with Bertram Taylor at nine-thirty."

"He's running behind. Take a seat." Mary Beth didn't

bother looking at me as she flipped open a worn romance novel. *Did everyone read those damn Whitney West books?*

Jo came out of the break room with a paper cup in one hand and a powdered doughnut in the other. Sugar dusted her cheek, her fingers, the hideous blazer, and the thighs of her pants.

"You're holding up the line," Mary Beth snapped.

There wasn't another damn person in this God-forsaken bank. I wanted to pitch a fit and wax poetic about how I personally managed more funds and assets than this bank saw in a decade, but that wasn't going to get me anywhere. Not when the pint-sized menace had single-handedly made me public enemy number one.

With great annoyance, I turned and took a mother-fucking seat in the empty lobby.

Jo was already seated and had a smear of raspberry jam at the corner of her mouth.

I wanted to lick it off.

Whoa, what the fuck? Where the hell had that thought come from?

At night I dreamed of plane crashes. I dreamed of the brakes on her truck failing, sending her careening over a cliff. I dreamed of her dying of dysentery. Making Jo shit herself to death would be a poetic end since she had been a royal pain in my ass from the moment I arrived in Maren.

But kissing her... That wouldn't do.

"What are you doing here?" I hissed as I took the seat across from her.

My back was to the window of Bertram's office. I could hear him on the aforementioned phone call, discussing fantasy football. The vinyl squeaked under my butt. I tried to look composed. Tried to stay in control. But the lumpy seat had other ideas.

My attempt to sit with my calf propped up on my knee was an utter failure. I had to resort to manspreading to keep from sliding out of the chair. Even I knew that I looked like a douche.

"I have a meeting," she said without a care in the world.

"No, *I* have a meeting," I clipped through clenched teeth. "You had an assumption that you could waltz in here, completely ignoring professional protocol, and disrespecting everyone's time by *not* making an appointment."

She grinned—the kind of smile I imagined a lioness having right before she pounced. "Wow. Are you really this crotchety in the morning, too? I mean damn—I knew you weren't an evening person... Or an afternoon person... But seriously? Not a morning person either? Do you just live in a constant state of misery all the time?"

"Much like how you live in a state of delusion rather than the state of Texas."

We were speaking in hushed tones, careful not to let our voices rise over the decibel deemed appropriate for banks and libraries by polite society.

Jo glared at me as she inhaled the rest of the doughnut. "Better delusional than dead." She made direct eye contact as she sucked the powdered sugar off her fingers.

My god. I had never seen something so erotic in my entire life.

"And for your information, I'm here to talk to Bert about a loan." The hometown smile was brief enough to quell the nervousness in her voice. "You know, so that we can square up."

The door behind me opened, and a paunchy man with a graying handlebar mustache poked his head out. "Morning, JoJo! Mary Beth said you wanted to talk?"

Jo looked like she was going to throw up. I was fine with

that as long as she didn't do it on my shoes. It took half a day to get all the dust and animal feces off them after the morning marathon she made me take against my will.

She put on a smile that could charm a rattlesnake and stood. "Yeah. I've got a few questions, and I'd like some advice if you have the time."

He preened like a peacock. "Absolutely, sweetheart. Come on in. Did Mary Beth tell you we got doughnuts this morning?" While Jo laughed and made herself comfortable in his office, Bert looked at me like I was a piece of gum stuck to his shoe on a hot day. "Sorry. Runnin' late. I'll get to you when I get to you." And with that, he slammed the door.

I muttered something that resembled, "Take your time." I wasn't rolling over and playing dead. I was simply biding my time until I could come up with a way to more thoroughly tame the Hell beast.

I flipped through my notes, detailing my plan to get the farm out of the red. With my investment, we were on more stable ground with the bank. Stable like quicksand, but at least it wasn't the swamp it had been. Still, I needed to get an aggressive plan for repayment in place. Profits would be nonexistent this year, but a slim year was better than going under completely.

Jo's laugh penetrated the wall between us. She was buttering up poor Bert, and he had no idea. Then again, he probably didn't care. A little attention from a pretty young thing like Jo and he was probably choking on his tongue.

"Let's get down to business," she said. "I wanted to see about qualifying for a loan. What do I need to do to get it?"

Bert was quiet for a moment, or perhaps I couldn't make out what was being said. Faint tapping came from the keys of his computer, then a heavy sigh. "I'll be honest, JoJo. I like you, kid. But you're not there yet."

More muffled talking. I practically had my ear pressed to the wall.

"Look, you're on the right track. A few more years and you'll qualify no problem. But right now, your debt-to-income ratio is still far too high, and your credit score leaves a lot to be desired. You've done well digging yourself out of the hole, but now you need to build yourself up. If I could give you the loan today, I would. I know how hard you work. Unfortunately, who you are doesn't hold much sway when it comes to who we can approve. If it did, you would have had it when we talked about it a few months back."

There was desperation in her voice and it made me sick. "I've doubled my clients. I work from sun-up to sundown. With my cost of living, I make enough to pay it back in half the time."

"I know that, Jo."

"I serve nearly every farm in this part of the state. With this loan I could buy out—"

"Like I said, sweetheart." He sighed. "It's a complicated situation. If it was just the credit, maybe I could overlook that. But you're self-employed. That already makes it an uphill climb. Add in the fact that everyone knows the Thompson Farm is in jeopardy, and it's not a good investment for us to give you that loan. If the farm goes under, so does the money we'd be loaning you."

Jo didn't say anything else. I heard the scraping of chairs and shuffled feet.

"Work on your credit. Lower your debt. Find a different property to live and fly out of. If the loan isn't dependent on the Thompson's staying in business, the next time you ask, it might be a yes."

"Thanks, Bert," she said softly.

"Word of advice, JoJo?" He paused. "I heard through the

grapevine that George's oldest told Vulkon where they could shove their sweetheart deal. I don't think the farm will be getting another one. The vultures will probably just wait out the farm. That city boy pissed 'em off real good. I'd be careful. Wouldn't want him to drag you down, too."

Motherfucker.

10

VAUGHAN

"You gonna turn that thing off, or am I gonna have to pitch it into the wheelbarrow when I muck the stalls next?" Cash said, pointing at my phone.

Another call from Vulkon.

I smashed the button and sent it to voicemail.

"Did you forget to tell him to change?" Ryman asked Cash.

Cash raised his hands defensively. "I told him. He flipped me the bird and told me to fuck off."

Did they seriously think I couldn't hear them?

When Cash told me they were taking me for drinks at The Silver Spur after the day ended, I thought nothing of it. I'd have a beer with my half-brothers, then head back to the farm to finish working through a new client I was onboarding. Tamara—the godsend—had managed most of the details, I was just giving the account a personal touch. It let them know that I cared about their investments as if they were my own.

But here I was, not doing my job because I was trying to... what was that term? Make an effort?

The line outside the bar shuffled forward. I cuffed my sleeves as we waited patiently for IDs to be checked.

"Whatever. It's fine," Ryman clipped. He peered under the rim of his Stetson and assessed my business wear.

I was in pressed black slacks, a crisp button-up, and a matching gray vest. The sleeves of my shirt were cuffed at the elbows, and my tie was silk. It was a stark contrast to their nearly whitewashed blue jeans, plaid shirts, and over-sized belt buckles. While their boots were Ariats, I was in Paul Smith Oxfords.

"You could totally get laid tonight, bro," Cash said as he stared at the sea of ladies waiting. "You want a wingman?"

I wasn't oblivious to the female gaze; I just didn't care about it.

"That won't be necessary," I said as we moved forward in line.

Cash grinned from ear-to-ear as he lifted his hat and pushed his floppy blond hair out of his face. "Ah, I get it. You got those city boy moves. You don't need a wingman."

"Nope." I shoved my ID in the bouncer's hand even though I was clearly over the age of twenty-one. "Not interested in taking any souvenirs back to Chicago."

Ryman exchanged a few quiet words with the bouncer before grinning. "We're good to go. No cover tonight."

Cash fist-bumped his brother. "Dude, you have it fuckin' made. You flirt with the bouncers and get the cover waived. Flirt with the bartenders and get free drinks. I wish I was bi."

Ryman grinned. "It has its perks."

"Better work your magic," I grumbled as I squeezed my wide shoulders into the narrow door frame and scanned the crowd. People were sandwiched together as they waited for the bartenders to sling drinks.

"Bull riding night is always like this," Cash said. "Don't worry. Ezra and Jenny have it covered."

As if he had willed it into existence, Ezra stuck his fingers in his mouth and let out a sharp whistle. "Thompsons!" He held up an ice bucket full of beers.

"Fuck yeah, dude," Cash said as he elbowed his way through the crowd and grabbed the bucket. When he waded back, nearly swimming through the sea of people, he tipped his chin to Ryman. "He wants you to text him when he gets off."

"Eh. We'll see," Ryman clipped as he snagged a primo table right next to the padded ring that housed the mechanical bull. He still seemed irritated at the game of cat-and-mouse Ezra seemed intent on playing.

"Ry, what have I told you?" Cash asked. "You can't go burning bridges. This is the only bar in the whole fuckin' town, and you know I hate driving to the city."

Ryman grabbed the bottle opener that was tethered to the side of the ice bucket. "Ez and I are good. Just work different hours is all. He's getting off work when I'm going to work. Trying to deal with that is more effort than it's worth."

My phone rang again, and I glanced at the screen. *Vulkon.*

I took the call. "Vaughan Thompson."

"Mr. Thompson, this is Gerald calling from Edward Ellington's office at Vulkon Incorporated."

"Yes, I'm aware of that, Jerry," I said as I reached for a beer. "You've been tying up my line for three days now."

"Mr. Ellington would love to have a sit-down with you when he comes to Maren. I think you'll be interested in what he has to say."

"I highly doubt that."

Gerald chuckled, unfazed by my rancor. "I know how it

can be—family ties and all that. But you're not a farmer, Vaughan. Can I call you Vaughan?"

"You can call me Mr. Thompson."

"Let's just say that my boss isn't just interested in the property."

The subtext raised my hackles, and Ryman and Cash eyed me curiously. "It's about time he latched onto something else. The property isn't for sale."

"How's next Tuesday at three in the afternoon?" Gerald suggested. "I'll follow up with the venue for the meeting."

"How about you go fuck yourself," I said as I took a swig of my Lonestar. "And tell Ellington to go and do likewise." I ended the call and dropped my phone on the table.

Cash looked like the wide-eyed boy he used to be. "Did you just—"

"Tell the president of Vulkon to go fuck himself?" Ryman finished.

"I told his assistant to pass along the suggestion, yes."

"Holy shit," Ryman breathed over the lip of his beer bottle.

"Badass," Cash said as he shook his head.

I downed half of my beer and wiped the foam from my mouth. "Just doing my job."

"Yeah, but you told the *president of Vulkon* to go fuck himself!" Cash exclaimed. "That's like walking up to the gates of hell, waving at Satan, and flipping him the bird."

"He's an old man in an office. He's not Satan. It's just business."

"It's the suits," Ryman said. "I've seen that dude around here. Man rolls through town in a six-figure SUV. Ain't nobody 'round here wearing expensive as hell suits to look at farmland. He's corporate Satan."

I looked down to the four out of five pieces of my suit, then back up at Cash and Ry. "And what am I?"

Cash grinned. "Corporate Hades."

I ... didn't mind that so much. In fact, I quite liked it—especially when I thought back to seeing Joelle at the bank. She was pretending in that god-awful pantsuit. It was a costume to her. But to me, my suits were armor. My watch was a weapon. My knowledge—that was power.

I knew enough about men like Edward Ellington to know that I wasn't afraid of him. He could throw his weight around all he wanted.

But he wasn't touching my farm.

I tried to dismiss the notion. It wasn't my farm. It was my family's farm. I was just here temporarily.

No souvenirs, I reminded myself.

"Ladies and gentlemen!" A woman's voice called from the stage. "It's five o' clock, the work day is done, the beers are cold, and it's time to ride!"

Cheers went up across the packed bar.

Ryman's eyes were on his phone. Cash nudged him with his elbow. "Is she coming tonight?"

Ryman grinned. "Oh yeah. And she's in rare form."

"Figured," Cash muttered as he drained his beer and went for a second. "She was flying like a goddamn kamikaze today. Only does that when something—" he peered at me "—or *someone* royally pisses her off."

I strangled the glass bottle in my hand. "Who?" I asked even though I knew damn well who he was talking about.

Her.

As if I'd conjured her, the lights dimmed and a spotlight beamed on the worn saddle that covered the back of the mechanical bull. Cigarette smoke clouded the vinyl padded arena. The speakers thumped with the heavy bass of a country tune that was dark and broody.

"Y'all know the drill!" the DJ called over the guitar riff. "Only one hand on the bull. Get rowdy for the riders you like! Five hundred dollar cash prize to the rider who puts on the best show!"

The bar went from ambient murmurs to stadium cheers as curtains parted on stage and Jo appeared. She circled the arena, trailing her hand along the edge of the wood pallets that separated the rider from the crowd. Shadows covered her as she strutted around the ring, working the crowd. Her smile flashed in the dim bar like a spark of electricity. Her hair hung in loose waves down her back. Her legs were painted in dark leather.

That was until she stood in the light.

Cheers nearly busted my eardrums as she stepped into the spotlight.

She was in a tiny leather vest that stopped just below her cleavage. What I thought were pants, were actually chaps.

Beneath the leather was the tiniest of G-strings.

The chaps framed her bare ass like it was the goddamn *Mona Lisa*. She bent and brushed nonexistent dust off the toes of her boots. Bills started raining down on her like a high-roller strip club, and she hadn't even gotten on the bull yet.

Jo caught my eyes. Like the devil she was, she grinned like this was all part of her plan to kill me. Like she knew that seeing her put on a fucking show, exposing all those curves and hidden places, would kill me.

And God help me, it might.

Cash elbowed Ryman. "Dude. She's gonna fuckin' kill it tonight."

My blood flowed hot and violent at the thought of my brothers—*half-brothers*—watching her.

"Bro, do you need a handful of Aspirin or something?"

I guess it was Ryman who had asked, but I wasn't completely sure. His voice sounded like it was a hundred miles away. All I saw was her.

Her climbing onto that bull.

Her ass peeking out of those chaps.

That string disappearing between her cheeks.

The vest that barely concealed her tits.

The tits that I had seen when she was sprawled out in her back porch stock tank.

"You look like you're having a heart attack." That was definitely Cash talking to me. "You sure you're alright? That vein poppin' out of your skull ain't normal."

I pressed my beer bottle to my forehead. Cool droplets of water nearly sizzled on my skin.

I was feverish. That had to be it.

That, or I was having a heart attack. I was sweating like I'd just run a marathon in the midday sun, and my breath was choppy like I was drowning.

Definitely a heart attack.

The music switched to something with a fast beat as Jo backed away from the bull, then ran. She leaped into the air, legs separating in a near-split as she landed on the saddle. Her breasts peeked out from under the open vest.

Fuck me, she wasn't wearing a bra. Not even goddamn pasties.

With each flash of her tits, the crowd grew more and more rowdy. The DJ moved back to the control panel and flipped a switch. The bull shuddered, jolting back and forth. Jo tipped her head back, laughing as she jiggled from side to side. Her ass bounced on the seat, golden skin teasing me.

Topless bull riding at the Silver Spur Saloon had been a Maren institution since I was in diapers. If I had known that it was like this, I would have tried a hell of a lot harder to sneak into the bar in my teenage years.

But it wouldn't have been her, and that's what made the show so fucking erotic.

Jo was having the time of her life, swinging around on that bull as she put on one hell of a show.

The arena was a sea of green. Dollar bills covered every square inch as she whipped around, keeping a steady grip on the bull.

The DJ grinned, tossing her bleached-out mullet over her shoulder as she manned the controls. She wasn't trying to throw the riders off, I realized. She was helping Jo put on a show.

The bull stopped shaking side-to-side and switched to a deep rocking motion. Jo slid to the front of the machine and leaned forward, offering an unobstructed view of her ass. When the bull tipped up, she slid backward and arched her spine. The flaps of the vest fell apart and her tits came into full view.

Ryman let out a sharp whistle, and Cash whooped.

My mouth felt like I had eaten cotton.

She drew her knees up, and planted her boots on the saddle.

"Holy shit," I muttered as Jo stood up straight on the back of the bull.

Cash was grinning from ear-to-ear. "She's good, right?"

She was ... something.

Jo practically surfed the back of the bull, keeping her hips loose with each rock and twist of the machine. Her eyes met mine and, as if to say, "Watch this," she grinned.

The DJ flipped a lever and the bull spun in a circle. Jo

jumped, spreading her legs and dropping down onto the saddle, catching the bull as it whipped around.

The DJ alternated between making her tits shake by having the bull vibrate side-to-side, and making her slide up and down the back of it. Jo's eyes closed, and her lips parted in a lazy smile as if she was enjoying this. As if she was getting off on it.

As if she was riding a man. Not a machine.

All I could imagine was her up there with my handprint marking her ass like a brand.

They could look, but they couldn't touch.

The song ended and Jo was still on the bull. No way would any other rider beat that.

No way could any other woman beat that.

Ho-ly shit.

Instead of picking up the cash that had been thrown at her—which was way more than the five-hundred-dollar cash prize for the winner—she strutted over to our table.

I opened my mouth to say something, but Jo paid me no mind. She grabbed Ryman's Stetson, plopped it on her head, and then turned and kissed Cash square on the mouth.

I wanted to throw her over my shoulder like a possessive caveman, then punch Cash in the face.

Her Cheshire grin as she pulled away taunted me.

Ryman and Cash jumped over the partition, into the arena, and grabbed the push brooms propped up against the wall. They corralled all the bills and shoved them into a corner.

The DJ offered them a trash bag for Jo's haul.

The mingling scent of sweat, Jo's perfume, and the smoky aroma of hellfire and brimstone lingered as she leaned on the arena's wall. Someone shoved a beer in her hand and she took a swig.

"You enjoy the show, city boy?" Jo asked. Her voice held a low, seductive rasp.

Her teardrop-shaped breasts dangled over the edge, dark pink nipples teasing me. I watched as her lips wrapped around the bottle and she tipped it back.

Her throat constricted with the swallow and I imagined her swallowing my cum.

I leaned back in my seat, and took a casual pull from my bottle. "I've seen better."

Jo's grin was feral as her eyes flicked to my crotch. "You keep telling yourself that."

"I tip good strippers with Benjamins." I reached into my pocket and pulled out my wallet. I thumbed through the stack of petty cash I kept on hand and pulled a single bill out. I reached over the partition and stuck one dollar in the waist of her chaps. "Go buy yourself some class."

11

JOELLE

The six-pack in the passenger's seat clinked as I shifted gears, easing the truck off the road. I dimmed my headlights as I pulled through the Thompson Farm gates.

By my guess, Cash and Ryman would still be at the saloon with that ass potato they were unfortunately related to.

Buy yourself some class? How fucking dare he.

My knuckles turned white against the steering wheel. The only thing that was grounding me to reality was the fact that my thong was fusing itself to my butt crack. That, and the garbage bag of cash I'd shoved into the floorboard for safekeeping during my quick run into Jay's for beer.

Of course, Vaughan would take any opportunity to get in a jab. In his defense, I would have done the same. It wouldn't have mattered if he had a bad day like the one I had. It wouldn't have mattered if he was forever stuck in a shitty hole.

If I saw him dancing like he was on *Magic Mike,* I would have taken the opportunity to knock him down a peg, too.

Do unto others, right?

But no matter how much I tried to ignore the sting, I couldn't. Hence the alcoholic Band-Aid sitting beside me.

Usually after I cleaned house riding the mechanical bull and flashing my tits to all of Maren, I would have stuck around and played pool, hustling some unassuming newcomers out of their paychecks.

I never let myself get anything more than a light buzz at the bar, but tonight I just wanted to get wasted.

Instead of stopping at my cabin, I drove out to the property line. It was far enough away from the big house that no one would see my truck lights. Far enough away that no one would hear me cry.

That was, if I even could cry tonight.

I wanted to.

I made it through the clearing and coasted to a stop. A lone figure sat on a stump, poking at the fire pit I had dug out.

It wasn't Cash or Ryman's blond hair.

It was dark.

"Get out," I snapped as I hopped out and slammed the truck door, towing my beers behind me.

Vaughan looked over his shoulder, then tipped a bottle back, downing a swig. He was still in that stupid vest and tie, though the tie was loosened around his collar.

I wanted to strangle him with it.

"No." The syllable wasn't slurred, but it was close. He took another pull from the bottle.

The glass glinted in the moonlight, and I got a better look at what he was drinking. Top shelf Scotch straight from the bottle while sitting on a rotting log in the woods. *Classy.*

"You're in my spot," I snapped. "But if you're intent on

staying here, I can arrange a permanent place for you. I've got a gun and a shovel."

Fire burned beneath Vaughan's brown eyes, glowing like a bonfire. "This isn't your land."

"It's not yours either," I shot back. "You can throw your money around all you want, but it doesn't change the fact that this isn't your home. It's mine." I was shouting, and I hated that. I wanted to have the calm, cool, collected façade that he did.

Instead of countering with something snarky, he turned away and took another drink.

Two could play that game.

He detested my presence. If he wasn't in the mood for verbal sparring, I'd simply annoy him with proximity. He didn't deserve the luxury of drinking in peace. Not after acting like a complete jackass at the saloon. I dropped the tailgate to the truck and hopped up. Fishing the bottle opener out of my bra, I popped the top on the first bottle and downed half of it in the first sip.

"Shouldn't you still be moonlighting as a slutty cowgirl?" he called over his shoulder.

I snorted. "Come on, Thompson. Even you can do better than that." I laid back on the truck bed. The bumpy, corrugated metal bit into my back and shoulders. "I expected more from you."

It sounded like he murmured, "Everyone does."

His shoulders were hunched, and reckless pieces of dark hair hung in front of his face. For a few minutes, we sat in silence. The dance of alcohol sloshing in glass filled the night air like wind chimes.

Finally, he huffed and stood. His shoes—*probably those fancy ones he always wore*—scraped against the dirt and loose rocks. "What are you doing out here?"

"I don't owe you an explanation," I said as I cracked open my second beer.

"Yeah, well, it's apparent that neither of us are leaving, so you might as well tell me what you're doing. Shouldn't you be in that pile of sticks you call a cabin, counting your winnings?"

I laughed as a warm buzz washed over me. "Eight hundred and forty-three dollars and fifty-six cents. That's not counting the five-hundred-dollar prize for being a fucking badass."

Vaughan cracked a grin. "Someone threw change at you?"

I snickered. "Don't look so surprised. It was probably you. Hell—next month you'll probably show up with a sock full of nickels and pelt me off that bull."

He downed more of the Scotch. "I didn't throw anything at you."

Slipped it into my chaps, but that was semantics. I would have rather he kept the dollar and left my dignity intact.

"I swear," he said as he listed to the left, then grabbed onto the tailgate for support. "I didn't throw fucking coins at you. I was too busy watching you."

What's that thing folks always say? The only honest people are toddlers and drunks?

Things were about to get real honest.

"I know."

Vaughan raised an eyebrow as I chugged the rest of my beer, then opened another one.

"I saw you watching me."

His eyes dropped to my cleavage. I was still in the cut-offs and flannel I had worn to the Silver Spur, but I hadn't bothered buttoning the flannel after I finished my ride and got dressed. At least my bra was cute.

"You think I perform like that for just anyone?" I continued. Vaughan shrugged and I couldn't stifle my beer-fueled giggle. "Only people I want to torture. How's your dick, by the way? An erection lasting that long can't feel good."

"So, I'm special, huh?" he said as he eased his well-toned ass onto the tailgate.

I stared up at the sky full of endless stars. "I don't hate anyone quite the way I hate you. So if that makes you feel special, then by golly, you're special."

His grin was that of an alligator's. "Glad to hear it, Tinkerbell."

"Tinkerbell's blonde!" I exclaimed at a decibel that was far too loud for how close we were. I elbowed my way up from the half-prone position and sat up. "You can't be so drunk that you actually think I'm blonde."

"Not 'cause you're blonde, Tiger," he grinned. "Because you've got an attitude that matches." Vaughan's eyes lingered on my face. I could tell he was studying the jagged scar that slashed across the side of my head. "Got a tiger stripe, too."

Without breaking his gaze, he raised the half-empty fifth of Scotch to his lips and drank. His Adam's apple bobbed as he swallowed.

My bottle was still pressed to my lips, but I didn't dare take a sip. Watching him was far more intoxicating.

"Why do you do it?" he rasped.

"Do what?"

There was a heavy pause. " Why do you ride?"

It was interesting that he didn't say, "Why do you flash your tits and show your ass to the town and have money thrown at you?" I knew that's what he was getting at. But he simply said, "Ride."

I preferred it that way. There were two different answers he could have pulled out of me, especially fueled by the booze. I erred on the simple side since words were swirling around my head like alphabet soup in a blender.

"Pays the bills."

"I know what you charge to fly." Vaughan's eyes bore into me. "I did the math. I know what you make. You don't need to do shit like that."

But he didn't know the whole story. "I ride once a month and live off the winnings. The rest of my income goes into the business and paying shit off."

"Are you really that irresponsible with money?" he jeered.

Easy for him to say. It was easy to do things like throw money around or qualify for loans when you weren't already in a hole.

I rolled my eyes. "Just shut up and drink yourself to death already. It'll be easier to bury you if you're not squirming around."

Vaughan called me Tiger, but it was his grin that was feline. "I like you, Joelle."

He was definitely drunk off his ass.

He slid off the tailgate, but didn't walk away. Instead, he faced me. The bottle of Scotch hung from his fingertips. It wasn't quite as empty as I thought it was.

"No, you don't," I countered with a swig of beer.

"I think about you more than I think about anyone else," he said as he laughed at the stars. "I think you like it."

"Probably—" I poked him square in the chest "— because you like keeping your enemies close."

His hand wrapped around my wrist, holding my finger against his sternum. My breath caught in my throat. "Nothing you've done before now has pissed me off as much as it pissed me off to see you kiss Cash. It was low, I'll give you that."

A slow, satisfied smile crept up the corner of my mouth. "What can I say? He's the better kisser out of the Thompson boys." *Although, Vaughan looked like he'd know what to do with a woman.*

His tongue darted out and wet his lips.

Just to drive the knife in deeper, I added, "But I've never kissed Bristol. Maybe I should give her a try before I make any judgments."

Vaughan's nostrils flared, and he gritted his teeth. "You've kissed Cash *and* Ryman?"

I could smell the liquor on his breath. The bottle of Scotch clinked against the truck bed as Vaughan set it down. Warm hands wrapped around my knees and spread them apart. He took a step forward and stood between my legs. His palms slid up from my knees and held my thighs in a steady grip.

Tipping my chin up, I craned my neck to try and meet his gaze. "Yes."

I caught the slightest glimpse of Vaughan's glassy eyes before he lowered his lids, focusing on my mouth. "How can you make a judgment about which Thompson boy is the better kisser when you haven't kissed all of them?"

I leaned forward, grazing my lips against his. "I guess I can go make out with your dad. I don't think Ms. Faith will mind."

Vaughan clicked his tongue. His nose bumped against mine. "You know, one day your mouth is gonna write a check that your ass can't cash." His fingers flexed around my thighs, digging into my skin.

I fingered the textured fabric of his vest. *What kind of a man wore a suit vest in Maren, Texas?*

The air was as hot as asphalt in the middle of July.

He glanced at the space between us, where my fingers grazed the buttons that dotted the front of the vest.

"You should take it off," he rasped.

"What?"

"Take it off me," Vaughan growled. "You said it yourself. That little show you put on—you did that to get at me. Take my vest off."

Electricity flashed down my spine.

His eyes were completely open now, dark and full of lust as he stared at me.

"And then what?" I whispered into the night air.

He tilted his head, and his lips met my throat. "And then you're going to put it on and give me my show."

There were a hundred ways I could have efficiently killed him using the random things I kept stashed in the truck. Instead of reaching for any of the implements that came to mind, I unfastened the first button.

Vaughan bit the underside of my jaw. "Keep going."

I whimpered and undid the next one. He pushed my flannel off my arms.

"Two more, tiger." His hand raked my scalp as he fisted the bulk of my hair at the base of my neck. Vaughan tilted my head back, exposing my throat.

My breasts strained against the plunging bra I had on. With clumsy fingers, I undid the final buttons while he kissed my throat. Vaughan shucked off the vest. His tie hung recklessly from his neck, mussed and disheveled.

Without warning, he grabbed my hips and lifted me, taking my place on the tailgate and dropping me on his lap, facing him.

My knees settled on either side of his hips, and I nestled up against his erection. I grappled at his shirt, trying to get it off him as fast as humanly possible.

"Nuh uh-uh," he murmured, grabbing my wrists in one large hand and yanking them high above my head. "Put your claws away, tiger."

I whimpered. *Fucking hell.* I had *whimpered* and he hadn't done anything but kiss my neck and plop me on his lap. *How pathetic.*

His hand flexed around my restrained wrists. "Are you going to behave?"

"Fat chance of that," I clipped as I ground into his erection.

Vaughan grinned. "I'll take my chances." He dropped my wrists and pushed my bra straps off my shoulders. Faster than any man ever had, he reached around and unfastened the hook and eye.

"Are you a boob guy or an ass man?" I asked as he yanked it off my arms.

"Ass," he said without hesitation.

"Lucky you," I breathed as he worked his vest around my arms, letting it hang open over my torso. "If you were a boob guy, you would be sorely disappointed."

His hand skated up my ribs and cupped my small breast. "I'm not disappointed."

The happy buzz I had been riding was slowly fading. I needed something stronger. Something to make me forget that I was dry humping my mortal enemy.

I reached for the Scotch, but Vaughan had my hands pinned behind my back before I could blink.

Then again, I was blinking *really* slowly. I blamed the beers.

"The only way you're drinking that is if I let it drip into your mouth from my lips."

"Then you better drink up," I rasped.

He hooked two fingers in the waist of my shorts, keeping

me anchored to him as he reached for the bottle. Vaughan tipped the bottle back and took a drink. Without warning, his mouth crashed into mine.

Liquor dribbled down our chins as his tongue swept into my mouth. The burn of the Scotch was mellowed by the instant chaser of lust.

His lips were strong, dominating and leading me in the kiss. It consumed me. Every particle that composed my body exploded like an atomic bomb had detonated.

I snaked my arms around his neck and tangled my fingers in his thick hair.

His hands found my hips, guiding them side to side, forcing me to rock against his throbbing cock.

Vaughan's tongue swept into my mouth again, lapping at mine. I savored every taste of Scotch. Something about drinking it straight from the devil's mouth made it exponentially more powerful.

"Vaughan—" I whispered his name as I quickened my pace, rubbing my cunt up and down his covered dick. We were like teenagers, sneaking out to the back forty to get frisky.

"Are you gonna come like this?" he said in a guttural rasp that sent sparks skittering across my skin.

I nodded. "Uh-huh."

He pulled my hair, a sharp tug that brought my ear to his mouth. "Tell me the truth. You nearly got off while riding that bull, knowing that you made me hard as fuck. You got off on kissing my brother in front of me."

I didn't bother pointing out that he had called Cash his *brother* instead of *half-brother* like he usually did.

"Yes," I said. It was barely audible. I was so close. I wanted that orgasm so badly.

"Tell me something, Tiger," he said. "Tell me who's the better kisser now."

I whined, my eyes rolling back as I reached the pinnacle of pleasure.

Vaughan palmed my tit and gave my nipple a sharp tug.

I yelped, nearly collapsing into him.

"Tell me," he said in a tone that was more of a threat than a request.

"You are," I spat, lacing the words with as much venom as I could. I hated admitting it, but my body wasn't about to let me lie when he was about to give me a male-induced orgasm.

"Hating me is a fucking aphrodisiac for you, isn't it?"

I tried to find his lips again. To savor the way it felt to be kissed by him. The way it made me float.

"Answer me," he growled, using my hair as a tether to keep my mouth millimeters away from his.

"Yes," I breathed. I was so close. I could feel the wave of euphoria cresting. I was almost—

Vaughan grabbed my hips and lifted me off his lap. My crotch hovered an inch above his.

Damn him and those muscles. My clit throbbed like a kick drum. One touch and I would come.

Just one more touch.

Vaughan set me on the edge of the tailgate, dropped to his feet, and grabbed the Scotch.

He took a swig, then poured the rest into the dirt before turning back toward the path to the big house. "I hope that hate keeps you warm at night."

12

VAUGHAN

"You're up early," Bristol said as she moseyed out onto the porch, sipping on a mug of coffee.

I rested my forearms on the cedar railing, clutching a mug of my own. "I'm always up early."

She snickered. "Not *this* early."

Maybe Bristol had a point. I was an early bird, but not a farm early bird. I was a *wake up at six, get in a workout, breakfast, and a shower before heading to the office* kind of guy. I wasn't the type to wake up before the rooster.

But today I was.

"So," she said between sips. "Why are you up?" She eyed me suspiciously. "It isn't about Meredith, is it?"

I wrinkled my nose. "Fuck no."

To my knowledge, Bristol had met my ex-wife a grand total of two times. Once at our wedding, and once when we visited Maren for Christmas at the behest of Ms. Faith.

"Good," she muttered. "I never liked her."

I raised an eyebrow at Bristol, but held my tongue. It had never occurred to me that my baby sister—*half* sister—had opinions about my marriage. She was a kid when I had been with Meredith.

I nudged her with my elbow. "How're you doing?"

Her brows furrowed, forming a tiny groove above her nose. "What do you mean?"

"You know ... with your breakup."

Bristol looked momentarily surprised, then stared back into her coffee. "Fine."

"I'm sorry for losing my shit on you the other night."

"I think you owe most of that apology to Jo," she said without skipping a beat.

I grunted something unintelligible. *No chance of that.*

"Not like I had anyone else to go to," she said quietly.

I scoffed. "You had—"

"Cash and Ryman?" She laughed. "Please. Do you think I'd actually go to those two bozos for boy advice? They're more likely to kill the guy and lock me in my room until I'm forty."

She had a point.

"And you and I don't really talk since you never come around," she added on quietly. "Mom's been worried about Dad's recovery. And Jo's just... She's always been there."

My stomach soured. "Bris—"

"I know I'm not your whole sister," she clipped. "I don't take it personally. We didn't grow up together."

I rested my coffee mug on the wood railing and hooked my arm around her neck. "C'mere, kid."

Bristol tucked into my side.

"There's two things you need to know. First, I'm a better shot than Cash and Ry. So, if anyone's putting a bullet in some prick, it's me. Second, I was eighteen when you were born. And I remember going to the hospital and holding you."

She looked up at me. "Yeah?"

"Did your mom ever tell you how you got your name?"

She shook her head.

I sighed. "Before my mom died, I remembered her talking about wanting us to go on a road trip to Bristol, Tennessee because it was the birthplace of country music. There's a—uh—big museum there. She really loved music... We never got to go, but I remember thinking that if we got the chance, going to Bristol would be the best thing that ever happened, because it meant that she was getting better. She didn't, but I held on to the idea of Bristol, because it gave me hope that things would be good again."

She wrapped her arm around my waist and squeezed. "I didn't know that."

"Dad and your mom hadn't decided on a name yet, and they asked me if I had any ideas." I rested my chin on top of her head. Her hair was the same dark shade as mine. "So, I asked if they would name you Bristol."

She sniffed, and I realized that she was crying. I took her mug and set it beside mine before wrapping my arms around her. "I love you, Bris."

"I like you better than Ry and Cash," she murmured into my chest.

I laughed.

She sniffed, wiping her eyes. "And I love you, too."

The sweet moment was shattered by the ear-piercing screech of metal on asphalt. Birds evacuated the trees in flocks at the racket.

"Sweet Jesus, what is that?" I asked as I let go of Bristol and downed the rest of my coffee.

"Jo opening up the hangar," she said as if it was just another day. "I think the hangar door is warped or some-thing and it makes that noise when she's rolling it back."

I raised my eyebrows. "You *think*?"

Bristol shrugged. "Just needs some WD-40." She paused and added, "*A lot* of WD-40."

I paid the comment no mind as I pulled my phone out of my pocket and opened the app that monitored the trail cameras stationed across the farm. There was one in particular, I had noticed, that pointed right at Jo's hangar.

Last night had been an anomaly, I decided. I was horny, drunk, and let it get the best of me when I kissed the Angel of Death.

But fuck, that woman could kiss.

My fingers tingled at the memory of making her strip out of her clothes and put on my vest.

I never got the vest back, but if a piece of clothing was the price for feeling her bare tits in my hands, I'd happily empty my closet.

Not that I'd ever admit that out loud.

The single thought made me feel like I needed to go to confession.

Maybe it was the self-loathing that made me do it, but as I stumbled out of the clearing, leaving Jo behind, a wicked idea popped up in my mind.

Things were a little too chummy between us. I needed to redraw the boundaries. Needed to add fuel to the fire.

I wasn't waving a goddamn white flag. I was going to obliterate her.

This was war.

There would be no truce. There would be no prisoners. There would be no survivors.

The renewed purpose was why I had broken into her cabin, crept around the bow-tied lump of fur she thought was a guard dog, and stolen her Dollar Store lipstick.

A banshee screech pierced the air, startling me out of my

thoughts. I studied the trail camera feed as a smirk drew up my mouth.

"What the hell?" Bristol murmured as she popped up on her toes, trying to figure out what made Jo's voice carry across the farm.

I was grinning from ear-to-ear. On the grainy night vision feed, I watched as Jo hauled her plane out of the hangar.

In a bright shade called Red Rebel, I had scrawled, *Save a horse, ride a cowgirl.*

Bristol gasped as she craned around my arm and studied my phone. "Vaughan!"

Her mug tipped off the edge of the railing and shattered on the flower bed pavers below. Shards of glass exploded, spraying across the mulch.

"Did you do that?" she screeched.

I took a screenshot for posterity, then pocketed my phone. "Do what?"

"Well, I know it sure as hell wasn't Cash and Ry." She planted her hands on her hips. "Vaughan..."

Her tone had an eerie resemblance to Ms. Faith. It felt like I was back to being an eight-year-old, getting scolded for sneaking out of the big house to walk the property at night.

"An eye for an eye is never the answer, Bris," I said. "But sometimes it is *an* answer."

"And what did Jo do to you?" Bristol snapped more aggressively than the snoozing pit bull in Jo's cabin. "*Recently,*" she tacked on.

We all knew Jo wasn't innocent in this turf war. She started it. *But I was going to finish it.*

"What did she do *recently* to deserve *that*?"

Make me want her, I thought to myself. There was something about those blue eyes... She was so full of life. I thought being flighty was a bad thing, but if flighty was her, then... *Fuck*. I wanted her.

I wanted to play with fire.

I didn't want to extinguish it. I wanted to fuel it, then control it. I wanted to see how close I could get without being burned.

Then again, part of me wondered what it would be like to be marked by her fury. A dark part of me wanted to know how much I could let her flames wrap around me before she consumed me entirely.

One taste of her lips. One touch of her bare skin. One moment of fleeting pleasure while I listened to her quiet gasps and pleas as she worked her cunt along the outside of my shaft...

Fuck her for getting under my skin and not letting go.

Bristol's face showed absolutely no humor in the situation. "Make it right." She crossed her arms. "My Momma would have a conniption if she knew you did that, and from what I've heard about yours, she would have too."

———

THE SUN HAD JUST BEGUN to lift over the horizon when I hopped in the borrowed farm truck and headed to Jay's.

Bristol must have called ahead and given him permission to serve me because there was no push back when I stepped up to the counter and ordered a sack full of breakfast tacos. Still, Jay glared at me as he filled the paper bag, wrote Jo's name on the front, then stapled it shut.

As if I would try to poison her.

Then again... Nah. I wouldn't poison her. Poison was too easy to trace. One toxicology panel and you were done for.

Besides, there was a hog farm not too far away. Hogs were great for disposing of bodies.

My shoes crept silently along the cracked runway as I strode to the hangar. The doors were rolled back, and the sounds of Blues Saraceno drifted from the boombox in the corner.

Jo—in a pair of red rubber boots, the same cut-offs she had been wearing last night, and a sports bra—stood with a hose in hand as she rinsed off the front of the bright yellow plane.

Suds pooled on the concrete below, slowly swirling down the drain. I could still make out the 'w' in cowgirl. She probably hadn't been able to reach it from either side of the plane.

It had been a bitch to climb up there and scrawl the message while I was tipsy. Hell—it was a miracle I hadn't fallen and broken my neck.

Jo would have probably walked in on my paralyzed body, yelled at me for getting blood in her hangar, then thrown a mop at me and told me to clean it up myself.

She probably would have kicked me in the nuts for good measure.

I winced as I got closer. The music was far too loud for this level of a hangover. The consequences of getting drunk after thirty sucked.

"Don't make me turn this hose on you," Jo clipped as she whipped the tail end of the coil out, giving her a little more lead to wash the 'W' off of the windshield. "I'm not in the mood."

"Could have fooled me," I clipped as I shoved one hand in the pocket of my slacks.

The Rolex on my wrist glinted in the morning sun, sending rays of light dancing along the corrugated metal walls. She was probably feeling just as shitty as I was. Granted, she'd been downing beers. I went straight for the hard liquor.

"Figured you could use some hangover food." I lifted the grease-soaked bag that had 'JoJo' scrawled on it.

She kinked the hose in one hand and cocked her hip. "I never thought I'd see the day when you actually felt guilty about something."

I snorted. "Guilty? I don't feel guilty."

Okay, I felt a little guilty, but it was mostly because of Bristol's face when she saw the trail camera feed.

Jo rolled her eyes. "Get out of my hangar, dipshit."

"If I felt guilty, I would have been out here washing it off."

"Let me guess," Jo mused with a wicked grin. "You came by to bribe me with brisket tacos so you could get your precious vest back."

I watched as she scaled a ladder, grabbed a gray washrag that was stained pink, and craned over the nose of the plane to finish scrubbing the lipstick 'W' off.

Without thinking, I walked over and stood at the bottom of the ladder, keeping my weight on the bottom rung to stabilize it.

The last thing I wanted was for my mortal enemy to fall to her death. Fucking with her was too much fun. It'd be a pity if she died by something other than my hand.

"You smelled like a brewery last night," I clipped. "I'd appreciate it if you had it dry-cleaned before you returned it."

I looked up and stared unabashedly at her ass as it wiggled back and forth. My dick twitched at the thought of how it felt to have her bouncing on my lap, trying to get off on my cock. I thought about the way she had straddled the mechanical bull in those assless chaps, her tanned cheeks on display under the spotlight.

Something wet and heavy slapped my face.

I stumbled away from the ladder as dirty water streamed down my face, ran into my collar, and soaked me to the bone. "What the—"

"So-rry," Jo sing-songed. "You shoulda known better than to let me wear anything that can't go in a washing machine."

I peeled the wet rag off my face and, to my horror, discovered that she had been scrubbing that rusted-out flying death machine with my favorite vest.

Dirt, lipstick, and soap stained the once-luxurious fabric.

She was...

Oh, I was going to...

Joelle fucking Reed would rue the day she decided to pull over on the side of the road.

The sopping wet vest hit the ground with a *plop*.

"Word of advice, Mr. Thompson," she said, sweet as sugar.

Jo climbed down from the plane. Her rubber boots splashed in the puddle at the base of the ladder. Water the color of chocolate milk dotted the hem of my slacks and stained my crisp, white dress shirt.

"If you keep fucking around, you *will* find out." She grabbed the hose and sprayed off the rest of the suds, seemingly unbothered by my presence.

I dropped the damp bag of tacos on a work table as the song on the radio switched to something about the singer's woman being sunshine mixed with a hurricane. That could have been said about Joelle Reed—sunshine mixed with a hurricane. But only if that hurricane was Katrina.

"Do you think I'm out here crying over you calling me names or thinking I'm a whore?" she clipped with a laugh that wasn't at all sarcastic. "I've been called far worse, city boy." Jo cut the water to the hose, and turned to face me. "I'm not a delicate little butterfly you can trap in a jar or squish under your heel. I'm a fucking velociraptor."

A slow smile crept across my mouth. My palm smoothed along the abrading stubble on my cheek as I slowly strode closer to her. "Is that what you think?"

Jo crossed her arms, pushing her breasts just a little bit higher.

"That's fine. You're a velociraptor," I said magnanimously. I leaned close, letting my mouth graze her ear with the lightest touch.

She let the slightest intake of breath slip.

"Just know that your days are numbered. I'm the asteroid that's gonna end you."

Instead of backing away like I thought she was, Jo tipped her chin up. Dark waves spilled down her back, and heavy lids shielded powder blue irises.

"You're not an asteroid, Vaughan," she said.

A wicked smile curled up on her lips as she ghosted them over mine. She had stolen my breath by simply saying my name.

Before I could come to terms with what those feelings meant, Jo finished her thought. "You're just an ass."

13

JOELLE

Vaughan's brown eyes flashed with fury as he backed away from me like I had bitch slapped him. Little did he know, I didn't slap. I punched.

Daddy didn't teach me much, but he did give me a shining example of how to throw a mean right hook. *I got first-hand experience on what it felt like to take that punch, too.*

Daddy didn't like it when I started hitting back.

My eyes flicked down to Vaughan's crotch. He got off on this just as much as I did. The evidence was straining against his zipper.

My panties were uncomfortably wet, and it wasn't from hosing down the plane.

Maybe we were both toxic. Maybe we were just too similar. We weren't opposite magnets, attracted to each other. We were the same negative pole, pushing at each other relentlessly.

Ms. Faith probably would have said we were dancing on the line between love and hate.

But it was far more elementary than that.

We simply brought out the worst in each other.

Sure, it was fun screwing with him. And yeah—maybe I'd miss him when he hauled ass back to Chicago.

But when he went back to Chicago, I wouldn't have someone fucking with my livelihood.

His gaze warmed my skin. I craved that heat. Craved the way his attention made me feel electric.

Last night had been... I didn't know how to wrap my head around what I'd done.

I was no stranger to one-night-stands, and I knew my way around a dick. But I wasn't the kind of woman who dry humped her mortal enemy in the middle of the woods.

Even *I* had standards.

We stood frozen; both paralyzed in thought of how last night could have ended. Vaughan made no move to cover his erection, and I didn't bother pretending like I wasn't looking.

He stumbled back to assess me, then apparently changed his mind and stepped forward. Vaughan towered over me like a skyscraper. His booming voice quieted to a low growl. "How'd it feel to go to bed with your pussy still begging for me to finish you off?"

Here we were, yet again. My back was pressed against the side of the plane, and Vaughan was caging me in. Wide palms braced against the fuselage.

I tipped my chin up, refusing to cower. "How do you know I didn't finish myself off?"

His grin was Machiavellian. "Because if you had gotten off, you wouldn't be this mouthy."

"Don't flatter yourself."

Vaughan's hand came down and squeezed my breast. I couldn't help the whimper that escaped my lips. My eyes rolled back as he worked his thumb over the swell in a slow massage. I was vaguely aware of his other hand dropping from the fuselage. He grabbed a fistful of hair at the base of my skull and tugged. Strong lips grazed the corner of my mouth.

"Trust me, kitten—" he tightened his grip on my hair, edging the pleasure toward pain as he worked his thumb across my spandex-covered nipple "—I would fuck this attitude out of you."

I barely caught my breath as he released me from his grip and stepped backward, then turned on his heel and walked out of the hangar.

As he stepped into the sunshine, his phone rang. "Thompson," was his cursory greeting. My heart was still racing as he strode out without so much as a second glance.

————

MY EYES WERE weary when I finally slammed my laptop shut. I had done some aircraft maintenance after scrubbing Vaughan's lipstick graffiti off my Ag Cat, then retired to my cabin to finish a mandatory refresher that kept my pilot's license in good standing. I topped off the day with a boatload of invoices billed to my clients, and put in a whopper of an order for fertilizer, pesticide, and fungicide.

It was a good thing I didn't have to fly today. Between the hangover and the Vaughan-over, my head hadn't stopped swimming.

Heavy machinery had been whirring outside all day. Maybe George had finally decided to have the boys clear the last five acres and drop seed before it was too late in the season.

"Do you need to go out?" I asked Bean, who was lounging across the foot of my bed. I pushed the TV tray I used as a desk out of the way and rolled off the mattress.

Bean hopped down and trotted to the door. His nails were a shade of red I liked to call Fuck-You-Vaughan. His bowtie matched.

I cracked open the door, and Bean wobbled out. Glancing at the kitchenette that I was slowly turning into a kitchen, I spotted the remnants of my lunch.

"Don't want any more ants," I said with a sigh as I scooped the crumbs and crust from my peanut butter sandwich into the trash can, then wiped the countertop with a washcloth.

Outside, Bean growled.

That was odd. I mean, sure—he was a pitbull. But Bean never growled at anything. Much to my dismay, he didn't even growl at Vaughan.

"What is it, Beaners?" I hollered.

Another low growl resounded from the porch.

I huffed. *Probably just a rat.* He'd be okay. "I'm too hungry to deal with your weirdness, dude."

I didn't cook much. If I wanted a big, homemade meal, I would usually just crash dinner at the big house. Ms. Faith always made plenty and they always had a place set for me.

I could go to Jay's. Out of pure obstinance, I refused the tacos Vaughan brought to the hangar. I'd let myself starve before I ate something he provided. *But the tacos smelled so good...*

Jay's it was.

I toed on a pair of flip-flops, grabbed my keys, and poked my head out to call Bean inside.

"Hey, boy—"

Holy fuck knuckles.

My heart stopped, and my blood froze in my veins.

No. He. Fucking. Didn't.

Bean was stationed at the base of the porch steps. His snout was pointed at the runway.

A shiny new billboard had been erected just shy of the strip of blacktop. In oversized letters, it read, *FUCK YOU, JO.*

A bucket truck was still parked beside the wide pole. *I bet the paint was still wet.*

That twat goblin!

Fuck him!

My paralyzed pulse began to thrum fast and hard. Sweat broke out on the back of my neck, and all I saw was red.

I yanked my phone out of my pocket, the screen flashing with text after text from every Thompson except the soon-to-be corpse.

My phone wouldn't stop buzzing as message after message and consecutive call attempts clogged the screen. I jammed my finger against the button to turn it off. I didn't need apologies from George, Ms. Faith, Ryman, Cash, or Bristol.

The desire I'd had clouding my mind faded, and all I felt was unadulterated hatred.

The rage was still pulsing hot white when I pulled back through the farm gates after grabbing dinner at Jay's. I'd even done a few loops around some backroads with the windows down to try and mellow my temper. My knuckles were bleached as I strangled the steering wheel.

I wasn't everyone's cup of tea. Hell, I wasn't even everyone's shot of tequila. I was more like a ghost pepper that frat boys were dared to taste and stupid enough to try.

The truck bumped and bobbed along the dark path. The sun had set in cotton candy pinks and blues, leaving the way back to the cabin shrouded in deep shadows.

I reached across the steering column to cut my headlights on when a dark ball scampered across the dirt path.

Oh hell no. I was not dealing with an armadillo collision today.

I jerked the steering wheel to the left, edging toward the grassy shoulder and away from the demon cannonball.

The truck shuddered, and a muffled, "Fuck!" echoed from outside.

I threw the gear shift into park and hopped out. Vaughan—in black athletic shorts and a black t-shirt that seemed a tad too snug—stood on the side of the road. He was hunched over, his hand wrapped around his bicep.

"Did you just *hit me* with your truck?" he bellowed.

Any ounce of remorse immediately vaporized. I was half tempted to back up and try again.

"Not my fault you were walking in the middle of the road!" I shouted.

Vaughan straightened, brown eyes searing me like a laser. "I was on the side of the road, you jackass!"

"Well, call an optometrist because you're blind as a motherfucking bat if you think you were on the *side* of the road!"

"You swerved!" he yelled.

"I was legally occupying the lane!" I countered at a decibel louder than his.

"You fucking *tried* to hit me, didn't you?" Vaughan was backing me up against the truck with each furious stride.

I stepped out of dodge and headed back to the driver's side. "I didn't try to hit you, but I wish I had!" I jumped behind the wheel but, before I could slam the door, Vaughan grabbed the frame.

"You're reckless," he spat.

I pointed to the road ahead. "Why don't you go ten paces that way and I'll gun it? Go all Evel Knievel on your ass."

He pointed to his bicep. "You hit me with your truck!"

"You put up a fucking billboard beside my runway!"

"*My* runway," he roared. "And don't you forget it. Your livelihood is hanging by a fucking thread. You keep testing my patience and I don't think you'll like the consequences."

Those athletic shorts weren't doing him any favors. His flag was quickly rising to full mast.

"You're all bark and no bite, Thompson," I said as I grabbed the door handle and tried to pull it shut.

Vaughan didn't budge.

"What are you even doing walking on this part of the property?" It wasn't like it was anywhere near the big house or the main fields. "Let me guess. You were trying to come up with a dig to put on your little billboard that's more than three syllables? Word of advice—next time you spend an easy ten grand on pissing me off, do it where other people will see it."

That's what I didn't understand about the billboard prank. Why go all in on something that big when I was the only person who neared that side of the property? Sure, his family would see it, but it wasn't like it was anywhere near town.

His eyes were midnight black and his voice grew husky. "I was out here to clear my head, which has been royally fucked up, thanks to you."

I stuck my lower lip out, pouting dramatically. "Aww, is being away from your butler and gold-plated commode too stressful for you?"

"You know what's fucking stressful, Joelle?" Vaughan reared back, raking his hands through his hair. "Getting a goddamn job offer from the company trying to buy the land that holds the only good memories of my mother." His chest heaved. "You know what's stressful? Trying to keep people employed while trying to keep the bank from foreclosing on the farm." His eyes were wild and, for the first time, I saw him as a man.

Not the bane of my existence. Not a cartoon villain.

I saw him as George's son.

As Cash, Ryman, and Bristol's brother.

Then again, he was also the guy who had started this whole mess, and Momma didn't raise a quitter.

Vaughan gritted his teeth as he grasped the top of the truck and leaned into the cab. "And for some godforsaken reason, my old man has me seeing to it that you're not homeless and jobless, no matter how much I want to put you out on your ass."

"Vulkon's trying to poach you?" I said out of nowhere.

His nostrils flared. "That's what you took away from all of that?"

A lump started growing in my throat. "You can't ... you can't sell. What will George and Ms. Faith do? What about Cash and Ry? They love this land."

Something akin to surprise flashed across his face. "Vulkon has job offers on the table for them. Full-time. Benefits—more than they have now. They want locals running the quarry site. They need puppets to make the town think that it's a good thing for them to snatch up farmland."

"It's not," I whispered. "It's ... fuck. That's fucking messed up."

He backed away from the truck and slammed my door shut. "Maybe open your fucking eyes next time. I've got a shit ton on my plate, so you had better believe I'm gonna be walking the fucking land a lot." His stare was heated, and I couldn't tell if it was familial passion, lust, or both. "It was my home before it was yours."

I didn't say anything as I threw the truck back into drive. I'd give him a pass tonight—even on the billboard.

I'd bide my time and come up with a far more fatal form of retaliation.

I pressed the gas and lumbered down the road, heading back toward—*thump!*

"You fucking hit me again!" Vaughan howled.

I craned my head out the window and found him pressed against the front corner of my bumper. Apparently, the dumbass never learned to walk *behind* moving motor vehicles.

"I *barely* tapped you!" I shouted back.

"What the fuck is your problem?" he yelped.

"My problem? What is with you and walking in the middle of the road!"

Vaughan stomped across the dirt path, heading in the direction of the big house. "I hope your truck stalls!"

"I hope you get bit by a rattlesnake!"

His voice grew more distant. "I hope your plane crashes!"

I leaned my head out the open window and hollered, "I hope you get exactly what you deserve, Thompson!"

"Go to hell, Reed!" he called as he disappeared into the field. I swear I heard him laugh under his breath.

I leaned my head against the seat, closed my eyes, and grinned.

14

VAUGHAN

"How's it going?"

I looked up from the screen that was quickly darkening the bags under my eyes. The blue light had given me a headache, so I resorted to taking my contacts out and putting on my prescription glasses that had a blue light filter. They made me look ten years older but fuck it—I didn't care.

Scrubbing my hands down my face, I sighed and pushed away from my dad's desk and faced him. "It's going."

He grunted something unintelligible as he held on to the door frame with an iron grip.

The old stained-glass banker's lamp flickered on the lacquered wood desk. The heavy coat of dust and the lingering musty smell made it obvious that my dad never used his office.

Ms. Faith was probably the reason it was as organized as it was. She helped with the books and payroll for the farm, making sure that everyone's checks were ready on time each Friday.

Much like his other two sons, Dad preferred to be out in

the fields, working the land. He judged the success of the harvest by the quality of the crops—not the quantity.

Unfortunately, quality crops didn't keep you in business. He needed to up his game.

"Got off the phone with Bert down at the bank. They're pleased with the progress and are holding off on foreclosing."

Dad let out a sigh of relief. "That's good."

"For *now*," I clarified.

As much as I hated to say it, my money wouldn't last forever. I could afford to buy the farm outright. Granted, I couldn't match the price Vulkon Incorporated was willing to pay. I could only buy it at-cost. Then again, what good was that if it fell into a pit again? The point wasn't to keep the farm from failing once. I needed to make it sustainable.

I leaned back in his rickety desk chair and laced my hands behind my head. My lower back ached from hours spent hunched over. "You should be resting."

He huffed and adjusted the tension of his oversized belt buckle. "All I ever do is rest."

I raised an eyebrow and turned back to the screen. "I need to know that when I go back to Chicago, you're ready to keep this place moving. If you're fucking up your back a few weeks after surgery, you won't be able to keep the operation rolling because you'll be back in physical therapy."

Conceding, he leaned his hip on the edge of the desk. The wood groaned as it took some of his weight.

"Where were you last night?" he asked, crossing his arms.

I didn't look up from the screen. I had too much work to do to dabble in small talk. As soon as I got through the quarterly sales reports for the farm, I had to jump on a conference call for the firm. Tamara was a ruthless dictator when it came to my schedule. The woman knew how to pack every minute of my day. And pack it, she did.

"Took a walk."

"You were out awful late."

I shrugged. "Needed to clear my mind."

"I'll bet," he said with a wheezing chuckle. "Heard about that little stunt you pulled with JoJo's lipstick."

"Bristol needs to learn what happens to snitches," I muttered under my breath. Both of us knew that it wasn't a real threat. I wouldn't dare lay lands on a woman, much less my baby sister.

Good thing Joelle Reed wasn't a woman. That gremlin was pure evil.

I wanted to lay my hands on her in all sorts of ways.

Fuck.

No, I didn't.

I just wanted to lay them on her long enough to squeeze the air from her throat, then toss her in a shallow grave.

I'd get her a headstone in the shape of a middle finger.

Here lies the body of a complete cunt.

Then again, I'd have to put it in the dirt upside-down so it would point at her. If there was an afterlife, there was no way Joelle Reed was going up. No—that brat would stomp through the gates of Hell, flip off the devil, and complain about it being too chilly.

She'd probably strut around the lake of fire in her birthday suit.

Great, now I was thinking about Jo's tits, and my dick liked that picture.

A lot.

"When are you two gonna stop pickin' at each other like children?" he asked.

"She started it," I countered.

His lip curled, highlighted by graying stubble. "Boy, you know I raised you better than that." He crossed thick arms over his barrel chest. "You keep bothering that sweet girl and I'll send you out into the field with a sling blade and have you harvest the old-fashioned way. It builds character. And apparently, I didn't make you do it enough in your younger years."

Or I could sell my majority share of the farm to Vulkon, walk away, and leave you to fend for yourself.

It was a horrible, intrusive thought, but I couldn't help that it had slipped into my mind.

"Sweet like chloroform," I grumbled as I closed out of the spreadsheets and pulled up the file Tamara had sent over, scanning it before she called to loop me into the conference call.

"Play nice," he gritted out, easing off the desk. "I'm heading out. Cash said one of the balers is actin' up."

"You'd better not climb on that thing," I snapped as he turned for the door. "Ms. Faith will have your hide and mine if you get up there."

He snorted. "Don't I know it. Don't worry—Momma's driving me out there in the truck."

Momma. He had started calling Ms. Faith that after Ryman was born. After Cash made his dramatic entrance into the world, Dad sat me down and said I should call her that, too.

But I was obstinate.

Ms. Faith had always been good to me. Probably better than I deserved. But she wasn't my mother.

"Take it easy," I said as he wandered out the door.

Dad tipped his chin back toward me. "Make it right with JoJo. Don't be a jackass."

And with that, his boots thumped out the door.

———

BY THE TIME I got off the conference call, I was seeing double and I had a headache that was steadily encroaching on migraine territory. One glance at the clock told me why.

It was half-past four in the afternoon, and all I'd had to sustain me was a cup of coffee. *This is why I needed Tamara back in my life.*

If my ass was glued to my desk chair, she'd stomp in and shove a take-out box in my face. If I was on a call and couldn't risk high-roller clients hearing me with a mouthful of deep-dish, she'd come by with one of those fru-fru green smoothies that were chock full of protein powder and kale.

Ms. Faith didn't believe in kale, but she did believe in cowboy stew.

I slammed my laptop closed and eased out of the desk chair. With Ms. Faith taking my dad out to check on the baler, Bristol on campus for classes today, and Cash and Ry in the fields, the big house was blissfully quiet.

I rounded the large island that Ms. Faith piled high with supper each night and made a beeline for the fridge. I had watched her scoop the last remnants of cowboy stew into an old Cool Whip container after dinner last night.

Leftovers would give me fuel for a late-night work session and an excuse as to why I didn't need dinner with the family.

But the spot where leftovers were neatly stacked was empty.

Gone.

I glanced at the sink and spotted the empty Cool Whip container. Dad had probably cleaned it out for lunch.

Before I could convince myself that I didn't need sustenance, my stomach let out a rip-roaring growl.

Dammit.

I cursed the fact that Willard's still hadn't fixed my car and grabbed the truck keys off the hook by the door.

Maybe I'd swing by and rip the mechanic a new one for obediently following orders given by the tyrant of Maren, Texas.

I needed food first.

The shocks on the truck squeaked and groaned as I bumped along the dirt path, heading for the two-lane road that edged the front of the property.

A car passed, honking as it cruised by. The driver probably thought I was my dad, or maybe Cash or Ryman in the truck.

It didn't matter what my last name was. Jo made it clear that I was public enemy number one, and that was that.

Jay's Gas-N-Go was packed when I pulled in. The bell on the door never stopped jingling as patron after patron filtered in and out, arms full of dinners to-go, drinks, and convenience store snacks. I held the door open for a mother with a toddler in tow. Even the little snot rocket glared at me like I was the Grinch.

Wave after wave of warm air was laced with brisket smoke. The aroma of baked beans and the signature smell of oil-filled deep fryers wafted over me as I made my way inside.

The line to place orders was backed up to the row of drink coolers that lined the wall. Jay, with his ball cap on backward, danced between the flat-top and fryers, slinging orders as fast as he could while folks shouted what they wanted at him.

His back was turned, but the moment I fell in line, his spine stiffened and he peered over his shoulder as if sensing a change in the atmosphere.

I immediately figured out why.

Jo was two aisles over, grabbing a bottle of wine out of the wire rack. She looked around, sensing something looming over her like a bad omen, but quickly returned to deciding between a cheap Chardonnay and an even cheaper Pinot Grigio.

Both were abysmal.

I studied her for a moment. It was rare that I got a chance to look at her without her being aware—and proud—that I was doing so.

Jo had her hair down. Dark waves swished across her back as she shifted from her left foot to her right. They weren't styled curls. It was more like she'd had her hair in a braid all day and took it out when she finished flying.

How did I know she had flown today? The flyover wake-up call at the wicked crack of 4:30 this morning clued me into that.

Fuck her.

I swear I hadn't gotten a good night of sleep since the day before I left Chicago. The woman was a menace. She occupied my every waking thought, and the majority of my nightmares.

And dreams.

She wasn't in denim shorts today, I noted. She was in a pair of black leggings, sneakers, and a tank top. The sleeves had been cut off down to the hem, exposing her ribs and stomach on either side. I stared at the side of her strappy black sports bra for far too long, but the slight swell that peeked out was too tantalizing to look away.

Deciding on the Pinot, Jo slid the other bottle back on the wine rack and grabbed a bag of corn chips. *Classy.*

"Should have picked a Reisling," I clipped over my shoulder when she joined the line.

Jo scowled and rolled her eyes. "Are you the wine pairing police? It's four-dollar gas station wine. I don't think the kind of grape matters." She took another look at the bottle. "It's probably not even made of real grapes. They probably used a "grape-flavored product." You know—like Cheez Whiz. It's not real cheese, but who cares? It gets the job done."

"Are you ever not combative?" I shifted my weight backward and let the heel of my loafer smash her toes.

Jo yelped and jumped back. The line of gas station diners turned and stared at me. I stood with my hands in my pockets, innocent as a baby lamb.

Jo popped up from behind me like a bridge troll. Her elbow connected with my kidney. I groaned as she cut in front of me. "Ladies first."

I elbowed her back, shoving her behind me. "That would imply that you're a lady. Last time I checked, you were just a pile of shit."

Jo snorted and muttered, "Like you haven't drooled over my tits."

She wasn't getting away with keeping that comment to herself. I grinned from ear-to-ear as the line shuffled forward. "Don't flatter yourself," I said at a volume that wasn't appropriate indoors.

Heads across the tiny convenience store spun.

"Pretty sure the whole county's seen your tits." I tipped my chin down and gave her a curt once-over. "Not that there's much to see."

That did it. Before I could brace, her fist was swinging. Knuckles crashed into my temple. She had to get on her tiptoes to get that jab in, but *damn*—Jo Reed could throw a punch.

My head throbbed like I'd just been kissed by a

wrecking ball, and my eye started to swell. That punch was a bell-ringer.

Before Jo could get a sucker punch in, Jay hollered over the commotion. "Hey!"

We snapped to attention like two kids caught rough-housing on the playground.

"That shit don't fly in here," he snapped.

A quiet squeak escaped when Jo opened her mouth to argue. Jay pointed a greasy spatula at her. "You know better than to pull that kind of behavior in here, JoJo."

He chucked a brown paper bag at the customer standing by the dinosaur of a register. Instead of leaving, the woman took her order and shuffled off to the side, opening a foil-wrapped taco to snack on and watch the show like she was front row at fight night.

I hid my grin behind my fist.

Jay glared at me and pointed the spatula at the door. "Get out, Thompson."

Was he fucking serious? I was the one who got punched!

"That was assault," I said calmly as I pressed my forearm to the incessant throbbing on the side of my head. Nothing like a little head trauma to make me forget about the migraine.

I was going to have to get a better health insurance plan if I was going to spend any more time in Maren.

Hell, I'd probably need to double my life insurance policy.

It wouldn't surprise me if Jo had a hidden room in the cabin that was plastered with black-and-white photos of me with the eyes scratched out and *die* scrawled in red marker.

She probably had a nice little manifesto typed up and everything.

Jay tossed the spatula onto a cutting board. *Shit.* He

looked like he was about to haul ass across the counter and drag me out. "I don't care if she cut off your nuts, baked them in a pecan pie, and served you every bite. Out of my store. *Now.*"

Jay looked like a little league coach with the backward ball cap, gym shorts, and Maren Armadillos t-shirt, but he was a big guy. The last thing I wanted was for him to ban all of the Thompsons from his little establishment.

The food was good, and Ry, Cash, and Bristol would kill me if they were cut off.

But if I was the only one banned, I could probably convince Bristol to sneak me a taco or two when she was on her way home from class.

Jo held the wine bottle over her mouth to hide her giggle. She did a shit job of it because Jay shot her a warning look.

Looks like I'd be having dinner at the big house with everyone wondering why I was sporting a shiner.

I gritted my teeth so hard I thought I was going to crack a molar. "Better watch your back, Reed," I hissed before storming out.

15

VAUGHAN

I toed my shoes off on the porch, yanked the front door open, and stormed inside. My stomach growled, threatening to devour my intestines if I didn't get some sustenance soon.

Ms. Faith was at the kitchen sink when I blew through without so much as a hello. Bristol peered out from behind the fridge door cautiously.

Even Cash and Ryman gave me a wide berth when I stomped past them.

My dad was the only one who was seemingly unperturbed. He peered up from the issue of *Farm Show* he was thumbing through. "I'll take it that making peace with JoJo didn't quite go as expected?"

"This whole town can go fuck itself," I clipped as I crossed the wide living room. The ceilings were vaulted with thick beams crisscrossing at the peak. Warm afternoon light filtered through the window panes. "And as for her? She can die in a ditch for all I care."

Dad lifted his hand off the recliner's armrest, and I skidded to a halt.

I was a grown man, and I had been on my own for a long time. Still, one lift of my dad's hand—his silent way of saying, "Now, you hold on just a second,"—and I stopped in my tracks.

Bristol peeked in the room. "Vaughan! What happened?" She popped up on her tiptoes and went wide-eyed. "You have a black eye!"

Shit. I'd been so preoccupied with my justified hangry rampage that I forgot about Jo punching me in the candy and chip aisle at Jay's.

I touched the tender skin around my eye and winced. "You can thank your *bestie* for that," I sneered.

"Hey, now," Ryman said in a low warning as he threw a protective arm around Bristol.

Ms. Faith appeared in the doorway between the kitchen and the living room. "This nonsense between you and Jo has gone on long enough."

Dad nodded. "Momma's right."

I raised my hands. "In case you all missed it, I didn't touch her. She's the one who decked me."

Bristol crossed her arms. "And what did you *say* to provoke her to do that?"

Either the little shit was psychic, or I was predictable.

"Well, your timing is perfect, Vaughan," Ms. Faith said. "I was going to call Jo and tell her to come over for dinner and dessert. It's been a while since she's had a meal with us. Why don't you go over to the cabin and invite her? I saw her truck come down the path not too long ago."

Out of the corner of my eye, I could see my dad glowering over the magazine pages, daring me to defy Ms. Faith's request. Ryman, Cash, and Bristol stood shoulder-to-shoulder, a united front ready to defend Jo.

Ms. Faith wiped her hands on a dish towel, quietly waiting out my temper tantrum.

I was half-tempted to stomp into the office, call Tamara, and have her put me on the first flight back to Chicago. Willard's could keep my car.

They'd probably give it to Jo. She would fill it with tannerite and blow it to kingdom come.

When I didn't move, my dad spoke up. His tone was decisive and left no room for an argument. "Jo is part of this farm. Same as you. Go make nice with her and invite her back to the house for dinner, or find your own meal while you're out."

He knew I was perfectly capable of providing for myself, but the underlying message was clear.

Don't come back until you grow the fuck up.

Without a word, I blew out of the big house and headed across the yard.

I didn't bother taking the truck out to Jo's cabin. I needed the walk to release the pressure that was reaching critical. But with each step, my righteous indignation grew. By the time her ramshackle cottage came into view, I was well past fuming.

I took all three front porch steps in one stride and pounded on the door. "Open up, Reed!" I bellowed.

The door whipped open like she had been waiting for me. Jo had changed out of her workout clothes and stood on the other side of the threshold in a pair of denim shorts and a tank top. Her eyes were still blazing, not satisfied with the one jab she already got in.

"Come back for seconds, Thompson?" she sassed.

"You're lucky I don't hit women," I clipped as I took one step over the threshold, crowding her space.

Instead of moving to the side or shoving me out the

door, Jo took a step back. "I'll let you get a shot in," she teased. "Fair's fair. Besides, if you hit like you kiss, I'll barely feel anything."

Oh, she was fucking in for it.

I took another step forward. It didn't take much for the two of us to make it halfway across the cabin. Her living space was the size of a match box. The back of Jo's knees hit the edge of her bed. Her sharp intake of breath was the only sound that filled the space.

My gaze locked in on her lips. Everything else was a blur. "I think you just admitted to feeling something."

"I believe what I said is that I barely felt anything," she countered in a slightly more unsteady tone.

I leaned down and let my lips graze the corner of her mouth with each word. "You're a brat."

Her lips turned up in a smile. "That's pretty unoriginal. Get some new material."

This woman...

I wanted to kiss her ... then choke her.

I wanted to fuck her ... then kill her.

I wanted to pin her against the wall and tease her until she was completely and utterly under my will.

I wanted her ass in the air, red from my hand.

I wanted her on her knees, begging for my cock.

I wanted to keep her under my thumb just so I could toy with her. Play with her. Control her like a puppet.

Jo's back was arched. She was trying her best to keep from falling backward onto the mattress, but I was towering over her. Her pale blue eyes flicked down to my crotch.

Slowly, she reached between us and squeezed the bulge in my pants. I barely restrained my groan. *Fuck, that felt good.*

"You're like an annoying-ass phoenix who keeps rising

from the ashes no matter how much I try to burn you down."

Her grin was malefic. "I'm not a phoenix, city boy." She tipped her chin up, meeting my unforgiving gaze. "I'm a cockroach lumbering through the wreckage, unable to be killed, even when death would be easier."

My hands clenched into fists at my side. If I touched her, I wouldn't be able to stop myself. Jo's tiny hand squeezed at my cock again. My toes curled inside my dress shoes. She kept at it, like she knew that single touch packed more of a punch than a right-cross.

"You wanna know how to kill a cockroach?" I growled. Her eyes widened as I grabbed the back of her thighs and threw her on the bed. "You get it on its back."

Without hesitation, Jo rolled. I grabbed her ankles and pulled her back.

"You get off on this, don't you?"

When she started to claw at me, I grabbed her wrists and pinned them to her sides.

Her hips thrashed, but there was a maniacal smile on her face. "You do, too."

"Tell me 'no,'" I said as I let go of her wrists—only partially worried that she would try to strangle me with my necktie—and spread her thighs.

She opened them willingly.

I reached in my back pocket and tugged a condom out of my wallet. "Just to make it perfectly clear: if you keep doing what you're doing, this—" I held the foil packet between us "—is how it ends. I'm giving you one more chance. Tell me to stop."

She responded by yanking on my tie, crashing my lips to hers. She tasted like bad wine, brisket, and salsa. I slid my tongue along her lips, prying them open to taste her again.

Fucking delicious.

My head swam with lust. I couldn't get my bearings. Joelle Reed had turned my life upside-down against my will. Now, I wanted her to turn me inside out. She sucked my lip between her teeth and—

"You bit me," I hissed, rearing back from her.

Jo grinned and yanked me back down for another kiss. "You liked it."

She wasn't wrong.

"You've been fucking with me for weeks," I hissed. "It ends today."

"Aww," she cooed, mocking me. "I didn't think you'd wave the white flag so soon."

I fisted her hair, yanking her head to the side. Jo cried out in surprise. "This is the furthest thing from surrender, Tiger."

My mouth latched onto her neck. I sucked and nipped until I had marked her skin in purple and blue.

Her high-pitched whimpers continued as her body stopped whipping back and forth and settled into a steady, wanton rocking. Her knees were bent and parted, beckoning me to settle between them.

My mind floated back to when I had seen her in her redneck bathtub; her pussy peeking out from beneath the bubbles.

"Don't get soft on me now, city boy," she jeered, bringing me back to the present.

That was enough to snap me out of my haze. I fisted her hair and pulled her off the bed. "On your knees, kitten."

She dropped to my feet without hesitation, the wood planks groaning beneath us. For a split second, Jo looked up at me with wide eyes and complete reverence.

At that moment, I made it my life's mission to see that look again.

"You want my cock so bad? Take it out." I shifted my feet shoulder width apart. She didn't know it, but it was an act of trust on my part. For all I knew, she had a switchblade hidden in her bra and would slice my dick off so that she could grill it like a smoked sausage.

Jo reached between us, nimble fingers working my belt apart. I studied her as she concentrated on undoing my pants. The belt fell away with a clink from the buckle. She thumbed the button of my slacks and pulled down my zipper. As if asking for permission to continue, she looked up at me. I gave her a nod.

Jo's fingers curled around the elastic edge of my boxer briefs, and tugged. My erection sprung free, bobbing inches away from her lips. A bead of moisture leaked from the head. She opened her mouth, tongue darting out to lap at it. I used her hair to jerk her head away. She whimpered in delight.

"Hands in your back pockets."

She opened her mouth to argue, because of course she would. I grabbed her throat, squeezing along the graceful lines where her arteries pulsed. "Do not test my good will." The threat was low and venomous.

Almost reluctantly, she reached back and slid both hands up against her tight little ass.

I stroked her cheek with the back of my knuckles. "See? Was that so hard?"

Fury flared in her eyes, and I knew one sure-fire way to snuff it out. With one hand, I stroked my shaft. With the other, I reached down and squeezed her cheeks. "Open."

Her lips parted and I didn't hesitate to slide my cock to

the back of her throat. She liked to talk a big game. It was time to put her to the test.

Her mouth was warm, and her tongue was silken along my length. *So fucking good.* I only gave her a moment to adjust to my size before threading my fingers in her hair; withdrawing my dick, then thrusting back in.

Jo gagged, her eyes watering as the head of my cock hit the back of her throat. She moaned, thighs clenching together for relief.

Another thrust.

She whimpered around my cock when I held deep in her mouth. Her cheeks were flushed the prettiest shade of sunset pink. Eyes the color of faded denim stared up at me through thick lashes. Her fingers curled beneath her rear, desperate to grab onto me or relieve the ache between her legs.

A single look from her was a shot to the heart.

She swallowed around my dick to clear the saliva in her mouth, and I nearly came on the spot.

I tugged on her hair and pulled her mouth back. "Up."

My cock slipped from between her lips, the veins glistening from her mouth.

Jo stumbled trying to get to her feet and I caught her in my arms. She was so small compared to my large frame. So breakable.

I wanted to be the one to break her.

To tame her.

I yanked on the sides of her shorts, ripping them down her legs. The simple briefs she had on underneath were the sexiest things I'd ever seen.

Jo pulled her tank top over her head, her perky tits filling up the cups of her sports bra.

I grabbed the condom from the bed, tore it open, and rolled it on.

Jo turned and made a move for the bed, but she didn't get to choose how this went down.

I hooked one arm around her middle and yanked her against my body. My dick pressed into her spine.

"Good girls get orgasms on the bed," I growled into her ear.

She rocked her ass, teasing me with the motion. The hint of a smile curled on her lips. "And what do bad girls get?"

"Bad girls get bruises on their backs from being fucked against the wall, and bright-red asses from getting spanked."

Jo turned and tilted her head, easing up onto her tiptoes and kissing me. It was soft, and the way she melted into me had me half-tempted to lay her out on the mattress and bury my face between her thighs until she was delirious.

And then she bit my lip again.

I chuckled under my breath. "Bend over, tiger. Hands on the wall."

With shaking steps, she turned away from me and faced the wall. She planted her hands on the wood slats and arched her back. I stood a step behind her, watching the way her tight ass swayed. *So fucking gorgeous.*

Jo looked over her shoulder as I assessed her posture.

"Eyes down," I snapped, smoothing my hand over her panty-clad rear. Jo turned her head down, keeping her gaze on the dusty wood beneath her feet.

I hooked my fingers in the top edge of her underwear and yanked them down, leaving them around the middle of her thighs.

I gave her no warning.

My hand clapped against her cheek, and the moan she let slip made my cock painfully hard. The head of my cock nudged against her cunt, teasing her. If she hadn't been so drunk in lust, she would have been fighting me tooth and nail.

But this side of Jo... The feisty, yet submissive side...

She was irresistible.

I spanked her ass again, letting my fingers swat at the puffy entrance to her pussy. She was swollen and soaked.

Jo whimpered, squeezing her legs together.

"No," I said sternly as I wedged my foot between hers and eased her ankles apart. "Take it like you're supposed to." I leaned down and let my mouth ghost along the shell of her ear. "Take it like you want to."

I kissed the side of her neck as I spanked her. Again and again, over and over. The only sound filling the air was my palm connecting with her ass and each accompanying moan. It was filthy and erotic, and fuck—I loved it.

I smoothed my hand over her bright pink ass, my heart pounding out of my chest. Letting my fingers slip lower, I slid two between her soaked folds, gently stroking.

Jo's breath caught in her throat. "V-Vaughan—"

My name on her lips was my favorite sound.

I liked hearing her tease me. I loved hearing her fight me. But I *needed* to hear her want me.

The pad of my finger found her clit. I worked it with a gentle touch for just a moment, and had her knees trembling. Her fingers clawed into the wall, desperate for purchase.

"You're so wet, kitten," I murmured, teasing her as I dipped my finger into her pussy, but never giving her any satisfaction. "Fighting with me turns you on, doesn't it?"

Jo bit her lip, trying to hold back any kind of affirmation. That wouldn't do.

I grabbed her hips and spun her to face me. Her bare back slammed into the wall, knocking a picture frame to the ground and rattling the random knick knacks cluttering the place.

"Arms around my neck," I ordered as I pulled her panties off her ankles and tossed them across the room. "Don't strangle me."

Jo's smile was wicked. "No promises," she said as she looped her arms around me and jumped. I caught her ass in my hands and wrapped her legs around my waist. I slammed her back into the wall as I thrust into her. Her head smacked the paneling, eyes rolling back in ecstasy.

I pulled out and slammed back in, ramming her into the wall again hard enough to knock the air out of her lungs. *At least it kept her from running her mouth.*

Her soft pants were a quiet accompaniment to my grunts as I fucked her deep and hard. I felt the knot in my chest loosening as I held her up, pinned her to the wall, and rutted inside of her. Her forehead pitched toward me and rested on my shoulder. The collar of my shirt stifled her whimpers.

Her cunt tightened around my cock, squeezing me and drawing me to within an inch of my sanity. "Vaughan," she whispered again, breathless and desperate.

I dug my fingers into her ass cheeks as I pressed her back against the wall, grinding into her clit. "Come for me."

It only took another shallow pump to get her there. Jo shattered in my arms, clinging to me as I poured my release into the condom. I was soaked in sweat, and my arms ached. Still, my blood pressure was the lowest it had been since leaving Chicago.

I pressed my forehead against the wall, breathing deeply as Jo rested against me, trying to catch her breath. The walls of her pussy were still fluttering around my dick.

I lowered her to the ground, holding on to her until she found her balance on shaking legs.

I spotted a small trash can beside her bed and took a step back, my eyes never leaving hers as I dealt with the condom. The taste of brisket on her lips had me amending the invitation I was sent to deliver.

"Ms. Faith wants you to come to the big house for dessert."

Jo stood there in only her bra, staring at me with dazed eyes. "Uh—"

Before she could argue, I zipped my pants, tucked my shirt back in, buckled my belt, and crossed the room. I crooked a finger beneath her chin and lifted it, forcing her to meet my eyes. "You *will* come to the big house and have dessert."

She nodded, still wide-eyed.

I plucked her underwear off the floor and knelt in front of her, waiting patiently as she stepped into them. I shimmied them up her muscular legs and smoothed my hand across her ass before turning and walking out.

I spent the walk back patting down the wrinkles on my clothes, tucking my shirt in, and running my hand over my hair. When I stepped into the big house and five pairs of eyes landed on me, I knew there was no way I could hide what I had just done.

Everyone looked back at their plates, trying to act as though they didn't notice, but Cash grinned from ear-to-ear. "How was it?"

I steeled my expression and crossed the room, calmly filling my plate from the pots and platters spread out on the kitchen island. "Have you ever stuck your dick in a tornado?"

Cash choked on his food. "Can't say I have."

I sat with my family and hid my smile behind a bite.

16

JOELLE

I stood in the middle of my cabin watching, shellshocked, as Vaughan strode out the door. Bean didn't even stir. *Some guard dog.*

"Get a pit bull," they said. "They're protective," they said.

I should have gotten a chihuahua. Those pint-sized demons would snap a person's ankles clean off.

My pussy throbbed. The delicious ache from a good fuck lingered between my legs. I was shaking and cold. Wrapping my arms around my waist, I watched the door slam shut.

The corner of my mouth trembled, but Bean's snore from the other side of the room snapped me out of the post-sex haze.

I had never felt a hormone crash that hard after an orgasm.

I didn't bring men back to the cabin. *Ever.* Any hookups I indulged in happened in town.

Sex with Vaughan happening in my most private space was...

I shook my head, dismissing the thought. Sex was sex. It filled a need and nothing more.

I had wanted him to fuck me, and he did. There was no sense in making things more complicated than they had to be.

I stepped into my coffin-like shower and let scalding water cleanse me. I soaked in the little bits of steam that managed to cloud from the pathetic excuse for a shower head and played back the way it felt for Vaughan to pin me against that wall. The way he let me cling to him as we careened over the edge of ecstasy.

The fire in his eyes when he first stormed into the cabin had turned to simmering coals as he helped me back into my underwear when the deed was done.

I toweled off and ran a comb through my hair. Stepping outside would dry it faster than a blow dryer anyway.

You will come to the big house and have dessert.

I shivered as Vaughan's words echoed in my mind. The petulant side of me wanted to defy him and keep my ass at home. The other part of me wanted to see him.

I wanted to see if the fire between us still blazed, or if one hookup had smothered it.

And Ms. Faith's pecan pie was to die for. If the invitation was from her, it was because she knew I loved pie.

I changed clothes, fed Bean, and traipsed down the dirt path—opting to walk instead of drive so I had time to gather my wits.

My toes were a sandy brown by the time I made it to the big house. Hopefully, the boys would have dispersed, and it would just be George and Faith. Maybe Bristol.

After kicking my flip-flops off and opening the front door, my heart fell.

Cash and Ryman were huddled around the kitchen island. Bristol was at the fridge, and Ms. Faith was at the sink. George and Vaughan sat at the oversized farm table, talking quietly.

Ryman's eyebrows winged up as soon as he spotted me. "JoJo—"

Ms. Faith cut him off as she turned from the sink and dried her hands on a dish towel. "Hey there, sweetheart. We're just cleaning up from dinner, but I can heat you up a plate if you're hungry."

I shook my head, twisting my fingers in front of me. "Oh, no ma'am. I already ate."

At the sound of my voice, Vaughan looked up from the table. His gaze rooted me to the floor.

"Well," she said with a smile. "You're just in time for dessert. I've got pecan pie and Bluebell. Why don't you wash up and join the boys at the table? Ryman and Bristol can take care of slicing and scooping." She tipped her head toward the dining room.

Vaughan watched me like a hawk.

"Yes, ma'am."

I could feel Cash and Ryman's gawking stares as I stood at the sink and washed my hands. I cut the water off and turned, nearly running into a brick wall covered in a dress shirt. The smell of his cologne made my knees buckle. I had indulged in the scent when I buried my face in the crook of his neck.

Vaughan reached around me, not waiting for me to move as he dropped his dishes into the sink.

"You came," he said quietly

I tried my best not to breathe him in, but I failed miserably. "You told me to," I whispered.

Ryman stood wide-eyed and muttered, "Ho-ly shit,"

before turning to grab the tub of vanilla ice cream out of the freezer.

Ms. Faith stuck an ice cream scoop in his hand and hissed something that sounded a lot like, "Hush."

Vaughan's hips pressed into my stomach. His brown eyes searched mine for any show of emotion. He was probably looking for any show of weakness he could exploit. "Good."

As I pushed past him to get to the table, our hands grazed. If we had been made of metal, sparks would have exploded between us. Electricity zipped up my arm, making me shudder from deep within my bones.

Bristol peered at me curiously as I passed her by. The Thompson family was eerily quiet, and that was never a good thing.

"JoJo," George said when I dropped into the chair beside him. "How're my crops looking'?"

I smiled as I picked at a thread dangling from the corner of a plaid placemat. "Like the cattle are gonna be fat and happy this season."

That made him grin. "Good, good. The ol' Ag Cat holding up on you?"

"As long as I treat her right." I watched through the open doorway as the Thompson kids bustled around. "I've got a few parts on order just in case, but she flies well."

"You headin' up to Wichita for WASP training soon?"

I shook my head. "They're holding one in Dallas this year."

I was part of a group of agricultural aviator pilots who used their aerial application skills to help ground firefighters suppress wildfires. My talent for flying low, fast, and dumping a payload of fluid on the ground came in handy during the dry season.

Protecting crops was my bread and butter. I helped

prepare the fields. I helped drop seed and fertilize the soil. When irrigation systems didn't cut it, I helped water the plants. And when Mother Nature whipped up a hell storm, I was ready to fight her, too.

My Ag Cat was the Clydesdale of biplanes, but most of the pilots who flew sleek little aircrafts still couldn't do the maneuvers I did.

Federal aviation set an altitude minimum of five hundred feet off the ground in rural areas, and a minimum of a thousand feet over cities.

In order to reduce chemical drift, my hard deck was eight feet.

When I finished a pass, then pulled up and rolled, I felt limitless.

"You stay safe up there, ya hear?" he harrumphed, patting me on the elbow.

I laughed quietly. "Yes, sir."

While the rest of the Thompsons piled into the dining room with plates of pie and ice cream in tow, Vaughan hung back.

"Something about his job back in Chicago," Ms. Faith said gently as she slid in beside me. "He'll come to the table soon. Even Vaughan can't resist my pecan pie. Never has been able to."

I jabbed my fork into the brown sugar custard and dragged it through the Bluebell. "No sane person would say no to this."

"Lord knows that one tried," she said with a wry chuckle, nodding toward Vaughan. "When he was little, he would have hidden in his room for days if we had let him. Sometimes it took a piece of pie to coax him out."

The image of a boyish Vaughan grieving the loss of his mom by hiding from the world did something funny to me. I felt... I felt sorry for him. I knew exactly what that felt like, except I didn't have Ms. Faith to tempt me with pie. I hid to survive, then I ran.

Cash, Ryman, and Bristol were in a boisterous conversation among themselves, drowning out the memories.

"You two have a lot in common," Ms. Faith said quietly.

The scar on my temple burned as though dredging up old memories had set it alight.

"Sorry," Vaughan clipped and made his way to the table, pocketing his phone. He pulled out the chair between Bristol and his dad and sat across from me. "Work."

The conversation flowed easily, but I didn't have much to say. Not with Vaughan staring at me like he was waiting for me to explode.

But I didn't feel like messing with him. Not now, at least.

Sure, I could have gotten in a jab about him living in Chicago. I could have made fun of the way he insisted on wearing suits and dress clothes when it was triple digits.

But I felt unsteady. I had used my best weapons against him—sarcasm, self-defense, and sex. Nothing fazed him.

I thanked Ms. Faith for the pie, and cleared my place at the table. I didn't like feeling this way. I didn't like someone else having control of my emotions. No way should a spur-of-the-moment tryst with Vaughan send me into a melancholy spiral.

"Don't worry about your dishes," Ms. Faith said. "We've got a dishwasher, ya know."

I laughed. "I know. Y'all live the high life out here." If I put a dishwasher in the cabin, it would either take up most of my lower cabinets, or it would have to sit in the middle of the damn floor.

I was just one person, and I didn't cook much. I could do without.

"You want a cup of coffee?" she asked. "I'm putting some on for Bristol. She's cramming for a test tonight."

"No, ma'am. I've gotta get to bed. Early wake up call tomorrow."

She snickered. "I won't bother setting my alarm then. I know you'll wake me up right on time."

"Thanks again for inviting me for dessert," I said. "I'm assuming you sent Vaughan over to my place to tell me."

A guilty smile was painted on her face. "He's a good man, JoJo. I know he can be a little..."

"Infuriating?" I supplied.

She laughed and pulled me into a maternal hug. "Something like that. But a good man just the same."

I melted.

Ms. Faith gave the best hugs. When I laid awake at night, I let myself wish she could have been mine.

Orange rays of light leaked through the windows, coating everything in a fiery glow.

"Did you drive over, JoJo?" George asked as he slowly made his way into the kitchen. It pained me to see him moving so slowly. I knew he couldn't wait to get back in the fields with the boys.

I shook my head. "No, I walked."

"Have one of the boys drive you back," he said. "One of the farm hands found a rattler in the south field. Don't want you gettin' bit."

I could handle most anything, but rattlesnakes made my skin crawl.

"I'll be fine."

"I'll drive," a deep voice clipped through the jingle of keys. Vaughan appeared out of nowhere like Bloody-freaking-Mary.

My heart pounded in my chest. I didn't know if I could

handle being in the tight cab space of the truck he had commandeered. I needed a minute to catch my breath— especially after putting on a front for the Thompson family.

As if Vaughan's declaration had decided things, Ms. Faith shoved a foil-wrapped plate in my hands. "In case you don't feel like cooking tomorrow," she said.

When I was younger, I thought that Ms. Faith was just really bad at estimating how much food to cook. She always made enough to feed nearly the whole town. Pretty soon, I realized she made so much just to have the excuse that she needed to give it to someone.

There's just too much. We can't possibly eat it all.

I was always that someone.

"Thanks," I said with a soft smile.

"Get some sleep, sweetie," she said with a pat on the arm. "I'll hear ya bright and early. Stop by tomorrow if you want dinner. I'm starting a low country boil. It'll be ready when y'all call it a day."

Vaughan trailed behind me as we made our way out of the big house and walked to the truck.

I clutched the plate like a lifeline. When I reluctantly peeled one hand away long enough to reach for the door handle, Vaughan beat me to it. Our hands touched, and I recoiled like he had burned me.

"You don't need to drive me," I said as he opened the truck door.

"I'm driving," he said dismissively. "If you get bit by a snake, it'll delay the fresh hell I have planned for you tomorrow. Wouldn't want to miss out on that, now would we?"

I stifled a smile and peered out of the corner of my eye. He was smiling, too.

"I need to go by the hangar and do laundry," I said. "You can drop me off there."

The cabin didn't have space for a washer and dryer, so I put them in the hangar. It made decontaminating my clothes way easier. On top of that, the hangar was closer to the big house than my cabin was. The sooner I stopped breathing the same air as Vaughan Thompson, the better.

He dropped into the driver's seat. "I'm taking you to the cabin."

I bristled. "You can take me to the hangar or I will walk to it myself."

Vaughan pinched the bridge of his nose. "Why do you choose to be so goddamn stubborn all the fucking time?"

I buckled my seatbelt. "You think you can come into my house, pin me down to the bed, and fuck me into the best orgasms of my life, then have me ready and willing to call you 'Sir' or 'Daddy?' Think again." I offered him a sickeningly sweet smile. "But you're more than welcome to call me 'Daddy.'"

His jaw flared with frustration. Picking at him and regaining some shred of control made me feel more like myself.

Besides, he needed to know that I wasn't rolling over and playing dead.

Vaughan twisted the key in the ignition and silence fell between us. I hated that. I wanted him to drop a killer comeback. I wanted him to drive out to a remote part of the property and make me dig my own grave. I wanted him to yank me out of the truck and bend me over the hood.

My nipples certainly liked that idea.

But Vaughan didn't do any of those things. His hand casually wrapped around the top of the steering wheel as he pulled away from the big house.

"Are you okay?" he asked calmly.

Was I okay? What the hell kind of cutting remark was that supposed to be?

"After what we did," he clarified.

Oh...

"I'm fine," I said, turning quickly to stare out the window. "I wanted it. You wanted it. Why would I not be okay?"

There was a flash of remorse across his face as I studied his reflection in the window. "I should have made sure you were okay is all."

I steeled my expression, ignoring the pang of longing in my chest. "I'm not the type of woman who needs to be cuddled after sex, if that's what you're asking. Walking away was for the best." The lump in my throat was barely manageable.

Because as much as I didn't want to admit it, I wondered what it was like to cuddle after sex. I wondered what it was like to be held and feel safe.

The cabin came into view, headlights dancing across the sagging front porch. I really needed to fix her up before the next storm, but I was flying sun-up to sundown most days. There just wasn't enough daylight.

I looked away from the window as he slowed to a stop. Brightness flashed from the center console as Vaughan's phone lit up. The screen read, *Meredith Thompson*.

17

VAUGHAN

Anger, white hot and potent, flared through my veins. *Why the fuck was Meredith calling? What the hell did she want?*

Jo's face went white, and I saw the assumptions racing across her features.

"You're married," she sputtered, eyes blinking in disbelief.

"Not anymore," I snapped when she made a move for the door. I grabbed her wrist and barely missed the swipe of her claws.

To my surprise, Jo didn't slug me. It would have been more in character for her to get a quick punch in. Instead, she swatted me away, scrambling for the door.

"Don't lie to me and tell me you're separated, or the papers aren't final yet, but soon." The myriad of possibilities she threw my way dripped with sarcasm and vitriol.

"That's my *ex*-wife," I snapped, jabbing my finger to end the call. "Our divorce is long since final. Ask Bristol. Ask Ms. Faith. Ask my dad. Ask anyone."

My argument was useless. Jo was already out of the truck and storming toward the cabin.

I got out and slammed the door. "Where do you think you're going?" I bellowed. "We're having this out."

"No, we're not," she said as she stomped across the grass toward the cabin. "I'm not going to be the other woman, and I'm sure as hell not going to be a convenient place for you to get your dick wet when you need a little stress relief."

"Jo—"

Her face was as bright as a tomato. "You should have told me," she hissed as she grabbed the doorknob and yanked.

"Should have told you what?" I growled. "That I'm divorced?" I tried to grab her arm, but she squeezed past me.

She kicked off her flip-flops, picked one up, and pointed it at me. "If your divorce is so final, why is your ex-wife calling you?"

"I don't know why the fuck she's calling!" I shouted. "And I don't care!"

The sole of her flip-flop smacked my cheek with a resounding *thwack!*

I stared at her, my face stinging from the slap.

"Whatever. You did your job. You got me here, now you can leave."

I yanked her flip-flops out of her hand and threw them across the room. They hit the front of her mini refrigerator and fell to the ground with a clatter. "You don't get to dismiss that accusation and walk away. You don't get to come at me about being truthful when you're anything but."

"Oh yeah? And how have I not been truthful? Because trust me, I wasn't lying when I said that I wanted to murder you." Her blue eyes blazed like flames—beautiful and deadly.

"You failed to mention how the hell you ended up living at the farm. I had to hear it from Ryman."

Jo rolls her eyes. "My momma killed herself, my daddy drank, and the county took me away. I'm the main character in a depressing country ballad."

There was an edge to her words, but little force. She was teetering on the brink, halfway between flying and falling.

Her shoulders were braced, her back to the wall as if she was taking up the best vantage point. Still, her hands trembled. Her mouth was soft; lips parted like she couldn't decide whether she was going to cry or cuss me out six ways from Sunday.

Joelle Reed was larger than life, but right now she looked small. Like I had broken her.

I thought that's what I wanted, but fuck—not like this.

I cupped her cheek in my hand, running my thumb along the silvery scar that slashed across her temple, slicing through her eyebrow and barely missing her eye. "How'd you get this?"

She stood stock still for the longest moment, her body tense as if waiting to see if I'd hit her. I kept my touch gentle, smoothing the pad of my thumb across the ridge of scar tissue.

"Daddy was drunk. He broke an ashtray and hit me with it."

Her voice was completely devoid of emotion. All that fury she pointed at me was nowhere to be found. She was robotic and stoic.

"How can you say it like that?" I rasped. I wanted to pull her into my arms, but I also valued my life and bodily well-being.

Joelle was a tornado. Unpredictable. Uncontrollable.

Wicked and destructive, yet enticing and captivating in every way.

"Pretty easy to regurgitate it when I've said it hundreds of times for teachers and cops and social workers and lawyers and judges."

"Ry said you testified against him."

She nodded.

"And you were emancipated?"

She nodded again.

"Jo..." My voice broke on her name.

Except for my palm cradling her cheek, our bodies barely touched. She didn't move closer, but she also didn't pull away.

"I was taking care of myself years before I got him thrown in jail. Not like it was a big change. Ms. Faith tracked me down and told me I could live with them."

"Did you?"

She shook her head.

My lips pursed. "How'd you end up here?"

"I dropped out of school and started waiting tables. Couch surfed every few days. Sometimes I'd find other places to sleep. I just... I pretended I was camping."

I dropped my hand from her cheek and tried to wrap my arms around her, but she planted her palm against my stomach and pushed me away.

I caught her with my forearm around her stomach and pulled her into my frame. Her eyes were glassy, but she never cried. No tears welled up in her eyes. She was stone cold.

"Your dad came into the diner I was working at and said he needed some help at the farm. He said he'd pay me under the table until I got on my feet. I worked odd jobs around here. One day he had me out on this side of the property and I saw the old cabin. It used to be a tool shed."

"I remember that," I said, stroking her hair as she flung her elbows, trying to thrash her way out of my grasp. "I was confused when they said you lived out here."

"George let me clean it out and fix it up. Said I could live in it if I wanted."

Fix it up was a gray term. The window unit battling the brutal Texas heat was on overdrive, the cracks in the wood-plank floor let in more of a draft than the windows or door, and I had yet to see an actual bathroom. Moonlight leaked through sporadic holes in the roof.

"I'm safe out here," she said. "No one bothers me."

Her words jogged the memory of Jo pulling a gun on me. I had been surprised at how quickly she drew it with no hesitation. What was she afraid of?

Jo tensed in my arms and tried to slip out again. "Don't pity me, Vaughan."

I loved my name coming out of her mouth in that soft, breathy way.

"When I was seventeen, George introduced me to an old ag pilot he knew. The guy helped me get my private pilot's license and get in all the additional training I needed to do crop dusting. They helped me fix up the Ag Cat and I got my business off the ground. Mostly, taking care of the fields here, then I started taking on more clients." She let out a tremulous breath. "I went back and finally got my GED a few years ago, and I make good money now."

Her GED.

A latent memory of the first time Jo and I met pricked at my brain. I had called her a GED-wielding country bumpkin.

Shit.

"Don't pity me, Vaughan. I already told you that once, and I will not say it again," she snapped as she wrenched out of my grasp and crossed the tiny one-room cabin.

Jo popped up onto her tiptoes, reaching into a cabinet for a glass. The one she pulled down had a chip in it. I watched as she stuck it under the faucet, filled it, and took a fortifying drink.

She emptied it in the sink and turned to me. "None of that scared me, so don't think you're going to scare me off either."

Her pit bull raised his head from the plush bed shoved in the corner and lifted a judgmental eye at me as if to say, "Get lost, loser."

To my surprise, he lumbered out of his bed and plopped in front of me, thumping his stub of a tail on the dusty floor. He was missing an ear.

Hoping that he wouldn't bite my hand clean off to prove his loyalty to his human, I offered my palm and let him sniff me.

"Traitor," Jo muttered as she glared at the dog. She stood across the room from me, keeping as much space between us as possible.

For the first time, I didn't see her as the pain in my ass woman who had tortured me from day one. I saw her as the little girl who had to put on a brave face far too young.

My gut ached as I imagined her at half her age, all alone in this shack. I pictured her curled up in the bed, hugging her knees as she listened to the howl of the wind and the creaking and groaning of the structure, wondering if she really was safe.

"You should go," Jo said with a thick swallow of emotion. And just like that, she was back to her annoying self.

"Thanks for the completely unnecessary and totally intrusive ride. Next time feel free to bypass stopping here, and find the nearest cliff to drive off of."

I wasn't perturbed, and I didn't move. Surprisingly, her snarky comment didn't elicit a single sarcastic thought for me to counter with.

"Jo—"

"Whatever mind-fuck happened today, let's forget it. Okay?" She crossed her arms over her stomach and leaned against the kitchenette counter. "Let's just go back to you trying to get me kicked off the land, and me trying to kill you. It's easier that way."

Simply because I knew it would piss her off—*and because I really wanted to*—I crossed the room and kissed her.

She raised her arms—probably to hit me—but I held them against her sides. Her lips were soft and supple—a stark contrast to her prickly personality.

"Night, Tiger," I whispered against the corner of her mouth when I pulled away.

Jo's cheeks were flushed the same color as the gingham curtains hanging in front of the windows.

She didn't say anything as I strode to the door. I twisted the handle, opening it just a crack. Turning, I gave her a pointed look. "Lock up."

Jo nodded.

A tight smile forced its way across my mouth. I didn't want to, but I couldn't help it. Something about tonight felt like a change in the wind. A glitch in the matrix. A turning point.

I pulled the door behind me, pausing to listen.

The quiet creak of Jo's footsteps racing across the floor

took me by surprise. Then, the *schnick* of the deadbolt and the click of the lock.

A muffled thump rattled the front of the cabin. Jo's shadow filled the crack at the bottom of the door. She slumped onto the floor, her back pressed against the wood. I stood, frozen, and listened as she let out a heavy breath.

Then a sniff.

And then nothing.

I waited a moment as she rested there, then moved away, heading back to the truck.

Her shadow cropped up in the left window as the headlights flashed to life. I studied the cabin for a moment before throwing the truck into drive and lumbering back toward the big house.

Two shadows sat in rocking chairs when I pulled up to the house. The faint glow of a cigar illuminated latent smoke rings floating toward the sky. Cash uncrossed his legs. The heavy soles of his work boots dropped onto the porch with a *thud*.

"What are y'all still doing up?" I asked as I slammed the truck door. Cash and Ryman rarely stayed up this late.

Ryman straightened, then rested his elbows on top of his knees. "Figured we needed to have a talk."

My brow furrowed. "About what?"

"JoJo," Cash said.

"What about her?" I tried to keep my tone even, but every word conveyed concern. Something about the last six hours had me on edge anytime someone so much as looked at her.

Ryman took a pull from his cigar, blew out a breath, and tapped the embers into a dish on the table between the two of them. "What happened between you two?"

I was the oldest by a long shot, but there was something about Ryman's posture that was authoritative.

They sure as hell knew what the two of us had done. It was written all over our faces, especially when Jo walked into the big house for dessert. She looked fresh from the shower, but the once-roaring fire that burned inside of her had turned into ash. She carried herself differently. The two of us hadn't been at each other's throats and everyone took notice.

"Do you actually expect me to tell you?" I asked as I made my way up the porch steps and leaned against the railing.

"Jo told me," Cash said.

I smirked. "No, she didn't."

He glowered. "Fine. She didn't. But it's pretty fuckin' obvious."

My fingers dug into the railing. "I'm not talking about it."

Ryman snuffed out his cigar and rose to his feet. "Let's get one thing straight," he said as Cash stood, too. "I don't care whether we're brothers or half-brothers. If you hurt her, we'll kill you."

"And her attempting to hurt *me* hasn't been a problem for you thus far?"

Cash crossed his arms. "You know we ain't talkin' about you two picking at each other like kids on a playground."

"Pretty sure kids on playgrounds don't hit innocent pedestrians with their vehicles," I muttered.

"Look. That girl's nuttier than squirrel shit, but she's a good person. Jo deserves to be treated like a fuckin' queen after all she's been through." Ryman pointed a finger at me. "You get me?"

I was done with this conversation. Cash and Ryman were just looking out for her, but they were doing it because of how little they thought of me. I didn't really care, but the reminder that they didn't know me hurt more than I expected it to.

"You know, I don't think she's a flowers and chocolates kind of girl." I brushed past them, heading toward the front door. "Maybe I'll bring her a plate of ExLax cookies, and a bouquet of poison ivy and barbed wire."

That shut them up, because I wasn't wrong.

18

JOELLE

Crosswinds whipped up, shaking the wings as I neared the tree line at the edge of the Thompson's north fields. I let out a breath, felt the pounding of my heart, then inhaled before pulling up on the yolk, tipping the nose of the Ag Cat straight in the air.

Intense pressure slammed my body against the seat as I fought gravity to make it above the trees. I rolled, narrowly avoiding the power line I cursed every time I saw it. I leveled out and opened up the throttle, blasting over the road that circled the far side of the property.

I glanced at the gauges, checking the level of my fluid payload. I had enough left over to get a head start on the east fields before the weather picked up. The wings tipped to the side as I turned to head across the farm.

I flipped the radio dial, settling on the frequency that Ryman, Cash, and the farm hands used on their radios. "Ground. Y'all got anyone in the east fields today?"

There was a burst of static before Cash's voice popped up. "They just wrapped up and headed back to the silos."

"I'm gonna empty my tank. Y'all stay clear."

"Copy that, JoJo." There was a long silence before he said, "You doing okay?"

I turned the radio off. Radio conversations were patched through the PA system at the big house.

Did I want Vaughan to hear that I felt a little wounded after our last conversation? Did I want him to know I didn't sleep at all after telling him about my past? Did I want him to know that every shadow, every scratch of a tree branch against the cabin, every whip of the wind scared the hell out of me?

Kind of.

There was something about the way he touched me. Something about the way he spoke to me when we weren't fighting. It made me feel safe.

But it also made me feel off-balance. Like he had shifted the axis of my world.

The big house appeared in the distance. Usually I would have dive-bombed, flying in fast and low to give George a show, or to piss off Vaughan.

But I didn't feel like it today.

I didn't really feel like doing anything today.

I sat my ass in the cockpit because I got paid to—not because it was the only thing that made me feel something.

Instead of shaking the windows in the big house, I circled around it, giving Vaughan a wide berth.

The east fields bloomed in the distance. Bright green rows of milo sprung up as far as the eye could see. I lined up with the edge of the field and dropped low, skimming down ten feet above the ground. I opened the nozzles and released the pesticide.

Suck it, headworms.

Cash had spotted the beginnings of a pest problem in a few of the rows yesterday. With the weather looking like shit for the next day or two, the plants could use a little protection.

I pulled up and rolled, lining up for another pass in the opposite direction. The nose dipped. I dropped low again, spraying down another section of the field.

By the time the tank gauge flashed with low fluid, I was spraying the last row. I pulled up and adjusted my heading back to the hangar.

Vaughan's massive *Fuck You, Jo* billboard was still on full display. George and Ms. Faith had apologized profusely, but I hadn't accepted it. It wasn't their stunt to apologize for. With his back still healing from surgery, George needed to take it easy. I pretended like it didn't bother me in the slightest. There was no sense in him getting worked up over something his spawn had done.

I touched down on the blacktop and skidded to a stop. I barely remembered going through the motions of getting the beast of a plane into the hangar, flushing out the tank and apparatus, and logging my flights.

It was like that eerie haze when you're driving and realize that you can't remember the last two miles.

My rubber boots sloshed through the puddles of water as I yanked the hose back and coiled it against the wall.

Keep it oiled. Keep it clean. Keep it safe. The words of Merle —the old timer George convinced to take me under his wing—echoed in my mind.

I took pride in my work. I had built something—a life. Made something of myself. I was the girl everyone expected to end up in juvie, or worse.

Maybe spite was the reason I'd stuck around Maren instead of trying to make it in Austin or Houston.

Spite, and the fact that I didn't have a vehicle to drive until I started working for George back in the day.

I had paid him back for the truck he lent me all those years ago. The one I still drove.

I didn't like having debts. Didn't like being under someone's thumb. I couldn't even count how many times I had tried to pay him rent on the cabin or the hangar, even when I couldn't afford to.

All he ever said about it was that taking care of the fields at-cost was payment enough.

The mental haze followed me back to the cabin. Back to the place where Vaughan made me bend over and plant my hands on the wall. The place where he held me in his arms as I broke into a thousand pieces.

Maybe I should just take a wrecking ball to the place. It was the only way those memories would be demolished.

Hell, I wouldn't even need a wrecking ball. I could wrap the tow chain under the porch and have the whole structure down in a jiff.

Deep waves of hurt washed through me as I drug my feet up the porch steps. Even Bean seemed to be on the lethargic side today. I wanted to blame the weather, but even I knew that wasn't why I felt this way.

I did what I always did on this day. I rummaged around the cabinets until I found a cellophane-wrapped cupcake. It was one of those grocery store snack cakes filled with vanilla cream, topped with a disc of chocolate fudge, and adorned with loops of white icing. It had been my tradition since I could barely cook for myself, much less bake.

The lone candle was still in the junk drawer where I had left it last year. I stuck it into the cake and fished around for my lighter.

The bed groaned beneath me as I sat against my pillows and stared at the flickering flame. "Happy birthday, Joelle," I whispered to myself, then blew out the candle.

Faint tendrils of smoke swirled through the air as pressure built behind my eyes. I wanted to cry. I wanted to mourn the loss of my life.

I missed my mom—or at least the mom she should have been. I missed my dad—the fictional one I had crafted in my mind when I would daydream about what it would have been like if he got sober.

I missed the life I should have had. The life where I had a childhood. A family. Maybe a boyfriend. Maybe I would have gone to college. Maybe I would've had kids or a husband by now.

Still, the tears never came.

The dripping wax had cooled, but the thought of taking a bite made my stomach turn. Why couldn't I let go? I *wanted* to cry.

The last time I had felt a tear roll down my cheek had been fifteen years ago. I still remembered the sound of his voice as he smashed the ashtray on the doorframe, pointing the jagged edge at me like a knife.

Don't you dare cry, Joelle. If you're gonna cry, I'll give you something to cry about.

Rage boiled through me at everything that should have been mine. I couldn't contain it. I crushed the cupcake in my hand, pulled my arm back, and screamed a guttural battle cry as I threw it at the wall. The cream filling stuck to the paneling with an unsatisfying *splat*.

The candle rolled, stopping along a crack in the floorboards.

What was wrong with me?

The urge to cry was quickly replaced with unfettered anger. It was too dark to fly, and I needed something to take the edge off before I exploded.

———

BRIGHT LIGHTS GLOWED from inside the liquor store as I passed it and took a left, heading into town. I passed Jay's, then Willard's—cruising into Maren's little downtown district. If you could even call it a downtown. It was more like a single block with a few niche shops and town hall.

The western pin-up girl glowed in the distance as I came to a screeching stop in front of The Silver Spur.

It wasn't a bull riding night, but hell if I wasn't going to make it one.

"What are you doing out and about?" Ezra hollered as he waltzed between the taps. "You're not usually here this late."

Late was a subjective term. It was just after seven.

I ignored him and tipped my head toward Jenny, his partner behind the bar. "Want some entertainment in this shit hole?"

She raised an eyebrow. "You planning on singing karaoke? Our cover band canceled."

"Fuck no," I said as I made my way to the other side of the building. There was a side door behind the stage. It led to a makeshift green room for the talent, or a dressing room for the girls who stripped for topless bull riding.

"Jo—"

I pushed through the dressing-room door, ignoring Jenny calling after me. I wasn't going to bother with the chaps or the vest. I took off my bra, then put my flannel back on. Instead of buttoning it, I tied it in a knot between my breasts.

Through the wall, I heard the screech of the sound system and Jenny's muffled voice as she barked at patrons to get out of the padded ring.

She barely had time to get the machine turned on and a song queued up before I stomped out into the ring. The silver-plated toe of my boots hooked in the stirrup. I swung my leg over the saddle, my denim shorts already riding up my ass.

Cigarette smoke clouded the bar, turning a packed house into nothing more than unidentifiable figures.

This wasn't about them. I rode the mechanical bull and flashed my tits for one person and one person only.

Me.

Jenny flipped a switch and shook the bull side-to-side. She usually began with something that would make my assets jiggle. It got the crowd going and set me up for a trick.

But I wasn't giving them an easy flash of cleavage tonight. I planted my palms on the saddle, the worn leather giving me purchase as Jenny turned the lever and made the bull whip around in a tight three-sixty.

There was a reason the machine was surrounded by thick padding, and it wasn't to soften the blow when drunk frat boys gave it a go.

Jenny knew what I was about to do. I had only done it a handful of times, and managed to stick the trick about half of that.

I popped my boots out of the stirrups, squatted with both feet on the saddle, then jumped as she spun the bull as fast as it would go.

My palms slapped the back of my knees as I tucked into a tight backflip. My eyes were glued to the bull, spotting the landing as I rotated mid-air.

My feet hit the saddle first. I spread my legs and settled astride the bull. The crowd cheered, pressing against the partition as Jenny whipped me around again.

A few drinkers threw dollar bills at me, but I paid them

no mind. Usually, I would play up the crowd and wring their wallets dry, but not tonight.

A tall figure stood along the half-wall, bracing his hands against the edge. I teased the rest of the barflies by tugging on my knotted flannel. Cheers of 'take it off' were raised in unison.

But not him.

Vaughan stood out among the smoke and chaos. He was steadfast and resolute.

I locked eyes with him as Jenny made the bull shake. It was her signal for *get naked or move on*.

I tugged on the knot while I slid down to the back of the bull and laid on my back. I pushed up into a handstand, turned, and landed sitting in the opposite direction. Vaughan had moved along the wall, chasing my undivided attention.

I gave it to him.

He didn't flinch when I wedged my finger through the loosened knot and tugged. The sides of my shirt fluttered open, giving him a full-frontal view of my cleavage.

Jenny turned the machine, taking me away from Vaughan and giving the rest of the bar a peek. Bills rained down like confetti on New Year's Eve.

Riding usually gave me a rush. I loved the attention; loved making some easy cash. Why did I feel so empty?

The anger at failing to experience any sort of vulnerable emotion, even after storming into the Silver Spur, hadn't been quenched.

Through the mayhem, Vaughan never moved. His hands stayed braced along the partition. His gaze covered me like a blanket. I finished my ride and dismounted the bull, stepping on crumpled bills. My shirt was still open, flashing everyone as I made my way to him.

He straightened as I approached. A green bill was pinched between two fingers.

"What are you doing here?"

I caught a glimpse of Benjamin Franklin's mug on the front of the note.

His expression remained neutral. "Meeting in town. Decided to have a beer before I headed back to the farm." Vaughan's eyes darkened as he studied my chest. "Didn't know I'd get a show, too." He reached out, his fingertip grazing the lower swell of my cleavage.

I shuddered from the electricity skittering across my skin.

"Did you enjoy yourself?" I rasped.

Vaughan lifted the hundred-dollar bill. "I did."

His honesty made me take a step back, but Vaughan wasn't having that. He reached over and hooked a finger through my belt loop, tugging me against the wood half-wall that separated us.

All eyes were on the two of us as he slid the hundred dollar bill into the waistband of my shorts.

"Why are you out here tonight?" he asked.

My eyes darted to the floor.

Vaughan crooked a finger beneath my chin and tipped it up. "Tell me what you're doing here, Tiger."

"Why do you call me that?"

"What? Tiger?"

"You called me 'kitten' the other night, too."

Vaughan nodded. "I did."

"Why?"

He stroked my cheek with the back of his knuckles. "Because I like it."

Something about his touch fed the craving to feel something.

Vaughan pressed the pad of his thumb against my lower lips. "I like seeing you let down your defenses."

"Who says I've let them down?"

A feral smile crossed his mouth. "I did." He leaned in, his stubbled jaw scraping my cheek. "And as much as you like fighting me, you get off on obeying me."

19

VAUGHAN

I gripped the edge of the wood partition with white knuckles as I watched Jo slip her feet out of the stirrups, crouch on top of the moving bull, and do a backflip.

That reckless daredevil...

My fury burned white hot when she landed astride the machine. A self-satisfied smirk graced her lips.

Eyes the color of the pale blue neon sign locked with mine. She had noticed me.

I didn't show up to the Silver Spur with the intent of watching her flash her tits for petty cash. I had been at the bank for a meeting that went less than optimum. I wanted to take the edge off before I went back to the big house, lied to my family, and told them that everything was going to be fine.

On top of the problems on the home front, a billionaire was playing fast and loose with a company he was trying to buy, and the uncertainty of that situation was fucking with the value of some of my clients' investments. Of course, Tamara couldn't talk them down. It was all on me.

Everything was fucking on me.

Making my clientele obscene amounts of money.

Saving the farm from foreclosure.

Turning a profit so the money that I dumped into the land wasn't a waste.

Setting my dad up for the rest of his life.

It was all on me.

But there she was, holding on to that bull with just her thighs as she prepared for her next trick.

Jo tugged on the knot between her breasts as she eyed me up and down, daring me to flinch.

The two of us had been playing a game of chicken since day one. Now that I had a taste of her under my control, the stakes had never been higher.

Why did I fear losing something that wasn't even mine to begin with?

Maybe one of us would walk away. Maybe we would wreck each other.

I was many things, but a coward wasn't one of them.

She finished her ride with her tits on full display, dismounting the bull as it rained dollar bills. The patrons hadn't shown up expecting a show. But they sure as hell knew a good one when they saw it.

Her breasts bounced with each stride she took toward me, the sides of her flannel flowing behind her like a cape.

"What are you doing here?" she asked, her eyes flitting down to the bill I had pinched between my fingers.

I steeled my expression as I tried not to choke on my tongue. *So fucking beautiful.* "Meeting in town. Decided to have a beer before I headed back to the farm." I paused, looking my fill. "Didn't know I'd get a show, too." I reached out, my fingertip barely ghosting over the curve of her breast.

Jo shivered. "Enjoy the show?"

I lifted the hundred-dollar bill. "I did."

She took a step back, but I didn't let her get far. I reached over the partition and hooked a finger through her belt loop, yanking her against the wood half-wall that separated us.

With the speed of a tortoise, I slid the hundred into the waistband of her shorts.

"Why are you out here tonight?" I asked.

She studied the floor like it was the most interesting thing in the world.

I crooked a finger beneath her chin and tipped it up. "Tell me what you're doing here, Tiger."

"Why do you call me that?"

"What? Tiger?"

"You called me 'kitten' the other night, too."

"I did." I had loved her reaction when I called her 'kitten.'

"Why?"

I couldn't help myself. I stroked her cheek with the back of my knuckles. "Because I like it." I pressed the pad of my thumb against her pillowy bottom lip. "I like seeing you let down your defenses."

"Who says I've let them down?"

I grinned like a predator about to pounce on its prey. "I did." I leaned in and let my stubbled jaw scrape her cheek. Her subtle intake of breath was a green light. "And as much as you like fighting me, you get off on obeying me."

My palm slid around her bare ribs, and Jo swallowed. "You're not allowed to touch the riders in the ring," she whispered.

My thumb grazed the side of her breast. "Maybe I'm trying to get us both kicked out," I countered.

Her eyes lowered. They were too heavy with lust to stay locked on mine. "I..."

All eyes were on us as I whispered in her ear. "Does the 'no touching rule' apply to the people in the ring?"

Her lips parted, but no sound came out.

I swung my leg over the partition, hopping into the ring. "Go get your clothes. *Now*."

She let out a quiet gasp when I palmed her ass, claiming her in front of the whole fucking saloon as I marched her across the vinyl-covered pads to the stage.

I ducked under the door frame that led down to a narrow hallway. It was lit by a single exposed bulb.

The blonde DJ who slipped out from behind the bar to work the bull and fuel Jo's antics popped her head through the door. "You good, JoJo?"

She turned, dark hair whipping between us as she peered around me. "I'm good, Jen. Thanks."

Jen eyed me suspiciously, then turned her attention back to Jo. "You need me to call one of your boys for a ride?"

"Vaughan's going to take me home. Someone will come get my truck tomorrow."

My heart swelled with pride, but I kept my face grim. "Let's go."

Jo dipped into a room the size of a closet and plucked her bra from a rickety table. She shucked off her flannel and went to put it on, but that wasn't fucking happening.

I snatched her bra away from her. "Trust me," I said as I scanned the room for anything else that belonged to her. I grabbed her keys and phone and slid them into my pocket. "This is the most clothed you'll be for the foreseeable future."

Jo had slid the flannel back on her arms like a jacket.

Nimble fingers that were deftly fastening the buttons froze. "Maybe we should just get it out of the way now."

I grinned and ripped my finger down the front of her shirt, sending buttons flying across the room. "It's funny that you think you're going to call the shots here, Tiger."

"What?" she teased. "You gonna make me bend over with my hands on the wall and spank me again?"

I threaded my fingers in the back of her hair and tugged, putting a delicious pressure on her scalp. "By the end of the night, I'll be calling you kitten, and you'll be calling me 'sir.'" I rolled my thumb over her nipple, and she gasped. I pinched the bud. "Get in the truck."

"Like this?" she asked, looking at her tattered shirt.

"I don't fucking care," I clipped, turning her toward the door. "You can get off on them looking, but I'm the only one who makes you come. Understood?"

"There's a back exit," Jo whispered.

"Get going, Tiger."

The truck ride back to the farm was made in silence. Jo sat with her hands in her lap, and I didn't dare reach across the seat and touch her.

If I did, I'd have to pull over and take her on the side of the road.

I took a sharp turn when I pulled beneath the wood and metal ranch gate that marked the entrance. I followed the dirt path to the cabin rather than heading toward the big house.

No way in hell was I fucking her in the tiny bed I was temporarily occupying with my family on the other side of the walls.

The brakes on the truck screeched as I came to a stop in front of the cabin. Dim lights glowed from inside.

"Do you want me to go back to the big house?" I asked. I didn't want her to say yes.

There was something about the way she carried herself tonight that set off warning sirens in my mind. She usually waltzed through life as if she didn't have a care in the world. As if Maren was her kingdom.

Tonight, her shoulders slumped with an invisible weight. When I had watched her bull ride, she wasn't doing it for fun. She was exorcising demons.

It looked like she went out there to let off steam. Because if she didn't, whatever was going on inside would eat her alive.

"No," she said, her jaw locked.

"Jo—"

"I said 'no,'" she snapped, fury radiating off her shoulders like waves of heat. "So either haul my ass inside and fuck me, or get lost. I don't rely on others for anything, especially not orgasms."

That was it. I ripped open the door and jumped out. Jo's feet had just hit the dirt when I grabbed her by the waist and threw her over my shoulder.

She let out a squeak, air leaving her lungs as I skipped the porch steps and leaped onto the landing with her keys already in my hand.

I jammed two in the lock with no avail before finally finding the right key and shoving the door open.

The damn dog was braced on the other side of the entrance, low like he was ready to maul whoever it was to death. Realizing it was me, he huffed and waddled over to the corner, grabbing a stuffed armadillo to nibble on.

Fucking armadillos got me into this mess...

I threw Jo onto the mattress, the frame creaking under

the unexpected weight. I had an inkling that I'd break her bed by dawn.

It would be worth it.

"Clothes off," I snapped as I started working on my own. I kicked my shoes off and unbuttoned my dress shirt.

Jo was already halfway there. "You're not going to do it for me?"

I grabbed her jaw, my fingertips flexing in her cheeks. "I had multiple orgasms planned for you tonight, but if you're going to sass me, maybe I'll tie you up and keep you on the edge while I paint your tits with my cum."

A wicked smirk flickered at the corner of her mouth. "Don't threaten me with a good time."

This fucking woman. I wanted to kiss her... And kill her.

"Clothes. Off. Now."

She did as she was told as I looked around the room. Women usually kept their stash of sex accessories in a bedside table.

Jo didn't have a bedside table.

The little tornado had a lamp perched on top of a stack of books beside her bed in lieu of actual furniture.

I went for her dresser. The underwear drawer was a safe bet. Instead of neatly folded and organized undergarments, it was a reckless mess of tangled thongs and briefs. But I found what I was looking for.

I grabbed the bottle of lube she stored next to a small vibrator and an average-looking dildo, and crossed the room.

Jo sat in the middle of the bed with her legs crossed, hugging a pillow. She eyed the lube and arched an eyebrow. "At least you're humble enough to know you'll need help getting me wet."

My tongue slid over my teeth as a nefarious grin spread across my mouth. "Sweetheart, I'm going to have you dripping and begging for me."

I set the bottle on her book stack and unbuckled my belt but left it hanging in the loops for just the right time.

I grabbed her ankles and yanked her to the edge, spreading her thighs and throwing her legs over my shoulders. Jo gasped when I licked up her slit.

"Wow," she choked out between labored breaths. "You really don't bury the lede, do you?"

I answered by sucking on her clit.

She writhed in the sheets as her desperate moans filled the air. Her cunt dripped with arousal, coating my mouth as I ate her pussy.

"What was that about me not being able to get you wet?" I teased as I slid my finger deep into her core.

Her inner muscles fluttered, clenching around my finger in response. I stroked upward, methodically memorizing her like a map. It was all part of my diabolical plan to win this feud. At least, that's what I told myself.

Know the enemy.

I had especially wanted to know what she tasted like. Now that I did, I knew I'd never get enough.

"V-Vaughan—" Her plea was strained.

I added another finger to pushed her further. "Tell me what you want, kitten."

Jo's fingers threaded into my hair, locking me in between her thighs. Her nails scraped across my scalp, sending floods of shivers down my spine.

I delved my tongue into her entrance, circling the tender flesh. Jo's feral cries turned to stifled whimpers. I looked up long enough to see her biting her lip, trying to silence her reaction.

I kissed the inside of her thigh. "If you hold back on me, I'll make you regret it." I leaned forward and kissed across her pubic bone, making her shiver as I rolled my thumb across her clit. "I want your fury."

She let go like a supernova, knees locking around my neck as she tensed, riding each wave of pleasure as it slammed into her.

Jo arched her back, a reverent, "*Fuck,*" escaping from between parted lips.

"On your knees, kitten." I stood, licking my lips for one more taste of her before wiping my mouth with my shirt sleeve.

She was boneless from her release, panting to catch her breath.

I flipped her onto her stomach, grabbed her hips, and yanked her up. "I said *on your knees.*"

Dark hair flew like a tumbleweed as she whipped her head around to look back at me.

I slapped my palm against her rear. "I want this ass nice and high. Present it to me."

Jo braced with her forearms, trying to regain her composure after one hell of an orgasm. "What?" she wheezed as she arched her back. "You think one arguably good orgasm and I'll turn into your little pillow princess?"

"That's exactly what I think, kitten." I chuckled, tapping my palm against the inside of her thighs. "I want these apart. Show me that pretty cunt."

Jo did as she was told without argument.

She was a fucking sight to see. Ass in the air, thick waves of mahogany hair spread across the pillow, her cheek flushed a sunset pink. Her eyes were closed, and her lips were parted with anticipation.

I sat back on my haunches, smoothing my hand up and

down her back as I watched her tits bounce in the space between her body and the mattress.

She started to relax under the ministrations. Her breathing steadied, her shoulders slumped, and her ass lowered.

I spanked her ass with a clap that echoed across the small cabin. Jo cried out in surprise, her skin instantly pinking up from the contact.

"What do you say?" I growled as I fisted her hair, yanking her head off the pillow.

I spanked her other cheek when she didn't respond. "You've given me shit since the moment I set foot in town," I growled before giving her another swat.

Her cry of surprise turned to whimpers full of desperation.

"What's that old saying? Don't do the crime if you don't want to get fucked?"

Jo let a smile slip. Her ass rose to meet my hand on the next spank. Her pussy was dripping with fresh arousal. "It goes something like that."

I squeezed her reddened skin in my palm. "Back to what you're supposed to say." I braced my free hand by her shoulder and leaned over her. My cock, still restrained by my pants, nestled comfortably between her cheeks. I brushed her hair away from her face and let my lips graze the shell of her ear. "The proper response is *'thank you, sir.'*"

Jo whimpered when I thrust my tented crotch against her.

I reached between us and ripped my unbuckled belt out of the loops. The clink of the metal blended with the whip of the leather in harmony.

Goosebumps flooded her bare back.

I pressed a kiss to her spine. "If it's too much, all you have to say is 'please.'"

She gritted her teeth. "Never."

I chuckled. "Very well, then."

20

JOELLE

Leather whipped against my pussy. The snap of pain that melted into uncontrollable heat had me gasping for breath. It was too much and not enough all at the same time. Nothing had made me feel this alive in years.

Not flying like a goddamn kamikaze. Not flashing my tits and doing backflips on mechanical bulls. Not playing fast and loose with the random assholes I'd hook up with in the back room at the saloon.

Whether we were fighting or fucking, Vaughan made me feel alive.

He pulled my hair again, making my spine light up like a sparkler on the Fourth of July. I grinned like a lunatic when he threw his belt across the room.

Vaughan had been edging me for the better part of an hour. *Or at least I thought it was an hour.* I had lost track of time three potential orgasms ago.

My ass burned like the surface of the sun. My shoulders and back ached from holding the position he had put me in. My thighs trembled as I felt the crest of an orgasm coming closer and closer as he played with my clit.

Smack!

His hand left my pussy and painted my ass with another red print before I could reach a release. "What do you say?"

I cried into the pillow, angry that he delayed yet another orgasm.

I wanted it so badly. I wanted *him* so badly.

"T-thank y-you, sir," I panted.

"Say it, kitten," he said in a timbre laced with husky amusement. "Say 'please' and I'll let you come."

I didn't know why that one word was my last bastion of resistance, but I was holding on to it like a fucking lifeline. Strands of hair stuck to my cheeks, plastered to my skin by sweat and tears of pleasure.

My heart raced like I was on the last mile of a marathon. "No."

His laugh was dark and devious. "Very well, then."

The bed bounced as he eased off of it. Out of the corner of my eye, I noticed that he had lost his pants and shirt at some point. The man was built like Adonis—broad shoulders strapped with muscle, narrow hips, thick thighs, and the tightest ass I had ever seen.

He grabbed the bottle of lube from my book table and popped the top.

Fuck... He didn't need that. I was drenched. If he used even a drop, I'd barely feel his dick if he gave me mercy and stuck it inside of me.

Vaughan eased back behind me, his cock poking at my entrance. It was a sick tease.

But if *this* was the consequence for all the hell I had given him, I needed to find where to bulk order brimstone and pitchforks.

I loved it.

Cool liquid drizzled down my skin, starting at the top of my crack until it disappeared between my ass cheeks.

"Say 'please,' kitten," he soothed in a taunting voice as he gathered the lube on his fingers and worked it against my hole.

I mewled at the pressure as he tested and teased the puckered muscle.

"Say it."

"No," I gasped.

His thick finger pushed inside. "Say. It."

"If you're too chicken to fuck me there, *just say so*," I gasped.

Mouthing off to him was the worst—*and best*—idea I ever had.

Vaughan fucking smiled. I could see the flash of bright white teeth when I peered behind me. Without warning, his finger pushed inside past his thick knuckle. I keened at the snap of pain, burying my face in the pillow to stifle a scream.

"Not so sassy now, are we?" he quipped.

I sucked in a heady gulp of oxygen. "That erection can't feel good after this long."

He snickered as he withdrew his finger from my ass. "You've had me hard for weeks, kitten. I'm used to it."

Without warning, two lube-slicked fingers entered me. I pounded my fist against the mattress as heat and lust boiled deep inside. Arousal dripped from my cunt, leaving a wet spot on the sheets.

I didn't even care. I just wanted to come.

I needed it more than I needed my pride.

Vaughan pumped his fingers in and out, fucking my ass with one hand while he reached around and teased my tits with the other. He didn't even let his cock graze my pussy, like he knew one millisecond of contact would set me off like a firecracker.

"*Vaughan*," I whispered in desperation. Tears leaked out of the corners of my eyes.

"Say it, kitten," he rasped, his need just as dire as mine.

"Make me come," I cried, my words choking off as he thrust his fingers into my tight rosette again. I wanted to feel him fill me. I needed it like I needed to breathe.

"*Say it!*" he barked.

I screamed. "Please!"

Vaughan ripped his fingers out of me as my limbs gave out. I collapsed into the mattress only to be flipped over like a rag doll. His tight boxer briefs were off before I could blink. Either I was delirious or he had pulled a condom out of thin air like a magician. He rolled it down his thick shaft, parted my legs, and positioned himself at my entrance. One quick thrust and he was home.

"Fuck..." My eyes rolled back in ecstasy as he filled me to the hilt.

Sweat dotted his brow as he pounded my cunt.

I couldn't do anything but lay there and take it. Pleasure, lightning fast and incessant, blazed across my pelvis.

Vaughan slowed, grinding against my clit while his cock was deep inside of me.

"Yes," I whispered as I felt the orgasm building quickly.

He dotted the side of my neck with a tender kiss before pulling out and slamming his cock inside of me again. His fingers dug into my hips as he rocked, changing the angle of penetration as he worked my clit with the base of his shaft.

The orgasm hit me like a plane careening into the side of a mountain. I cried out as every atom in my body exploded.

The force of it was nuclear.

I reached out for him, nails digging into his bicep and shoulder as I shuddered. When I opened my eyes, he was coming. Everything around us was covered in soft clouds of bliss.

Vaughan dropped to his forearms, hovering above me as his cock pulsed inside of me.

I expected him to laugh. I expected a glib joke or a cutting remark. I expected everything except his lips on mine.

His palm cradled my cheek in a warm caress. Firm lips led me in the kiss, helping me descend from the high without crashing.

"You okay?" he whispered as he pressed his forehead to mine.

I nodded as I began to shiver.

Vaughan drew the quilt over me as he pulled out, swinging his legs off the side of the bed to go deal with the condom. "Where's your bathroom?"

I pointed listlessly across the room. "Door by the kitchen."

He padded across the cabin, then opened the door that most folks assumed was a closet.

It kind of was.

Vaughan barely fit his massive frame into the tiny space. He reached up and tugged on the string that was connected to the exposed lightbulb above his head. It was almost comical to see him try to fit in there. He braved the claustrophobia and closed the door.

I had only just closed my eyes, soothed by the white noise of the sink running, when I felt hands on me. My instinctive reaction was to fight.

"Whoa!" Vaughan said as he dodged my arm. His hand clapped around my wrist and lowered it down. "It's just me, kitten."

I peered through bleary eyes. "Oh."

His lips pressed against my temple. "How do you feel?" A cool wash rag pressed against my flushed cheeks.

I smiled lazily. "So good."

He chuckled. "Yeah?"

I nodded. "Really good."

With tender care, he wiped away my sweat. Cool air flooded my damp skin when he peeled back the quilt. Vaughan swapped the cool washcloth for a warm one and cleaned my pussy.

"Can you roll over?" he asked softly.

I didn't have an ounce of energy left, but I managed to flop onto my stomach, resting my cheek on his thigh. He used the warm washcloth on my ass, cleaning up the lube and the stray remnants of my orgasm.

I whimpered when the fabric grazed my ass. "I'm gonna be sore tomorrow," I murmured.

He bent low enough to dot the edge of my ear with a kiss. "Good."

Vaughan discarded the washcloths and took my hand, helping me to my feet. My knees wobbled as I made my way to the bathroom. When I came out, he had just finished changing the sheets. Vaughan smirked with satisfaction as he eyed the welts that striped my ass.

I wore them like a badge of honor.

Vaughan made sure I didn't die on my way back to the bed, though a small part of me considered whether the kind gesture was a trap. When I eased back down, he manhandled me onto my back.

I was about to tell him he could leave, but then he slid under the quilt and wrapped his arms around me.

I stiffened and tried to roll away, but he kept me locked

in place. When one hand left my waist to caress my thigh, I thrashed, desperate to get out of his arms.

Vaughan grunted as he fought against me. "Just calm— *Jesus, fuck—*"

I swung my elbow backwards. A sense of impending doom washed over me. I couldn't shake it. The intimacy—it was too much. Vulnerability wasn't safe. Vulnerability meant I wouldn't survive.

I kicked and fought, but I was no match for his strength. "I just need—"

"Let me hold you," he gritted out, yanking me backward against his chest.

I clawed at the sheets, but the moment my bare back hit his chest, my racing heart slowed. Vaughan took up the proactive position of pinning my arms to my sides. After a minute of simply breathing together, he reached down and laced our fingers together.

"Do you need water?" He kissed my temple. "A snack?"

"No." I was a little hesitant before I admitted, "This is... nice... though. I guess."

Vaughan held me close, my back sandwiched between his chest and his arms. I was almost on the precipice of sleep when he said, "You're really fucking amazing, you know that?"

I smiled and let myself relax. "I suppose I'm woman enough to admit that *maybe* you're not the human hemorrhoid I thought you were."

He pinched my ass, and I squealed.

"I'll make you pay for that," he growled into my neck.

I giggled. "Looking forward to it."

For a while, we lay together, listening to the wind whip outside the cabin. Vaughan stroked my hair, gently lulling me into the sweet abyss of sleep.

"Jo?" he said out of nowhere. His voice was thick with exhaustion.

"Hm?"

"Why is there a cupcake stuck to your wall?"

I let out a heavy breath. I didn't want to unload on him tonight, but the simplest version of the truth couldn't hurt, right?

"It was my birthday today."

He didn't make a peep. Didn't so much as breathe. But the protective tightening of his arms around me was comforting enough. In a strange way, it felt safe.

I reached backward and pressed my hand against his leg. "If you're going to pity me, you can leave."

Vaughan grabbed my hand, wrapping my arm across my stomach and holding it in place with his. The submission hold was dominating. But more than that, it was caring.

"I'm not leaving," he said in a gravel-filled baritone.

Pressure and heat built behind my closed eyelids, but I knew that trying to cry was useless. Besides, I didn't have it in me to get angry again. Vaughan had sapped all of my energy. I'd need three full business days before I'd be ready to go toe-to-toe with him again. At least, if I wanted to win.

"Why?" I whispered into the midnight air. The drafty doors, ill-fitting windows, and the holes in the roof let in a cool breeze. It made up for the window unit only working half the time.

Vaughan turned my body, cradling me in his arms as I burrowed into his chest. He kissed the top of my head, then tucked it beneath his chin. "Because no one should be alone on their birthday."

If anything could have made me cry, it was the gentleness in his voice.

But it didn't.

———

I woke to gray skies and an empty bed. I had fallen asleep in Vaughan's arms last night, only to find myself wrapped in cold sheets. I couldn't mull on it for long. Rain pounded on the tin roof, stray drops finding their way through the holes and splattering inside in an ambient rhythm.

I wiped the sleep from my eyes and looked around. Bean was snoring peacefully in his doggie bed. Vaughan's fancy corporate clothes were gone except for his white undershirt, which was folded neatly on top of the pillow he had commandeered last night.

It's easier than finding something clean in my drawers, I told myself as I pulled it over my naked body. The faint aroma of his cologne and the latent smell of the saloon surrounded me like a hug.

A raindrop pelted Bean on the head. He roused with a displeased huff and eyed me with annoyance. *And that was my cue to stop being a melancholy lazy ass.*

I tiptoed across the cabin, dancing around the wet puddles that were pooling on the floor, wincing with every step. I was sore all over from a night in bed with Vaughan. My shoulders screamed as I reached for the bowls and buckets I kept on hand for rainy days. My thighs throbbed as I knelt and stood, wiping each of the puddles and setting out bowls to catch any rain that leaked through the colander I called a roof.

No one should be alone on their birthday.

Vaughan's gruff kindness made me shiver, as did the memory of him holding me until I fell asleep. He probably snuck out and went back to the big house to keep the rest of the Thompsons unaware of our dalliance.

He probably didn't want anyone to know he had succumbed to sleeping with the enemy.

But he left his shirt...

As much as I didn't want to admit it, part of me wanted that to mean something.

I had never slept with someone before. Sure, I'd had plenty of sex, but neither of us ever stayed the night.

Vaughan—my mortal enemy—had stayed.

And then he left.

The loneliness began to creep in. The emptiness. The self-loathing. The longing for things to be different. The pathetic wish for life to not be so fucking hard.

I wrapped my arms around my stomach. For a moment, I stood in my cabin—alone—and let myself ache for all those things.

Bean pawed at the front door, begging to go out and do his business. Luckily, he wasn't a persnickety dog when it came to the rain. He was just spoiled rotten regardless of the weather. There was a small patch of mulch that was shielded by the lip of the roof. He'd scurry out, do his business, then run back in.

I dismissed the melancholy cravings and crossed the cabin. I twisted the knob and realized that, in our haste to get naked, neither of us had locked the door.

Oh well. No one dared trespass on the Thompson's land.

Bean whined again, his claws tapping on the wood floor as he danced and tried to hold it.

"Go on," I said as I yanked the door open. "Take care of your business."

Bean's path to the porch was immediately blocked by a tall figure in jeans. He wedged past the legs and bolted into the yard.

I looked up with wide, surprised eyes as I met Vaughan's eyes.

Grocery bags lined his arms, and I didn't miss what looked like an overnight bag on his shoulder.

"You came back." I was just as surprised as he was at the relief in my voice.

A devilish smile curled at the corner of his mouth. "What are you doing out of bed, birthday girl?"

21

VAUGHAN

I laid awake, staring at the shadow on the wall that was a demolished Little Debbie. Streaks of moonlight danced across Jo's cheek. Her gentle breaths whispered across my chest. Neither of us had said anything after she admitted it was her birthday.

Jo shifted, stirring in her sleep, and I tightened my hold. I liked holding her close. She couldn't find a makeshift weapon to stab me with if I was cuddling her. Win-win.

With her unconscious, I could allow myself to breathe easy. My head was still spinning from the night. The orgasm was great, but Jo... She was...

I let out a breath. *She was incredible.*

Never had I been with a woman who took ever lick of sexual depravity I inflicted and begged for more. I liked her fight, and I craved her fire.

There was nothing mediocre about Joelle Reed. She was the match and the gasoline. Napalm flowed through her veins and she ate C-4 for breakfast.

But seeing all that power harnessed? Controlling it long

enough to make her detonate? It was a symphony that wrecked me inside and out.

I slept beside her on and off as storms rolled across the plains. Every time she would stir or snuggle closer, seeking my body heat, I wished I could take a snapshot and save this moment forever.

Mostly to prove to her that it actually happened.

Before dawn broke, Jo had rolled onto her side, away from me. I eased out of bed, found my pants and button-up, and quickly dressed.

I didn't want her to think I wasn't coming back, so I left my undershirt on the pillow. I cupped my hand around the flashlight on my phone, trying to ward away the wonky shadows that danced across the cabin as I pawed through her cabinets.

The woman lived off canned goods and a handful of frozen TV dinners. Granted, a dollhouse probably had a more functional kitchen. But still—she was thirty.

I stole Jo's keys and snuck out to my truck with only a mild look of derision from the dog. So what if I had railed my mortal enemy? Who was he to judge?

The ground was wet as I trudged to the truck. I didn't want to wake her when I cranked it up, but the chances of her rousing after the night we had were slim. She looked exhausted.

I pulled away, mud sloshing on the tires as I drove to the big house. Lights were on in the kitchen when I pulled up. Probably Ms. Faith and Ryman.

Rainy days—especially gully washers like the one they were calling for today—were unofficial holidays. There wasn't much that could be done at this point in the growing season when a downpour came along. There was no sense in risking getting equipment stuck in the mud. A few chores would be done to take care of the livestock on the property and make sure nothing had gone haywire in the fields.

"Morning, sweetie," Ms. Faith said when I opened the front door. She was seated at the table in the breakfast nook, sipping on a cup of coffee.

I braced my hands on the doorframe as I toed off my muddy shoes. It was more than obvious where I had come from—still dressed in last night's clothes—so I didn't even bother lying.

"Morning," I said, tipping my head to her as latent raindrops rolled off my hair. I glanced at the puddle that formed on the kitchen floor and gave her an apologetic look. "I'll get a towel."

She waved her hand dismissively. "A little water won't hurt. Besides, you know when the two Neanderthals wake up, they'll be tracking mud all over the place. I swear. Those two are hopeless. There's still a chance for Cash, but it'll take some magical man or woman to get Ryman to clean up after himself."

I cracked a smile.

"I wasn't sure if I'd see you today," she said.

My brows furrowed. "Oh?"

She shrugged and stuffed her hands in the pocket of her Baylor sweatshirt. "You used to always make yourself scarce when it rained." A faint smile laced with sadness painted her lips as she recalled my childhood.

I remembered those days. Especially the rainy ones. Activity on the farm always gave me a place to be or a place to hide. But when everything stopped, I felt exposed. Like Cash, Ryman, Bristol, and Ms. Faith looked at me like I was an outsider.

They didn't, of course.

Ms. Faith had been nothing but good to me. Amazing, even.

My standoffishness had never been about her, and always about me.

"You look like you've got something on your mind," she said, patting the seat beside her. "Wanna sit a spell and tell me about it?"

For a moment, I felt more like the skittish eight-year-old who lost his mom and less like the thirty-six-year-old man who had been called in to save everything.

I grabbed the back of the kitchen chair and lowered into it.

Ms. Faith's smile grew as the silence echoed around us. Finally, she broke the tension. "I know you weren't out walking the fields like you used to, Vaughan."

I nearly choked on my tongue as she let out a dry chuckle. "I, uh—"

"I'm aware that my kids are adults with their own lives," she said, patting my hand. "Even Bristol."

I muttered something colorful under my breath, and she laughed. I *hated* that Bristol was an adult.

"You were always one of mine, even if I wasn't yours." Her tone was serious. "I hope you know that."

"I know," I rasped.

Unexpected emotion clogged my throat. I'd lost my mom. Grown up and moved away. Got married and divorced. But something about hearing Ms. Faith say that to me even after all the years and miles between us hit me like a freight train.

I picked at a groove in the table as I asked. "Did it ever bother you that I never picked up on calling you 'Mom?'"

Ms. Faith shook her head. Gold and silver strands fell from the clip that held her hair back. She perched her reading glasses on her head and turned to face me. "I knew when I started seeing your father all those years ago that you and I were gonna have an uphill climb ahead of us." She sighed. "I remember the day your father said that he had told you to call me 'Mom.'"

I stared at the table.

"Your daddy and I haven't ever had a more explosive fight than when he said that. I remember yelling at him and saying that if you were gonna call me that, it had to be on your terms."

"It was never because of you," I admitted. "I just—" Visions of my mom floated through my mind "—I couldn't let her go."

"I know, sweetheart." She squeezed my hand. "And that's okay. I never wanted to replace her. I just... I wanted to be whatever you needed."

"And you were," I said quickly.

"I tried to be that for Joelle, too," she added. "Though, her situation was a little different from yours."

I opened my mouth to ask for Ms. Faith's side of Jo's story, but I was cut off by the scrape of her chair on the floor.

"But you'll just have to talk to JoJo about that," she said with a coy smile as she rose to her feet. Looking me up and down, she snickered to herself. "And it looks like you two might be getting along a little better."

I said nothing.

She cocked an eyebrow. "Am I wrong?"

I let a smile slip. "You're not wrong."

"Good. Then you'll see to it that the profane billboard you had erected by the runway gets taken down as soon as the rain clears. Your father tried to get the company out there to remove it, but *apparently* they only deal with you since you bought the darn thing."

I chuckled as I stood. "I think it looks nice. Really freshens up the place."

Ms. Faith just rolled her eyes.

Ryman stepped into the kitchen, wiping sleep from his eyes.

"Do me a favor?" I asked as I fished around in my pocket for Jo's keys.

He eyed me suspiciously. "What are you doing up so early?"

I tossed him the keys. "Can you take Cash or Bris with you and pick up Jo's truck from the saloon?"

"The fuck?" he spat as he caught the keys mid-air.

"Language, dear," Ms. Faith chided.

"Wait..." Ryman's head looked like it was about to explode. "Is this some kind of prank or did you... No." He shook his head. "It's a prank, isn't it. Because the only other reason you'd have her keys is if you and her—"

"Not a prank," I said as I strode out of the kitchen and headed to my room.

I brushed my teeth, changed into something more comfortable, and rolled on some deodorant. I hurried through packing a few things in a duffel I found in the closet that had been there since the nineties.

After a quick trip into town, in which only three Mareners gave me the stank eye, I arrived back at Jo's cabin.

The sky was still a miserable gray when I hopped out of the truck and loaded my arms with the bags of groceries I'd picked up in town. Rain drizzled down my neck as I trudged up the stairs.

I reached for the knob, but the wood door creaked open first.

"Go on. Take care of your business," I heard Jo say.

Bean wedged his snout through the crack, but stopped when he ran into my shin.

Jo, in nothing but the shirt I'd left her, stared up at me with surprise. "You came back."

Bean bolted outside, but neither of us moved.

I grinned and kicked my shoes off onto the porch. "What are you doing out of bed, birthday girl?"

She clammed up, crossing her arms over her middle as I pushed my way in and began unloading the bags on the kitchen counters.

"What ... what are you doing here?"

Rain clattered on the tin roof. It was accompanied by the *thwop* of droplets in buckets that had been scattered about. The cracks that had let moonlight dance across her like a disco ball showed just how rickety the structure was.

"I was gonna make us breakfast, but I'm not really a canned-ravioli-in-the-morning kind of a guy." I held up the grease-soaked paper bag. "So, I went by Jay's."

Standing in the middle of the cabin, drowning in my oversized shirt, Jo looked small.

Sure, she was tiny—a little five-foot-two wicked pixie. But nothing about Jo, other than her frame, was small.

I paused. "What's the matter?"

Her eyes darted around like she was looking for an escape.

Bean trotted back inside, ran straight up to me, and plopped his rear down. Thanks to my shrewd reconnaissance over the last few weeks, I was prepared.

I reached into the bag and grabbed the foil-covered taco labeled with a *B*. I unwrapped it and tossed it to him.

Bean gobbled it down in one snarf.

Her eyes widened. "Wha..." She rubbed her eyes. "How did you—"

"Brisket and eggs for Bean," I said as I dug in the bag and handed her two tacos. "The works with extra pico for you."

She stood there, dumbfounded. "Vaughan—"

Before she could argue or stammer anymore, I had her pinned against the wall. My hips held her down while I caressed her ribs with one hand and used the other to tip her chin up and keep her attention on me. "You're grounded."

Her face turned from confusion to petulant anger.

I kissed her softly, leeching some of the tension from her. "It's gonna be storming all day, it's not safe to fly, and it was your fucking birthday and you didn't tell a goddamn soul." My thumb stroked her throat, eliciting a quiet gasp. I kissed her again. "Get back in bed."

"Or what?" she asked, testing me.

I slid my palm to her ass, and squeezed. Jo's teeth sunk into her lip, desperate to hide her whimper. "You really ready to go another round, Tiger?"

She looked up at me through thick lashes and shook her head.

I squeezed again—gentler this time, but still firm enough to give her a reminder. "That's what I thought. Now get in bed."

We sat side-by-side, eating our gas station breakfasts in companionable silence.

She finished her first taco and balled the aluminum foil in her hand. "How'd you know what I like? And what Bean gets?"

I chuckled as I wiped my mouth. "I know everything about you, kitten."

She rolled her eyes in a *yeah, sure* kind of way.

"Don't believe me?"

She shrugged. "I think you like to think you know everything."

"Try me."

"Fine," she sighed. "How do I take my coffee?"

"Black."

Her eyes narrowed. "That was an easy one. Everyone knows that." She thought for a moment, then asked. "Where did I adopt Bean from?"

"You didn't," I said with a laugh. "Rumor has it, you broke into a dogfighting puppy mill and stole him."

She grinned like the happiest little felon on earth.

I arched an eyebrow. "It's true?"

She giggled. "It's true."

I let out a low whistle and took a bite. "Next?"

Jo hummed. "Who was the last guy I dated?"

"Never have. Always single. You never bring guys back here either. You hook up in town or go to their place. Which, let's be honest, is really fucking stupid. Rule number one is that you never let a serial killer take you to a second location."

"Takes one to know one."

"Touché."

"What did I score on the GED exam?"

I paused with the last bite of my taco halfway to my mouth, then dropped it back in the foil and set it aside. "You got a perfect score."

Jo stared at her lap.

"Is that a sore spot for you?" I asked gently.

She nodded. "I always liked school. I did really well. It sucked having to drop out. Being labeled the kid who was trouble..."

"There's a difference in being trouble and being troubled."

The corner of her mouth quivered, but she didn't say anything else.

I draped my arm around her shoulder, pulled her into my lap, and wrapped my arms around her. "I, uh, I see where we may have gotten off on the wrong foot when you stopped to help me out of the ditch."

"We?" she snapped, tensing up. "Calling me a 'GED-wielding country bumpkin' like I was the scum of the earth was *all you*."

"Please. I can admit my guilt in all this, but you're not innocent in the slightest."

"Fine. So maybe we bring out the worst in each other."

"Maybe tit-for-tat got a little out of hand," I murmured into the crook of her neck.

"I'm not the one who rented a fucking billboard."

I grinned against her skin. "I think I'm gonna leave it up."

"You would," she muttered.

I brushed her hair to the side and kissed up the side of her neck. One night with her—hell, one *taste* of her—and I was addicted. "Think of it as a promise every time you take off and land."

Jo shivered as my lips skated across her skin. "It says 'Fuck you, Jo.' Is that a promise to make my life a continuous living hell?"

"No, ma'am." I nibbled on her ear. "A promise that I'm going to fuck you."

Under the blankets, she crossed her legs and squeezed her thighs together.

"You're thinking about it, aren't you?" I murmured.

She nodded.

"Are we good?"

Jo craned her head back. "Good? You and me?"

I nodded.

She cackled. "Not in the slightest! You have some serious groveling to do!"

"You're the one who hit me with your truck!"

"It was barely a love tap!"

"You have a backwoods mechanic holding my car hostage."

She grinned. "It's been fixed for weeks. I just told them not to let you pick it up until I had you running out of town with your tail between your legs." Her voice softened. "I didn't expect you to stay and fight."

"I like fighting with you," I admitted as I cradled her cheek and kissed the spot on her temple where her scar slashed across her skin like a lightning bolt.

"I like fighting with you, too."

22

JOELLE

"**T**ell me something." Vaughan's voice was low and gritty like sandpaper. His fingers tangled in my hair as he stroked it away from my face.

We had been lying together for the better part of an hour. Breakfast was long gone. The groceries—or whatever the hell he had procured in town—were still sitting on the counter. Bean was happily gnawing away on a bully stick that Vaughan had tossed him.

It was like I had been captured in a freeze frame, complete with a record screech, right before a narrator popped in and said, "Yep. That's me—snuggling with the human twat waffle. You're probably wondering how I got here."

Everything about this scene made my skin crawl.

But then his hand found my hair and started stroking. *Oh, sweet Dolly Parton— I was a goner.* I closed my eyes and curled into his side.

Vaughan stayed upright, fielding emails and the occasional phone call from his uppity job doing whatever the hell demons did when they weren't possessing people.

Maybe that's what I could blame this on. Vaughan had possessed me when we had sex.

At least I had some kind of reason as to why I was cuddling his thigh like a koala clinging to a tree.

When he came back to the cabin, wearing jeans and a t-shirt, I realized it was the first time I had seen him in something normal. I had just assumed he was a robot who thought suits made him more human.

The possessive arm that pinned me to his side was so strong, strapped with layers and ridges of muscle.

"Hm?" I grunted, reluctantly peeling my eyes open to glance up.

The shit-eating grin he pointed at me was feral. "Tell me —is this rock bottom for you?"

A laugh ripped out of my throat, and I cuddled closer. "I think so." I rolled onto my back, leaving my head in his lap. "What about you? Rock bottom?"

He chuckled and set his phone on my book stack table. "Nope."

I raised an eyebrow. "No?"

"I hit rock bottom after my divorce was final ."

"And what is rock bottom for Vaughan Thompson?" I said with a yawn before burrowing under the covers. Rain plunked into the buckets scattered around as gusts of wind rattled the windows.

"I got really into paint-by-number projects and tried to go vegan."

My eyes shot open. The laugh that escaped me was more suited for a foghorn than a lady, but no one ever accused me of being a fucking lady.

"You're kidding!"

"I shit you not, Ursula." He stroked my hair again. "I stopped lifting and started doing yoga. Did a juice cleanse."

I giggled. "So, your rock bottom was having a hobby and shitting yourself from liquid kale?"

"My assistant caught me painting a picture of Betty White in my office in the middle of the day. She staged an intervention."

I howled. "I don't believe you."

He plucked his phone off the books and scrolled through his photos before showing me the screen.

"Damn," I said through my laughter. "It's actually really good!"

"I know," he said with a chuckle.

"So, my guess is the vegan thing, the yoga, and the juice cleanses didn't stick?"

"Nah." He burrowed down under the quilts with me. "But I have a cabinet that is stuffed full of completed paint-by-numbers."

"I'll believe it when I see it," I murmured into his chest.

Without skipping a beat, Vaughan asked, "How do we not know each other?"

"What do you mean?"

"I mean, I know I moved away. But I spent the first eighteen years of my life here.

"There's what—six or seven years between us? We didn't run in the same circles."

"It's a small town, Jo." He looked down at me. "How did I not know about you?"

When I didn't immediately pipe up with an explanation, his hold on me tightened.

There had never been any pretense around us. We showed our asses, let the worst parts of ourselves run wild.

And yet, we still ended up here.

Maybe that's how I knew I could trust him. He didn't pretend to be anything other than exactly who he was.

"People like to think that, if they ignore things that make them uncomfortable, they don't exist."

He pressed a kiss to the top of my head, and I melted.

"My Momma killed herself when I was twelve. My daddy never recovered from that. I'd like to think that it's what made him drink as much as he did, but everyone knew he wailed on her for years before she took her life. When she was gone, I took her place."

"Jo—"

I shook my head. "You remember how I said I was good in school?"

He nodded.

"I was good in school because it was safe there. I got to eat lunch. Nobody touched me. I'd stay after school and tell my teachers I needed tutoring." I sighed. "I didn't need the help. I was just biding my time. Staying there as long as I could. I'd skip taking the bus and walk home just because it took longer."

His hand caressed my arm, stroking up and down in a steady rhythm. The touch was soothing. It had been a long time since I regurgitated this part of my life. I didn't particularly like thinking about it, much less bringing it up.

"When I was in eighth grade, my math teacher noticed some bruises. I lied and told him I fell out of a tree."

"And he believed you?"

I shrugged. "For a while. But there's only so many fictional trees a girl can fall out of before it's too big to hide. It was about a month after that when my daddy hit me with the ashtray." Without even thinking about it, my fingers made their way to the scar I wore like a middle finger. I grazed the mottled skin and closed my eyes.

"I didn't have any money and we didn't have any first aid supplies at home. It was too far to walk to a doctor's office or the hospital, so I tried to deal with it with toilet paper. When a child shows up with a deep cut down the side of her face, a lot of phone calls get made."

"Baby..." Vaughan's voice broke.

But I didn't cry. I couldn't.

"Cops and social workers showed up to the school and pulled me out of class. I sat in the guidance counselor's office for five hours. After that, they sent me to the hospital to get checked out. I had to stand naked while a nurse took pictures of everything. There was so much more that I hid under my clothes. I had a broken arm that had to be reset and put in a cast."

Vaughan let out a slow, tremulous breath.

"Cops found my daddy passed out at home. The ashtray was still in his hand and had my blood on it. They hauled his ass to jail and put mine in an emergency foster home. I don't know which of us had it worse."

"What do you mean?"

"There aren't many foster families in this town. The social workers tried to keep me in my school zone, so the options were even slimmer. There were so many kids in that house. They kept the food locked up. The older kids were supposed to be caregivers for the little ones while the foster parents kept collecting government checks. When the social worker showed up with me, they were scrambling to put on a good front. I stayed overnight, went to school the next day, and then ran away. Cops found me walking out of town. My social worker found a foster family outside of Maren that wasn't complete shit and stuck me with them while my daddy was tried. I testified against him. Got him locked up for a while."

"How long is a while?"

"Twenty years."

I could tell he was doing the math. "Less than five years until he's a free man."

"Shit."

"Yeah. Last I heard, the judge laughed when his public defender tried to get him out on parole."

"Is that why you carry a gun?"

"Yes. And it's why I know how to use it." I smiled at the memory of him disarming me when Bristol had crashed my cabin. "I'm surprised you know how to, city boy."

He chuckled. "I still grew up here. I might be rusty, but I'll bet I can outshoot you any day."

"I stayed in the system until I could convince a judge to emancipate me. And I think you know the rest. Couch-crashing, working dead-end jobs before I could legally drive. George and Ms. Faith trying to convince me to move into the big house. They did more to raise me than my folks did."

"Tell me about it," he said without an ounce of hesitation.

"Why?"

He sighed and stared at the leaking roof. "For the love of God, I can't figure it out myself." Vaughan tipped my chin up and kissed me. "But I want to know everything about you."

"I moved into the cabin when I was sixteen. I didn't know how to drive, so George taught me. When I freaked out because I got my period for the first time, Ms. Faith managed to convince me to come over to the big house. She spoiled me with brownies, ice cream, chick flicks, and a bubble bath. Then she talked me through pads and tampons. I knew the mechanics of sex, but she was the one who sat me down at seventeen and made sure I understood consent and birth control and disease prevention. George helped me fix up the plane and the hangar, and called in a million favors to his buddies so I could learn how to fly."

"I hope you're a better pilot than you are a driver," he quipped.

I smacked him in the chest.

"I came back to visit a few times," he said. "I never knew you were living out here."

I shrugged like it was no big deal.

I remembered those times. Bristol would fawn for weeks, ecstatic that her big brother was coming home from Chicago. Then, for a few years, he didn't so much as grace the state of Texas with his presence.

I was curious about those years.

"Bristol always wanted me to meet you," I admitted. "She'd show me pictures and talk about how cool you were. After a while, she dropped it. I guess it's when you got married."

He sighed. "Meredith hated coming out here. She hated small towns—being out in the middle of nowhere. If we came for the holidays, she'd insist we stay at a hotel in Austin or Houston. Even Waco was too 'cowtown' for her. Eventually we stopped visiting."

"Bitch," I muttered under my breath.

He snickered. "You're not wrong there, Tiger."

The groceries on the warped kitchen counters caught my eye. "Why'd you get all that?"

"Hmm?" He was stroking my hair again, and it made it nearly impossible to form complete sentences.

"The bags from the store."

"Because your cabinets are empty."

"I don't cook a lot."

He chuckled. "I know." Pressing a kiss to my temple, he

whispered, "I've been spying on you and gathering intelligence for weeks."

I smirked against his chest. Not satisfied with the t-shirt between us, I wiggled the cotton up his stomach and laid my hand on his abs.

"You eat *a lot* of canned ravioli," he joked.

Acid boiled in my stomach. It was the discomfort that always rose when I thought back to how stunted I was as an adult.

"It's safe," I admitted quietly.

His brows furrowed and his mouth tensed. "What do you mean?"

"I have the cooking skills and palate of a six-year-old. Ravioli was always safe. It was cheap and filling. It has a pullback lid, so I didn't need a can opener. All I had to do was microwave it. And back then, if the electricity got shut off, it didn't taste too bad straight out of the can."

Vaughan cupped my cheek, stroking his thumb back and forth across my skin. "I'm sorry, I shouldn't have—"

"It's fine. It doesn't bother me," I interjected. "You do what you have to do to survive, and you don't apologize for it."

Curled up in my bed, listening to the pitter-patter of the rain on the roof, it felt like we were having church. Vaughan's hand skated up the hem of the pilfered shirt I was in and caressed my ribs.

"Are you okay after what we did last night?" he asked.

I knew what the hesitancy was about. He was scared that I had actually let him hurt me.

I draped my leg over his, giving him the chance to grab my ass. I was sore, and I still had a handful of marks lingering from his hand and his belt. "You gave me exactly what I wanted. I would have stopped you if I needed to."

"What was it that you wanted?" he asked as he gently caressed my butt.

"To feel something." I kissed his chest. "You made me feel alive."

"You would tell me if I was taking it too far, right?" he asked into my hair.

I grinned. "I punched you in the face, didn't I? How many times do I have to tell you? I'm not some delicate little butterfly."

"Trust me. I know," he said with a chuckle. "You're not delicate like a butterfly. You're delicate like a landmine."

Nature called in the form of growling stomachs after a heady make-out session.

I sat on the counter while Vaughan whipped up something that looked borderline healthy for lunch. While we sat side-by-side in bed, chowing down on grilled chicken wraps, Vaughan updated me on the situation with the farm.

"I thought things were good," I said when he had finished. "At least for the time being. You know, with you being a majority owner now."

He sighed and wiped his mouth. "The money I put in was like throwing a handful of dirt into the Grand Canyon and expecting it to fill it up."

"Shit," I muttered as I spat out a piece of lettuce. *Gross.*

"Yeah." He hesitated, then added. "Can I trust you to keep something to yourself?"

I snorted. "I know what happens to snitches."

"If I can't figure something out soon, we'll have to take Vulkon's offer. Even my dad knows it."

The blood drained out of my face. "I'd have to leave."

"Yeah," he admitted. "Everyone would. The deal is enough to set everyone up financially. Hell, my dad would make a pretty penny with what they're offering for the land.

It's better than waiting it out, then having the bank auction it off for pennies on the dollar."

This land ... it was my safe haven. It's not that I didn't have any other options. I could get a little place in town that was hella nicer than the cabin, but it wouldn't be this. I didn't want to have to leave my piece of heaven.

"Over my dead body," I murmured.

That made Vaughan smile. "I, uh, have something to ask you, though."

"Hm?"

His smile grew to an ear-splitting grin as he grabbed a napkin and wiped dressing from the corner of my mouth. "Can I take you out on a date?"

My eyebrows winged up, and I choked. Vaughan patted my back as I spewed my bite of tortilla, chicken, lettuce, and Caesar dressing onto the paper plate perched on my lap. I sputtered as I reached down to the floor for my drink. "What?"

"A date, Tiger. You have heard of them before, right? You know, two people get dressed up. There's usually a meal involved. Sometimes sex after."

"I'm aware of the concept, yes."

"So, are you in?"

"I'm not the dress-up type, mister." I spread my arms wide. "What you see with me is what you get."

Vaughan rolled his eyes. "Are you in or not? Consider it a belated birthday present if you don't want to call it a date."

"Can we still have sex after?"

He grinned. "We can have it before, after, in the car, in the restaurant bathroom—"

I squealed as he leaned over and started kissing up my neck, making me shiver in delight. "Okay, okay! Fine!"

"Is that a yes?"

I laughed. "Yes."

"One condition," he said, nipping just below my ear.

"What's that?"

"I'm not driving that fucking truck to take you on a date. You have to give me my car back."

23

JOELLE

"I can't believe you convinced me to take a day off work for this," I grumbled into my pillow.

Vaughan stretched out beside me, his back cracking as he twisted on the mattress. He snaked his arms around me, dragging me backward into his chest.

"Get moving, kitten," he murmured against my neck as he left a trail of wet kisses down my shoulder.

Goosebumps raced from the top of my head down to my toes.

His hand wandered across my stomach until he found my right tit and squeezed.

"If I'm taking a day off, I should get to sleep in." I wiggled my ass, teasing the erection that was quickly tenting his boxer briefs.

He chuckled. "If you don't get moving, Bris is gonna come over and drag your fine ass out of the bed herself."

"If she wants to trespass and see me naked in bed with her brother, that's fine."

He snorted. "C'mon, Tiger. Do it for Bristol and Ms. Faith. Up and at 'em."

Vaughan had me there. I'd do just about anything for them. Still, I whined and closed my eyes again. I couldn't let him think that we were all chummy now that we had slept together every night for the past few days.

He pinched my nipple, and I squealed.

"What happened to the diabolical early bird who'd wake up when it was still dark and terrorize the farm by flying fast and low?"

"She wasn't getting laid," I grumbled.

"Should I start denying you orgasms?" he asked without a hint of amusement.

I peeled back the covers and rolled out of bed. "I'm up."

Vaughan grinned and laid on his back, lacing his fingers behind his head. His biceps bulged like pillows. "That's what I thought." The sheet covered his waist but exposed one muscular thigh. It was the kind of thigh I wanted to sink my teeth into.

If I had seen Vaughan completely naked weeks ago, I wouldn't have been able to hold out as long as I did. I was only human, after all.

I huffed. "I just need to get a shower."

The bed creaked and groaned as Vaughan got up and tugged on a pair of sweatpants. "You going over to the big house to shower?" Mugs clinked and clattered as he started the coffee pot.

"I have a shower, thank you very much."

"You have a toilet and a sink jammed into a closet, and a stock tank on the back porch." He grumbled something about his dad letting me live here in squalor, but I didn't deign it worthy of a response.

I wasn't going to be shamed for where or how I lived. If he had a problem with how I made it work, he could fuck right off and take his rich ass back to Chicago.

"Ye of little faith," I said as I set up the shower.

I closed the toilet lid and moved the floor tile that hid the open drainpipe. I pulled out the rubber tubing connected to a shower head that I found on the internet.

I think it was supposed to connect to a bathtub faucet so a person could spray down tile after cleaning it, or maybe for camping and showering outdoors. Sure, it was no hand-held sprayer with a jetted massage setting, but it was twenty bucks and did the job. A hook was fastened a few feet above my head to hold it up.

I snapped the rubber hose to the sink faucet like a latex water balloon and cut on the hot water. The hose jerked as water slowly rose to the shower head. I stripped out of the t-shirt I had been sleeping in since the night Vaughan hauled me home from the bar.

Water spattered on the sink, the mirror, and the toilet as I stood in the pint-sized bathroom and rinsed off. I managed to do a decent job of shampooing my hair, and ran a razor over the parts that mattered.

When I was satisfied that I didn't smell like three days of sex, I turned off the faucet, drained the hose, coiled it up neatly, and used an old towel to mop up the water that hadn't made it down the drain.

Vaughan stood just outside the door, shaking his head and muttering curses under his breath as he handed me a towel. I returned his indignation with a *told you so* smile.

"Did Bristol tell you what y'all are doing today?"

I snickered as I filled Bean's water bowl. "You said 'y'all.'"

He cracked a smile as he thumbed through his phone. "I guess it was only a matter of time."

"What? A matter of time before your accent came back? Because you still sound like Chicago. If you say 'pop,' I might have to hit you with my truck again."

Vaughan grabbed my hips and spun me to face him. His lips crashed down on mine as the bowl fell out of my hands and hit the sink with a *splash*. "No, kitten." His pelvis pinned me against the counter's edge, removing any option for escape. "It was only a matter of time until I realized it's gonna be hard to leave."

I pushed away from him and yanked open a dresser drawer.

"Hey..." Vaughan grabbed my arm.

I pulled it away.

"Where are we going tonight?" I asked, effectively cutting off all talk of feelings and the like. This was just sex, even if he wanted to take me out to dinner first.

"It's a surprise," he said through gritted teeth. The annoyance was palpable.

"I need to know if I should wear my dressy jeans or my normal jeans or my casual jeans."

Vaughan glanced around. He was probably looking for my nonexistent closet full of poofy dresses.

"If you asked me out because you think I'll put on a dress and suddenly be a different person, you're sorely mistaken. This isn't like in the movies, city boy. This isn't the moment where the mousey girl lets her hair down, puts on a dress, and everyone realizes she's actually hot. I'm already hot. I just don't own a dress."

I realized that halfway through my monologue he had pinched the bridge of his nose. "Are you through?" he huffed.

I tossed my towel into the dirty clothes pile, crossing my arms as I stood stark naked in the middle of the cabin.

He looked down and started texting someone.

He should be calling the coroner to let them know to have a fridge slot ready for a body, because if he got that attitude with me one more time...

"I will tell Bristol and Ms. Faith where I'm taking you tonight. They can help you figure out if what you want to wear is appropriate."

I rolled my eyes.

"Oh, and Jo?"

I raised an eyebrow.

A wicked smile spread across his mouth. "I will punish you for that attitude later."

————

"SPILL EVERYTHING," was the first thing that came out of Bristol's mouth when she hopped in the front seat of Ms. Faith's SUV and slammed the door.

I snorted under my breath. "I don't think you want all the details."

Ms. Faith tossed me the keys. "You drive, JoJo."

I hopped behind the wheel and pulled away from the big house, leaving Vaughan standing, arms crossed, on the porch. He had changed into his Satan suit for the day—slacks in a charcoal gray, a white button-up, and a vest.

Damn him in those vests.

I squeezed my legs together and thought about something other than him making me wear that vest and nothing more.

Cottage cheese. Cow shit. Bean's post-taco farts.

"Don't hold back on my account," Ms. Faith said from the back seat. "I want the details, too. Vaughan was awfully tight-lipped the other morning."

It was no secret that he had stayed over at my place. It

was also no secret that neither of us had been seen at the big house together for dinner.

In the mornings, I would get up and go to the hangar while Vaughan went back to the house to work. When he heard me do a low pass over the house, he knew that was my way of telling him I was done for the day. He usually beat me to the cabin and had my clothes off before he even said hello.

When he told me that Bristol and Ms. Faith wanted a day for girl talk and shopping before our first date, I couldn't really say no.

"I need to know where he's taking me, and y'all are going to tell me."

The two of them exchanged knowing smiles.

"You're going to have a lovely time," Ms. Faith said. "Nothing too fancy, but maybe a new blouse and a pair of heels with some jeans."

Bristol rolled her eyes. "Geez, Mom. He's taking her to dinner, not to church. Get something sexy."

"I will be getting something off the clearance rack. He's seen me naked. I don't have to seduce him. That ship has sailed."

Bristol's face said *I know something you don't know,* but her mouth stayed shut.

"So. I take it you two have worked out your differences?" Ms. Faith asked, then quickly added, "*Before* things became ... intimate."

Bristol giggled as she watched the GPS.

I waffled. "Before ... d*uring...*" I waved it off. "We're good now ... mostly."

"I'm sorry he still hasn't taken down the billboard. Vaughan can be quite spirited and stubborn when he wants to be."

"Mom, just say he can be an ass," Bristol said.

She pursed her lips, but there was a faint smile across them.

"It's alright," I said as I neared the spaghetti bowl of Austin highways. "It doesn't bother me. Besides, I still have his car under my command."

"Isn't he supposed to be picking it up today?" Bristol piped up. "I heard Cash say he was running Vaughan out to Willard's to get it back."

"One call," I whispered maniacally. "One call and they'll 'lose' the keys to Vaughan's car forever."

Ms. Faith dropped her head into her hands. "Dear heavens, if you two ever have babies I fear for the rest of humanity."

Bristol and I cackled.

"So, are you two like ... a thing?"

I shrugged. Truthfully, I didn't really know. I liked the way I felt about myself when I was around him. He gave me shit, but he didn't make me feel like shit. That was good, right?

"We're just ... I don't know. I guess I should be setting an example and saying things like 'don't have casual sex' and 'make sure it's with someone you love,' but—"

"Pshh, that ship has *sailed* for me."

"Oh, dear Lord," Ms. Faith whispered to the heavens, as if begging for help.

We drove the rest of the way alternating between the country station on the radio and Bristol's rapid-fire questions about me and Vaughan.

Were we in a relationship? No.

Was he going to stay in Maren? No.

Was I going to go to Chicago? Hell no.

But Bristol didn't seem particularly perturbed. It was almost like she was up to something.

"Turn here," she said when I flew off the highway so a tractor trailer didn't rail me up the ass.

I pulled onto a service road that led into an upscale shopping area. I frowned, looking for the outlet stores. "Are you sure you put the address in right?"

"Yep!" She pointed to a strip of stores covered in light stucco. "Park there."

"Bris, this isn't the—"

"Oh, for Pete's sake," she huffed. "Park the fucking car and get out. We're not going to the outlets."

"But you—"

She reached into her purse and pulled out a small black card. "Jo," she said cautiously, as if she was a zookeeper approaching a hungry lion. "I'm going to tell you something. And when I do, you have to promise not to kill me." She craned her neck and looked at Ms. Faith. "You too, Mom."

My eyes narrowed onto her. "Start talking, Little Lucifer."

She wore the moniker like a badge of honor. "We're not shopping *yet*." She pointed to the stucco building that, upon closer inspection, I realized was a day spa. "Vaughan had me call and set up appointments for us." Bristol looked at me. "He wanted you to get pampered before your date tonight —" she turned around to look at her mom "—and he wanted you to relax as a way of saying 'thank you' for everything."

Ms. Faith teared up. "What about you?" she asked as she dabbed her eyes with her sleeve.

"Oh, hell yeah. I'm not getting left out. He's treating me because I'm his favorite."

She wasn't wrong. Vaughan had a soft spot for very few things. Bristol was one of them.

"Jo?" Bristol eyed me suspiciously as she unbuckled her seatbelt. "Are you mad?"

"Mad?" I shook my head. "I'm ... I'm not mad."

I didn't know what I was. Every emotion inside my head swirled around in a mass of unstable chaos. I wanted to cry happy tears. I wanted to feel loved—or at least cherished and appreciated... But I didn't know how.

As if I had conjured it, my phone chimed with a text.

> **Lucifer:** *Don't overthink this. Just enjoy it, kitten. You work hard. It's okay to accept good things when they come your way. Let me spoil you.*

————

So, this was what breathing felt like. The massage therapist worked my lower back with the strength of a bulldozer and the precision of a principal ballerina.

I let out a soft sigh and closed my eyes again. I was completely and utterly relaxed. I was fairly certain I'd have to be forcefully removed from the table because my bones had disappeared, and my face had drooped into the padded toilet seat like a melted ice cream cone.

I had stood to the side as Bristol marched up to the receptionist and informed her that the Thompson ladies had arrived for their scheduled appointments.

Plural.

I hadn't gone for so much as a trim in three years. My nail beds looked like I had never heard of a manicure. And my back, as the massage therapist so kindly described, was so knotted up that it resembled a fast food playland ball pit.

The esthetician who did my facial nearly had a coronary when I told her that my skincare routine began and ended with generic hand soap and drugstore sunscreen.

Now, I had been buffed and polished. My face had been chemically peeled off. My knots and kinks had been untied. All that waited for me was for a hairstylist to tackle the nest of tangles that always managed to form at the nape of my neck.

"Alright, Miss Reed," the massage therapist said in a soothing voice as she pulled the sheet over my shoulders and smoothed her hand down my back. "We're all finished. How do you feel?"

It took me a minute to find my words. My tongue had gone into relaxation-induced hibernation.

I let out a slow breath and blinked a few times to get my bearings. "So good."

It was probably a blasé response, but I couldn't possibly be the one at fault when she had massaged my vocabulary out of my brain.

"Excellent," she said softly. "Take a few minutes and just breathe. Then dress and head to the salon when you're ready. Down the hall and back through the lobby. It's on the other side of the water feature."

I breathed. I dressed. I chugged a gallon of cucumber water and wasn't even bothered by the fact that they had put vegetables in it.

When I arrived in the salon, Ms. Faith was sitting under the blow dryer with her hair in rollers. She smiled over the top of her gossip magazine. "How was your massage?"

I stretched my arms over my head and let out a breath.

"Immaculate. That woman did some *work*. I was all jacked up."

She chuckled. "I got the hot stones. It was so relaxing."

"Where's Bristol?"

"I believe she's getting her facial. Sit a spell. I think you're up next." She patted the empty chair beside her and handed me a magazine from the stack.

Why did I get the one with a feature story about baking for the holidays while she got the one with the good headline about MMA star Miles Zhou winning the fight of his career?

I mindlessly thumbed through the pages, my eyes glazing over the recipes and tutorials on dining room tablescapes. Who the fuck cared about personalized place cards written with a quill pen that had been plucked from bespoke, conflict-free geese?

"For someone who just got the Sam Hill massaged out of her, you sure look tense."

"Who? Me?"

She side-eyed me in a way that only a mom could.

"I'm not telling you about the sex," I blurted out.

Ms. Faith smiled and let her reading glasses hang from the chain around her neck. "I appreciate that very much. There are some things that I don't need to know." She reached over and patted my knee. "And I know you're good at taking care of yourself." When I didn't say anything, she asked, "Does he know this is your first date?"

I curled the edge of the magazine in my hand. "No."

"I see," she said in the way she always did before she prepared to drop some homegrown wisdom on me. "And you're feeling a little ... scared?"

"Stunted."

She cocked her head, the rollers tapping against the dryer bowl above her.

I shrugged. "He was *married*. He did the whole thing—dating, engagement, marriage. I guess he was one step shy of the baby carriage, but who am I to know if the rhyme is true? And me? I've never been on a single date. What kind of thirty-year-old hasn't gone on a date before?"

I stared at the white marble floor. I'd never been to a spa before. I'd never been to a salon this nice. My idea of getting my hair done was trimming it up myself over the kitchen sink with a pair of dollar store scissors and a YouTube tutorial.

"What if I'm too messed up for him?"

Ms. Faith pursed her lips, shifting in her seat so that she could look at me as best as she could. "Listen here, Joelle, and listen good."

My spine tingled every time she called me Joelle.

Usually, it was JoJo. Sometimes Jo.

"You don't get to decide what someone else can handle. You don't get to tell Vaughan how much of you he can take." She squeezed my knee, emphasizing her point. "Don't hold on to the past just because you've spent a long time living in it."

My throat tightened. I heard the hair stylist calling my name, but I didn't move.

"Tornadoes don't bother themselves with the opinions of breezes."

I smiled. "Did you just call Vaughan a breeze?"

She chuckled. "Oh no, dear. He's no breeze." After thinking for a moment, she closed her magazine and pointed it at me. "Vaughan is the lunatic standing in the middle of the storm with a smile plastered on his face, ready to take it head-on. He's not afraid. You shouldn't be either."

24

VAUGHAN

I waited outside my car, arms crossed, as the girls pulled up to the Buc-ees in Temple. Jo was behind the wheel, the reflection of the evening sun gleaming in her knockoff Aviators. I had given Bristol my credit card with the expressed intent of the three of them treating the shit out of themselves.

Bristol was the only one I could trust to actually see to it that they did. Ms. Faith would hem and haw about me not needing to spend money on her. Jo would act like I had asked her to disarm a bomb.

Bristol, however, could be trusted to make sure the two of them didn't bitch and moan about me sending them to the spa, lunch, and shopping.

She was first out of the SUV, her long hair now a short, glossy black.

I tugged on the ends when she threw her arms around me. "This is new."

"You paid for it. Don't think I'm not taking advantage of a fancy haircut when I get the chance."

I hugged her back. "Looks good, kiddo. Where's your mom?"

Ms. Faith slid out of the back seat. Her blonde and silver hair was a bit shorter, but looked a little more modern. "Sweet boy," she said as she came in for a hug. "You didn't have to splurge like that. Certainly not on me."

"Absolutely on you," I said as I hugged her back. I was about to say something else, but she cut me off.

"Come by the house tomorrow and we'll talk. I know I'm not the lady you want to see right now."

She wasn't exactly wrong. Bristol grabbed a handful of shopping bags out of the SUV and moved them over to my car. They must have been Jo's.

Ms. Faith leaned in. "Be gentle with Jo. She might be feeling a little raw right about now." Her palm pressed against my cheek. "This was good for her, Vaughan."

I wasn't quite sure what she was getting at, but I had a feeling whenever Jo stopped hiding in the car, I'd find out.

I pulled Ms. Faith into another hug simply because I wanted to. "Thanks for looking after her. And... And for looking after me. I love you."

She jerked back ever so slightly, like she had touched the electric fence that surrounded the farm. Then, she squeezed me harder and choked out, "I love you, too."

The driver's door to the SUV opened, and Jo slid out.

"Well," Ms. Faith said as she dabbed her eyes with her sleeve. "Bris and I are gonna head back. You kids have a good night."

They loaded up back up and pulled out of the parking lot, leaving Jo standing a few paces away in the empty parking space.

"I don't wear dresses," she blurted out.

"I didn't expect you to," I said as I slowly strode toward her.

She was in a pair of blue jeans that were artfully and intentionally distressed—not just riddled with holes because she wore them in the hangar day in and day out.

The black camisole that was tucked in at the waist was a thin satin that could have doubled as lingerie in a pinch. It had my mind racing at all the possibilities for how this date would end.

Jo was a few inches taller in the chestnut-colored wedges on her feet. She still didn't come up to my shoulders, but the heels made her legs and ass look even more fantastic than they already did.

I cupped her cheek, threading my fingers into her thick hair. It was a warmer color, a few inches shorter, and had layers that framed her face. Still her, just refreshed.

"You look fucking stunning," I murmured as my eyes raked her body.

Her cheeks pinked up at the attention. "Yeah?"

"Yeah, Tiger. You ready to go?"

She walked carefully to the car, trying to keep from face planting in the heels. I opened her door and ogled her legs when she slid in. I let her revel in the luxury interior before finally calling her on her shit.

"See?" I said as I pulled onto the highway. "You could have been riding in style this whole time. Instead, you had to fuck with me for weeks and hold my car hostage."

Jo smirked like the little devil she was. "Yeah, but then who would have sandblasted your sweaty ass when you finally dragged yourself through the gates?"

I reached over and wrapped my hand around her thigh. "You're a formidable adversary, Miss Reed." I pulled onto a private drive that led to a dirt road. "You ever been here?"

Jo leaned forward to study the massive sign that read, *The Griffith Brothers Ranch.* Just below it was a marker that guided visitors down a bumpy two-lane road. "I've heard of it. I think the farm supplies some of their cattle feed."

I nodded. "Ryegrass for the winter months. I'd like to convince them to buy more from us. Staying local and all that."

"And we're having dinner here or is this business?"

"There's a restaurant on the grounds. They've made it into somewhat of a tourist destination. Cabins and a lodge, too."

"Wow." She blew out a breath when the lodge came into view. "It's gorgeous."

I took Jo's hand as we made our way to the restaurant. The upside of her attempting to walk in heels was that she didn't fight me when I reached for her hand. Floor-to-ceiling glass walls shrouded by stonework gave guests an unobstructed view of the rolling plains.

I checked in with the hostess and kept my arm around Jo while our table was readied.

"Why do you look so nervous?" I asked quietly, hiding the question with a kiss to the top of her head.

I stood behind her and rubbed her arms, warming her skin. Really, I just couldn't keep my hands off her. All those speculative sayings about the thin line between love and hate were quite accurate.

When the two of us finally stopped fighting, we realized that all that passion and energy was put to better use when we were on the same side.

"I'm not nervous," she snapped, her defensive words tumbling out one on top of the other.

"Bullshit."

Jo huffed. I could see the restraint she was invoking to keep from stamping her foot.

"You might as well just tell me, because you know I'm not going to let it go."

"Vaughan..." she whined.

"Tell me, kitten."

It was enough to coax her into leaning back into my body. I wrapped my arms around her.

Jo rubbed her temples like my mere presence was undoing all the relaxing she had done all day. "*I've never been on a date before,*" she said under her breath.

"What was that?" I leaned down, goading her into confidently sharing something instead of deflecting.

Jo huffed. "I know you can hear me."

I tapped my ear. "I'm sorry, you must have ruined my hearing with your loud-ass flyovers. Say it again?"

She rolled her eyes. "I've never been on a date before. Okay? Happy?"

I was ecstatic, but I didn't tell her that. It brought out something primal in me. I liked knowing that I was the first of something for her.

And it was something good.

"Have you eaten food in a public setting before?"

Jo looked over her shoulders and shot daggers at me with her eyes. "Yes."

"It's just dinner, Jo."

The hostess called out for Thompson, party of two, and we followed her through the building.

The hostess looked over her shoulder as we wove through the dining room. "Is the rooftop okay for you two tonight? The sunsets have been so beautiful lately, and the weather is perfect."

"Sounds great. Thanks." I placed my hand on the small of Jo's back and guided her through the maze. We made our way up to the open-air dining space to a table against the iron railing. Candles dotted the white linen, the flames flickering in the breeze.

When I pulled out Jo's chair and waited for her to sit, she looked at me like I had lost my mind. I waited patiently, nodding subtly to encourage her on.

"There's no prices on the menu," she said when the sommelier left with my order for a bottle of red to share.

"That's fairly common for a place like this."

"But how are you supposed to know how much it's gonna be?"

I reached across the table and laid my hand over hers. She had a death grip on the leather-bound menu.

"How about I order for the both of us?"

"What if I don't like it? What if it's got something weird like snails or spinach?"

I raised an eyebrow. "Spinach is weird to you?"

She glared at me.

"It's a steakhouse. You can't tell me you're a Texas girl who doesn't like a good steak."

She made a move for her steak knife, and I held my hands up in surrender.

"If I promise no snails or spinach, will you let me order?"

"Fine," she said as she looked out over the pastures. Cattle dotted the land, grazing peacefully. The scenery seemed to soothe and ground her.

"Hey." I gave her hand a squeeze. "You're doing great."

"What kind of thirty-year-old doesn't know how to go on a date?" she said under her breath. The frustration was there, but so was the way she tangled her fingers in with mine.

"Look at me, Jo."

Her eyes were glassy when she finally peeled her gaze away from the cows.

"It's okay to stop and enjoy life occasionally. You don't get bonus points for running yourself into the ground."

She eyed me curiously. "Aren't financiers notorious for running themselves into the ground? Snorting cocaine and jacking off in the office bathrooms to keep the stress down?" Her finger grazed the top of my hand. "I had you pegged as an 'all work and no play' kind of guy."

"That stereotype is mostly true," I said as we lazily thumb wrestled, mostly just finding an excuse to keep touching each other. "I held on to the idea of 'work hard, play hard' even after I left the farm and moved to Chicago."

"Why Chicago?" she asked.

"My grandparents lived close by. They passed a few years back."

"I'm sorry to hear that," she said. "Are those George's parents?"

I shook my head. "No, they were my mom's folks. I guess I figured if I was closer to them, in some way I'd be closer to her. They lived about an hour outside the city in a little town called Lily Lake. I'd spend a week or two with them every summer when I was a kid, and decided to look at colleges in the area. I just stayed."

The waiter returned and took our order. I took the liberty of choosing a spread for us to share. Hopefully, she didn't have aversions to *all* vegetables.

"And how would you like your steak, ma'am?" the waiter asked as he closed his notepad.

"Rare," Jo said definitively. "Just walk it past the grill real fast. It's okay if it's still mooing."

He stifled a smile and looked at me.

"Same way," I said.

"Of course, Mr. Thompson," he said before turning to put the order in. On his way to the hidden server's station, a man at a table a few yards away flagged him down.

"So, is that where you met your wife?" Jo asked when the waiter was out of earshot.

"Ex-wife," I clipped. The hair on the back of my neck stood on end like I had been zapped with a cattle prod. "And I'll give you a hint—exes usually aren't first date talk."

"I don't care," Jo said as she took a fortifying sip of her wine. "You've eaten my pussy. We're well past appropriate date talk."

I couldn't help but laugh. If I hadn't hated her for so long, I was pretty sure I would have been in love with her by now.

"I met Meredith when I was in grad school. She had just finished her undergrad. It was a whirlwind. We dated for a few months, I proposed, and we got married."

"And when did you realize you married a raging cunt?"

I nearly spewed merlot across the pristine white tablecloth.

She grinned. "Bristol talks."

"Somewhere around our third anniversary," I spattered, trying to regain my composure.

Before I could further explain the downfall of my marriage, a tall man with a full silver beard rose from a nearby table and crossed the space. His heavy cowboy boots thudded across the floor. The belt buckle he wore was nearly the size of a dinner plate.

"Pardon me," he said as he stood at our table.

Jo looked at me curiously. I slowly tore my gaze away from her and looked at the cowboy.

"I apologize for interrupting your evening," he said. "I couldn't help but overhear—are you a Thompson?"

I nodded. "Yes."

"Any chance you're kin to the Thompson Farm? Thompson Grain and Feed?"

I nodded. "One and the same." I extended my hand and shook his. "Vaughan Thompson. This is my date, Joelle Reed. She owns and operates the agricultural aviation business that cares for the land."

Jo preened, proud as a peacock.

His beard split in a grin as he shook my hand. "No shit. Christian Griffith. I believe we spoke on the phone a few weeks back." He tipped his chin to Jo. "Pleasure to meet you, ma'am."

Before I could get a word in edgewise, Christian Griffith continued, "How's your growing season looking this year? I'll tell you what—I need to remember to give you a call. We're expecting a big calving season, but you know how dry it's been, save for the storm a few days ago. You'll probably be hearing from us when winter rolls around. Hell, we might just clean out your silos. We try to source local feed, but sometimes the herd has an appetite bigger than the little farms close to us can grow, and our main supplier's been actin' a little squirrely lately."

Compared to the Griffith Brothers Ranch, the Thompson Farm was a pint-sized operation. Jo perked up. A good calving season from one of the biggest ranches in Texas meant money.

Money gave us a chance to dig our way out of the hole.

I reached into my pocket and found a business card. "Give me a call anytime."

He took it and tucked it into his shirt pocket. "I'll let y'all enjoy your dinner."

"Holy shit," Jo whispered when Christian Griffith sat back down at his table.

I let out a breath. My head was spinning at the possibilities. I had just realized what hope tasted like.

25

JOELLE

"**W**hat in Dolly Parton's world is '*haricot verts?*'" I hissed as soon as the waiter waltzed away.

Vaughan smiled in amusement and draped his napkin over his thigh.

I glanced around the rooftop dining area and spotted a blonde woman sitting across from Christian Griffith. She wore a dress paired with killer heels that looked like they had no business being anywhere near a ranch. Her napkin was draped over her lap.

She looked like she knew what she was doing, so I tried to copy her. I studied the way she cut her food into microscopic bites and daintily placed them in her mouth, one by one. She didn't stuff her mouth full—which is exactly what I wanted to do.

Instead of sitting crisscross-applesauce in the chair, I draped my napkin over my bouncing knees and tried to sit up straight and still. I was fairly certain the cloth napkins had a higher thread count than all of my sheets combined.

"They're just green beans," Vaughan said with a kind smile as he sliced through his steak.

He didn't even need the machetes they brought out for us to use as steak knives. The slab of meat melted like butter.

"They're so ... green," I said in dismay. "And there's nuts on them."

He chuckled. "Green beans are usually green. It's in the name."

"Yeah, but not *this* green. Aren't they more of a dingy, military green? Did they add food coloring to these?"

"If they're canned, they're not as bright. But these are fresh. Blanched, then sautéed and tossed with toasted almonds. Try it. You'll like it."

I blinked at him.

Vaughan speared one with his fork and held it out to me, expecting me to eat it just like that.

I wrinkled my nose. "Are you one of those guys who gets off on treating their partner like a helpless little lamb? Because I am *not* into that."

"Trust me, Tiger. You're no lamb." He edged the fork closer to me, insisting that I try a bite.

Part of me wanted to tell him where he could shove that green bean. Instead, I leaned forward and nibbled off his fork.

Vaughan sat back and raised his eyebrows. "So?"

I dabbed my mouth with my napkin, trying my best to *Pretty Woman* the hell out of this situation. "It's ... crunchy."

"And?"

I swallowed and washed it down with a sip of wine. "And I kind of liked it."

He smiled proudly. "Good. Eat up." With a twinkle in his eye, he leaned forward and whispered, "You're going to need your energy."

That fucker made me blush. I looked down at my place setting and froze. "Vaughan?"

"Hmm?" His mouth was already full of steak and, from the looks of it, it was an orgasmic experience.

I cut my eyes down to the eight thousand utensils laid out on either side of my plate. My neck burned with embarrassment. "Why do I have three forks? Is one fork not good enough? What's wrong with just licking it clean?"

"Work from the outside in. Salad fork is the furthest one to the left. Just skip it. The big one in the middle is your dinner fork. The one closest to the plate is for dessert."

I picked up the dinner fork and momentarily considered stabbing myself in the jugular.

Lucky for the surrounding diners, I caught a whiff of my steak and decided to eat instead.

I tried to maintain some shred of decorum while inhaling the best meal of my life. My potatoes, tinged pink from the steak, were clouds of buttery heaven. The pretentious green beans weren't half bad, either.

We split a plate of what was supposed to be pecan pie for dinner. The waiter had droned on about their deconstructed "take" on pecan pie made with molecular gastronomy and unicorn tears—or whatever the hell he had said.

Frankly, I didn't care if that plate had been to space. It was fucking delicious.

Vaughan sipped on a tiny cup of espresso while I finished my wine. The bill had been paid, and we sat in quiet companionship, watching cotton candy skies fade to navy twilight over the ranch.

String lights glowed overhead, bathing us in flashes of gold as a gentle breeze rocked them back and forth.

"I want to talk to you about something before we get

back to the farm," Vaughan said as we stood from the table. He offered his arm—a wise move on his part since I was bobbling on heels thanks to the better half of a bottle of very expensive wine.

Truthfully, I couldn't tell the difference between the triple-digit bottle Vaughan had picked, and the ten-dollar box I could get at the Gas-N-Go.

His button-up was stretched tight across his chest and wrapped around his arms like a second skin. I squeezed his bicep as we made our way down the stairs to the main floor.

"What do you want to talk about?" I asked as we strolled to the parking lot.

"Your business. The hangar and the plane."

I pressed my hand to my cheeks, trying to cool them from the wine buzz. The last time Vaughan had mentioned either of those things, he had been trying to evict me and repossess them.

"What about it?"

We stopped beside his car. Vaughan slipped his fingers in the belt loops of my jeans and tugged me against his body. "Let me help you get a business plan together. I can get you your loan."

"What are you—"

"I overheard your meeting at the bank."

That motherfucking weasel. My nostrils flared as bile rose in my throat. I tried to choke it down, but all that did was make the pit in my stomach grow.

"Just listen," he soothed as he sifted his fingers through my hair, cupping my cheek. His thumb pressed down firmly, forcing my attention to be locked on him. "If the farm goes under—"

"But it's not," I shot back. "It's not going under. You can't

—that's my home." I was shaking my head and backing away from him like he had slapped me.

But Vaughan wasn't having that. He pulled me into his chest and locked his arms around me and dipped his head to the side. His mouth grazed my ear as he murmured, "I'm doing everything I can. But you need to be doing everything you can to secure your livelihood. Let me help you."

I pushed away from him and made a move for the car door. "I don't want to talk about this."

"Jo—"

I yanked on the handle just as he clicked the keyfob and locked the door.

That motherfucker...

His hands slammed on the top of the car, caging me in.

"You worry about the farm, and let me worry about my own damn business," I said as I crossed my arms. "I've been surviving just fine on my own. I don't need you coming in here, acting like a white knight when all you've been is the villain. You tricked me into letting you pay for a spa day. You told Bristol to use your card to pay for all of it and the lunch I had with her and Ms. Faith. I'm just fine living the way I live. I don't need you to fix it." Barely restrained rage leaked from my words like a blown gasket at a nuclear plant.

The look of self-satisfaction on his face told me I was spot-on.

"As long as you're with me, I will treat you like a goddamn queen, and I will not apologize for it."

"And what if I'm not yours?"

"Too late." His forehead pressed against mine, his breath coming in feral beats. "I will burn down the fucking world to protect what's mine."

"And what about Vulkon?"

A lazy smile grew on his stupidly handsome face. "I was always the kid who liked playing with fire."

Vaughan kept his hand on my thigh as we cruised back to Maren. I had to admit, the car was a fucking dream. If I'd known how things would turn out between us, maybe I wouldn't have held it hostage for so long.

There was no bench seat spring getting intimate with my ass, the air conditioning worked, and the interior was silent.

Blissfully silent.

The silence was exactly why I could tell that something was up with Vaughan.

"You okay, mister?" I asked nonchalantly as I stared at the street lights that whizzed by.

The only thing he offered was a grunt, but the right-handed grip he had on my thigh tightened.

I squeezed my legs together in response. "Fine, then. Act like your caveman brothers."

"You look stunning," was all he managed to grit out.

I raised an eyebrow.

Vaughan reached for my hand and laced our fingers together. His thumb brushed the glossy polish Bristol picked out for me—a very feminine black.

"I like your hair. It's different, but it's still—I don't know. You?"

I caught a glimpse of my reflection in the side mirror. My hair was a little lighter. Ms. Faith had convinced me to take off a few inches and warm it up with highlights that the pretentious stylist had referred to as "brûleéd cinnamon." Shorter pieces on top gave me the appearance of volume without any effort.

As a bonus, I could still throw it in a ponytail without too much hassle.

He turned onto a back road that circumvented the main part of Maren.

"I'm sorry I didn't wear a dress or something fancier."

I didn't know why I apologized, but I felt like Vaughan was disappointed in me. He had sent me on this epic shopping excursion, and I came away with a pair of jeans and an overpriced tank top.

Sitting in the restaurant at the Griffith Brothers ranch, I realized that I would always fit in better with the farm hands.

The car jerked to the side, startling me out of my thoughts. I grabbed the "oh shit" handle and studied the road. "What's the matter? Another armadillo?"

Vaughan's face was positively lethal as he pulled onto the shoulder and threw the car into park. "Don't apologize to me, Jo. Don't you dare fucking apologize for being anyone but you."

Headlights blazed across the darkness as a truck blasted past us, laying on the horn.

His chest heaved as the words exploded out of his mouth. "If you think for one second that I'm trying to change you, you're fucking wrong. Don't ever change, Tiger."

I stared at him, wide-eyed and blinking.

"Out of the car," Vaughan snapped as he unlatched his seatbelt and popped open the door. Instead of waiting for me to unbuckle, he did it for me, grabbed me under the arms, and hauled me out the driver's side door.

"What the hell?" I squeaked.

It was like being kidnapped, but kind of hot. My back slammed into the side of the car as Vaughan pinned me against his body. The thick outline of his cock was evident in the front of his slacks.

His gaze roamed my body like he couldn't decide which piece of me to devour first. I placed my hands on his chest and felt the rapid percussion of his heartbeat against my palm.

He played with the short strands of hair that framed my face before raking his fingers across my scalp. A quiet moan escaped my mouth as he tilted my head up and kissed me. It was soft at first. His hands caressed every part of me, chasing away the goosebumps and creating new ones in their wake.

The kiss turned desperate as he started pulling at my clothes—untucking the satin tank and fiddling with the button on my jeans.

"Don't you dare apologize to me, Joelle Reed. Not for anything before this and not for anything after. I want you exactly as you are. Loud and obnoxious and infuriating and unashamed."

"Wow," I mused without an ounce of humor. "You really know how to make a girl feel special."

He grinned as he worked my jeans down just below my ass, then lifted me onto the hood.

I kicked my jeans off and spread my legs. Vaughan's belt clacked as he yanked it open and unzipped his trousers. "I crave every part of you, just as you are. And anyone who tells you to change can't see how fucking spectacular you are."

He made a condom appear and rolled it on his cock. "Look at me."

I was too mesmerized by his dick to pay attention.

His hand shot out and he grabbed me by the throat. *"Look at me."*

My eyes were wide as I studied his face in the moonlight and the glow of the car interior. The latent *ding, ding, ding,* alerting us that the key was in the ignition and the door was open was the only sound for miles.

Vaughan hooked his finger in the soaked gusset of my panties and pulled them to the side. With one, longing look at my pussy, he exhaled in reverence. "You make me fucking crazy, you know that?"

I grabbed his tie and yanked him in. "Right back at you, Thompson."

Vaughan grabbed my hips and lined up with my entrance, slowly working his thick shaft into me inch by glorious inch.

"I know you can give it to me harder than that," I said, grinning between labored breaths. "If you're going to fuck me on the side of the road, don't be a pussy about it."

I loved making him snap. I lived for it. Maybe that's why I had screwed with him for such a long time before we finally fucked. I liked seeing how far I could push him before he teetered over the brink. Little did I know, channeling his rage into orgasms was far more satisfying.

Vaughan roared as he grabbed my thighs, bruising my skin as he rammed into me. My back hit the hood. The metal sent a zip of pain through my spine, but I didn't care. I loved it. I craved it.

Tires rumbled in the distance, a sobering reminder that we were very much in public.

"Vaughan—"

"You'd better come for me, kitten." He slammed into me and held deep, grinding against my clit. Pressure and need built like a chemical reaction. I couldn't control it. The head of his cock tapped my G-spot over and over again as he stayed buried inside of me and teased me with quick pumps, just barely pulling out.

He hit the deepest parts of me that no one had before.

He saw me like no one had before.

I cried out as my body seized, then rode out the after-shocks of the orgasm.

Vaughan grabbed me by the waist and thrust hard, making my tits jiggle and bounce with each pump. He grunted, the animalistic sounds choking off as he spilled into the condom.

"Goddamn," he said after catching his breath. He yanked me off the hood and pulled me into his arms. "So fucking good."

I laughed, still half-dazed from the unexpected tryst. "Are you trying to get us arrested?"

He gave me a half-baked grin as he discreetly stashed the tied-off condom in an old coffee cup and righted his clothes. I did the same just as a tractor trailer flew down the road, honking as if the driver knew what we had just done.

But I was too stupid in lust to care.

Vaughan opened my door this time instead of yanking me across the seats. "At least we'd get booked for something good."

26

VAUGHAN

"Rise and shine, city boy." Jo's whiskey voice made my skin prickle.

I grunted into the sad excuse for a pillow. Even though I knew Jo kept the sheets and pillow cases clean, everything still smelled musty. I blamed it on the cabin being unfit as a permanent residence.

I really needed to bring some of my stuff over from the big house. It wasn't a secret that I had been sleeping at Jo's. It hadn't even a secret the first time we did it.

But bringing my things over would make this arrangement more permanent than it was. I hadn't mentioned to Jo that I needed to go back to Chicago. For the life of me, I couldn't figure out why I couldn't bear to bring it up.

"Why?" I asked.

But Jo didn't care. She just danced around in my button-up, dishing out dog food for Bean and splashing water on her face.

The time on my phone was obscene. "It's three-thirty in the morning, kitten. Get back in bed."

Her laugh was half-snort. "That's my wake up call, and

you're coming with me. Don't worry—I'll have you back on the ground before the markets open."

I raised a bleary eyebrow. "What?"

"You're flying with me today," she said as she stripped off my shirt and pawed around in her dresser.

I chuckled. "Fat chance of that. Was this your diabolical plan all along? Seduce me, take me up in your plane, and then kamikaze into the ground and take us both out in a blaze of glory?"

She grinned. "What a way to go, am I right?"

Bean snarled and nipped at the covers that draped over my foot. I knew good and well if I didn't get out of this bed that the damn dog would see to it that I did.

"Get lost, buddy," I groaned as I rolled over and buried my face in her pillow. It smelled like the fancy salon shampoo still lingering in her hair, mixed with something that was uniquely *her*.

I breathed in her scent and closed my eyes, drifting off into the blissful abyss of sleep.

Her sharp whistle pierced the air. "Bean, get him up."

Fuck. I didn't even have time to brace. Bean jumped like he was light as a feather and landed square on my chest. I groaned as sixty pounds of spoiled canine cannon-balled on top of me, then pranced around on the bed. When I didn't immediately hop to it, Bean army-crawled up the blankets, put his slobbery snout in my face, and barked.

"Fine," I griped while I slung the covers back.

Jo was focused on wiggling into a pair of denim shorts when I came up behind her and slid my palms across her chest, cupping her breasts.

"We don't have time," she whined as I rolled her nipples between my fingers.

"We have time," I murmured against her neck, giving the buds a quick tug.

She braced her hands against the edge of the dresser and widened her stance, inviting me into her shorts.

I played with her tits until she was panting and could barely keep her feet apart. I massaged them, scraped my fingernails down them, and twisted and teased her nipples until they were puffy and red.

"Vaughan," she whimpered as she rested her forehead on the dresser. "Please—"

"You know what," I said as I cupped her breasts, stalling my ministrations. "I think you're right. We wouldn't want to get off schedule."

"You jackass!" she shouted, stamping her foot on the ground.

I grinned. "I'm just helping you be responsible."

"You know I have to go to Dallas for WASP training after this!" she whined. "You're seriously gonna leave me like this all day?"

"That's exactly what I'm going to do, kitten," I soothed as I placed a kiss to the top of her head. "Give you a little motivation to keep me alive long enough to get you off again."

I stepped into a pair of jeans that had become my "cabin pants" and pulled on a day-old undershirt. I didn't exactly come prepared for manual labor. Tom Ford and organic fertilizer didn't mix.

It was still dark when we rode into town in Jo's truck. Given my history with armadillos on dark roads, I was okay with riding shotgun. It felt like the most normal thing in the world to wake up before the sun with her. To feel up her tits before getting dressed for the day. To ride into town with her for breakfast tacos and coffee.

I swear, the woman survived on breakfast tacos, canned

ravioli, and not much else. She was a picky eater, but given her history, it wasn't all that surprising. Apart from the occasional dinner at the big house, she didn't eat a lot of food that didn't come out of a can. Breakfast tacos seemed like an easy way for her to fill up on something that was somewhat fresh.

My heart broke for the girl who was forced to survive, and the woman who didn't know that she had.

When I yanked open the door to Jay's and held it for Jo, everything stopped.

The group of old biddies who liked to congregate around the coffee bar as they caffeinated for a day of trucking stared at me, slack jawed. I had the distinct notion that they were mentally preparing to throw hands in the name of defending Jo's honor.

Jo straightened her spine, marched inside, and elbowed her way to the coffee dispenser.

"Mornin' JoJo," Hank Jackson—the tow truck driver who had hauled my car off—muttered under his breath. His glare never left me.

Another burley man sided up to him and crossed his arms. They were not so subtly positioning themselves between me and Jo.

"What'chu want this morning, JoJo?" Jay hollered from behind the counter. His spatula slapped against the flat-top grill as he flipped a row of pancakes.

"Four regulars and one for Bean," she hollered without turning around.

"Damn, girl that's more than you usually..." He turned and spotted Jo as she hip-checked the gang of trucker bodyguards and weaved between the aisles to hand me a cup of coffee.

I took a sip and tried to disguise just how terrible it was.

Jo grabbed the front of my shirt and hauled me down, planting a raunchy kiss on my mouth. Coffee sloshed out of her cup and spilled on my hand. I winced as it nearly blistered my skin, but hid it by taking her kiss and upping the ante.

Was it mature to make out in the middle of a gas station? No.

Was it effective? *Absolutely.*

Jay cleared his throat and waved his spatula. "Don't make me turn the compartment sink sprayer on you two," he warned.

Jo flipped her hair over her shoulder and grabbed my hand. "Any questions gentlemen?"

They all had good enough sense to keep their mouths shut.

Jo snatched her bag of breakfast tacos from Jay while I paid up. It was the least I could do.

While Jo drove fast and loose back to the farm, I forced myself to sip the sludge she had served me. It was atrocious.

Bean was waiting on the front porch when she pulled up to the cabin. His bow tie—a paisley peach color—matched the fresh manicure Jo had given him the night before. He bounded off the front steps and jumped into the truck bed. Jo pulled away and headed toward the hangar.

"He's coming too?" I asked as I peered out of the postcard window that peeked out into the truck bed.

"Nah, I don't take him up in the 'Cat. He just chills in the hangar for a change of scenery. If I'm taking the 150 up, he can ride if he wants."

I raised an eyebrow. "The 150?"

We passed the Fuck You, Jo billboard as she slowed to a stop. It still brought a smile to my face.

I held the breakfast bag and coffees while Jo unlocked

the hangar door and rolled it back. It took every bit of strength in her tiny frame to get the metal door to open, but she was nothing if not determined.

"I have a Cessna 150," she said, pointing to the tarp-covered lump in the corner. "I did aerial photography for a while to pay it off. It's what I fly when I don't have to take this lard ass." She patted the side of the bright yellow aerial application plane.

"So, you're doing photography today?" I guessed. It was still dark, but I guessed by the time she got in the air, it would be daybreak.

Jo grinned as she began her pre-flight checks. "Nope."

I sat beside Bean, reluctantly scratching behind his good ear as we watched Jo inspect every inch of the plane, check her flight logs, study the weather radar, and get dressed in an absurd amount of protective gear.

Jo shooed Bean out of the hangar and handed me a respirator to wear while she measured and mixed the proper parts-per-million ratio of two different chemicals. I stood off to the side while she filled the tank with the fungicide that was going to be sprayed across a field a few farms over. She doused herself with a hose while she was still in her plastic PPE before stripping it down and clapping her hands.

"Ready, city boy?" She pointed to the ladder that led twelve feet up to the cockpit.

I raised an eyebrow. "You're serious?"

"As a heart attack." Then, in her most diabolical move yet, she batted her eyelashes at me. "Please? I wanna show you what it's like."

Damn her and those irresistible ice blue eyes.

I grabbed the ladder and climbed in. When I peeked

over the edge into the cockpit, I looked back down at Jo. "There's only one seat."

"Yep. Get a move on. We're burning daylight."

"Fucking insane woman," I grumbled under my breath. Maybe she was just planning on showing me how to run it up or something like that.

Once I sat down, careful not to touch any of the eleventy million switches, pedals, and knobs, Jo climbed up and plopped her fine ass into my lap.

"Uhh—"

She paid me no mind as she closed the cockpit and started flipping switches.

"You comfortable, baby?" she asked as she fastened her headset over her ears. She used a splitter to plug in a second headset and handed it to me. I put it over my ears and adjusted the microphone in front of my mouth.

"Not in the slightest. What the hell are you doing?"

"Taking you flying."

I kept my hands firmly on her hips so I wouldn't accidentally bump anything. "This can't be safe. Or legal."

"I usually have to sit on a stack of phone books anyway. You're just more comfortable."

I looked up and closed my eyes. "Sweet baby Jesus, take me now."

"You're not gonna piss yourself or need a barf-bag right?" she yelled over the whirr of the engine.

"No promises," I shouted as she buckled us both in.

So, this was how I was going to die. I always expected it to be from a premature heart attack or aneurysm due to too much stress.

Dying in a plane crash piloted by a certified lunatic wasn't how I imagined going. But here we were.

I clenched my eyes and my ass as the plane started to move. Shadows pulled back as she eased out of the hangar, into the pre-dawn twilight. Jo acted as if this was just another day as we taxied onto the runway. Which, for her, I suppose it was.

"Any last words, Thompson?"

"If you're going to kill me, make it quick."

Her raucous laughter was the only thing in my mind as she gunned it down the runway and pulled into the air. Gravity sandwiched us together, slamming her ass into my lap. I grunted and wrapped my arms tight around her waist.

I peeled my eyes open and peeked out the side. The farm looked like a postage stamp as we gained altitude. My ears popped, then popped again when she dive-bombed toward the big house.

For the bright yellow plane being such a cantankerous beast, she maneuvered it with the skill and dexterity of a seasoned fighter pilot.

She flipped a radio switch and grinned. "Good morning, Thompsons! This is your captain speaking. If you're not already up and at 'em, get a move on!"

So, that's how she connected to the PA system in the big house.

Cash's voice echoed in my ears. "You take Vaughan up there with you today?"

"Hell yeah!" Jo said as she pulled up and circled the house.

"How's he doing?" That sounded like my dad.

Jo peeked back at me, smiling like an adorable little menace. "Looking a little green. Breakfast tacos probably weren't a good idea."

"Yep," I groaned, letting out a calculated breath. "Definitely a bad idea." When the urge to vomit all over the back of Jo's head passed, I said, "You told them you were going to torture me?"

"I'm pretty sure she's been torturing you since you set foot in town," Ms. Faith said, chiming in on the conversation. "You kids stay safe."

"Yes, Ms. Faith," Jo and I said in tandem.

I kept my mind away from impending doom by caressing her thighs as she peeled away from the farm's airspace and headed north.

"I'll give it to you," I said as I watched rolling plains fly by. "You fly better than you drive."

Jo beamed. "I'm choosing to take that as a compliment."

"Eh, it was—"

"Hold on, city boy!" she squealed in delight.

I panicked. "Hold on to what?"

"Me!"

And with that, she tipped the nose of the plane at the ground. I watched the altimeter spin out of control as orchard trees grew closer and closer.

"Jo—"

With one hand, she pulled up, barely missing the top of the fruit trees. With the other hand, she flipped a switch.

Clouds of fungicide plumed behind us as we zoomed over the field, barely cruising over the earth's surface. Power lines loomed at the edge of the field, close to the last row of trees.

I squirmed in the seat. "Tiger—"

The power lines grew closer.

"Jo—" I could count each individual line now. "Joelle!"

She pulled up at the last second, simultaneously cutting the flow of fluid to the sprayers under the belly of the plane while rolling to the left. We slid in the cockpit seat through the maneuver.

"You are fucking insane!" I shouted when she leveled out again and lined up for another pass.

She went through the same process again, getting as close to the treetops as possible to reduce the chemical drift. As soon as the last tree had been sprayed, she pulled up and rolled, barely missing the power lines.

Somewhere around the fifth pass, I stopped feeling like my vital organs were about to be regurgitated and began to relax. Hell, I even smiled when she let out a banshee, "Whoohoo!"

"Be honest," Jo said as she did one last flyover of the property. "You don't get that kind of rush from sitting in an office, adding commas to bank accounts.

I chuckled as she changed her heading to fly back to the hangar. "Wanna know something, Tiger?" I said as I ran my hands along her bare thighs.

"What's that?"

"I think you're the best kind of rush."

27

JOELLE

"JoJo!" Ms. Faith's voice echoed through the hangar. "Where are you at, sweetie?"

I groaned from the corner where I was hiding while I sifted through invoices, trying to make sure I was paid up. The last thing I wanted in this financial mess was to have my vendors pissed that I was behind on payments.

"Joelle?" she called again.

I signed my name at the bottom of a check and stuffed it in an envelope. These Thompsons and their well-intended niceties were dancing all over my last nerve today.

All I wanted was to call it a day, lock myself in the cabin —alone—and snuggle with a heating pad.

First, it was Bristol wanting to go out to breakfast and gab when all I wanted to do was pop a handful of Midol and sleep in. Then, it was Cash blowing up my phone, asking if I was going to the Silver Spur to see a cover band we both liked.

And, of course, he couldn't take no for an answer.

Then it was Ryman dropping by the hangar to ask me a

mechanical question about one of their combines. *I work on planes, not large farm equipment, dumbass.*

Every hour it was someone new. One of the farm hands, one of my clients, hell—even George moseyed down and talked my ear off for damn near two hours.

I was half-tempted to jump in the Ag Cat and take off even though I didn't have any flights today.

Every time someone called my name, every ding of an incoming text, every little red bubble notification that demanded a response fueled my already sour mood.

It was a good thing Vaughan was tied up with his actual job today.

Bean was the only one with the good sense to give me a wide berth. He plodded out to the back porch this morning and hadn't been seen since.

"Oh, there you are!" Ms. Faith said as she bustled through the hangar, a plate of something in her hand. "Cash said you hadn't left here all day. Have you eaten?"

No, because my uterus declared war on the rest of my body.

"Cash needs to keep his mouth shut," I muttered under my breath. I sighed and looked up from the stack of budget reports I had generated. "No. I'm gonna head home once I finish up here."

"You feeling okay, sweetie?" she asked, pressing a hand to my cheek. It took everything in me not to recoil.

"Fine. Just my period." *And smothering, overbearing, nosey people.*

"Those were the days," she said, fanning herself. "If you think periods are bad? Let me tell you, Hon—just wait until menopause. Hot flashes during Texas summers nearly took me out."

I muttered something unintelligible, but it sounded close enough to an acknowledgment.

My phone dinged with a text from Bristol about a boy she had a crush on. It was immediately followed by another text chime from Cash, asking if I wanted him to change the oil in my truck. The sound nearly made me come up out of my skin.

I was about to throw the damn thing in the fire pit and light it up.

"You need anything? Medicine? Brownies?" Her face lit up like she had the most brilliant idea. "I tell you what— why don't you and Vaughan have dinner at the big house and then you, me, and Bristol can hang out while the boys clean up? That way you don't have to mess with cooking supper."

Ravioli—probably cold because I was feeling lazy—was the only thing that sounded good at the moment.

Ravioli and being alone.

As much as I hated to admit it, Vaughan wasn't terrible company. We got along about sixty percent of the time. The other forty was spent picking at each other just so we could have sizzling hate sex, then make-up sex. Best of all, he didn't stick his nose in my business.

That was until an email came through with his royal pain in the ass-ness as the sender.

FROM: *Vaughan Thompson*
  To: *Joelle Reed*
  Subject: *Business Plan for Reed Ag Aviation*

AND THAT DID IT. I slammed the checkbook shut, threw it back in the under-desk safe, and kicked the thick door shut. "I think I'm going to stay in," I said through gritted teeth. It was all I could do to keep from losing my shit on her.

"Well," Ms. Faith said, patting the top of the foil-wrapped plate. "This is still warm. I'll leave you to it. Let me know if you need anything. I can have one of the boys run into town for pads or tampons or those fancy new pairs of underwear that just soak it all up."

I snorted at the thought of Cash and Ryman debating the merits of tampon absorbency, menstrual cups, and wings versus no wings.

Sometimes I wondered if Ms. Faith realized that I was older now than she was when she started having kids. Some days, she still looked at me like a helpless, stray teenager.

"Thanks," I said, taking the plate. "I'll be fine, though. I'm just not feeling social. But I'll make sure Vaughan shows up for dinner." *And that he stays far, far away from me, lest he incur the wrath of my menses.*

I usually wasn't one to call it a day before the sun went down, but we had another round of storms on the horizon and I needed to get as much work done as possible.

On top of all of that, my hormones were raging. I needed to turn my phone off before the annoying notification sound sent me into a murderous rampage. I especially needed to hide from anyone with the last name Thompson.

When I got back to the cabin, I stuck the plate Ms. Faith had given to me in my mini fridge and turned off my phone. I was clocked out for the day. Anything else could wait until morning.

The cabin was blissfully quiet. I popped a handful of ibuprofen and splashed water on my face. It would have to do since filling up the stock tank or setting up the sink shower were out of the question with the forecast.

I threw my tied-off pillowcase full of rice into the

microwave and warmed it up before burrowing down into my bed and snuggling the hell out of that thing.

I had just drifted off into the best REM cycle of my life when the tapping started.

And then the whacking.

And then the slamming of metal on metal.

I peered through half-closed lids, daring whoever was making that ruckus to fuck around and find out.

Unfortunately, my ability to mentally shove someone off a roof still needed some work. My only hope was that a large gust of wind made whoever it was fall off the edge and die a slow, painful death.

I closed my eyes and wished the roof trespasser a long bout of paralysis, during which I would visit them every day and annoy them with random sounds.

Bang, bang, bang!

"Motherfucker," I spat as I threw the covers back. The heating pad flew onto the floor. The last nerve that stood between me and people who decided to hover around me and smother me was long gone.

I threw the back door open and stormed out onto the porch. "*Hey!*" I bellowed.

The incessant pounding stopped, and, to my surprise, only one set of boots clobbered over the peak.

Vaughan appeared, dressed in a pair of dirt-streaked jeans and no shirt. He flashed a grin, wiping the sweat from his face with his thick forearm. "Hey, Tiger."

Smiling? *Oh, I was going to kill him.*

It was a good thing the farm had a backhoe, and I knew where Ryman kept the keys. I did *not* feel like hand-digging a Vaughan-sized hole six feet down in my cramped PMS state.

Before I could ream him for making a ruckus louder

than a tornado full of wind chimes, he disappeared over the apex of the tin roof. I heard the scrape and groan of a ladder against the side, then feet hitting the ground.

I hoped he fell and snapped his neck.

I turned and stormed inside, slamming the door behind me. The force rattled every window in the shack. Vaughan entered from the front door, his stance wide like he was waiting for me to run into his arms.

I glowered at him from the kitchenette. *The audacity of that man to climb on my roof and do God knows what—*

Vaughan glanced at the bed and spotted the heating pad in the middle of the sheets.

"Oh, shit," he muttered. His stupid, handsomely chiseled face marred with concern. "You not feeling good?"

Before I could get a word out, he crossed the cabin and was rifled through my cabinets.

"I already took ibuprofen," I snapped. "Not that anyone around here cares that I'm perfectly capable of taking care of myself."

Vaughan reared back, holding his hands up in defense. "Whoa, I just asked if you weren't feeling good."

"Oh yeah?" I crossed my arms. "And why are you looking through my cabinets?"

He had the good sense to look guilty.

I was about to give him a thorough dressing down—*and not the sexy kind*—when my uterus decided to cave in on itself.

I grabbed the edge of the countertop and squeezed my eyes shut as the cramp hit me like a sucker punch to the gut. It stole the breath out of my lungs, rendering me speechless just long enough for Vaughan to put his hand on my back and bend down with soothing words on the tip of his tongue.

"I'm fine!" I shouted, shoving away from him. "I don't need someone to babysit me. I don't need anyone's help performing truck maintenance. I don't need food to be cooked for me. I don't need to be coddled. I don't need anything. I can take care of myself."

"Joelle," his tone was full of warning, but I didn't bother heeding it.

"And do I even want to know what the fuck you were doing on my roof?"

"I was patching the roof so it wouldn't leak. I knew you were busy today, and I rearranged a few things so I could get up there and take care of it for you." Vaughan cracked a smile. "I know you think I'm just a suit, but I did learn a thing or two before I left Maren."

My skin prickled like it absorbed the electricity that buzzed through the air before a big storm. Everything that just came out of his mouth raised my hackles.

"Why would you think I wanted you to do that?" I blurted out. "What about me screams, '*Damsel in distress*?'"

Vaughan's gaze narrowed. "It's called being *thoughtful*, Jo."

He had called me a litany of names over the weeks that we had been at each other's throats, but the one I hated the most was when he called me Jo.

It was so... impersonal.

"I don't *need* your help. I'm fine." My skin was clammy, and my chest felt like an elephant was sitting on it. I couldn't catch my breath.

"You're not." He drew closer, apparently not caring very much about his personal well-being. I was known to use my claws when fists didn't cut it.

"Vaughan—" I warned with an outstretched hand, begging him to keep his distance. I was feeling rather fragile

—the one state of existence I hated with every fiber of my being. It was also when I lashed out the most.

"What's going on with you?"

"Nothing!" I shouted. My throat burned from the rage that lit up my vocal cords. "Why can't everyone just leave me the fuck alone? Is that too much to ask?"

"Baby," Vaughan's tone was soft and full of concern. "You're shaking."

"Yeah, well, I'm fucking pissed!" I slammed my hand on the countertop, seething in frustration. "And *apparently* that's something I do when I'm so furious I can't see straight."

His hands wrapped around my arms, gently but firmly pinning them down to my sides. "Breathe."

"No!" I screeched as I shoved away from him.

Vaughan grabbed hold of my wrists and pulled me into his sticky, sweat-soaked chest. "Come here."

"Don't fucking tell me to calm down," I choked out as I clawed at his chest.

Vaughan never flinched.

Something burned my eyes, but I couldn't tell if it was his aura of salty sweat or fifteen years of unshed tears. "I'm *fine*."

Every time I would rip free of his grasp, he would pull me in again. Over and over, never giving up on the fight.

Maybe I wanted to think that it wasn't just beating me in our battle of wits that kept him coming back.

Maybe a small part of me wanted to think that he wanted to fight for me.

I whipped to the left, trying to work my way out of his hold. "I'm fine—"

"Hey," he grunted as he dodged my elbow. "Settle down and talk to me."

"Just leave me alone!" I shrieked.

His tone was resolute. "No."

"Please—" I begged in a whisper as my knees buckled beneath me.

"I'm not leaving you, Joelle. Don't you think that if you were going to scare me away, you would have done it by now?" He stroked my cheek with the pad of his thumb.

I couldn't stop the word vomit that spilled out of my mouth. "Everyone does. It's only a matter of time until you will, too. So, do us both a favor and let me get back to looking out for myself."

"No."

I wanted to kiss him, *and then kill him.*

My body shook. My veins pulsed with lava. My vision blurred, but the tears never fell.

Through chattering teeth, I gritted out, "You don't get it."

"No, sweetheart. I do." With cautious, fluid movements, he released his grip on me and sifted one hand through my hair, cupping my cheek and tilting my head up to meet his eyes. "Cry for me. It's obvious that you've never cried a day in your life, and that's a damn shame. These walls you've built around yourself... It's not who you are. It's a shell, not a skin. Deep down there's a little girl who's still hurt and she was never safe enough to cry about it."

I stared at him, wide-eyed as the corner of my mouth trembled. Breath escaped my lungs in quick gasps. His gaze was unwavering and undeterred by everything I had thrown at him.

I had taken shot after shot at him, and yet, he stood there, begging for more.

He cradled my head against his chest, and pressed his cheek to my temple. "You're safe, Joelle." His other hand stroked up and down my back, keeping me firmly planted against his chest. "I promise you that. You're safe with me."

Pressure built hard and fast behind my eyes, burning everything like a roaring wildfire. My breath hitched, and a lone tear rolled down my cheek.

The *thud* of his heartbeat against my cheek was enough to make me detonate.

28

VAUGHAN

"You're safe, Joelle." I gently rubbed her back, still holding her tight against my chest. "I promise you that. You're safe with me."

The first sniff was faint; like she didn't quite know what to do with herself. A tear glimmered against her skin like a diamond in the desert.

"What's happening to me?" she whispered through clenched teeth before burying her face in my sweaty chest.

I kissed the top of her head and cradled her in my arms. "I think your body knows that it's okay to let your guard down, and your brain is finally catching up."

A handful of tears rolled down her cheeks as she silently heaved in my arms, trying her best to inhale choppy breaths.

"Hey," I said, smoothing my hand down the back of her hair. "Just slow down. Breathe. You don't want to hyper-ventilate."

Giving a grown woman who was emotionally stunted directions on how to cry was quite possibly the dumbest thing I had ever done.

Her knees buckled. Jo's cry was more of a scream. It was feral and wild as she collapsed in my arms. I wasn't sure what had brought on the wave of pent-up emotion, but it seemed to be decades overdue.

I scooped her into my arms and carried her to the bed, easing down slowly so I could sit with her on my lap.

Even through her sobs, Jo tried to wipe her eyes and scramble out of my arms. It was as if she had just realized she was actually trusting someone, and it scared the shit out of her.

Her ankle tangled in the sheets, looping around her like a leash. She reacted to being restrained like a rabid raccoon caught in a trash bag.

I caught her around the waist and kept her flush to my body with one arm. It was like wrestling a pissed-off anaconda. With the other hand, I unwrapped her ankle from the sheet and pulled the blankets over both of us.

Pink lips parted as she sucked in staccato breaths. Her long lashes glistened like the thin tree branches covered in a crystalline coat of ice that lined the walk from my apartment to my office back in Chicago in the winter.

Her cheeks were stained with rivulets of tears. I pressed my mouth to the corner of her eye, tasting the salt lingering on her skin. "I've got you."

Jo cupped her hands over her mouth, trying to close the floodgates. But they were already open. It was like a levee breaking in the midst of a hurricane. There was something too powerful cresting over her to be held back.

Nor should it be.

"I'm sorry," she whispered through blubbering breaths. *"I'm sorry. I'm sorry. I'm sorry—"* She sniffed, trying to quell the tears.

I tucked her head beneath my chin, shrouding her with

my body. "Don't think for a second that you're going to scare me away. You've tried and failed. Accept it."

We lay together, Jo crying in my arms, for what felt like an eternity. Gut-wrenching sobs that turned to quiet gasps slowly became silent weeping. I whispered soft reassurances as her rigid body became soft and pliant.

I shifted, laying her on the mattress and straddling her. I braced my arms on either side of her head, pressing my forehead to hers. With a feather-light touch, I kissed every tear-stained streak that slashed her cheeks. I kissed the scar that stretched across her temple and forehead. I kissed the corners of her eyes where unshed emotion lay like buried diamonds. I pressed my lips to hers, tasting salt. I kissed the corner of her mouth. Her jaw. Her neck. Her throat. Her chest.

I held her hands and kissed each one of her fingers.

"I'm sorry," she whispered as she wiped under her eyes and tried to sit up. "I—I don't know what just happened." She sniffed and used her sleeve to wipe her nose. "I guess I'm just PMS-ing really hard today."

To hell with the excuses.

I shook my head. "Stop that."

She dabbed her eyes again. "Stop what?"

"Blaming how you feel on your hormones." I shook my head, then laid a kiss on her forehead.

Jo let out a trembling breath.

I brushed her hair away from her face. "From the looks of it, all of that has been inside you for a long time. Maybe your body just decided it was time to let your guard down."

"I never cry."

"Everybody cries, kitten."

Jo shook her head. "Not me. I haven't cried since I was a kid. I thought I forgot how." A rogue tear rolled out of the corner of her eye and into her hair, disappearing into midnight tresses like a shooting star. "Crying never fixes anything."

"That's where you're wrong," I said as I eased off of her and propped up the pillows against the wall. I pulled her into my arms and had her reclining against my chest before she could fight me on it. "Crying feels pretty damn good."

"I usually just get angry."

A thought pricked at the back of my mind—the night Jo stormed into the Silver Spur and jumped onto the bull without warning. It had been a stark contrast compared to the first night I watched her ride.

The night she went rogue, there was a brutal fire burning inside her. She wasn't performing. She was *fighting*.

"Anger is a fuel, sweetheart. It's like energy—you never really burn it off. It simply changes form. Tears are a purge. Sometimes you have to flush it out of your system."

She let out a weighted breath, the corner of her mouth quivering. "Is that what you learned when you went all *Eat, Pray, Love* after your divorce?"

I knew she was trying to pick a fight with me, and usually I would have jumped in with both feet. Fighting with Jo was fun.

But not now. I wasn't giving in to her.

"No," I said, dropping a kiss to the top of her head. "It's something Ms. Faith taught me when she moved in with me and my dad. I thought that being a man meant that, even though my mom died, I had to act like nothing had happened. Like my world hadn't just come crumbling down." I brushed her hair aside and kissed down the gentle slope of her neck. "I used to sneak out at night and walk the fields so my dad wouldn't see me cry."

She perked up, her chin tilting ever so slightly.

"One night, I walked all the way out to the property line and sat there for hours so I could cry."

"The spot where I found you drinking Scotch?"

I nodded.

The corner of her mouth quirked like a fond memory had floated through her mind. "The spot where we kissed."

I chuckled. "The very one. It's always been my thinking spot."

"Mine too. It's far enough away from everything, but it's still on the farm, so it feels safe."

"When I finally walked back to the big house, it was midnight and Ms. Faith was sitting out on the porch."

Her brows knitted together. "Did you get in trouble?"

"I thought I was going to." I sighed. "But, to my surprise, she asked if I wanted to sit a spell."

A soft smile painted Jo's lips as she closed her eyes and rested her cheek against my chest. "What did y'all talk about?"

"My mom," I said almost reluctantly. "It didn't scare Ms. Faith to hear me talk about her. She listened to me tell her about all the good memories. I told her all the things I was afraid of—that at some point I would forget what her voice sounded like or the way she smelled. And that eventually all I would have were blurry snapshots of her in my mind."

"What did she say?" Jo whispered.

"Nothing." I let out a breath and took a moment to compose myself. "She, uh... She didn't say anything. But she hugged me for the longest time."

Jo laughed. "She gives the best hugs, doesn't she?"

I couldn't help but smile. "Yeah, she does. It was the first time I remember letting her give me a hug."

"Really?"

I nodded. "I held out for a long time. I guess I thought

that if I didn't let Ms. Faith in, my mom wasn't really gone. And to her credit—she never pushed me. Just waited until I was ready. She never told my dad when she heard me creep down the stairs in the middle of the night. Just sat on the porch and made sure that I came back. Sometimes I'd get it all out of my system on the walk. And sometimes I'd sit down with her and she'd let me cry about it."

"You're lucky, you know," Jo said, looking up at me with red-rimmed eyes.

"Yeah. I—uh... I'm realizing that."

———

I LEFT Jo to rest while I slipped over to the big house to shower and change my clothes. The sky was an ominous gray as storm clouds loomed in the distance.

After a quick peek inside to find her fast asleep, I made a spur-of-the-moment trip into town for reinforcements before the weather picked up. Jo was testy on a good day. I didn't want to risk life and limb with a hungry Jo.

Wind whipped through the trees along the last five acres that shrouded Jo's cabin from the property line. I slid grocery bags up both arms because second trips were for wimps. When I edged through the front door and dropped the groceries, Jo was nowhere to be seen.

I did eventually find her sitting in a rickety rocking chair on the back porch with Bean curled up at her feet.

"What the hell are you doing, Tiger?"

She raised an eyebrow, looking at me as if I had said we were going to start farming Skittles and M&Ms. "Uh, sitting on the porch?"

I pinched the bridge of my nose. "I can see that. We're in a tornado watch."

"Yeah, I know." She waved at the sky. "I'm watching for it."

"Jesus Christ," I muttered as I shook my head. I said a quiet prayer of thanks when she followed me back inside with Bean on her heels. I started unloading the bags, stocking her shelves with cans of ravioli before tackling the few perishables I crammed in the mini fridge.

Jo tentatively eyed the stack of buckets and bowls she scattered all over the cabin during storms.

"You won't need those, Tiger," I said as I wadded the grocery bags together and shoved them under the sink into the plastic bag graveyard.

"Right..." Her finger trailed along the rim of a five-gallon seed bucket. "You... Fixed the roof." She looked like she was about to come up out of her skin. "You didn't have to do that. It's on my to-do list. I'm perfectly capable of—"

I slammed the door to the sink cabinet and turned to face her. "I know you're perfectly capable of climbing on that roof and patching it yourself." I pinched her chin between my thumb and index finger. "But you need to get used to the idea that sometimes I will do things for you just because I want to."

"But shouldn't you be holed up in George's office doing —well, I don't know what you do all day."

Sighing, I tipped my head toward the bed. "Lay down."

"I'm not tired anymore."

"*Just lay down,*" I hissed as I threw her redneck heating pad in the microwave and pawed through the pile of snacks I brought in.

Jo stamped her foot—only lightly this time—and did as I said. I grabbed the bag of mini peanut butter cups and carried them to the bed, unwrapping one as I went.

Jo was lying on her back, propped up by pillows. I

pressed the candy to her lips. Her eyebrows winged up, but to my surprise, she didn't bite the hand that fed her.

"Wush dah for?" she mumbled as she chewed.

The microwave dinged, and I grabbed the heating pad out. "Roll onto your side."

"This is suspicious," she hollered as she rolled away from me. "Are you going to smother me to death?"

"Nah, you're a flailer. You'd kick me in the nuts or something. Poisoning you protects my physical well-being," I deadpanned. "I'll just have to pay off the coroner to not run a toxicology panel."

She cracked a smile. "Hence the chocolate. Arsenic, probably. Tasteless... Odorless..."

I laid the heating pad against her lower abdomen and dropped a few of the chocolates in front of her. Jo repositioned the pad and drew her knees up, just below the fetal position. I rolled up the hem of her shirt and laid behind her, working my thumbs into her lower back.

Jo tensed like a cat who just realized it was going to get a bath.

I brushed her hair away and kissed the back of her neck. "Relax."

Slowly, the tension unfurled, and she melted into the bed. I resumed the massage, working the stiff muscles in her lower back.

She let out a low groan. "That feels amazing." Her eyelids fluttered closed as I worked slow circles around the dimples on her lower back. After a few minutes, she tried to roll to her back. "Do you want me to do you?"

I laughed under my breath and kept her on her side. "Is it helping?"

"Helping what?"

"Your cramps."

For a moment, she stopped breathing. "You did this because I have cramps?"

"You said you were PMSing. I figured it couldn't hurt."

She fingered a foil wrapper. "Sometimes I forget that you were married before..."

"Does it bother you?"

"No," she said honestly. "It's just... It's weird to think about you doing all this with another woman in a much more serious relationship. You've been a lot of firsts for me, and I guess I'm just now realizing that I'm not that for you." As if the next admission carried the weight of the world, she said, "It scares me a little."

"Something actually scares the infamous Joelle Reed?" I kissed her scarred temple.

"You scare me," she admitted in the smallest voice I'd ever heard.

"Why do I scare you?"

"You make me feel things that I haven't been able to feel in a long time. You make me feel things that I've never felt before. It scares me, Vaughan."

"Hey..." I rolled her over so we were nearly nose-to-nose. "Look," I said with a sigh. "I don't know if we're nearing 'big conversations' territory yet." I found her hand and twined our fingers together. "But I think that whatever *this* is... It's worth a shot."

"But you'll go back to Chicago eventually."

"Pretty soon, actually."

Her eyes widened with surprise and flashed with hurt. "Oh..."

"Everything I've been doing here—I'm at a standstill. I'm just waiting on some subsidy funding to come through. I've done all I can."

She turned away from me and hugged the heating pad.

The gap between us might as well have been an impassable chasm. "When do you leave?" It sounded like she was about to cry again, but her eyes were glued shut.

I laid my hand on her hip and gently worked my way under the hem of her shirt, desperate to keep the connection to her skin. "The end of the week. There's an event I need to attend in the city."

"Okay."

"I want you to come with me."

"I underst—*what?*"

"I said I want you to come with me." I kissed her shoulder, then the shell of her ear. "Come to Chicago with me."

Jo swallowed and shook her head. "I can't. I have work, a-and—"

"Things are slowing down for you. It's almost time for the harvest, kitten. You have a little longer before it's time to drop seed for cover crops and winter grasses. Move your jobs around and come to the city with me. It'll just be a few days, and then you'll be back."

"What about you?" she asked. "Will you come back, too?"

I sighed and wrapped my arms around her. In a perfect world, I wouldn't have to choose.

But it wasn't a perfect world. Just a messed up one with a perfect woman in it.

29

JOELLE

"I don't know, kitten," Vaughan murmured into the crook of my neck. "I still have a few irons in the fire to try to get the farm in the black, but I can manage them from Chicago. I've been working my ass off to get things in order here."

I lay still as a statue. "Oh."

"I'll still be managing the business side of the farm," he said. "But I need to get back to my actual job before my assistant throws me in the Chicago River with cinder blocks tied to my ankles."

I should have laughed, but nothing about it was funny to me. Having Vaughan around had become a sort of comfort. Fucking with him... *Fucking* him...

I pulled the covers up to my chin and closed my eyes. It was stupid to think that all of this meant something to him when I didn't even know what it meant to me.

"So, what do you think? You gonna come with me?"

I wanted to. The last few weeks had been a whirlwind and I felt as though I was on a crumbling cliff, desperate to grab onto something sturdy. Maybe leaving the farm for a while would give me a little perspective.

That, or I'd fall further down the rabbit hole.

Vaughan's hand slid up my thigh, slipping under the thin pajama shorts I wore. He palmed my ass, firmly laying claim to his favorite part of my body.

His cock pressed against my thigh, the thickness of it constantly stealing my breath. I pushed back into him, wiggling my butt against his dick.

Vaughan let out a low groan that reverberated deep in his chest. He pushed one thigh up, separating my legs, and cupped my pussy outside my shorts.

"You know what happens when you tease me, kitten."

I snorted and egged him on even further. "You gonna spank me, Daddy?" I teased. "Take me to the city and show me your red room?"

Vaughan grinned into my hair. "What makes you think I have a red room?"

"You seem like the type," I said, finishing with a gasp when he grabbed the front of my panties and yanked them up, pinching my folds between the fabric. "You look like the kind of guy who's into whips and cuffs."

"That's where you're wrong," he said with a devious laugh. "I prefer doling out punishments with my hand. The only impact toy I need is *me*."

I shivered, my breath exhaling in a wheeze.

"And as for the cuffs..." He hooked a single finger around my hair and pulled it away from my neck. His breath was warm against my ear when he growled, "I don't need to restrain you. You will do exactly what I say because you know that I demand your obedience."

A single finger trailed down my side. I closed my eyes, imagining what the two of us looked like—him spooning me while whispering deliciously dirty things in my ear. The way his hand lackadaisically grazed my skin.

Vaughan slid his hand up my tank top and cupped my breast, keeping my nipple trapped between his fingers. He teased it gently for a moment before pinching it.

His voice was lethal. "And you know the consequences if you choose to act like a brat."

I whimpered, mewling at the lightning-fast pulses of pleasure that zipped through me. My boobs were always extra sensitive when I was about to start my period. My clit throbbed, begging to be played with.

"Don't tease me," I begged quietly, as though I was afraid of someone else hearing me bend to his will.

"What makes you think I'm going to tease you?" His knuckle grazed my wetness.

"I-I'm on my period—" I gasped when he slid a finger inside of me.

His lips were warm as he kissed the sensitive spot behind my ear. "Do you want me to put a towel down?"

I chewed on my lip. Was period sex an option? I just assumed that all members of the male species were like Cash and Ryman—scared shitless whenever Bristol or I hit that time of the month. I swear they tracked it on a calendar and intentionally avoided us for a week.

"Um, I'm not really bleeding yet. Just crampy and irritable."

"You know, I've heard orgasms can relieve cramps," he said in a rumble that told me that his motives were completely selfish. The desperation in his voice paired with his rock-hard erection was quite the aphrodisiac.

I wanted him to want me. I didn't want it to be easy for him to pack up and leave.

Texas looked good on him.

Whether Vaughan wanted to admit it or not, he had changed. Sure, he still woke up every damn day and put on a suit. *The weirdo had even packed a steamer to bring along with him.* But his true colors came out in the moments when he let his roots find soil again.

He sat around the table at the big house and laughed with everyone over dinner. He went to the Silver Spur with Cash and Ryman. He slipped Bristol a beer every now and then, and listened patiently while she unloaded collegiate drama on him. He hung out with his dad and shot the shit, talking tractors and farm equipment. I had even seen him throw his arm around Ms. Faith's shoulders and give her a completely unprompted hug.

"Let me make you feel good," Vaughan urged again, snapping me out of my daydream. He squeezed my hip. "Do you wanna lie just like this?"

"I don't know how to take this," I murmured into the pillow.

He laughed. "You don't have to do anything. Just let me make you feel good."

"I know how to take your cock, dumbass."

He ripped the covers back and spanked my ass. A flash of heat painted my skin without warning.

I let out a slow breath. "I like it when you make me get on my hands and knees and beg for you. I don't know how this works if it's not rough."

His hand slid up the column of my throat and grasped my jaw. Gently, he turned my head to look at him. "You still have to trust me, even when it's not rough."

Vaughan laid behind me and worked my tank top up and over my head. When I started on my shorts, he stopped me.

"Hands off, Tiger. That's for me to do."

He slid them down to my knees, then let me kick them off. Vaughan peppered my back with kisses while he yanked his boxers off. He grabbed a condom from the stack we kept on hand, gave his dick a few forceful strokes, then rolled it on.

"I want this knee by your chest," he said, tapping his palm against the leg that was covered by the blanket. "Bring it up so I can play with your tight little cunt."

The bed frame screeched as I readjusted and pulled one leg up. His hand was back on my pussy, stroking through my wetness with a single finger, then circling my clit.

Every sensation was heightened. The scrape of his chest hair against my back. The pad of his finger rolling over my clit. The pin pricks of pleasure that came in waves when he slid his other arm beneath me and toyed with my breast.

He was leisurely in his movements, exploring every intimate part of me as if he had all the time in the world to get to the main event.

Vaughan needed to get a move on. I hadn't been in the mood before, but something about the way he gently guided me into position lit me up like a Christmas tree. I ached for him to fill me. I wanted him to rut deep inside and pause like he always did. I loved the connection. The simple pleasure of being joined at the most basic level.

I reached back and found his hip first, then wrapped my hand around his throbbing cock.

"Nuh-uh-uh, Tiger. Hands to yourself."

I whined. "Vaughan—"

"You know better than to speak to me like that."

I bit my lip when he pinched my clit and rubbed it between two fingers, feeling the rush of an orgasm on the horizon. Of course, he stopped before it hit me. He always did. Vaughan got off on the control. On taming me. And, in some weird, twisted way, I got off on pushing his buttons before yielding to his will.

It usually paid off in the form of multiple orgasms. But there was something else I had learned about Vaughan.

I could trust him.

He never lied. Never pretended to be anything other than exactly who he was. And underneath all that bravado and his stuck-up exterior was a man who cared deeply and showed it grandly.

I tucked my hands beneath my cheek, bringing my elbows up so they didn't block his access to my boobs. "Yes, sir," I said on an exhale.

He rewarded me with two long fingers stroking inside of me. "That's my girl," he murmured against my cheek and stroked my walls. "Does that feel good, kitten?"

"Yes." My body relaxed as endorphins swirled around my mind.

"Good. Just breathe. I'm not going to let you come right away. Let it ebb and flow. Don't try to fight it or make your orgasm happen. I'll make you feel good." Vaughan's low voice was hypnotic. He pressed his palm over my heart and buried his nose into the back of my hair. "Trust me."

I nodded. "I do."

Vaughan went back to my center, twisting his fingers as he patiently searched for my G-spot. Lightning zipped up my legs and flashed across my torso when he stroked it. He felt the twitch in my body and slowly started pumping his fingers, dragging along that magical place with each thrust.

Instinctively, I clenched around his fingers, seeking out an orgasm. He paused.

"What did I tell you?" He didn't so much as breathe, not wanting to give me any more pleasure than what he allowed.

"I—I'm not—"

"You're holding your breath and tensing up." He pinched my nipple. "Relax or I'll hold you like this all night and never let you come."

I whimpered, half in pure annoyance and half in dissatisfaction.

"You say you trust me, but your body says otherwise." Vaughan nipped at my ear. "You need to learn to let someone else take care of you once in a while."

Instead of arguing with him or grabbing his dick and shoving it inside my pussy, I let out a breath and tried to clear my mind.

"Atta girl," he murmured, resuming his ministrations. Every crook of his fingers inside of me drew me closer and closer to the edge. When he pulled out and started massaging my breasts, I bit back a cutting remark.

It actually felt amazing.

My back melted into his chest as his hands roamed my body. I floated on clouds of euphoria, losing myself in his touch.

He went back to toying with my clit, working it back and forth with firm pressure until I felt the build-up of an epic orgasm. Of course, he let up. Instead of whining, I focused on the way his other hand had begun parting my entrance as he lined up and dipped his cock in and out with shallow thrusts.

"You're a dream, Joelle," he rasped. "I am fucking obsessed with you. Have been since the minute you rolled up and bent over the tailgate of your truck in those itty-bitty shorts." He notched the head of his dick into my cunt, but didn't push any further. "The first time I saw your eyes, you had me."

He pushed in and held. I didn't dare squeeze around

him. I focused on my breathing and the energy flowing between us.

I hadn't had many of them in my lifetime, but this felt like some sort of spiritual experience. The way Vaughan held me from behind while we were connected was vulnerable, yet incredibly safe.

He pressed his palm against my pelvis. I stifled the urge to react like a rabid chimpanzee at someone touching my stomach. His hips fell away from mine for the briefest of seconds before slamming back into my ass as he powered into my cunt.

The pressure from the heel of his hand pressing just above my pubic bone intensified. I sucked in a sharp breath as he did it again and again. Without thinking, my hand drifted down to my clit. I got two precise flicks in before Vaughan grabbed my hand and yanked away.

"Please," I cried out as he drove in again.

"If you touch yourself one more time, I will not let you come." There was a firmness and resolve in his tone that took my breath away. "This is your lesson, kitten. I'm not going to turn your ass pink and red tonight. I'm not going to make you thank me for each stripe I place against your skin. I'm going to make you do something harder than getting pleasure out of pain. You expect people to hurt you, so you brace for it and find a thrill in the pain. But not tonight." His words turned to a whisper. "I'm going to make you trust me. You're going to give your body to me completely. I want you to lay here and let me make you feel good because that's how I choose to show you how strongly I feel for you."

Tears rolled down my cheek, one after the other. The only sound filling the cabin was the groan of the bed and Vaughan's soft grunts as he pumped in and out of me.

He looped his arm beneath my thigh, lifting my leg slightly and deepening his thrusts.

I sucked in a heady breath, though it was drowned out by the whip of the wind outside. The quiet ambience of sex blended in a melody with the gentle patter of rain on the tin roof.

"There you go," Vaughan soothed when my pussy began to flutter around his shaft. "Just keep breathing. I'll get you there, kitten. I'll get you there."

"Vaughan—" My words caught in my throat.

"Come for me, beautiful."

All it took was a handful of slow thrusts and his thumb on my clit to make me careen into the abyss. I hunched forward, curling in on myself as every nerve in my body exploded. Vaughan continued to push in and out of my cunt while I detonated.

"Shit—Fuck—" Vaughan grunted, then went silent as he poured into the condom. He sputtered as he caught his breath, his chest heaving against my back. "You are incredible," he exhaled against the crown of my head. "Absolutely spectacular. Do you know that?"

I shifted, rolling to my other side so that I could face him, and let him see the tears on my cheeks. With a cloud-like touch, he cupped my jaw and kissed the tears away.

"Magnificent."

Vaughan waited while I used the bathroom before hopping out of bed to deal with the condom. When he joined me back between the sheets, it was with two bowls of microwaved ravioli.

I sat between his legs while we ate. When the bowls were scraped clean, we lay in companionable silence, listening to the rain.

"Hey, Vaughan?" I said, lifting my chin off his pectoral to look up at him.

He perked up off the pillow and arched an eyebrow. "Whatcha need?"

I laid back on his chest. "I'm ... I'm sorry I lost my shit on you today."

He let out a wry chuckle. "Tiger, you can lose your shit on me any day."

"I mean it. I'm not the best at talking about things that bother me, and today I was a camel trapped under a crap ton of straw."

Vaughan brushed my hair away from my face before tightening his arms around me. "I can't imagine having to grow up the way you did. And whatever your road to healing looks like, you have a hell of a lot of people in your corner."

I was never good at accepting encouragement or compliments. I didn't know how to react or what to respond with.

"Thanks for fixing up the roof."

"It was the most I knew I could get away with," he said with a chuckle that turned into a yawn. "You make me want to give you more than a cabin with a patchwork roof."

I didn't miss the way his hand wrapped around mine, his fingers tracing abstract lines across my knuckle.

He must have thought I had fallen asleep, because the next thing out of his mouth was, "You make me want everything I tried to leave behind."

How many times could a person get goosebumps before it was considered a skin condition?

30

VAUGHAN

"You're kidding, right?" I stood in the hangar with my hands on my hips. "No. Absolutely not."

"Oh, please." Jo rolled her eyes as if *I* was the one being ridiculous. "It's not like I'm flying you in the Ag Cat. It's perfectly safe."

I stared at the Cessna 150 Jo had been running through maintenance checks. "You're out of your fucking mind. Get in the car, we're going to the airport. I'll have Tamara book tickets on the way."

Jo cocked her hip and crossed her arms under her breasts, pushing them up. The clipboard she had been checking things off on was tucked under her arm. "This is my one condition. You want me to go to Chicago, then I'm flying us there."

Our bags were already packed, and we were *supposed* to be leaving within the hour.

Instead of keeping up the sassy attitude, she flipped like a switch and went for the jugular.

Jo batted her eyelashes and looked up at me. "Come on. You've flown with me before," she begged, bouncing back and forth from her toes to her heels. Jo set the clipboard on top of the wing and reached for my hands, tangling our fingers together. "If I'm not the one flying the plane, I'll be an anxious, nervous wreck."

I kissed the tip of her nose. "I know you're lying, but it's effective."

"Good!" she chirped.

"This is just fuckin' weird," Ryman grumbled as he strolled into the hangar.

"What?" Jo said, glowering at him.

He wagged a finger between the two of us. "Y'all acting like this. It's like seeing cats and dogs gettin' friendly with each other."

"You come by to wish us a safe trip?" Jo asked as she dropped my hands and grabbed the clipboard to finish her pre-flight checks.

"Momma wants y'all to come up to the big house before you head out. She fixed a feast. Doesn't want JoJo flying on an empty stomach."

I looked at her. "Do we have time?"

Jo glanced at the clock on the wall. "Yeah, I already looked at the radar. Let me finish up and load our shit and we can head up to the house."

"I'll load the bags in," I clipped as I strode to the pile of suitcases and travel duffels.

The clipboard smacked me in the chest. "You absolutely will not."

I shot a look at Jo that had her shaking in her boots. "You wanna try that again, Tiger?"

Jo scoffed and played it off with a flip of her hair. "Or what? You'll spank me? My plane, my rules, my packing method. Weight distribution matters, *sir*."

"Jesus Christ," Ryman muttered under his breath. He

scrubbed his hand down his mouth like he was trying to erase hearing what had just come out of Jo's mouth. Without another word, he disappeared from the hangar.

Jo's grin was full of mischief. "I love fucking with them," she snickered.

I chuckled and grabbed her by the belt loops. "I can see that. But just so we're clear, you can fuck *with* whoever you want. But I'm the only person you get to fuck."

She stared at the concrete beneath our feet, thick lashes shielding her eyes. "Are you saying we're... *this* is exclusive?"

I cupped her chin in my hand and made her put her attention solely on me. "I'm saying that I'm about to take you to an event where every man in the room will be salivating over the woman on my arm. They're the kind of people who are used to getting whatever they want." I tightened my grip on her jaw. "I'm making it clear that you are with me. I am not okay with you entertaining the idea of flirting with them just to get a rise out of me."

Though I didn't tell my dad or Ms. Faith, the main reason I was going back to Chicago this weekend was for a charity dinner where the who's-who of Chicago's elite would be in attendance.

The firm bought a table every year and sent the partners and a few upper employees. It was a good PR move, but I wasn't going this year because I wanted to look good to the partners.

I wanted to chum the waters. If I could bring in a few investors—sell them on the idea of the American dream, protecting the supply chain that got meat into grocery stores, and saving a small-town farm—I'd have a shot at saving my family's legacy.

Jo was a charmer at heart. She could butter up the snobs

with her Texas drawl and make it easy for them to open their wallets.

She trailed her fingers down the row of buttons on the front of my dress shirt. "Were you jealous when you saw me bull ride for the first time? Knowing that everyone in the bar was there to watch me flash my tits?"

My fingers dug into her ass as I pulled her in for a kiss. She tasted like coffee and toothpaste. The memory of waking up to her naked body around mine made my dick stir in my trousers.

"I have been a jealous bastard since the moment I saw you on the side of the road."

Her lips were swollen from the kiss, and her eyes were heavy. "Good."

When she finished the pre-flight checks, we loaded Bean and all the crap Jo used to spoil him into the truck and headed up to the big house. The scent of bacon and sausage wafted through the air as we trudged up the stairs.

I kept my hand on Jo's lower back since groping her ass before everyone had their coffee was probably impolite. When we stepped into the kitchen, all eyes landed on us.

"Morning, y'all," Ms. Faith chirped as she bobbed between the burners.

My dad kissed Jo on the head, then patted me on the back. "Mornin.'"

Bristol was perched on a stool pulled up to the island. Her legs swung back and forth, and she looked giddy. "I love everything about this."

Bean trotted right to her and plopped his furry ass down.

"It's weird," Cash chimed in as he stole a strip of bacon off the paper towel covered plate. "But fuck it—whatever butters your biscuit."

"It's unnatural," Ryman glowered. "Like a lion and a honey badger getting all snuggly."

Jo frowned. "Well, who's who?"

Ryman pointed to me. "He's the lion." He took a sip of coffee, then pointed to Jo. "You're the honey badger, obviously."

"Why don't I get to be the lion?"

He took another pull from the mug. "Honey badgers scare away lions by ripping their testicles off."

Jo paused, then shrugged. "That checks out."

"Alright, that's enough talk of testicles." Ms. Faith shooed everyone into the dining room. "Y'all dig in. Fill your mouths so you won't blab about ripping genitals off quite so much."

Jo took it easy on the soul-crushing, energy draining food, while I gorged myself on sausage kolaches and huevos rancheros.

It was probably a good thing she was flying the plane. Now that I had a full stomach, all I wanted was a nap.

We said our goodbyes, and I didn't fail to notice the lingering hug Ms. Faith gave Jo.

She gave me the same one, but without the whispered words.

Jo gave Bean a kiss on the snout and we headed back to the hangar. It was strange sitting stock-still in the passenger's seat while Jo flipped switches and mapped out the flight path.

"You sure you have a license to fly this thing?" I shouted into the microphone that was positioned in front of my mouth while Jo taxied out to the runway.

Her smile was ear-to-ear. "Eh, it's more of a 'ask forgiveness, not permission' situation."

My head spun so fast I was surprised when it didn't snap clean off.

Dark waves spilled down her back as she threw her head back and laughed. "Sit tight, city boy."

My heart didn't leave my throat until we were touching down at a little airport in Hot Springs, Arkansas. I stretched my legs and grabbed two cups of coffee from the diner inside while Jo refueled the plane. It tasted a lot like the sludge I had begrudgingly downed when I was making the sixteen-hour drive from Chicago to Maren. For some reason, it didn't bother me quite as much as it had then.

We were in the air for a few more hours before Jo decided she wanted lunch.

I listened to her chat with air traffic control as she circled an airport just south of St. Louis. They put us in a holding pattern until a commercial airliner had landed. Listening to her ramble off codes of numbers and words from the phonetic alphabet made my head spin.

I didn't know what the hell a squawk code was, but when Jo saw that hers was 6666, she keyed up the radio and politely asked them to change it. The woman on the other end of the radio laughed about pilots being superstitious, and rambled off a new code before we took off again.

"Isn't flying supposed to be faster than driving?" I asked as I tried to stretch my legs in the cramped seat. Jo was perfectly comfortable with her barely five-foot frame in the tiny Cessna. "It took me just over sixteen to drive down from Chicago."

We were close to Chicago, but nearing fourteen hours of travel. It was a good thing we took off from the farm as soon as the sun peeked over the horizon.

Jo smiled from behind her headset and microphone. "Maybe if you're flying commercial. But think about it like this: there's no road rage up here. No traffic jams. You probably had to stop for gas damn near a million times—especially in your swanky car. We've only had to stop twice. You're not staring at the same strip of pavement from sun up to sun down."

"True," I admitted. "But we could have just driven and not been stuck in a metal deathtrap hurtling over the earth's surface."

A faint smile quirked at the corner of her mouth, but she didn't say anything.

"Tell me why you really wanted to fly. Because if it was for efficiency's sake, we would have flown in the comfort of first class."

Jo was quiet. I would have given her the benefit of the doubt if she had been listening to radio chatter as we entered busier airspace, but the radio was silent.

Turbulence made the plane shudder, but her grip on the yolk never wavered. She was comfortable and confident up here.

When the ride became smooth again, she spoke up. "I wanted you to have to come back."

"What do you—" I stopped talking when the realization hit me. "You want me to stay in Maren?"

"I'm not asking you to," she snapped defensively, as if admitting she had feelings about the state of our situationship somehow made her weak in the dynamic.

"Joelle *I don't know your middle name* Reed." I reached across the cramped cockpit and draped my arm around her shoulders. "It's okay to admit that you have feelings for me." Nonchalantly, I added, "I won't judge you for it. I'm pretty hard to resist."

Her sunset pink lips pursed like she was trying to hide a smile.

"I'll let you in on a secret," I whispered. Static burst in our headphones. "I have feelings for you, too. Should I pass you a note that says, 'Do you like me? Check yes, or no?'"

She snickered. "I'd definitely check 'no,' and that shouldn't be a surprise. I tried to run you over with my truck."

Her quick wit never failed to make me laugh. "I'd expect nothing less."

Jo adjusted our heading, then relaxed in her seat. "Trisha," she said softly.

I couldn't quite make out the muffled word. I wasn't as used to hearing people talk through a foam-filled tin can as she was.

"What?"

"Trisha." Jo glanced my way and gave me a tight smile. "My middle name is Trisha. Momma was a huge fan of Ms. Yearwood."

I kept my arm around her shoulders as she coordinated with approach. We were close enough that I could see the distant Chicago skyline lit up in the sunset.

I brushed her hair off her shoulder and gently stroked her skin with my thumb. She would freeze when we touched down in Illinois. Autumn in Chicago and autumn in Maren were two completely different things. She hemmed and hawed when I insisted that she pack warm layers and coats, but I knew she'd be thanking me in a little while.

"It suits you," I said when the radio chatter went quiet.

What I didn't tell her was that the next thing that ran through my mind was what her name would sound like with Thompson added to it.

The thought scared me shitless, but it would have made her jump out of the damn plane.

Jo dropped us down onto the tarmac of a small, regional airport just outside of Chicago. It appeared to be mostly frequented by hobby and agricultural aviators. Jo knew how to find her people.

Tamara, wrapped up in a thick tweed peacoat, met us by the hangar Jo had rented to store the plane while we were in the city. She was fresh-faced, her brown skin glowing in the pre-winter chill.

It was probably due to me not being in the office, working absurd hours. That, and the spa package I had booked for her as a thank you since me working remotely had made her job slightly more complicated.

She handed me the keys to a sleek rental car, then tipped her head in the direction of Jo and the airport manager she was chatting up. "So, that's her, huh?"

I pocketed the keys and buttoned my coat. Months of blazing heat made me forget what a bitch Chicago weather was.

"What do you mean?" I asked.

Tamara smiled, her eyes crinkling at the corners. "The woman who made you human again."

Her Jamaican accent was a little thicker than usual. It came out more whenever she had been chatting with her mom.

I made a mental note to schedule her some time off over the holidays and send her to visit her family.

Jo danced from one foot to the other, clearly hating the cold. She said something that made the airport manager let out a rip-roaring belly laugh. The two of them swapped smiles like they were old friends.

We had been on the ground for less than ten minutes and she already had the man wrapped around her finger.

That made two of us.

"I think y'all would get along real well," I said, my Texas accent coming out strong.

Tamara raised her eyebrows. "Oh really?"

"She's a spitfire. Shame we won't be here long."

"When will you be back?" she asked, pulling up the calendar on her phone that coordinated my schedule.

I hesitated before admitting, "I don't know."

Translation: I don't want to.

31

JOELLE

"Wake up, Tiger. We're here."

I startled awake, rocketing upright in the passenger's seat of the rental car and smacking my head on the window.

"Shit," I mumbled as I cradled my skull.

Vaughan grimaced even though he was laughing. "Come here and let me see."

I leaned over the slick leather console that separated us and tipped my head toward him. His hands were gentle as he smoothed over my hair and timidly prodded around for any bumps. Satisfied that I had escaped without any serious head trauma, he kissed the crown of my head.

"Good nap?"

I nodded listlessly as I rubbed my eyes. "Sorry. Didn't mean to fall asleep."

"You flew the entire way here." He cut the engine and pocketed the keys. "Least I could do was let you drool on my arm for an hour."

"What?" I looked at him, wide-eyed as I searched his sleeve. I huffed, smacking his bicep. "You motherfucker."

Vaughan chuckled. "Come on, *country girl*. Let's get you inside before you freeze your tanned little ass off."

He wasn't kidding. My jeans were practically popsicles by the time we unloaded our bags and hustled inside. The elevator ride up to Vaughan's floor was blissfully warm. I stayed glued to his side, soaking in his body heat as he fished around for his key.

Having woken up in the parking garage, I had missed checking out the exterior of the high-rise. I had spent plenty of nights imagining what Vaughan's personal lair looked like. In my mind it was a lot like the Bat Cave, but the hallway we stepped into was anything but.

Exposed brick was warmed with art deco accents and reclaimed furniture. The narrow hallway table was accented with an arrangement of cream-colored orchids. There were only two units on this floor. Vaughan veered to the right, somehow managing to tow our luggage with one hand and keep the other securely on my hip.

My boots clomped across the slick tile. Vaughan, on the other hand, was quiet as a ghost in his patent leather loafers.

He had turned back into Chicago Vaughan for this trip. Gone were the blue jeans and pilfered flannels. He was decked out in his fancy suits and vests.

Not that I was complaining. The man looked like sin in a suit.

He unlocked the door and pushed it open, turning on the light as he led me inside.

"This is—"

"Not what you were expecting?" Vaughan filled in as he tossed his keys onto the coffee table.

I stood with my feet glued to the threshold. "Nope."

"You can come in and close the door whenever you're

ready," he said as he strolled through the space, completely unperturbed.

I looked around at the apartment that was oddly reminiscent of the big house. Brown leather couches were wedged together in an L-shape in front of a large flatscreen. The kitchen island had a butcher block top and a collection of copper pots and pans hanging from a rack above it. A blue metal star hung behind the stovetop.

Giant black-and-white photos hung on the walls. It took me a moment before I realized that they were aerial photos of the farm. Clean rows of plants were edged by the curving tree line that bracketed the field, separating usable dirt from the remaining five acres behind my cabin. It was of the east fields, if I had to guess. I could even make out the little dot of a shack where I lived.

"I had you pegged as a modern-minimalism kind of guy. You know... All glass. Weird square couches that you can't actually sit on. Black and chrome everything..." I turned and pulled the door closed behind me. "I thought you'd live in a penthouse and have a tank full of jellyfish that glowed at night. Or maybe a pet piranha."

Vaughan laughed as he finished turning on the lights. He took the bag that was looped over my shoulder and carried the rest of our things into, what I assumed was, the bedroom.

I followed curiously.

"I have 'fuck around' money. I don't have 'find out' money." As soon as he emptied his arms, his hands were on my hips, pulling me into him. "This isn't Gotham. I don't drive the Batmobile."

I started to laugh, but it turned into a yawn. It wasn't a cute yawn that reminded you of puppies and kittens. Some people are ugly criers, I was an ugly yawner. I looked like a snake that was trying to detach its jaw to more effectively slurp down prey three times its size.

Vaughan looped his arm around my shoulders and steered me toward the bathroom. "The grand tour can wait till tomorrow. Let's get you to bed, kitten."

We stood side by side in a bathroom that was as large as my entire cabin and brushed our teeth. Double sinks were topped with a light granite finish. The walk-in shower was the same size as my bed. To the side was a clawfoot tub that was made for soaking with wine and a book.

Vaughan took out his contacts and threw on a pair of glasses while I scrubbed a day of flying off my face. I really needed a shower, but it was nearing midnight and that was closer to my wake up time than my bedtime.

"You're quiet," Vaughan noted as he unbuttoned his dress shirt. He was the kind of psychopath that hung clothes back up rather than tossing them in *the chair*.

I shrugged. "Just tired."

He shot me a look that communicated that he didn't quite believe me.

"What?" I said as I stripped down to my underwear and pawed around for something to sleep in.

"You know what else is really quiet before it goes nuclear?" Vaughan produced a large t-shirt from his meticulously organized closet and dropped it over my head. "A bomb."

"You think I'm going to lose my shit because I left Maren?" I yanked the hem of the Chicago Cubs shirt down. It hung just below my butt. "I've traveled before. It's not like I've never left Texas."

The muscles of his chest rippled as he hooked a finger in the collar and tugged me closer. "You like control. You like routine. Consistency makes you feel safe."

"I can handle being on your turf," I countered. Pin pricks of heat and anxiety flooded the space between my shoulder blades. It took everything in me to keep from clawing at my skin to quell the sensation.

"I know you can," he said. "I wouldn't have brought you here if I didn't think you could handle yourself. I brought you here because..." He cursed under his breath. "I just wanted you here... With me. Maybe it's selfish, but I wanted you here with me."

We crawled in Vaughan's massive king-sized bed. I tried to be respectful and lie on my side, but it felt like a million miles of sheets separated us.

I liked the full bed I crashed on in the cabin. Sure, Vaughan woke up every morning with more back problems than the day before, but it was small enough that snuggling was the only way we both fit.

I didn't have to admit that I needed the comfort of lying in his arms. I didn't have to put that admission out there. I could maintain a shred of the control he had so precisely pointed out that I liked so much.

Before I could work up the courage to crawl over to his side, I heard his quiet snores. It must have felt like heaven for him to sleep in his own bed again, especially after the long day of travel.

I was so exhausted that it felt like going to sleep was going to be impossible. Rather than going insane, staring at the ceiling fan, I rolled out of bed like a ninja. The memory foam didn't even make a peep.

On silent feet, I tiptoed into the open-concept living room. He had left a few lights on, but I was drawn to the sliding glass doors that overlooked the bustling city.

Midnight at the farm was pitch-black and silent. The only ambient sounds were crickets. On the contrary, twenty floors below my feet, cars raced, horns blared, and lights glimmered, glowed, and flashed.

I knew the exact distance between Maren and Chicago, but it felt like I was on another planet. Maybe it was a good thing I slept during the drive into the city. The last thing I wanted Vaughan to see was me having a freak-out.

I crossed my arms over my body and hugged the Cubs shirt I was in. Even though it was fresh from his closet, it still smelled just a little bit like him.

A low gurgle bubbled in my stomach, reminding me that dinner had been a few hundred miles ago. Surely he wouldn't mind if I found a snack.

Then again, Vaughan had been gone for nearly two months. Everything in his fridge was probably rotten.

But maybe I could find a granola bar or some crackers to munch on. A quick bite, and then back to bed.

I was quiet as a church mouse as I eased through the kitchen, careful not to make so much as a breeze so it wouldn't disturb the pots hanging over my head.

If I left the cabin for two months, everything would be coated in dust and cobwebs. Vaughan's place was clean enough that I could eat off the floor.

The first cabinet I looked in was a bust. It was all protein powders and weird supplements.

Surely the man wasn't opposed to snacks...

I went through two more cabinets. One had an assortment of dry goods in labeled, airtight containers. I found pasta, legumes, flour, sugar, oats, and something weird called "quinoa."

Pass.

The other was filled with spices, oils, hot sauces, and vinegars.

Not quite helpful to me.

I was about to give up and hope my stomach didn't wake Vaughan up as I crawled back in bed when I spotted a narrow cabinet beside the refrigerator.

Aha—the holy grail. Chips, granola bars, crackers, and cookies galore.

I was about to go back to my theory about Vaughan being a robot, but the snack cabinet proved his humanity.

I was preparing to ripped into a pack of crackers when I saw it.

Lined up like soldiers, just below eye-level, were six cans of Chef Boyardee.

My heart popped like an engine misfiring.

I quietly pawed around the drawers for a fork, peeled back the aluminum lid, and curled up in the corner of the couch. I closed my eyes and exhaled all the anxiety that had been building up inside of me.

I was three bites of cold ravioli in when the bedroom light turned on.

"Joelle?" he said softly, though I could make out the concern in his voice. Before I could reply, he was out of bed and striding into the living room.

I looked up with wide eyes, like a kid who had just been caught sneaking out after curfew. It was the first time I had ever had that feeling. By the time I was of partying age, I was on my own, working to survive.

Worry was etched across his face. "What's the matter?" He knelt in front of me, his palm cradling my cheek as his gaze flicked down to the open can of ravioli in my hands.

I lifted a shoulder. "Couldn't sleep."

His other hand came up and wrapped around mine, his thumb stroking my wrist.

"Sorry," I said softly. "I know it was a long day and you've got that dinner thing tomorrow. I didn't want to toss and turn and keep you up."

Instead of saying anything, Vaughan stood and walked to the snack cabinet. He grabbed a can of ravioli, pulled the top off, and plucked a fork out of the utensil drawer. He sat beside me on the couch, our arms pressed against each other as we ate cold ravioli in companionable silence.

The man who had once said he wasn't a "canned ravioli kind of guy" sat beside me, in his boxers, with a coy smile on his lips as we shared a cold midnight snack.

I had never been in a relationship before. If I was being honest, I didn't know if we were in one. But whatever this was, I liked it. I knew it was okay to be a little scared, because Vaughan always made me feel safe.

My fork scraped the bottom of my can, and I called it. Vaughan was only two bites behind me. He took our cans to the sink, rinsed them, and then dropped them into the recycling bin. He left the forks for the morning.

"You still hungry?" he asked, bending over to give me a chaste kiss. I could still taste the tang and acid of tomato sauce on his mouth.

I shook my head. "No. I'm sorry I kept you up."

He cracked a smile and returned to sitting beside me, this time pulling me into his arms. "I woke up because I didn't feel you next to me." He pressed his lips to my temple and lingered. "I didn't realize how much I got used to having you in my arms."

"You have a really big bed," I murmured as my eyes closed. Apparently, this was what serenity felt like.

He chuckled. "I've never hated it until now."

The wry confession brought an honest-to-goodness smile to my face.

We brushed our teeth—again—at the double sinks.

Vaughan stood beside me this time and shared the one on the left.

When I walked back into the bedroom, I found him pushing our pillows together in the middle of the mattress. He had hauled long body pillows out of some hidden closet and put one on each side of the bed, making a smaller space for us to sleep.

"How's this?" Vaughan asked when he looked up and spotted me.

I rolled my lips between my teeth and nodded. "It's perfect."

"Then get your fine ass in here," he said as he laid down and opened his arms.

I turned out the lights, scrambled over the body pillow, and dropped into the space at his left side. I wrapped my arm around his torso, my palm resting over his heart. The repetitive *thump-thump, thump-thump* soothed me.

I'd nearly fallen asleep when Vaughan kissed my forehead. He let out a contented sigh and whispered, "That's better."

32

VAUGHAN

Bodies bustled past us as we hurried out of Carnicerías Guanajuato. When I told Jo that my favorite taqueria in the entirety of Chicago was in the back of a grocery store, she was sold. *Probably because her favorite barbecue place was also a gas station, but who was I to judge?*

I kept her hand in mine as we hurried down the sidewalk. Whenever I saw Jo in her little shorts and sports bras, she made me choke on my tongue. But Jo all bundled up in a fur-lined parka was even more adorable.

I, however, was strolling around without even so much as a blazer on. It was a balmy forty-nine degrees today, which meant Jo thought I had brought her to the arctic.

I opened Jo's door, then hustled around to the driver's seat. She had already stolen the keys from me and was cranking the heat before I could get in.

"You gotta toughen up, Tiger. This isn't even close to cold."

She shot me a look that could have cut steel as she held her nimble fingers to the air vents, thawing them out. "I don't plan on sticking around to see what *you* think cold is."

I pulled away from the curb and headed east. Jo dug through the bag, divvying up our haul: a lengua and an al pastor taco for me; carne asada and a chorizo taco for her.

I drove with no particular destination in mind, simply content to show her the sights as she ate. It was a lesson I learned early on: Jo was less argumentative when she had food in her mouth.

We passed Wrigley Field and snickered as a mustachioed man waved a *W* flag as his picture was taken in front of the stadium sign. The Sammy Sosa jersey he sported looked like it had seen decades of fandom.

I pried Jo's chorizo taco out of her hand just long enough to hop out at Tribune Tower and show her the stones embedded in the wall. She popped up on her tiptoes to read the placards denoting where each piece was from. *A stone from the Taj Mahal. A piece from Beijing's Forbidden City. A piece from the Parthenon. One from the Great Pyramid. A fragment of the Berlin Wall.*

Jo laughed as she studied one of the signs. "It's from the Alamo!"

I pulled my phone out and snapped her picture. I hated looking like a tourist, but the joy on her face at seeing a little piece of Texas was unmatched.

"There used to be a rock from the moon that was brought back on one of the Apollo missions," I said. "I think they removed it about ten years ago, though."

"That's a bummer," she said as she studied the next sign, mumbling to herself as she practiced saying, "Hagia Sophia."

I laid my fingers over hers, feeling the rough surface from thousands of miles away. "It's a mosque in Istanbul."

"Turkey." Her smile grew. "That's so cool. It's like I've been to all these places now."

We walked hand-in-hand down the sidewalk as we made our way back to the car. "Have you ever been out of the country?"

She shrugged. "I've been to Mexico, but it doesn't really feel like going out of the country when it's just over the border, you know?"

I took us in the direction of the riverwalk, trying to drive slow enough in the midday traffic for Jo to see everything. We made a quick escape from the car to snap a cheesy photo together in front of The Bean.

"Have you ever been out of the country?" she asked as she fastened her seatbelt again.

I nodded. "A while ago, but yeah."

"Where'd you go?"

"Greece and Italy." I rubbed the back of my neck. "It, uh ... it was my honeymoon."

Her eyebrows lifted. "Oh."

"I haven't traveled much after that." I cracked a grin to try and ease the tension. "I guess I work too much. Spending time in Maren to try and fix everything is the longest I've been away from Chicago in a long time."

Jo was quiet as I searched for a parking space. We finished our lunches in silence, then decided on a stroll down the Navy Pier.

Lake Michigan was a crisp aqua blue, sunlight glimmering off the ridges of water like it was made of glass.

"Do you regret putting your life on hold and coming back to Maren?"

I waffled for a moment, debating my answer. There were a lot of things I regretted in life: my marriage, shutting out people who genuinely cared for me, and leaving the farm to fall on hard times.

But going back? I didn't regret that at all. Especially because of the woman walking beside me.

I squeezed her hand three times. "Not even a little bit."

We spent some time exploring the pier and the waterfront. Jo reluctantly shed her thick coat as the afternoon sun warmed us. By the time we made it back to the car, she had even rolled her sleeves up.

"What do you do for fun?" Jo asked as I cruised through the Magnificent Mile, heading north to take us back to my apartment. "Stuff like this?"

I chuckled as I took a left before the light turned red. "Nah, I'm pretty boring. I usually end up going into the office and working on the weekends."

"Home and work?" she asked, peeling her eyes away from the window and turning to me. "Come on, Thompson. You can do better than that."

I grinned. "I think I'd get summoned by HR if I did topless bull riding."

That made her laugh. "I'd pay big money to see that."

"Think they'd make me wear the vest?"

She cupped her hand over her mouth, giggling uncontrollably. "You could get away with some tasseled pasties. Just say when, city boy. I'll call Jen and make it happen."

I grinned, leaning back in my seat and draping my hand over the top of the steering wheel. "Sometimes I'll go for a run along Lake Michigan if I want to change up my routine. If I close my eyes, it's a little like walking the fields at the farm."

"You missed it, didn't you?" she asked pointedly. "Is that why you decorated your apartment like you did? Or was that your ex?"

"Definitely not Meredith," I clipped. "She got the house in the divorce." Simply saying the words made my eye twitch. "The perfectly curated, designer-everything house. It looked like a museum. She'd pitch a fit if a speck of dirt made it inside."

Jo's smile was Cheshire. "My cabin is ninety percent dirt."

I slid into my designated space in the parking garage and waited patiently for the elevator doors to open. Jo stood in front of me, leaning back into my arms. It was so natural. Easy.

How had the world's most infuriating woman become the one person I couldn't stand to be away from.

I was drawn to her like a magnet. If she was in the same room as me, I physically ached until I touched her.

"So ... that charity dinner tonight?" Jo asked as we stepped off the elevator.

I fiddled with the keys until the door swung open. "Yeah, I figured we could hang out here until it's time to leave."

"Probably smart," she said as she toed off her shoes. "Fair warning, but I'm going to commandeer your bathroom for the foreseeable future."

I cupped her cheek and drew her in for a slow, languid kiss. I hadn't kissed her for at least an hour and that was far too long. "Don't fret about the dinner. Just wear whatever you're comfortable in."

"Ye of little faith." She smirked and patted my chest before strolling to the bedroom.

———

THE SOUNDS COMING from the bathroom didn't do anything to increase my faith. I could hear Bristol's voice coming through the speaker on Jo's phone. The two of them were yelling at each other over concealer and eyeshadow.

I pressed my ear to the door just long enough to catch Bristol shrieking, "You can fly a plane! Eyeliner shouldn't be that hard!"

"I can count on one hand the number of times I've worn makeup, and none of them have involved me sticking a pencil anywhere near my eye!" Jo shouted back.

It was probably a good thing they were separated by a few states.

I caught up on some work with my blissfully fast internet, and got ahead so Tamara wouldn't have me drawn and quartered when I told her I was leaving again and going back to Maren for a little while.

How long? I didn't know.

Hours went by and Jo hadn't emerged from the bathroom attached to my bedroom yet. It was a good thing I had a guest bath.

The dinner wasn't quite tuxedo-worthy, but I did pull a nicer suit out of my closet. I didn't mention any kind of dress code expectation to Jo. If she wanted to show up in jeans and work boots, I'd be honored to have her on my arm.

Still, the grunts and groans echoing from the bathroom made me worried about what she was getting herself into.

I stood at the mirror in my bedroom and ran a hand through my hair, then checked my watch. We needed to get going.

"Joelle, sweetheart!" I hollered across the room, hoping my voice made it into the bathroom.

It dawned on me that Jo had been quiet for a few minutes. I panicked, worried that she had passed out from hairspray fumes or had accidentally strangled herself trying to get dressed.

"You almost ready?" I asked while I fastened my Rolex—a gift from the partners of the firm last year.

The bathroom door swung open and Jo appeared. She was an absolute vision in a low-cut black dress.

Strappy high heels peeked out of the bottom as the hem swished across the top of her toes. It was form fitting, giving her stunning curves. The top, held up by two thin straps, dipped in a V between her breasts, showing off the slightest hint of cleavage. A slit split the dress clean up to the top of her thigh.

Her hair was pulled back in an ornate ponytail, braids crisscrossing around the band. Voluminous curls spilled out of the tail, grazing her bare spine as she wobbled from one foot to the other. Thin tendrils framed her face.

She wore a light dusting of makeup. Her eyes were smoky and seductive, and her lips were painted a glossy pink.

"I tried to cover up my scar," Jo said. "But I'm not that good at makeup." She gingerly touched her forehead. "Bristol tried to talk me through it, but I probably should have had her show me in person before we left."

I moved to her in one long stride. "You are absolutely breathtaking, Tiger," I said, finally getting my hands on her. I traced the delicate slope of her neck. Her shoulder. The dip at her waist. I held the back of her neck and kissed her temple where the jagged slash was formed into bumpy, raised scar tissue. "And I love your scar."

Jo looked down. "I don't wear dresses. This is Bristol's. I think she wore it to prom a few years ago. Ms. Faith took the lining out so it wouldn't be poofy."

I slid my hand up the slit, gripping her bare thigh. "You look incredible."

She teetered on her high heels, and grabbed my arm. "Maybe this isn't a good idea."

"I will carry you all night long if I have to." I wasn't kidding.

Her teeth sunk into her lower lip. "Are you sure I look okay?"

I knelt in front of her, putting us eye to eye as I held her hands. "You are perfect in every way, Joelle Reed. Absolutely flawless. I can't wait to show you off."

Jo grabbed a shawl and wrapped it around her shoulders. She tossed her phone and a few cosmetic reinforcements into a small clutch and snapped it shut.

"One question," she said as we made our way out to the elevator. "Is this the kind of fancy, rich people thing where they serve snails and fish eggs and call it dinner? Do I need to sneak a sandwich in my bra? Because I don't have boobs." She looked down the front of her dress and squished her tits together, then let them fall back to their rightful places. "See? There's plenty of room."

I laughed and shook my head as we made our way down to the car. "There will be dinner, and I promise you'll like it."

She waited patiently as I opened her door, then took my hand to help her sit down without toppling over. "You do remember that I'm kind of picky, right?" She pulled up the hem of the dress so I could shut the door.

I rounded the hood, smiling to myself because, as usual, I was one step ahead of her.

When I dropped behind the steering wheel, Jo continued. "I'm not trying to be high maintenance, I'm just not big into overpriced, tiny portions. I'd rather hit a drive-through on the way home."

She called my apartment "home" and I didn't know if she realized it.

But I did. And it was everything.

33

JOELLE

"This was a mistake," I muttered under my breath as I clung to Vaughan's arm for dear life. My ankles wobbled with each step.

Bristol tried to coach me on how to walk in high heels, but she would have had better luck teaching a fish how to drive a tractor.

"Don't look down at your feet," Vaughan said. "Pick a spot in the direction that you're going and keep your eyes on that."

"You have a lot of experience wearing stilettos that I don't know about?" I hissed, finding a tree covered in string lights to stare at. I silently prayed to the gods of impractical women's fashion that I wouldn't face plant on the sidewalk.

He grinned. "I had a baby sister who wanted to play dress-up whenever I came to visit. Yes, I have worn high heels."

"Bristol really has you wrapped around her finger, doesn't she?"

"Always has," Vaughan said.

He looked like sex in a designer suit. His hair was the

perfect blend of styled and messy. It made him irresistible. I wanted to tangle my fingers in it and yank him down to kiss me while I climbed him like a goddamn tree.

"You called her your sister," I noted.

"She is."

"You didn't say *half*-sister." I chanced a look up at his face and caught his brow furrowing before I had to look at my tree again.

Vaughan used his free hand to scrub the stubble on his jaw as he worked the distinction over in his mind. He seemed to be warring between admitting I was right and finding some shred of reasoning to defend his slip-up.

"I haven't spent this much time with them since I was a kid. And even back then, Bristol was so little she couldn't do much with me, Ryman, and Cash." He sighed, his breath clouding in the night air. "I guess as I've gotten older, I've realized that semantics don't matter quite as much as they do in my head. That people are going to take a place in your life whether you give them a title or not." With more conviction than I had ever heard him use, he said, "Bristol is my sister because I love her. Same with Cash and Ry. They're my brothers. Period." He hesitated a moment before adding, "And Ms. Faith... She's been so good to me all these years. Even when I didn't deserve it. And she voluntarily filled a role for more decades than my mom was able to."

I didn't want to risk reaching for his hand. I wasn't that confident in heels yet, and my toes were already starting to blister. Had it not been for the instant frostbite, I would have been in considerably more pain. Instead, I squeezed his bicep three times.

The warmth of the Drake Hotel was a welcome reprieve from the whipping Chicago winds.

The city lived up to its nickname. Add in some frigid temperatures and my evening gown didn't stand a chance.

I didn't even know why I attempted to dress fancy. You could put a big ol' bow on a bag of trash, but that didn't turn it into a Christmas present.

We hadn't even made it into the lobby before an older man in a black suit strolled up to Vaughan and slapped him on the shoulder. "Thompson! Good to have you back! You know, for a minute there I was worried you were using this time to look at other companies."

Vaughan plastered on the fakest smile known to man, but this guy ate it up. "Absolutely not, Mr. Devers. You know how passionate I am about my clients."

"Good man!" he said.

I'd never quite understood the phrase "chuffed to bits," but that was this wrinkly old guy to a T.

"And I'm sure you heard the big news," he continued. The mischievous twinkle in his eye told me he wanted to be the one to spill the beans.

Vaughan played along.

Mr. Devers cleared his throat. "You know Allegiant Holding Group from the twenty-eighth floor? Their CEO—Solomon something 'er other—is bringing in a new tech company. Gonna take up the rest of the building. You know what this means, don't you?"

"Lots of new hires with matched retirement plans," Vaughan said with a chuckle.

The pair of saggy balls in a suit grinned. "I knew you were a keen one. That's why I put your name up for partner."

Vaughan stiffened.

So, he hadn't been expecting that. Frankly, neither had I.

Part of me hoped there was a chance that Vaughan

would have reconnected with his family enough to want to stay in Maren. Maybe then we could keep whatever this was between us going.

But becoming a partner at his investment firm? That would pretty much tie him to Chicago forever.

As my toes began to defrost, the blisters started to burn. I used Vaughan's arm as a brace to wiggle up higher in my shoes to keep the straps from cutting into my feet.

Vaughan cleared his throat in an attempt to regain his bearings. "Mr. Devers, this is my date, Joelle Reed." He tipped his head to the side and introduced the bag of bones to me. "Jo, this is my boss, John Devers. He's one of the founding partners of Devers, Garcia, and Nguyen."

His hand was clammy. It was like greeting a dead fish, but I plastered the southern charm anyway. "Pleasure to meet you, Mr. Devers."

"Well, aren't you something..." He eyed me up and down, his gaze lingering on the dip at my cleavage. It took everything in me to not rip my stiletto off and stab him with it. "Where ya from, doll?"

"Little town called Maren, Texas. You should visit sometime. Mareners certainly know how to welcome newcomers."

Vaughan nearly choked on his tongue, but I kept right on smiling like a pageant queen.

"Is this your first time in Chicago?" he asked.

"Yes, sir. It's quite the city."

"Well," Mr. Devers said, looking between Vaughan and me. "Let's hope you like it. I think Garcia, Nguyen, and *Thompson* has quite the ring to it. Maybe someday Vaughan will be sitting in my office." He slapped Vaughan on the arm again.

And with that, he turned and walked away.

"What the hell was that?" I muttered to Vaughan as he led me further inside.

He was rattled, but quickly shook it off. "Welcome to the mind games."

———

"YOU LOOK LIKE YOU'RE HIDING," Tamara said as she sided up to me in the corner of the ballroom. Her velvet dress in a deep crimson was stunning. "Can I hide with you?"

I took a sip from my glass while I shifted between my feet, rolling one ankle and then the other. The burn of the bourbon was nice. The burn of the sores on my feet were not.

"Be my guest. Vaughan got snagged by another old guy in a suit. I'm hiding so I don't put my foot in my mouth." I looked down at my shoes. "Although, at this point, I think I'd rather chew my toes off than ever wear heels again."

Tamara snickered. "You hide it well. You and Mr. Thompson look good together."

Before I could get another word in, a mile-tall woman with sandy blonde hair pulled up in a stuffy French twist floated over to us. "Tamara, is that you?" She touched the gaudy necklace wrapped around her throat like she couldn't believe her eyes. "It's been so long! How are you?"

Tamara's smile was tense, and her eyes shot daggers. "Meredith."

Meredith? Like *Meredith* Meredith? Like the she-devil who used to be married to Vaughan? *My* Vaughan?

Fine. Maybe he wasn't *my* Vaughan, but he sure as hell wasn't hers. What was she doing here anyway? My mind floated back to the call Vaughan ignored from her, and the fight and confessions that ensued.

Meredith's exacting gaze turned to me and she held her hand out. A rock the size of a piece of gravel was perched on her ring finger. Apparently, she had lured another poor, unfortunate soul to meet a soul-crushing demise in miserable matrimony.

"Meredith Thompson. I don't think we've met. I'm on the board for Chicago Arts Preservation Society. Are you here with Devers, Garcia, and Nguyen?"

Hearing her use Vaughan's last name made me want to sock her square in her artificially perfected nose.

Across the ballroom, I spotted Vaughan at the exact moment he spotted Meredith. His eyes widened and he very clearly said, "Shit," in front of someone who looked like they thought they were important.

"No, I'm actually here with a charity of my own," I said, sweet as sugar.

Meredith's eyes twinkled like she just couldn't wait to add someone else to her Rolodex. "Oh how wonderful! What type of work do you do? Perhaps we could set up a lunch."

Vaughan was halfway across the ballroom. I had to make it quick. "I oversee the rehabilitation of men who escaped narcissistic relationships."

Vaughan's hand slid around my back as he pulled me into his side. "There you are."

Meredith paled. Her brain wasn't quite as fast at processing my insult as it was taking in the sight of her ex-husband with his hands on another woman.

"You—you're with the—" Wide eyes turned to thin slits as she poured all of her venom into a sharp glare. "Wow, Vaughan. I can see you really hit rock bottom with this one. Where did you find her? Some backwoods comedy club?"

"No, but you're close," I said as I took the champagne

flute right from her hand and downed it in one swallow. "He watched me ride a mechanical bull with my tits out." I looked down at the front of my dress. "My girls are real winners."

Vaughan choked. Tamara nearly doubled over in hysterics.

Meredith turned her ice-cold gaze to Vaughan. "I was hoping you'd be here. I've tried calling you a few times. I heard about your father. How is he?" Her words were sympathetic, but the poison dripping from them was unmistakable.

This woman had her eyes set on something. I was pretty sure all seven digits of her mark were sitting in an account in the Northern Trust Bank.

"Fine," Vaughan clipped, taking my hand. "Same as he was all the years you refused to visit my family. Same as he was when we ended our marriage. Now, since you're not going to be wringing so much as a nickel from me tonight, you can continue with your rounds. I'll be spending my evening with a woman who does not make me want to stick thumbtacks in my eyes."

"Holy shit," I giggled as Vaughan whisked me away. "I'm going to need an itemized list of all the things you saw in her because unless she has a platinum pussy, I don't get it."

To my absolute surprise, Vaughan cracked a smile. "Trust me, it's not that good."

"You're going to have to elaborate."

He lifted an eyebrow.

"Come on," I begged. "I know we're sleeping together, but you can talk shit about your ex to me. I love talking shit about people. It's one of my favorite pastimes. Especially when the people we're shit talking are shitty."

"I'm pretty sure you just set the record for the most uses of the word 'shit' at a charity dinner."

I elbowed him as we circled a table and found our assigned seats. "You love it."

Tiny place cards had *Mr. Vaughan Thompson* and *Ms. Joelle Reed* written in looping cursive that was so ornate I could barely read it.

Vaughan pulled out my seat, then nudged it in when I lowered down. He took the spot beside me, stealing a sip from the pre-filled water glass. "She scheduled sex."

I nearly spat out a sip of bourbon. "Seriously?"

Vaughan nodded. "Scheduled sex. Lights off and efficient. She wasn't big into foreplay, which is just fucking weird."

I held my clutch in front of my mouth to hide my laugh. "So, you were just her charger?"

He quirked an eyebrow. "A charger?"

I shrugged. "You plug in, get your fill, and go about your day."

Vaughan stared at me, dumbfounded, then tossed his head back and let out the deepest, loudest laugh I had ever heard.

When he finally caught his breath, he wiped his eyes and shrugged. "I, uh... I guess you're right. It was kind of like that. There was no emotion."

We had nothing but emotion. *Hate. Jealousy. Desire. Anger. Adoration. Fury. Ecstasy.*

Vaughan and I were everything but lukewarm. Everything but mediocre. Everything but indifferent.

We were hot and cold. On and off. Hate and—

"Thompson. Fancy meeting you here."

Vaughan peeled his eyes off me as a man in a bespoke suit took a seat at the opposite side of the round table. His hair was the color of fluffy snow, and his skin was the color of asphalt slush. There was something blank about his stare that made him look like a corpse. The white completely surrounding his pinpoint irises was unnerving.

Vaughan took a sip of water. "Good evening. Forgive me —you know me, but I don't think we've met."

The white-haired man's smile was vampiric. "We've spoken on the phone, and I believe you told my assistant to let me know that I could... How did you put it? Go fuck myself?"

Vaughan's eye twitched. It was his only tell that whoever this fucker was, had already gotten under his skin. "Mr. Ellington."

"Edward, please," he said magnanimously before turning his lifeless gaze to me. "And you must be Joelle Reed."

Something told me he didn't steal a peek at my place card. It was meant as an intimidation tactic. Trying to subtly get across that he knew more about us than we knew about him.

"Been working the room tonight, have you?" Ellington said as he grabbed the neatly folded cloth napkin from his plate and stuffed it down the front of his collar. "Trying to get some generous benefactors to donate to a lost cause?" He shrugged nonchalantly. "Not a bad idea. People love an underdog. Unfortunately underdogs don't stand a chance against bulldozers."

Vaughan didn't touch his water. His poker face never slipped. He stared Edward Ellington in the eye. "I'm glad to know Vulkon is such a supporter of the arts. I'll be sure to let the council's donation liaison know to expect your very generous contribution."

Vulkon.

It wasn't just one of the crows that had been pecking at farm owners for months. It was the vulture himself.

Ellington's expression was murderous. "Word of advice, Mr. Thompon—playing with fire is never a good idea. I offered you a candle, something useful. A way to get your family out of the hole they recklessly dug themselves into. A means to set them up for the rest of their lives."

"And I told you no. A wiser man would have taken that answer and walked away with his pride intact. But you just keep coming back for more rejections." Vaughan cracked a cocky smirk. "You're worse than a clingy ex-girlfriend."

Ellington wasn't bothered. He reached for a glass of something amber and took a sip. "Let this be a lesson to you, Thompson. I handed you a candle and you rejected it. But I'm still holding the match."

A chill ran up my spine when his beady eyes landed on me. It took everything inside of me to keep from clawing my skin off. His gaze felt disgusting.

"And from the looks of it, the Thompsons won't be the only ones who could get burned."

A couple dressed to the nines dropped into the two seats between me and Edward Ellington, and immediately started chatting him up. Vaughan slid his hand under the tablecloth and gave my thigh a comforting squeeze.

I could barely breathe. Had he just threatened me?

The butter knife at my place setting was useless, but I could do some serious damage to that man with my fork.

"Breathe, kitten," Vaughan murmured under his breath. "Just breathe. You're doing great."

"Mind games," I said just loud enough for him to hear. "That's what you said, right?"

Vaughan's pause was telling. "That's right."

34

VAUGHAN

The rest of the table filled up with employees of the firm, another Vulkon executive, and a woman named Blair Dalton who was part of the up-and-coming social scene in Chicago.

Chastity and Harold Bergstrom, a snooty couple who couldn't stop talking about how lovely the Amalfi Coast was this time of year, were the last to be seated.

As the first course was served, I kept my hand on Jo, anchoring her to me. It was all I could do when what I really wanted was to leap over the table and smash the obnoxious floral centerpiece over Ellington's head. I wanted to watch his skull crack open like a watermelon falling off of a truck onto the highway.

After a quiet stretch of clinking forks and mumbled conversation, servers swooped in, clearing the salad plates to make room for the main course. Jo's was completely gone, save for the spinach leaves.

"Your accent is so ... quaint," Chastity Bergstrom said with thinly veiled disdain as she looked Jo up and down. She had asked Jo what she did for work and barely kept herself from guffawing when Jo talked about being an Ag pilot.

"I grew up in South Carolina," Chastity said as she took a nimble sip from her goblet. "Charleston. Old money and all that. I took elocution lessons for years to get rid of my accent. Perception is nine-tenths of the law, you know."

Of course Meredith sat me with the Bergstroms. She knew how much I couldn't stand them and the way they thought their multimillion-dollar shit didn't stink.

But Jo, ever the shrewd little fox, didn't let the dig slip.

"Actually," Jo said, "it's *possession* is nine-tenths of the law." She offered a pitying smile. "But we all make mistakes. The same way you're mistaken about the way I speak. An accent does not indicate a lack of intelligence."

I wanted to grab her hand and raise it over her head like she had just won a heavyweight title, but Jo wasn't done yet.

"But I suppose having an accent is just one of many things that you think are classy if you're rich and trashy if you're poor. A lot like living in Chicago and—" Jo looked at her plate "—intermittent fasting."

Chastity paled and clutched the pearls at the base of her neck. "My stars. They're just letting anyone in here these days."

"Here's the thing, Chas," Jo said, pretending as if they were old friends. "I'm a Dixie cup martini. Not fancy on the outside, but I still taste good. But you? You're sewage in a champagne flute. It doesn't take long to see that it's just shit inside."

I was going to marry this woman.

Chastity excused herself, waltzing out in a cloud of Chanel No. 5 and disdain. Jo let out a sigh of relief as the servers began bringing out the main courses.

"What's for dinner?" she whispered, her eyes roaming over the plates.

Before I could answer, a server swooped in and daintily placed a crisp white plate in front of Jo. Her eyes widened at the sight.

"Your second course, Miss Reed," the server said. "Artisanal semolina envelopes filled with le bœuf haché, suspended in a bright heritage pomodoro. Accented with a snowfall of provincial Parmigiano Reggiano and hydroponic microgreens. Enjoy."

She stared at her meal. The crisp orange-red of Chef Boyardee's famous sauce really jumped off the plate. The garnish of cheese and whatever the hell microgreens actually were was a fantastic touch by the catering staff. The server gave me a knowing smile, sliding my dinner of scallops onto the charger in front of me.

Jo's pale blue eyes went glassy as she took in the artful plating that the chef de cuisine had come up with when presented with the can of ravioli I smuggled in.

"Thank you," she whispered as she confidently plucked the dinner fork from the array of utensils.

I leaned over and pressed my lips to her temple. "If you want to try my scallops, I'll share."

Jo smiled down at her plate. "I would rather wash my body with week-old tobacco spit from the Dr. Pepper bottle in Ryman's floorboard, than eat whatever the fuck scallops are."

I could see Meredith glaring at me from across the room. It made being here with Jo all the more fun. Especially because she looked absolutely miserable next to the stuffy alderman she was engaged to.

Jo wasn't a breath of fresh air. She was a goddamn cyclone.

I pulled away and speared a scallop with my fork. "I love your mouth, but I cannot wait to punish it when we get home."

And Jo fucking smiled.

———

I COULDN'T PEEL my eyes away from the way her dress spilled down her bare leg. That slit was going to be my damnation. I tightened my grip on the steering wheel, practically white-knuckling it back to my building. That dress had been a fucking cock tease all night.

Jo's high heels were in the floorboard. Her high-arched Barbie doll feet were propped up on the dash. Nothing but silken skin turned golden from the sun.

I shifted in the seat, waiting out the infinite row of red lights. My dick was painfully hard. It was becoming increasingly difficult to focus on anything but the way the black satin fabric pooled across Jo's hips. I adjusted myself and eased forward to the next light.

"Spread your legs."

Jo's hair whipped around as she turned from the window. "What?"

"I didn't say to open your mouth. I told you to open your legs. "

Her lips parted, but she didn't make a sound. She didn't even breathe. The light turned green and I pressed the gas. "Three seconds, Tiger."

Jo slid her left foot off the dash and parted her knees.

I reached over and pushed my hand under the layers of midnight satin and felt damp fabric. I hooked my finger through the gusset of her panties and tugged. "I want these off right now."

"Vaughan," she hissed under her breath, scolding me as if someone was in the car with us.

I cut my eyes to her before looking back at the road. "The windows are tinted. Now strip."

Her cheeks were flushed the prettiest shade of pink as she shimmied the little thong off her hips and untangled it from her ankles. I snatched it out of her grip and brought it to my nose, inhaling the scent of pure lust. Jo watched with dilated pupils as I wrapped the thong around my hand and continued to navigate through the bottleneck of traffic.

I didn't say another word to her as I pulled into the parking garage and cut the engine. I pressed the button that controlled the seat position and pushed away from the steering wheel. The interior light bathed us in a faint warm glow, highlighting her delicate features. Jo unlatched her seatbelt and reached for the door when I pressed the lock.

Her breath caught.

I unzipped my slacks and pushed my boxers down just enough for my dick to spring free. "Suck my cock."

Jo was taken aback and I watched as my sweet girl became a devil. "What makes you think I'm going to suck your dick? I think I should be the one demanding orgasms first. I'm going to—"

I grabbed her throat and squeezed, feeling her pulse throb and race in my hand. I kept my grip firm, but avoided her windpipe. "You're going to put that mouth of yours to better use than sassing me. And then I'm going to walk you inside, still dripping with need. You're going to take my dick in your mouth right now because when we get inside, you will be coming so much that your pleasure will feel like a punishment. Do you understand me?"

Jo tried to nod, but I kept her head trapped in my grasp.

"Use your words," I said with a growl.

"Yes, sir." Her head jerked back as I released her from my grip.

"That's my girl. Now..." I grabbed a fistful of her hair and tugged. "Down."

Jo's lips wrapped around the head of my cock, warm and wet.

I had been on edge since the moment I saw her step out of the bathroom in that dress. I had some tricks up my sleeve when we got inside, and there was no way in hell I could focus on her if I was thinking with my dick.

I felt a gentle tug on my balls and grunted, feeling the low roiling of pleasure threatening to turn into a volcanic eruption. I took a slow, steady breath and quelled it for the time being.

"That's it, kitten," I soothed as I brushed my hand over her hair, gently caressing her scalp. I brought her panties to my nose again and breathed her in, imagining her pussy around my dick instead of her mouth. "Fuck—you smell so good. I can't wait to bury my face between your thighs and eat your cunt."

Jo whimpered around my cock, her mouth stretched like a tight rubber band as she bobbed up and down, swirling her tongue around the head with each pass.

I threaded my fingers through the back of her hair and pulled her off my length. "Suck on my balls." I pushed her head lower and lifted my hips.

Jo's tongue darted out, searching for the delicate skin.

"Oh, fuck..." I gasped and choked at the same time as I felt the gentle pulls from her mouth.

She did it twice more before I was careening toward the point of no return.

I yanked Jo up, guiding her by her hair as I pressed my cock to her lips, and pushed back inside her mouth.

Jo gagged as I hit the back of her throat. She let out a stifled yelp, but the constriction of her throat was too good.

"Hold still," I clipped through gritted teeth.

I pumped between her lips again, loving the soft sounds she made as I claimed her mouth. I levered up, the head rubbing along the roof of her mouth. Her tongue laved up the shaft, stroking the sensitive underside.

"If you keep going, I'm going to come in your mouth."

When Jo didn't pull back, I tugged on her scalp. "Tiger."

Her eyes widened as she looked up at me with mischief twinkling in those blue irises. Her teeth scraped over the head of my cock and I nearly lost it.

I grabbed her head with both hands and drove in deep. My cock hit the back of her throat as I came hard.

Jo sputtered, plastering her hands against my thighs as she sucked down my release. Her hair was a mess and her makeup was smeared, but she had never looked more beautiful in her entire life.

She wore an untamable smile when she sat up. After a few calming breaths, she slumped against her seat and turned toward me with a lazy grin. "Please tell me we can do that again sometime."

I stared at her for a moment, dumbfounded. I thought I'd taken it too far.

Jo wiped her forearm across her mouth, mopping up the saliva and sweat that glistened on her cheek. She raised her eyebrows, uneasy with my lack of response. "Please?"

I couldn't help but laugh. "Tiger, we can do that anytime you want. But right now, I want your ass inside."

I marched her into the building, brazenly fingering her wet panties. Every so often, Jo would glance over her shoulder to steal a peek of me with her thong in my hand. I didn't care who we passed. I wanted the world to know she was *mine*.

The moment the door closed behind us, I pulled her down the hall. Jo stumbled on the hem of the dress, yelping as she stubbed her toe on a table leg. I didn't bother with asking; I simply threw her over my shoulder like a rag doll and carted her to the bedroom.

Jo squeaked when she tumbled onto the mattress.

I grabbed her hips and flipped her onto her stomach, frantically finding the zipper for the dress and yanking it down.

"Vaughan—"

My head swam and my vision blurred. I needed her like oxygen. Every moment without my hands on her felt like one where I was suffocating.

"Vaughan." Jo rolled over and braced her hands against my chest as she sat up. "Slow down."

I clawed at the straps holding up the bodice of the dress.

"*Vaughan.*" Jo's voice was firm as she clasped her hands around my wrists. Her grip was strong, but her blue eyes were calm like still waters.

I was unraveling at the seams and it was all because of her. I had never been like this—depraved and desperate. So fucking desperate. I *needed* her.

Jo locked with my gaze, her thumbs stroking the veins on the underside of my wrists. "We have time. I'm not going anywhere."

She blinked, as if waiting for me to sober up. Hours had passed since my last sip of alcohol, but it didn't matter. She had intoxicated me from the first time I laid eyes on her.

Slowly, she released my wrists and stood, brushing her hair over one shoulder.

"Go ahead," she said. "Take my dress off."

My hands trembled as I pushed the straps off her shoulders. I was losing it.

Black fabric pooled at her feet, leaving her wearing absolutely nothing. Jo turned and faced me, sliding her hands down the front of my suit. Her slim fingers curled around my lapels.

"Tell me where you want me," she said softly. The melodic soprano of her voice grounded me.

I buried my nose into the top of her hair and breathed in, closing my eyes. "I need every part of you. There is nothing about you that I can survive without."

She grasped at my hand and squeezed it three times. "You have me."

The gravity of those three words wasn't lost on me. Jo didn't trust easily, and it was something I would never take for granted. Hearing it from her cleared my mind like a rainstorm chasing away a haze of pollen.

"On the bed, kitten."

Without argument, Jo turned and crawled across the mattress. Her heart-shaped ass swayed with each stride.

"Stop." I planted my palm at the base of her spine.

Jo froze.

I circled the bed, trailing my fingers over her body as I moved.

She stayed stock-still, not daring to breathe until I granted her permission.

For a moment, my hands left her. I fucking hated it, but I needed to grab the box I had stashed under the bed.

The first thing I did was slip the blindfold over her eyes. It was a gunmetal gray silk with a lining that was as soft as a baby lamb.

"I want you to trust me," I said, and kissed her forehead. "Can you do that?"

Jo nodded and reached up to adjust the mask.

"Then lay on your back and spread your legs."

Jo grinned. I slid the box out of her way and gripped her hip, helping her spot where to lay since I had taken her sight.

"Vaughan?"

"Yes?"

"The things you just pulled out... They're *new*... Right?"

I chuckled. "Did I say you could peek?"

Jo blushed.

"They're new, kitten. I promise." The idea of my ice queen ex-wife using sex toys was comical, but I didn't say that out loud.

Meredith didn't matter. Nothing mattered. Only Jo did.

She nodded, a broad smile painting her lips as she adjusted the pillow behind her head. "Okay."

Her thighs were warm and pliant under my hands as I spread them apart. Her pinkened pussy peeked out at me. Obediently, she held the spread position as I stepped back and stripped out of my suit.

The first time I demanded Jo trust me during sex, she had fought me nearly every step of the way. Now, she was submitting to me, willingly giving me her body, knowing that I would give her nothing but pleasure. The peace that glowed from her was night and day compared to the sheer fear that had once been there.

I started at the foot of the bed, kissing up her body as I crawled to her. I started with the top of her feet, then kissed the delicate curve of her ankle. I kissed her calves, then the back of her knee. I kissed up the side of one thigh, then scraped my stubbled jaw up the other. As I moved toward her center, I reached into the box and felt around for the smooth bullet vibrator I had picked out just for her.

A soft hum filled the room. I let Jo adjust to the sound for a second before grazing the tip of the vibrator over her peaked nipple.

She whimpered, drawing her knees up as though she was seeking out the sensation.

I moved to the opposite breast and circled her nipple.

"Vaughan," she whispered on a heady breath. "Oh—"

Her attempt at speech was cut off with the first slow slide of my tongue through her center. I circled her clit then drew it between my teeth. Jo thrashed in the sheets, her fingers aimlessly grappling at my hair for purchase.

I loved the tug of her hands tangling in my scalp. I sucked on her clit while I parted her entrance and slid my fingers up and down, spreading her glistening wetness around.

"I—I'm—"

"Come for me," I growled. "Don't hold back."

I barely got my mouth back on her before she was quivering on the bed. I didn't wait for her orgasm to subside. I slipped the little vibrator into her pussy and held it against her inner muscles with two fingers. I kissed her clit before easing up onto my forearms, sliding my soaked fingers out of her cunt.

"How does that feel, kitten?"

Jo whimpered, biting her lip as she fisted the sheets.

"Not deep enough?" I slid my finger back inside her and methodically stroked her until I felt the rough patch of nerves. I moved the vibrator inside of her and pressed it against her G-spot.

Jo went rigid as profanity after profanity floated from her lips. I eased up and kissed the corner of her mouth. "Careful, kitten. Don't let that fall out."

She whimpered when I pulled away, a pitiful sound that

nearly broke my heart. But she didn't know what I had in store.

"Hands and knees, beautiful."

When she didn't immediately turn over, I plucked her nipple, rolling it between my fingers.

She gasped. "I— I can't. N-not with it in me."

"I didn't ask for your opinion, darling." I nipped at her earlobe. "I told you to get on your hands and knees."

35

JOELLE

My arms wouldn't work. I tried to get up, but between the orgasm and the vibrator cozied up to my G-spot, I was paralyzed with pleasure.

Every nerve in my body was on a hair-trigger. I was almost afraid that if I did manage to get to my hands and knees, I'd collapse again with another painfully hard finish.

"You can do it, kitten. Trust me. I won't push you past your limit, but we are going to meet it." Vaughan's gentle yet firm tone warmed me from the inside out.

Slowly, I tipped to my side and braced against the mattress before arching up onto my hands. The vibrator began to slip as my body tilted down. I clenched hard, then keened at the sensation boiling inside of me.

"There you go, Tiger." Vaughan's hand was warm against my bare back. "Arch this for me. Knees apart."

"But the—the vibrator," I said through heady pants. "It'll—"

"Then you'd better keep that cunt nice and tight and hold it in."

Shivers skated down my spine.

I heard him rustling around in Pandora's slutty box again. When he had pulled it out from under his bed, my heart raced. I had a few basic toys, but Vaughan's collection seemed rather curated.

"I thought you said you didn't have all that," I choked out as I tried to focus on my breathing and not the impending orgasm. I didn't want to come before he said so.

I... I wanted him to lead me. To guide me. To dominate me.

His chuckle was low, and I wished I could see his face. I didn't dare touch the mask, though. "You asked if I had a red room. Not if I had toys." I felt his touch on the small of my back. "This is going to feel cool. Just breathe."

I flinched when something icy and slick pressed between my butt cheeks. A rivulet of—what I assumed was lube—ran down my crack.

"Tell me," he said. "Have you ever taken someone back here?"

He worked the bulbous tip of a plug against my asshole, and I gasped. "Yes."

Vaughan never stopped massaging the puckered muscle with the silicone toy. "Did you enjoy it?" He pushed the tip in, a rubber band snap of pain ricocheting through me before melting into inconceivable pleasure.

A desperate whine broke free from my chest as I felt my body being stretched around the largest part of the toy. The vibrator shifted in my pussy, finding my G-spot again. My arms were like jelly. I couldn't last much longer.

"I was... so... drunk," I gasped. "It fucking *sucked*." I hissed as my asshole closed around the tapered side, sealing tight against the flared base.

Vaughan let out a primal groan. "I wish you could see yourself, tiger. You look..." His voice trailed off. "Radiant."

He kissed down my spine, and I cherished the warmth of his body blanketing mine. He smoothed his hand over my rear, then pulled back.

Without warning, Vaughan spanked me *hard*. "You'll look even more radiant when I'm balls deep in your ass, but we'll save that for another day." He reached between my legs and spanked my pussy. I cried out at the pinpricks of heat crackling across my tender skin. "I'll get you ready, kitten. So ready that one day you'll be begging for me to take you there."

"I need to come," I whimpered as he tugged on the end of the plug, jostling the bulb inside of me. Vibrations from the bullet in my pussy ricocheted through the plug in my ass, heightening every sensation.

"Then come," he said simply. "Don't stop it. If you need to come, then come."

I couldn't have held it back if I tried. My cunt clamped down on the bullet and wrung an orgasm out of me. With every flutter and contraction of my inner walls, the toy in my ass jolted inside the tight channel.

"Fucking stunning," he groaned as he watched me tremble.

I tried my best to stay on my hands and knees when all I wanted was to collapse into the mattress.

But the vibrator was still on. My body hadn't fully recovered from the orgasm, and here I was, careening toward a third.

Tears leaked from my eyes at the array of overwhelming emotions. I couldn't process it all. I didn't know where to start.

"Vaughan," I whimpered, pleading for some kind of final relief. I didn't know how much more I could take.

"You're doing so well, Tiger." His fingers slid into my cunt. The fit was tightened by the plug pressing against my walls. He crooked his finger and pulled the vibrator out of my pussy, turning it off. "Don't move. I'm just grabbing a condom."

"No—"

Vaughan froze. "Jo?"

I didn't even flinch. I held the position obediently, doing my best to prove to him that I was all in. "I'm on birth control. And I've never gone without."

His tone was kind and soft. "Are you sure?"

"Please," I begged. "Please fuck me. Just like this."

"Okay. I won't come inside of you. You've already given me mine."

"I wouldn't care if you did." Tears leaked from my eyes and soaked the blindfold. "Please, Vaughan. I want—I *need* to feel you."

He held my hips, guiding his heavy erection into my pussy with slow, methodical strokes. The plug throbbed as he pushed inside of me. The fit was excruciatingly tight.

Vaughan muttered expletives under his breath as he settled inside of me. "Jesus Christ."

Even though I was blindfolded, I closed my eyes, not waiting to miss a second. He pulled out at a snail's pace. Then, without warning, he slammed inside of me.

I tipped forward, screaming into the pillow as he thrust in me again. Vaughan let out a roar as he pumped in and out, the sound of sweat-soaked skin sticking to each other with each thrust. His hand left my hip and grabbed the vibrator. He held it to my clit, slowing his thrusts to a steady rhythm.

Ecstasy pooled like a dam on the verge of collapse. My body seized, and I shattered.

———

"How do you feel?" Vaughan murmured in my ear as he spooned me beneath the sheets. His hands never stopped roaming my body, aimlessly checking me over for any discomfort.

This was my favorite part of sex with Vaughan.

The foreplay was immaculate. The act was breathtaking. The thrill was unmatched. But his care afterward? It was *safe*.

I wiggled back into him, seeking more of his heat around my back as the aftershocks of the last orgasm wore off. "So good." I closed my eyes again as his hand slid down my rump, fingers delving between my cheeks.

"Bring your knee up to your chest." His tone was firm and patient.

My whimper was pathetic. "I can't go again."

He dotted the back of my head with a kiss. "Knee up."

My thigh trembled as I shifted. Vaughan slid his hand down my ass and delved between my cheeks. His fingers closed around the base of the plug and tugged.

I let out a high-pitch whine into the pillow as my muscles clenched and throbbed.

"Bear down, kitten." As Vaughan worked the velvety silicone out of me, he brushed my hair away from my face and murmured sweet nothings in my ear. I curled into him, feeling completely and utterly sated.

He fed me. Drew me a bath. Laid with me in the most luxurious jetted tub after washing my hair for me. He toweled me off and carried me to bed.

When we awoke, everything would be different. We'd be going back to Texas, but Vaughan wouldn't be staying. He'd be wrapping everything up, then coming back here. *Alone.*

Beneath the covers, Vaughan's hand found mine, squeezing three times. I returned the gesture, all while wondering if he knew what it meant to me.

————

THE FLIGHT back to Maren might as well have been silent. Sure, we made small talk, but it was nothing of substance. Vaughan was pulling back. Quiet and introspective.

I knew what he was thinking. He was probably trying to figure out how to let me down easy. He had always compared me to a bomb.

Now, he was just trying to figure out how to back away slowly without setting me off. I was sure of it.

On top of that, the leads he had been chasing at the fundraiser for investments into the farm turned out to be dead ends. We were going home empty handed.

The deep-dish pizza from Lou Malnati's that Vaughan insisted we bring along for lunch was long gone, as was the cup of coffee I had downed at our pit stop in Missouri.

More like misery.

The sun was low and blazing, painting the sky in swatches of orange and pink. The nose of my 150 lowered as I descended over the farm.

Bristol must have heard the plane coming in over the big house because an ant of a figure ran down the porch steps and waved both arms straight at the sky. I tipped the yolk, rocking my wings to wave back at her.

Vaughan cracked a soft smile. "Glad to be home?"

I let out a weighty sigh. "Yeah, I guess."

Chicago was fun, but the farm had always been my safe place. I couldn't imagine leaving it for long.

Instead of heading for the runway, I did another low loop toward the east field. "This is what I didn't want to miss."

Fields of gold.

Rows of milo that were ready to be harvested were lit up by the setting sun. The plants glimmered like God himself let a drop of heaven fall on Maren, Texas.

"Wow." Vaughan breathed out. "I—I've seen 'em from the ground but this is..."

"There's nothing like it."

I circled low over the fields before touching down on the runway. Vaughan's *Fuck You, Jo* billboard greeted me.

He took our bags to the cabin while I towed the plane into the hangar and prepped the Ag Cat for my early flights in the morning.

I flushed out the hopper to remove any residual chemicals, then set the hose to fill it with water. I'd mix in the pesticide tomorrow before takeoff.

While the hose steadily pumped two hundred and fifty gallons of water into the hopper of the plane, I ran through my flight plan. I'd be heading south to a farm that had quite the weevil problem.

Vaughan popped his head into the hangar. "You just about done in here?"

I looked up from the stack of FAA forms that needed to be addressed. "Yeah. I'll just be a minute."

He poked around the hangar while I finished my paperwork. "What's this?" he asked, pointing to the WASP certificate that hung on the wall.

I glanced up, then back down to the line I was signing. "Wildfire Aerial Suppression Program certification. It's

something I do with the Association of Agricultural Aviators. I'm trained to fly over wildfires and dump water to help
put them out."

"You shouldn't do that." Not that I expected rousing
applause, but I sure as hell didn't expect him to say that.

"And why not?" I clipped with a sarcastic huff. I practically stabbed the form with my pen as I dated it beside my
signature.

"Because it's dangerous."

I rolled my eyes. "Obviously. That's why I stay up-to-date
with the training and don't do vigilante shit."

Vaughan turned from the wall and crossed his arms. "I
don't want you doing those flights."

"Well, then it's a good thing it's not up to you," I snapped
as I closed the folder and set it aside.

He reared back. "What's that supposed to mean?"

"It means that it's a good thing I don't take orders from
you." When the hopper was at capacity, I cut the spigot and
pulled the hose out. "You don't get to tell me how to live my
life and I don't get to tell you how to live yours. Don't try to
change me. It will not end well for you."

He reached up and braced his hands on the wing. Anger
radiated from every millimeter of his posture. "Joelle—"

I whirled on him. "You're leaving." Ice coated each word.
"I don't take orders from anyone, but especially not
cowards."

"A coward?" Vaughan spat. "You think I'm a *coward*?"

"Yeah. I do. Only a coward would go back to Chicago
because he's too afraid to admit that he's fucking *miserable*
there. Do you think I'm blind? I saw you at that dinner. You
were there because it's your job. Not because you enjoyed
it."

"And right now that job is the only thing keeping this

farm afloat. Enjoy your pipe dream, darling. Because the only way you get to stay here is if I leave."

The comment felt like he had slapped me across the cheek.

His rumbling voice was low and direct, shaking the marrow in my bones. "Do not take those flights. I don't want to have to worry about you risking your life doing that, too."

"So, I don't get to tell you that I want you to stay, but you get to tell me to? That's not how this works."

So help me, if I started crying right now, I was going to murder someone. And it would probably be Vaughan.

Fifteen years of no tears, and suddenly the man had me spewing like a fountain at the drop of a hat.

"Jo—"

I was already walking out of the hangar. "Have a nice life, Vaughan." I paused and looked over my shoulder. "I hope you find what you're looking for. But trying to keep me on the ground because you're too afraid to fly isn't where you're going to find it."

It was just like it had been a few months ago. The reset button had been pushed.

I didn't belong to anyone. No family. No ties. Just me, myself, and I.

At the end of the day, I was the only person I could trust.

36

VAUGHAN

I hadn't slept in the big house for weeks. Now here I was, staring at the ceiling of my childhood bedroom while the woman who had turned my life upside-down was sleeping alone in her cabin.

I detested it.

I had stayed up for hours, staring at my laptop as I tried to get my head right to step back from the farm, pack up, and go back to Chicago. Probably for good.

In the deepest parts of my heart, I knew I wanted to visit more. I wanted to hang out with Cash and Ryman. I didn't want to miss any more of Bristol's life. I wanted to be there for my dad and Ms. Faith as they aged. But did I really have a place here?

I was just the fixer. I had done the best I could. I drummed up a little interest at the charity dinner at the Drake, but with Edward Ellington snipping every line I threw out, I didn't have much faith that anything would come of it.

Edward Ellington's smug face as he and his audacity sat across from Jo and I at dinner was burned in my memory.

There was something especially disgusting about people who preyed on the misfortune of others.

The warring thoughts about the farm, my career, and Jo kept me from drifting off to sleep. Eventually, I said "fuck it," tugged on an undershirt, and threw on a pair of jeans.

I crept down the stairs on silent feet and found my work boots by the front door.

Not the pair I had borrowed when I first got here.

My boots. I'd gotten them on a trip into town and broke them in during the many nights I'd spent walking the fields. I hadn't worn boots in nearly eighteen years. Now I had a pair that I was disappointed wouldn't fit into my daily life back in Chicago.

The earth was soft beneath my tread as I passed Ms. Faith's garden shed and headed for the field closest to Jo's cabin. Maybe if her lights were on, we could talk.

But talk about what? What a shitty situation this was? How it wasn't supposed to be like this? I was supposed to come in, save the day, and go back to life as usual. Instead, I fell for the girl, failed the farm, and didn't want to see the inside of my apartment ever again.

What kind of twisted fairy tale was this?

Even if I wanted to leave my job at the firm, if I couldn't keep this place from going under, there would be nothing for me here.

And Jo? She'd never be happy somewhere like Chicago. This was her home in every sense of the word.

"Goddammit," I yelled at the sky. This was some seriously fucked up shit.

I had been in love before. I wasn't naïve enough to deny knowing exactly how I felt about Jo.

Maybe that's why I lashed out at her back at the hangar. The thought of her doing something so reckless like those fire-fighting flights and me not being able to fix it...

I couldn't handle it.

I made my way down the dirt path that edged Jo's cabin, hoping to at least steal a peek at her silhouette. If she was up, I'd knock on the door and apologize. Part of me hoped she was sleeping like shit, too.

But the lights were off. I guess it was a good thing since she was working early in the morning. With one lingering look at the cabin, I turned and made my way back to the house.

Ms. Faith was sitting on the porch when I approached. A patchwork quilt was spread over her lap as she hunkered down in a rocking chair in her green and gold Baylor sweatshirt.

"Couldn't sleep?" she asked.

I stuffed my hands in my pockets and shrugged. The cloud of melancholy seeped into my bones as I plodded up the stairs.

She tipped her head to the empty rocking chair beside her. "Wanna sit a spell?"

I hesitated, but took her up on the offer and plopped down. It sure beat tossing and turning in bed.

She didn't wait for me to speak. "I'll take a gander and say that this is about JoJo, since you're back up in your room and not with her?"

I scrubbed my palms down my face, stretching my legs as far as they would go. The long day of travel had left me exhausted, which made the insomnia even more infuriating.

"Might've said some things I probably shouldn't have," I admitted.

"Ah." She nodded knowingly. "We all have a tendency to

do that. Usually it's rooted in love. But often it's fear masquerading as love."

I cocked an eyebrow. "Are you psychic?"

She chortled. "No, dear. I've just been around a time or two." Instead of pressing on, she changed the subject. "How was your trip?"

"Fine, I guess. I showed her the city. Took care of some business. May have found a little more money to put into this place." Even if my plan at the charity dinner worked, there were so many strings attached to that money it made me sick. I hated the idea of bringing in investors.

But if that's what it took, I didn't have much of a choice.

"Speaking of farm business, there's a business card sittin' in the office for you. Some rancher fella' you met a few weeks ago was in town and dropped by yesterday wanting to talk to you."

"Did you get his name?"

"Christian Griffith."

"Yeah, I ran into him when Jo and I went out to dinner at the restaurant they have on their property. I remember him saying something about a big calving season coming up. Probably looking to cut a deal on feed if they up their order."

Ms. Faith nodded. "Gotta keep the mommas fed so that they can feed their babies."

"I'll give him a call in the morning."

"And what about Jo?" she prodded. "Will you talk to her in the morning or is this the end for you two?" She wasn't holding any punches this time.

"Can it really be the end if there was never a beginning?" I hunched forward and rested my elbows on my knees. "It's not like we were ever seriously pursuing something."

"Oh, you were pursuing something alright," she muttered

with a dry laugh. "You were pursuing a deep sleep in a shallow grave. I was certain that if y'all didn't work out your differences that I'd wake up to a whole lotta crime scene tape one morning." She patted me on the knee. "I'm just glad that didn't happen. Lord knows your daddy can't handle much more stress. Not with his back and the finances." There was a pregnant pause before she added, "Between you and me, he needs to hand it over. Running this place..." She looked out over the expanse of blackness in front of us. "At his age, it's too much for him. I'm afraid the business side of things is gonna give him a heart attack. I'm hoping that some of that stress will go away when he can get back up on a tractor. That's always where he's been happiest."

"Ryman should take over," I said flatly. "He loves the land. Knows what it needs to make it through the season."

"Ryman said no," Ms. Faith stated gently. "He's too much like your father. Loves the land, hates the business. He'd rather have dirt under his fingernails than sit in an office crunching numbers and writing checks."

"I'll find someone to take it off his plate," I said. *Just as soon as we weren't on the verge of losing everything.*

Ms. Faith reached over and wrapped her hand around mine. She squeezed three times just like she had done since I was a kid—our silent way of saying "I love you" when I was too grief-stricken and confused to utter the words.

I'd started squeezing Joelle's hand the same way without even realizing it.

"Well, sweetheart," Ms. Faith said, and slapped her hands on the arm rests. "I'm not as young as I once was, and I need some sleep." She rose to her feet and draped the quilt over the crook of her arm. "You want me to put on a pot of coffee for you?"

I shook my head. "Nah. I guess I'm gonna try to turn in, too."

"Just holler if you need something." She offered a warm smile and started to say something else, but lights flashed inside and startled both of us.

Ms. Faith squinted, raising her hand to shield her eyes. "What in tarnation—"

I looked at the time on my phone. It was just after two in the morning.

Footsteps thundered down the stairs as Cash and Ryman nearly tumbled over each other. They were sprinting through the great room, then the kitchen as they pulled on clothes.

Ryman had his phone pressed to his ear, talking loudly to someone on the other end.

"What's going on?" I barked.

Ms. Faith looked terrified.

So did Cash.

"Fleming's south field is burning," Cash said. He jumped into his boots and grabbed a set of keys.

What the fuck? The Fleming's farm was north of ours, which meant that if their south field was burning, it was close to ours. Harvest for both farms began tomorrow.

That was money burning.

"Have them cut the irrigation system on," I said. "Turn on ours, too."

Ryman pitched a set of keys at me as he pocketed his phone. "They tried," he said. "Someone tampered with the line."

My stomach sank and my heart pounded. *Holy shit.* I looked out over the horizon where the faint glow of orange began to paint the night sky.

Cash looked at his phone. "Carlos is on his way. He's calling the other guys."

At least help was coming.

"Maybe put that coffee on after all," I said to Ms. Faith. I was already in my boots.

Cash, Ryman, and I sprinted off the porch stairs, running for the trucks.

I jumped into the F-150 I hadn't driven since Jo had Willard's release my car into my custody. We peeled away from the house. I followed Ryman's tail lights until we screeched to a halt outside one of the barns.

Everyone jumped out and sprinted inside with Ryman. We raided the place for anything that could be used to dig a fire line.

"Cash, loaded up the trencher," Ryman called as he threw a haul of shovels into the bed of his truck.

I hoisted a hose over my shoulder and grabbed some electrical tape. It wasn't a perfect fix, but if someone cut the irrigation line, maybe we could get it working enough to keep the plants damp.

If we lost the crop, the farm would go under. Simple as that.

Like us, the Fleming farm had been struggling this season. They had also told Vulkon where they could shove their offer to turn fertile farmland into a quarry.

The timing was all too convenient.

But I couldn't focus on that now. As we finished loading up the trucks, Ryman tossed me a walkie-talkie. I clipped it to my belt, jumped behind the wheel, and left the big house behind me in a cloud of dust.

In my rearview mirror, the faint glow of light inside Jo's cabin flickered on.

ORANGE HAZE RADIATED ALL AROUND. The sizzling crack and pop of burning grain sorghum echoed in my ears. Thick smoke hung in the air and scorched my lungs.

I lifted my sweat-soaked shirt and used the neckline to cover my nose and mouth. With all the force I could muster, I slammed my shovel into the ground. The metal bit into the earth, and I stomped on edge to press it as deep into the dirt as it would go. For a fire line to be effective, all the vegetation needed to be gone.

By a stroke of sheer luck, the fire hadn't touched too much of our land or our crops. We were on Fleming's land, helping them cut a line down the side of the south field to keep the fire from spreading any further.

Cash worked twenty feet behind me, helping dig the perimeter.

Ryman had just turned a corner with the trencher when the radios crackled with static.

Cash stilled his shovel and barked. "You need something, Ry?"

The noisy trencher stalled as Ryman let off and grabbed his radio. "I'm good. What's up?"

"Sounded like you clicked in."

"Wasn't me."

Cash and I looked at each other.

The radio crackled again. "Y'all are looking a little thirsty down there," Jo said.

No. I looked up, but couldn't see her. I grabbed the radio and smashed the button on the side. "Cut the fucking trencher off."

Ryman scrambled to turn it off and pulled it out of the

way. Through the whoosh of flames, I heard it—the buzzing of the Ag Cat propellers.

"*Who the fuck called her?*" I bellowed as I stomped my shovel into the ground. We couldn't stop now. Fear shot through my veins like an accelerant, and anger set it ablaze.

Cash raised his hands. "Not me."

"Probably Fleming," Ryman said as he jogged over and grabbed a shovel to help us connect the fire line. "She takes care of his fields, too."

Visions of her prepping the tank for her morning flight, flushing it out and filling it with water, floated through my mind.

"She's gonna water bomb the field," I said.

"Thank fuck," Cash said, peeling his shirt off and wiping his brow. "She can get here faster than the one measly firetruck Maren has."

"Look up, dumbass!" I shouted, pointing at the clouds of gray smoke that billowed around us. Heat began to singe my back. "Can you see her?"

Cash's eyes glowed, reflecting the sparks that danced in the air. "Shit."

The thrum of the propellers grew closer.

Ryman held his radio up to his mouth. "Jo, can you hear me?"

Static burst through the line, followed by a faint, "*Affirmative.*"

"The smoke's too thick. Keep your altitude high and turn around," Ryman said.

Static.

Cash spoke into his walkie-talkie. "Jo, pull up and turn around."

The rumble grew louder, but I couldn't see the flashing lights on the tip of the wings. The smoke was too thick. The south field was surrounded by power lines and trees on two sides. If Jo couldn't see them...

"No—"

A heavy wind whipped up new flames.

I winced. The three of us jumped back as a flare kicked up in front of us. The gust had temporarily cleared some of the smoke. I could see her now, coming in fast and low.

She was surrounded by smoke and flames like a phoenix.

Ryman stood beside me, holding his breath. Cash stabbed his spade in the soil and leaned on it.

Jo's plane was made to spray, not dump. But I remembered her telling me that she *could* dump. It was an emergency feature that allowed her to lose her payload if she thought she was going to crash. Apparently, dying on impact was preferable to dying in a chemical blaze.

A white wall of water fell from the sky, and I scanned the vicinity for the faint outline of the plane, lit up by the glow of the fire.

Voices shouted from the other side of the field as Fleming's guys hauled ass out of the way.

The plane shuddered at the sudden loss of weight, rocketing up. Jo hurtled toward the edge of the field, fighting gravity to keep it steady.

"Pull up," I whispered.

Cash swore under his breath, his eyes wide as he saw her nearing the row of power lines.

She was too low.

"Pull up!" he shouted.

"Fuck!" Ryman said, throwing his shovel to the ground and barking into his radio. "Pull up, Jo!"

She disappeared into a cloud of smoke.

"*Pull up, goddammit!*" I bellowed at the sky.

A light flashed from the corner of the biplane's left wing. She was gaining a little altitude, but still careening toward the power lines as she tried to level out from the water dump.

The sky grew darker as most of the flames were snuffed out. Only glowing embers remained, scattered across the field.

"Come on, Tiger," I whispered, bracing my hands on my knees. My eyes stung from the acrid air. "*Come on!*" I roared. The tears running down my cheeks could have been sweat. I didn't know. It was all too much.

Everything went silent.

Then I heard it … the sound changed direction. The nose of the biplane broke through a cloud of smoke. It rolled to the left to clear the trees and power lines with inches to spare.

"Sweet Jesus," Ryman said on an exhale and dropped to the ground on his knees.

A blast of air whipped my hair off my neck as Jo tore across the sky overhead. She turned toward the hangar, and my knees went weak.

37

JOELLE

"H'lo?" I grunted into my phone and rubbed my eyes as I stared, bleary-eyed, trying to make sense of what time it was.

I had just fallen asleep after crying for what felt like ages. I had one of those annoying headaches that apparently happened after you had an emotional purge.

"JoJo, it's Norman Fleming," the voice said, obscured by the rumble of an ATV engine in the background.

What the hell was he doing at this time of night? Before I could figure out what he was trying to tell me, a set of headlights flashed through the cabin windows.

Then another set.

And another.

Engines roared. It sounded like they were headed toward the north pasture.

A few moments later, the big house lit up like a Christmas tree.

I flung the covers back and jumped to my feet. "Norm, what's going on?"

"South field's on fire."

"I'm on my way."

"JoJo, if you can't—"

I trapped the phone against my ear with my shoulder and searched for a pair of shorts on the floor. "I've already got a hopper full of water and she's fueled up. I'll be in the air in a jiff."

"You sure, kid? There's an awful lot of smoke."

"The leaves are still green. They're gonna make a lot of smoke." I pulled on my shorts and jumped into a pair of boots, then hauled ass out of the cabin.

My trunk clanked and sputtered as I nailed every single pothole on the way to the hangar. "Where do you want me to dump it?"

"Middle of the field. Me and the fellas are heading to try to contain it. I called the fire department, but they're hung up with a tractor trailer that tipped over on Highway 79."

"I'm at the hangar. See you in a bit."

I ran through the pre-flight checks as quickly as I could before scrambling into the cockpit and taxiing out to the runway. I jammed on my headset and tried to click in with Ryman and Cash's radios. I assumed that's who had raced away from the big house like they were Dale Earnhardt and Richard Petty.

No response. They were probably coordinating with Fleming's guys to get a fire line started.

Smoke floated through the night air and wrapped around me like tendrils from hell.

I opened my baby up and rolled down the runway. I was barely off the ground when I spotted the glow of the hellish flames. I hit my ceiling, flying as high as I could over the south field to get an idea of what was going on down there.

Fleming wasn't lying—the smoke was thick. My plane had flood lights fixed to its belly and the spraying equipment, but they were useless in these conditions. The beams of light bounced off smoke particles and bits of charred ash, illuminating everything around me except the ground.

I reached for the switch and cut them off as I rolled and did another high altitude loop, surveying the field. The fire light gave me a better look at the ground as flames licked up from the corners of the field into the center. It looked like they had hoses out, trying to snuff the flames out from the edges.

I clicked into the radio again. "Y'all are looking a little thirsty down there."

Static, then a click. "Jo? Can you hear me?"

If I had to guess, it was Ryman.

"Affirmative," I responded.

I rolled again, turning so I could line up to come in fast and low. Next to the Thompsons, I treated Norman Fleming's fields more than any other client. Probably because of the proximity, but I liked to think that he had a soft spot for me.

With the direction of the flames, I needed to come in from the east. There was a dense tree line twined with power lines fifty feet from the edge of the field. It was one of the harder pieces of property to treat, and it made my ass pucker every fucking time.

It was also one of the fields I had trained on when I was getting my hours in to become an ag pilot.

The radio clicked like the boys were trying to say something, but all I heard was static. My system was old, and the smoke could have been fucking with it.

I inhaled a slow breath as I flew east and circled to the

right. I held that breath for four seconds as I tilted the wing down and rolled. I let the breath out as I lined up and dove toward the ground.

I kept one eye on the altimeter, staying a comfortable ten feet over the ground. I didn't want to decapitate anyone, after all.

Pull.

It was like aviator skeet shooting. As soon as I was in position, I jammed my thumb on the switch and dumped the payload of water.

Ash exploded into the sky like lava when it spills into the ocean. The cockpit windows clouded with gray soot, but I couldn't flip on the wipers.

The nose of the plane pitched up at the immediate loss of weight, but I held tight, fighting gravity to keep from hitting a coffin corner and stalling. The radio kept clicking, but I couldn't focus on that. The altimeter alarm blared as I dropped another two feet. The red line didn't even matter at this point.

It would really piss Vaughan off if I fell out of the sky when he specifically told me not to.

As soon as the rising pressure leveled out, I pulled up hard.

It felt like a cinder block slammed into my chest as I let out sharp, staccato breaths, hick maneuvering through the weight of the G-forces pressing down on me.

I was flying blind. The spatial disorientation struck more fear in me than I had ever felt.

It was the same sensation as divers who lose their sense of direction and can't tell if they're swimming up or down.

Breathe in. Four seconds. Breathe out. Four seconds.

I flipped the windshield wipers, then looked away from the windows.

Ten feet.

Fifteen feet.

The altimeter steadily climbed.

Twenty feet.

Twenty-five feet.

Thirty feet.

I jerked the yolk, rolling to the left as I climbed another ten feet to clear the power lines.

The cockpit windows were framed by a thick layer of ash and soot. I looked up, seeing the bright Texas stars beginning to peek through the smoke.

Then, clear night sky.

I broke free of the haze and made a wide turn around the gray billows.

"Holy shit," I swore. "*Holy motherfucking shit!*"

A manic laugh exploded out of me as I turned and did a low pass over the border between the Thompson's north field and the Fleming's south field, heading back to the hangar. Only then did I realize what I had put on when I jumped out of bed wasn't actually a pair of shorts. I had thrown on Vaughan's boxers.

Oh well. It wasn't like I had to go into an office.

I touched down and immediately got to work hosing ash off of the plane and checking over every nook and cranny before refilling the hopper. Might as well get a head start on the day since I was already up. I mixed up a nice little cocktail for the weevils, and took off for my morning flight.

The radio clicked halfway through my second pass. In my heart of hearts, I really wanted it to be Vaughan.

Instead, Ryman's voice came on the line. "You in the air, crazy girl?"

I adjusted the microphone in front of my mouth as I turned for another pass. "Kamikaze One to Ground. Over."

He chuckled. "You're fucking insane, JoJo."

I turned, dropping low to spray the last line of plants. "How's it looking out there?"

"Fleming lost most of the south field, but we kept it contained, thanks to you."

"Shit," I muttered.

"You gonna be up there for a while today?"

I turned and headed back to the hangar. "You know, I was, but I'm thinking I should probably get some sleep. Nodding off at the yolk is kind of bad for business."

He chuckled. "Momma wants everyone at the big house for a late breakfast."

My throat tightened. I wasn't ready to see Vaughan—not in front of everyone. But I couldn't say no to Ms. Faith.

"See you on the ground," I said.

I finished spraying, then did a flyover of the south field to assess the damage. When the smoke cleared completely, I'd come out and take some aerial photos to help Fleming file a claim on his crop insurance. The payout would take forever to process. Hopefully, he could hold on until then.

Harvest was supposed to begin today.

A lone figure stood at the end of the runway, catty cornered to the billboard that he had erected in my honor.

I didn't know if he was waiting to fight with me, fuck me, or fuck with me. But in all honesty? I wasn't in the mood for any of it.

I dropped down onto the runway and skidded past him before slowing up and heading into the hangar. I had just hopped into my red rubber boots to begin the decontamination process when Vaughan's silhouette appeared in the gaping doors.

His face was streaked in hues of gray and brown from soil and soot. His white undershirt was sweat-soaked into a dingy beige. His jeans were covered in ash and his boots were caked in dirt.

Vaughan in a suit was pure sin.

Vaughan completely naked was my obsession.

Vaughan looking absolutely feral like he couldn't decide whether he was going to devour me or murder me. That may have been my favorite look of all.

Filthy thoughts raced through my mind, but all of it was tamped down by the memory of the last time we stood in this hangar; just twelve hours ago when he told me to stay on the ground.

How dare he think he had any say over what I do when he wasn't staying? He made that very clear when he didn't even argue.

Of all the fighting we had done, that was the one fight I didn't want to walk away from.

But I had, and so did he.

"I told you not to do that," he said, still standing in the space left by the rolled-back hangar door.

I turned my back to him as I began to flush out the hopper and added an agent to neutralize the lingering chemicals. I let my respirator hang around my neck as I said, "I think that says more about you than me." I glanced over my shoulder. "A tiger can't change its stripes." I looked back down at the hose.

Vaughan's warm hands slid across my bare waist. "Have I ever told you how fucking thankful I am that you're a wildcat?"

I turned around, letting go of the hose as he pulled me into his chest.

His mouth pressed against the crown of my head. "You're tenacious and fucking fearless. You scare the shit out of me, and yet I can't stop being drawn to you. I'm completely spellbound by everything that you are."

He clung to me like a life raft. One hand held me captive against his body. The other tangled in my rat's nest of hair, cradling my head.

"I wish I was like you," he whispered.

"But you hate me," I said.

Vaughan pulled back long enough to look me in the eye. "Kitten, I don't think I ever hated you. I think I was scared of you." He pressed his lips to my forehead. "You're unapologetic. You live life the way you want to. You take risks and live like you're invincible despite knowing how fleeting life can be. And me?" He stammered. "You were right when you called me a coward."

"Vaughan—"

"No, listen to me." He pinched my chin between his thumb and forefinger with a firm grip. "I'm pissed at you. And I think I will be for a long, long time. Standing on the ground and watching you fly over that fire..." He let out a sharp breath. "I can't handle it."

He was saying everything I wanted to hear, but it wouldn't be enough. Not if he was just going to pack up and head back to Chicago.

"Don't do this." I sniffed and tried to wiggle out of his arms. "Don't pull me close just to push me away again. If you're gonna leave, just leave."

"But what if I don't?"

Ice froze my veins. "What?"

He wrapped his arms around me, tucked my head under his chin, and let out a heavy breath. "What if I didn't leave? What then?"

"I—I don't know."

"What if, instead of trying to hold you down, I flew with you?" Vaughan smiled. "Metaphorically, of course."

I rubbed my eyes. Adrenaline and emotion mixed in a heady cocktail that manifested in one massive breakdown. "Please talk to me in simple terms because I'm really fucking tired right now," I said, blubbering as tears leaked out of the corners of my eyes.

"Hey—hey now," he soothed as he cupped my cheeks and wiped away my tears, leaving black smudges across my face from the dirt on his hands. "Why are you crying? I'm trying to tell you I was wrong. You usually like that."

"I don't want you to leave," I confessed.

Those six words terrified me because with them, he could crush me. I finally put myself out there and I had never felt more vulnerable.

"Jo, I left eighteen years ago." He cupped my cheek and drew my lips to his. "And I think I spent every single day biding my time until I was ready to come back." His kiss was soft and tasted just the slightest bit charred. "And I think I found the best reason to stay."

I found his hand, tangling our fingers together as I squeezed it three times. Vaughan immediately repeated the rhythm.

"Jo—"

"It's something Ms. Faith used to do with me," I blurted out, sputtering through streaming tears. "She'd say I love you and squeeze my hand with each word."

"I know."

"I—" I looked up at him. "What?"

Vaughan grinned, sliding his hands into my hair and kissing me deeply. His tongue parted my lips as he tasted me with abandon—morning breath, soot, and all. "I know because she taught me the same thing, too."

His toes bumped mine as he walked me backward. My

spine hit the plane's fuselage as his hand slid up my back, cradling my neck to cage my lips against his.

"I love you, Jo," he whispered against my mouth.

Warm rivulets ran down my cheeks as he kissed me again and again.

"I love you, too," I confessed.

Vaughan's lips barely left mine, only parting enough for *I love yous* slipped in between quick pecks and long, languid kisses.

"Are you sure about this?" I asked on a whisper. "Staying?"

"I can't breathe when I'm not with you. I need you more than I can explain, and I want you more than I can fathom."

"What if I'm not enough for you?" I asked, feeling small and meek with him towering over me. My insecurities were showing like cracks in my carefully honed armor. "I'm not wife material. I'm not proper or well mannered. I'm a wreck, and I don't want to wreck you too."

"You got something wrong the last time we were in this hangar," he said. "I don't want to change you. There is nothing you need to change about yourself to make me want you. You are exactly what I crave with every breath I take." Vaughan chuckled, smiling against my lips. "I'm not looking for a gentle breeze, kitten. I want you in all your fury. You're a tornado, and every time I've tried to control you, you end up knocking me on my ass. But you know what?"

"Hm?"

"I like getting up and trying again because I like feeling the full force of everything you are."

"This is..." I shook my head. "This is crazy. We're crazy."

Vaughan kissed me again. "Your crazy is safe with me."

I shook my head, tears streaming down my face as I silently disagreed. "But—"

"Stop it, Jo," he whispered, cradling my jaw in both hands. "Just stop it, okay?" His thumbs brushed away my tears, kissing the path of salt and shine. "Stop wondering what'll happen if it doesn't work. I wonder what it would be like if you just chose happiness."

38

VAUGHAN

We were a damn sight to see.

After finishing the decontamination process, Jo and I rolled up to the big house in exactly what we had been wearing earlier.

Me—in work boots, jeans, and an undershirt—covered in dirt and sweat. Jo strode into the kitchen wearing my boxers, a sports bra, and tall rubber boots.

Ms. Faith nearly dropped a platter of French toast when she spotted us, then jumped again when Cash and Ryan appeared in the doorway, equally filthy.

"Sakes alive," she gasped.

Dad shuffled between the kitchen island and the coffee pot. He froze in his steps when he saw us piled up in the kitchen entrance, looking like we'd been rolling around in a pig pen.

My arm hooked around Jo's shoulders, and she leaned into my side.

The French toast plate clinked against the countertop as Ms. Faith set it down. "Everyone shower. I'll keep the food warm."

Cash was the first to whine. Apparently, nothing had changed since we were kids. "Seriously, Mom? We're just gonna go back out and get dirty again."

Ms. Faith popped her hands on her hips and raised an eyebrow, daring him to take that tone with her again. "You will not sit at my table as filthy as you are."

"It'll take forever for all four of us to shower," Ryman said, a little more amenable.

"Just a quick rinse," she said. "And change your clothes. You smell like an ashtray. Ry, you can use the bathroom in Dad's and my room. Cash will use Bristol's bathroom." Being the only girl, she got the room with its own bathroom while the boys shared the big one. "And Vaughan and JoJo can use the main bath in the hall upstairs."

There was a reason we called it the big house.

Jo stiffened at the mention of the two of us sharing a shower, but I kept a tight hold on her. The little thing was wily, and I wouldn't put her making a run for it past her.

"I need some 'yes, ma'ams' and moving feet," Ms. Faith said. "If y'all aren't back down here in two shakes of a stick, I can't guarantee much food being left. I'm awful hungry this morning."

"Yes, ma'am," Cash and Ryman grumbled in unison as they loped through the kitchen. They both kissed their mom on the cheek, then disappeared into the house.

Ms. Faith raised an eyebrow, a coy smile on her pursed lips. She had assessed the fact that Jo and I were standing side-by-side peaceably, and not in a bloodbath, brawling on the tile floor.

I could tell Jo was a little uneasy with being in the big house. After one of our late-night sexcapades, she confessed that coming over for meals made her uncomfortable. Not because of the food—Ms. Faith was a wizard in the kitchen

—but because it made her feel like a stray pet they some-times let into the house.

Still, she did it to be polite because she never wanted to seem ungrateful.

Nothing could have been further from the truth. In the eyes of my dad and Ms. Faith, Jo was just as much a Thompson as any of us.

"Vaughan, JoJo—get a move on," Ms. Faith said as she draped tea towels over the food to keep it warm. "You know, if Cash and Ry get back here before y'all do, there won't be a lick of food left."

Jo nodded sheepishly. "Yes, ma'am."

I slid my hand into Jo's and laced our fingers together, tugging her with me. I stopped where Ms. Faith stood and kissed her cheek like my brothers had done.

"Thanks, mom," I said.

Jo's body bumped into the back of mine, and she looked stunned.

Ms. Faith's eyebrows shot up and her wide eyes went glassy. She sniffled. "Oh—oh, Vaughan..." She threw her arms wide and smashed me in a hug.

"I'm filthy—"

She swatted my chest and went right back to hugging me. "I don't give a rat's ass. Let me have this."

I couldn't help but laugh.

Finally, she let me go and pulled Jo into a tight embrace. "Thank you for bringing him back to us."

Jo smiled softly and her eyes crinkled at the corners. "I didn't bring him back. I tried to scare him off."

Ms. Faith straightened up and put her hands on Jo's shoulders. "You gave him a good reason to stay."

"I hope so," Jo whispered. Her eyes were watery. "Can I call you 'mom,' too?"

"Well, shit," Ms. Faith said as the waterworks kicked in again. She bobbed her head for a moment, blonde hair swaying back and forth, before hugging Jo again. "Of course you can, sweetheart."

Jo let out a quiet, exasperated laugh. "'Kay."

Ms. Faith grabbed a tea towel and dabbed at her eyes. "Go get cleaned up, now."

My dad had come to stand behind his wife and put his hand on her shoulder. He gave me a curt nod and dabbed at the corner of his eye with his sleeve.

I took Jo's hand and led her upstairs. We grabbed towels from the hall closet then shuffled off to the bathroom.

When the door closed, I dropped the towels on the countertop and fisted the front of Jo's sports bra. "C'mere, Tiger."

She let out a little squeak as I yanked her into a kiss. "Vaughan—"

That was all I allowed her to say. I devoured her mouth —tasting and teasing her until she was putty in my hands. She turned soft and malleable, melting into me as we kissed.

"You're not a good reason, kitten," I whispered against the corner of her mouth. "You're the best reason." I kissed her again. "You're the only reason I would stay."

"We need to hurry," Jo said as she began to push me away. "I don't want them to think that I—"

"That you're what?" I grabbed the floof of bed head piled on top of her scalp and tangled my fingers in her hair. "That you're in here on your knees with my cock between your lips?" I thumbed the soft, pillowy pout that was the prettiest shade of pink.

"I don't feel comfortable fooling around in here," she clipped.

I backed off and cut the shower on. "That's fine, kitten," I said as I shoved my boxers off her hips while she toed off the ridiculous red rubber boots that nearly came up to her knees.

Jo stripped out of her spandex bra and stepped over the lip of the tub while I got undressed. When I joined her under the spray, I couldn't resist turning her, putting her back against my front so I could cup her perky breasts.

"But I need you to get comfortable with the idea of staying here for a little while," I said as I rolled my thumbs over her pert nipples. The that water pooled at our feet was murky brown from the dirt, ash, and soot rinsing off my skin.

Her body went rigid. "Why?"

I stepped back and let the water splash against her head. She relaxed when I started massaging her scalp.

"Because I quite like being in the shower with you," I said, turning her around to face me. "Which means you need an actual shower in the cabin. And that means—" I tipped her chin up "—we're gonna take a wall down and expand it. Put a full bathroom in. Maybe even a tub. Get a full-size fridge in there and a stove. Because here's the thing, kitten—I will make sure that the cabinet is stocked with canned ravioli for the rest of our lives, but *I* cannot live on Chef Boyardee alone."

Slowly, her hands worked up my chest, fingers grazing the dips and ridges on my torso. "You... You wanna move into the cabin with me?"

"For now," I said, pulling a wet strand of hair off her cheek. "But seeing as I own seventy percent of the dirt that it's on, I'd say there's a good chance I might evict you once we build a proper house."

Her eyebrows darted up in surprise. "What?"

I shrugged. "You like the farm. I like you. It just makes sense."

When the water streaming down our bodies turned clear, I grabbed a towel, unfurling it and wrapping it around Jo. I wrapped mine around my hips and grabbed our clothes off the floor. We tiptoed back to my room and I shut the door.

Jo looked around, her eyes wide as she took it in. "This is your room?"

"Yeah," I said as I pawed around the dresser for a fresh pair of boxers and an undershirt that hadn't been charred. "Why?"

She trailed her fingers along the carved wooden headboard. "I stayed in here once. I guess I just figured it was a spare room."

I yanked the shirt over my head. "When was that?"

She sighed, tightening the towel around her chest as she sat on the edge of the bed. "I was sixteen, I think. I had just come to live on the farm. A hurricane hit Houston and we got a few days of really bad rain, heavy winds, tornadoes— the works." Her eyes darted down to the floor. "I was scared. The weather was so bad that no one was working in the fields for days. There were no jobs for me to do, so I just stayed in the cabin." Jo sniffed, dabbing the corner of the towel at her eyes. "I don't know how she knew, but she did."

"Who?" I asked, and took the opportunity to sit down behind her and pull her into my lap.

"Mom," she said softly, as if she was still testing out how it sounded on her tongue.

I held her a little tighter.

She breathed deep and relaxed into me. "I remember the rain being so bad that I couldn't even see the truck she drove over to the cabin. Just the glow of the headlights. She let herself into the cabin and found me huddled up in the corner. I had made myself a little pallet of blankets and pillows because there was a leak in the roof right over the bed and I couldn't move it by myself."

I rested my forehead into the crook of her neck and let out a hushed string of curses. "You were a child," I choked out. "There was no fucking reason for you to be out there alone." A flare of protectiveness flashed inside of me.

What I wouldn't give for a time machine.

"There's something about being hurt over and over again by people who are supposed to love you and care for you that changes how you think," she said. "When I was emancipated, I knew it was going to be hard. I knew I was going to be hungry. I knew I was going to struggle. I knew that if I was going to make it, I couldn't trust anyone but myself." She let out a sharp breath. "You have to understand —I didn't know George and Faith that well. All I knew was that this lady pestered my case worker enough until she passed along a message that they had a place for me to stay. When I didn't immediately jump on it, George tracked me down at the diner I was slinging coffee at and offered me a job. Everything seemed too good to be true, but at least it wasn't a total handout. In my world, people didn't track down homeless teenagers and offer them a bed and a job."

"So you picked the cabin instead of sleeping in the big house?"

"I thought about running away more than once," she admitted. "Not that it would have been considered running away. In the eyes of the state, I was fit to be on my own." Her lip quivered. "But I was scared, Vaughan. And I remember that storm like it was yesterday. She came in and told me that Bristol was begging for a movie night and was hoping I'd come over. She was four or five years old.

Little did I know, Bristol was already asleep and Ms. Faith had already made up this room for me to stay in until the storm was over. So, I stayed in here for two nights." She smoothed her hand over the flannel sheets. "Slept in this bed. And when the storm passed, I went back to the cabin."

"Why didn't you just stay?" I asked. "Ms. Fai—*mom* wanted you here."

"Good things don't happen to people like me. Good people don't want people like me."

She couldn't have been more wrong if she said the sky was magenta and we had unicorns in the barn.

"I want you."

Jo turned and tucked her head into my shoulder. "I want to believe you, but—"

"No '*buts.*' The only question is if you want me."

She nodded without hesitation.

I tipped her chin up and kissed her softly. "How about we stop pretending like we're bad people? That maybe we're just people who do the best we can with the cards we're dealt. How about we stop believing that shitty circumstances make you a shitty person? Because nothing is further from the truth. You're fiercely loyal. You're a hard worker. You fucking brilliant. You have this light inside you that, no matter how hard some have tried, no one has been able to extinguish. Not even me." I kissed her again. "How about we start believing that tomorrow is gonna be a good day and that you're worthy of it."

While I pulled some clean clothes out of the dresser for myself, Jo dressed in a pilfered pair of leggings and a t-shirt from Bristol's closet.

By the time we made our way down to breakfast, Cash and Ryman had already devoured half of it like locusts.

They were on their way out the door to meet up with the rest of the farm hands to begin the first day of harvest.

Jo sat beside me at the table, nibbling on a piece of French toast while I told my dad about running into Edward Ellington in Chicago and my suspicions about the fire in Fleming's south field. Coincidences didn't just happen, especially with the comment he made about holding matches.

I kept my hand on Jo's thigh while we ate. After a few minutes, she slid her hand into mine and laced our fingers together.

"Oh, sweetheart," Ms. Faith began, then pushed away from the table. She hustled into the office and returned a minute later with a business card. "I almost forgot. Here's the number for that Griffith fella."

I nodded, taking the card and slipping it into my pocket. "Thanks. I'll give him a call first thing." I squeezed Jo's hand. "I'll be in the office most of the day. I've got some things to take care of."

"You flying today, JoJo?" my dad asked as he scraped his plate clean, shoveling in the last bite of eggs.

Jo nodded. "Yes, sir. I'm gonna take a cat nap first, then fly two properties that need fertilizer sprayed before they plant winter crops. If the light holds, I'm gonna do some aerial shots for the Flemings. Hopefully, it'll help them get the payout for the crop insurance sooner rather than later."

My dad just shook his head. "Can't believe they lost the south field the day before harvest..."

"Seems convenient to me," I piped up.

"We all know who did it," Jo said, stabbing her eggs. "Vulkon's been pulling that shit ever since they set their sights on the land around here. And before them it was that company pushing GMO seeds. They'd hire people who wanted to make some quick cash to spread the modified seed on farmland that's certified organic and get their organic status revoked. And that's not even the worst of it. They would hire thugs to go intimidate farmers who had bought their seed in seasons past if they caught a whiff that they were planning to switch seeds or crops."

My dad, mom, and I stared at her, open-mouthed. Ms. Faith was the first one to speak. "How do you know all this, sweetie?"

Jo just shrugged. "I've been flying these farms for damn near a decade. You'd be shocked at the things I know."

39

JOELLE

The neon lights of the Silver Spur glowed, painting Vaughan in blue and purple. He slid off his stool and gave me a peck on the lips.

"Hey, you," he said.

I popped up onto my tiptoes and returned the kiss. "Hey. How was your day?"

Vaughan wore his shirt unbuttoned. His tie was loose, and his usual vest-and-suit-jacket getup was nowhere to be found. He had cuffed his sleeves just below his elbows. Seeing him loosen up and raise a bottle of beer to his lips at the end of the day was undeniably sexy.

"JoJo in the house!" Cash said as he rounded the table, carrying an ice bucket of beers.

I stole one and popped the top.

"Dude, I'm fucking starving." Ryman shoved away from the table. "I need food."

"Bullshit," Vaughan and Cash muttered between themselves as they watched their brother weave through the after-work crowd to the bar.

Of course ... because Ezra was back there.

"You got some catching up to do, Tiger," Vaughan said, tapping my beer. "You're late."

I smirked and took a long pull. "I was waiting on a part to get delivered. I was at the hangar until Bristol called and said they had accidentally delivered it to the big house."

"What was it?" Cash asked.

"Some bolts for the landing gear on the Ag Cat," I said. "They're backordered from the manufacturer, but I found a pilot from some little beach town in North Carolina who has a biplane. Different model, same landing gear, so he sold me his spares."

I took a long drink from my beer and wondered if I could telepathically communicate with Ryman to order me something to eat while he was flirting with Ezra.

"I got you," Vaughan said. *Apparently, my telepathic abilities weren't half bad.*

"Chopped brisket, white bread on the side, beans, and creamed corn?"

I smirked. "My hero."

"See?" he said with a chuckle as he slid off his stool. "All that reconnaissance I did on you is paying off."

Cash stayed quiet until Vaughan was out of earshot. "So..."

I leaned forward. "Is this weird?"

"Fuck yes," he said with exasperation, flopping back in his seat. "So fucking weird. Like... I've seen your boobs and now you're dating my brother? Just hooking up? Fuck."

I giggled and finished off my first beer. "Don't think I'm letting you off the hook for bull riding nights. I still need someone to sweep up my haul so I don't have to kneel on the floor and pick up all those bills."

His smile was soft. "You happy?"

"Yeah," I said as my eyes roamed the bar until I spotted

Vaughan and Ryman in a rather intense conversation with Ezra.

"Just making sure," he said. "If you weren't, I'd have to kick his ass."

I had just popped the top on a fresh beer, and choked on the sip. "Trust me. If he fucks up, I'll be doing the ass kicking. But you're welcome to get in line."

"I wouldn't doubt it for a second," he said as we clinked bottles.

"How's harvest going?" I asked.

He sighed. "Had a hard time getting everyone out of the fields today. After what happened to Fleming's field, we're all a little paranoid. Wanna get the crop out of the ground and into the silos as soon as possible. Some of the guys went to help Norm harvest the rest of his property when we called it a day."

"Y'all still got those trail cameras up?"

He nodded. "Just haven't had time to go through the video feed."

"Send it to Don Draper over there and have him go through it," I said as I tipped my head in Vaughan's direction. "I'm sure he'd love to destroy someone else's life now that mine is off the table."

Cash chuckled. "You two are a match made in hell."

"Something like that."

The throngs of people jockeying for a spot at the bar parted as Vaughan and Ryman stormed away from Ezra.

"The fuck?" Cash muttered over the lip of his bottle.

"I need to step out and make a call," Vaughan clipped as he grabbed his phone off the table and disappeared out the door.

My brows furrowed. "What was that about?" I asked when Ryman sat down in a cloud of fury.

"Ezra knows who did it," Ryman said under his breath.

Cash stood up so fast he nearly knocked his stool over. "What? He knows who torched the south field?"

"Keep your voice down," Ryman hissed. "He said one of his barflies came in this morning, flushed with cash, and has been drinking ever since." He cut his eyes to a lump of man in a dull green coat who was passed out in a plate of chili cheese fries. "Ez heard what happened and thought it was suspicious when he came in smelling like a bonfire. So, he kept feeding him drinks until he was liquored up enough to spill everything. Apparently, some guy in a suit caught him leaving this place last night and offered him five grand to douse some plants in gasoline and drop a cigarette."

My blood ran cold.

"Fleming wasn't the target," Ryman said in a hushed tone. "*We* were. He said he came in through the front gate. The suit told him to light up the field that's closest to the big house, but he got disoriented—probably still drunk—and ended up in our north field. Poured gas on the property line and tried to light it up, but the wind changed and lit up Fleming's field instead. With all the plants being ready to harvest, it didn't take much accelerant to get it burning."

I peered around the crowd, searching for Vaughan's dark hair bobbing above the rest. I didn't see him, but I did see Ezra keeping a watchful eye on the snoozing arsonist.

"Apparently, Vaughan has connections in the FBI," Ryman said. "He's calling in a favor."

Cash frowned. "Wouldn't this be a local thing?"

Ryman shrugged. "Vulkon is an international corporation. Something about industrial espionage."

"Vulkon has serious money to throw around. If they're hiring locals to torch fields, it could get a lot worse," I said.

Cash finished his beer. "We need to finish the harvest."

"So that all of our money is conveniently packed in silos?" Ryman raised an eyebrow and shook his head. "I don't know what the answer is." He reached for a beer, shaking the ice off the bottle, then popped the top and took a swig as he peered around the bar. "I'm just paranoid as fuck."

There's no right answer when you don't know what the devil is up to.

Vaughan appeared, sliding onto a stool. "It's being handled."

"What are we supposed to do?" Cash said, edging on unhinged.

Vaughan seated him with a glare. "Nothing. You pretend like nothing's wrong and go about your business."

"Fuck that shit," Ryman said as he stood and popped his knuckles one by one. "I'm gonna go find the motherfucker who hired that piece of shit."

"*Sit. Down.*" Vaughan's tone made me seal my ass to my stool, and he wasn't even talking to me. "It's being handled. What you don't want to do is spook him."

Ryman's jaw flexed as he stared down Vaughan. For a moment, I saw the resemblance. The fire. The allegiance. The resolve. "And if he sets foot on our land?"

Vaughan's slow, deceptively charming smile was smug. "This is Maren. We handle our business our way."

I looked around and spotted Jay and Hank walking in with Norman Fleming, looking like they were planning a battle of their own. Behind the bar, Ezra looked positively murderous. There was an undeniable tension in the air but, stronger than that, was loyalty.

"Hey, Jo." The wire-thin voice of Clint Morgan made the hairs on my neck prickle. He was one of my former back-room hookups.

I turned and gave him an assessing up-and-down glance. "What do you want?" I said flatly.

He scoffed, laughing awkwardly as he took in the felonious looks that Cash and Ryman were shooting him. Vaughan didn't know that I'd hooked up with this chuckle-fuck, but the other boys did.

Clint tipped his head toward the empty mechanical bull. "You gonna put on a show tonight?"

"Not the kind of show you want."

He had the audacity to open his mouth to argue with me, but I cut him off. "Oh for the love—just shut up, Clint. Aren't you lactose intolerant? Don't act like you can handle me when milk is too spicy for you."

"C'mon, JoJo." His smile was smarmy as he tried to regain his dignity in front of the Thompson boys. "Last time was pretty good." *Last time* wasn't referring to the last time I hopped up on the mechanical bull.

Dignity-schmignity. Not on my watch.

"Pretty good?" I scoffed. "You lasted for thirty seconds, and I didn't even get close to finishing. Half of that time was you trying to shove that pencil in your pants into my thigh. Because apparently you have as much trouble finding a woman's vagina as you do in taking 'no' for an answer right now."

"Jesus," he sputtered, his face turning as red as the neon Budweiser sign.

Vaughan looked like he couldn't decide between laughing hysterically and throttling the prick. Cash and Ryman were doubled over, clenching their stomachs as they howled.

"Oh, and here's a tip." I lifted my index finger and wiggled it back and forth. "That's all you need. Not your whole hand. A clitoris isn't a bump you're trying to smooth down by treating your hand like sandpaper." I picked up Vaughan's beer and took a sip. "The next woman stupid enough to drop her panties for you will thank me."

Vaughan choked as he pressed his fist to his mouth to hide his laugh. I grabbed his loosened tie and yanked his mouth to mine in a raunchy kiss. I ended it with a *pop*. Vaughan blinked for a moment as he regained his bearings.

Clint looked like he wanted to vomit.

"Bye now," I said with saccharine sweetness and a fake pageant girl smile.

As soon as Clint's back was turned, Vaughan grabbed the front of my shirt and kissed me again. "I fucking love your crazy ass."

I did end up on the bull that night, but only at the behest of Cash and Ryman when Vaughan told them about the backflip I did the last time I had jumped in the ring.

Vaughan offered to hold my shirt while I threw a few tricks, but I decided to keep my clothes on. While I finished the last of my dinner, he went up to the bar and paid the tab.

The bell on the door jingled as a man and a woman in matching windbreakers strolled in.

Vaughan caught sight of them and tipped his chin. He flagged down Ezra, who exchanged a few words with them before pointing them in the direction of the man passed out in a corner booth.

"They're gonna take him in and sober him up before they question him," Vaughan said quietly as he pocketed his wallet and took my hand, helping me off the stool. "They'll probably want to come to the farm and take a look. We should head back."

Since Vaughan's ride with Ryman and Cash had already left, he hopped in the passenger's seat of my truck for the drive back to the farm.

"Did you ever get up with Chris Griffith?" I asked as I took a left out of the saloon's parking lot. "What did he want?"

Vaughan scrubbed his hand down his face, but it wasn't in frustration. It seemed like... Like relief. "A partnership."

I peeled my eyes off the road just long enough to steal a glance. "What do you mean?"

"They want exclusivity in exchange for a buy-in and expansion. We'll get some of their land on the ranch in Temple and start growing on it out there. Their main grain supplier really fucked them over this season because they sold their land to Vulkon before the harvest. The Griffith's need winter grasses and stored feed for their herd throughout the winter, and they're willing to pay through the nose so that they don't risk losing their supplier with the calving season coming."

I chewed on it for a moment. "Exclusivity like—"

"We don't have to worry about distribution. If we grow it, they buy it. If there's excess that they don't need, we can sell it off to whoever but they always get first dibs. In return, they'll take on some of the debt. I had a lawyer draw up a pretty ruthless partnership agreement." He sighed. "We'll see if they sign."

"That could—"

"That could save the farm," he admitted, though it was a little hesitant.

"What about you?" I blurted out. I had been thinking that, with him being the majority owner, he'd be sticking around. "And your dad—I mean—would the Griffiths own the farm?"

He shook his head. "No. We retain ownership, and the contract can be revisited every five years to adjust for inflation and any additional needs." When I pulled into the farm's entrance, Vaughan pointed to the big house. "Mind stopping there so I can grab something out of the office real quick?"

I let the truck idle while he ran in. He returned a little while later with a stack of paperwork in one hand and some clothes in the other.

"Thanks," he said when he dropped into the seat again.

I pulled away from the house and headed down the dirt path to the cabin. "What's all that?" I asked, tipping my head toward the stack of paperwork.

Vaughan cracked a smile. "It's your loan approval."

The truck brakes screamed as I stomped down on them, staring at Vaughan like he had four heads. "What did you just say?"

He handed me the thick file. "It's a copy of the loan approval. You need to go down to the bank and talk to Bert on Wednesday to go over the terms and sign everything. The appointment's at nine. I checked your schedule to make sure you didn't have any flights."

I thumbed through the pages, dumbfounded. "H-How?"

His smile was cocky and devilish. "I'm quite good at my job, Tiger."

"So, you'll *officially* be my landlord," I said.

"No," he said, and pulled another slip of paper from his pocket.

It was worn and weathered with age. In faded chicken scratch, it read, *Hangar deal is good.*

"The agreement you struck with my dad stands." He tapped the manila folder with his index finger. "This is for your future. You can get a better plane. Get another plane. Bring on another pilot. Expand. Maybe teach if you want to." His hand draped around mine. "And it's yours and yours alone. I'm not your cosigner. I'm not going to be your business partner. I'm *your* partner. Your future and your success belong to you. But I'll be damned if I'm not going to be beside you and cheer you on."

"Vaughan..." My voice faded into the night as we sat in the truck cab. Emotion clogged my throat.

"The line Bert gave you about your credit was bullshit. I looked over your numbers," Vaughan said as he stared into my eyes with an unbreakable gaze. I felt his confidence in my soul. "All you needed was to rework your business plan a little bit. But the potential is there. I believe in you, and the bank does too."

The papers spilled out of my lap and into the floorboard as I leaped across the cab to hug him.

Vaughan's arms wrapped around me, and he squeezed, letting out the first relaxed breath I had ever heard from the world's most uptight man.

"You've been busy today," I murmured into the crook of his neck.

"That's not all," he said, gently pushing me back into my seat so we could look at each other. "You remember Mr. Devers?"

"Your boss—one of the partners I met in Chicago."

He nodded. "I had a conference call with him today."

"Oh."

Sometimes I forgot that Vaughan had been juggling two very demanding jobs. It explained the bags under his eyes, but the demands of it all didn't affect his ferocity in bed. If anything, it made him more insatiable, looking for that stress relief.

"He was calling on behalf of the partners and the board to officially extend an offer to become a partner."

My heart dropped and got tangled somewhere in my intestines. Everything went dull like a blown-out neon light.

"That's—" tears welled up in my eyes "—that's great." I turned away and quickly dabbed at my eyes. "That's ... wow. C-Congratulations."

"Look at me." Vaughan's voice was firm but kind as he tried to coax me out of the shell I was recoiling into.

I didn't look at him. I didn't even turn back to face him. It wasn't that I couldn't cry this time. It was that I could, but I didn't want him to see it. He didn't need to feel guilty for taking a job he'd busted his ass for.

"Joelle." He placed his hand on my back. "*Look at me.*"

Slowly, I turned and faced him.

He crooked a finger under my chin and forced me to look up at him. "Tell me that you want me to be here long term."

The corner of my mouth quivered. "I want you to stay."

"Good," he said with a rising smile. "Because I quit."

Everything went swirly and, for a moment, I wondered if this was what a stroke felt like. "You ... you quit?"

"I quit," he said as if it was the simplest thing in the world. "Technically, I gave my notice and I'll be doing both jobs until the end of the year." He pressed his lips to my forehead. "A lot of early mornings and late nights, but I'll be here." He cupped my cheeks and kissed me, pouring every ounce of his heart into it. "You reminded me what home is."

I rested my forehead against his. Our noses bumped against each other. "You're mine, Vaughan Thompson."

He grinned ear-to-ear. "I'm your what?"

I pecked his lips once more. "You're my home."

40

VAUGHAN

I nearly ripped Jo's seat belt from the side of the truck interior, desperate to get her in my lap. She squealed as I clawed at her hips and thighs, trying to untangle her from the restraint. It wasn't the fun kind of restraint, either. It was the kind that made me turn into an animal because it withheld the one thing I wanted most.

Jo scrambled across the cab and straddled my hips, wrapping her arms around my neck and slamming her lips to mine.

"Please," she whispered when she broke away, sucking in a gulp of air. She wiggled against my erection, desperate for a little pressure between her legs.

"Please, what?" I asked as I wrapped her hair around my fist like a tether and kissed up the side of her neck. My lips lingered on a tender spot beneath her jaw until she was practically boneless, then I nibbled my way up to her ear.

She moaned, breathless and needy. "Please, sir."

I growled as I licked behind her ear, pleased with how she retained what I had asked of her.

Jo trembled in my hands.

I could manipulate her. Mold her. Shape her and twist her as I wrung orgasm after orgasm out of her. She'd never make it easy on me, but that's what I loved about her.

I craved her fight.

"Very good, kitten." I kissed up her jaw until I found her mouth again, then slid my tongue between her lips.

She glowed and settled on top of me, following my lead. A contented sigh escaped her as she submitted to the kiss.

"It's been too long since I've been inside of you," I murmured against the gentle slope of her throat. My palm grazed between her legs, then cupped her sex. "I miss this pussy."

A snarky smile twisted up on her lips. "We had sex the night before we left Chicago. It's barely been over twenty-four hours."

"Too long," I said, and pressed my thumb against her denim-clad cunt, rolling it back and forth. "Five minutes without you is too long. One breath without you is too long. Every day before I met you was one that I was alive, but I wasn't really living. And now that I know what living feels like, there's no way I'm ever going back."

"I love you," she whispered, like a reverent confession.

In my previous marriage, my ex had only cared about what other people thought about us as a marketable unit. How lavish our wedding was. The events we attended together. The number of zeros in our bank account. It was never choosing who we were as human beings.

Everything was different with Jo. Our love had never depended on what we'd gain from the other person. We saw each other through the harshest lens possible, examined our flaws, and chose love anyway.

"I love you more, Joelle." I pressed my lips to hers one

last time, then popped open the door. "Now get your ass inside."

We crashed into the cabin, tripping over strewn clothes and shoes as we tumbled toward the bed.

"On your knees," I bellowed as the back of my legs hit the edge of the bed. I shackled her throat and shoved her to the wood plank floor.

Jo gasped and her hands caught the edge of the frame for balance.

I swung my leg over her head and settled on the edge of the mattress.

She kneeled before me.

My erection throbbed against my pants at the sight of her submission. I unzipped my trousers and pulled out my cock, pumping it with one hand as I cupped her chin. My thumb pressed against her lips until I replaced it with the head of my dick. Evidence of my arousal leaked from the tip, and I swiped it down her cheek. I pried open her mouth with two fingers and pressed them against her tongue.

She didn't move. Didn't dare flinch.

"Suck them," I ordered. "Show me what you're going to do to my cock."

Her pale blue eyes fluttered closed and she teased my fingers with the flat of her tongue.

I groaned deep in my throat as I stroked my cock. "Such a good little whore."

Jo whimpered in delight. The hint of a smile curved her lips as she took my fingers deeper in her mouth. But her mouth wasn't made for my fingers.

Just like her knees were meant for kneeling, her lips were made to be wrapped around my cock.

"You like when I call you that?"

Jo nodded fervently.

I pulled my fingers out and pinched her cheeks until her mouth opened, then I filled it with my dick. I fisted the back of her hair, pushing her to take me further and further until her face was flush against the apex of my thighs and the head of my cock was pressed against the back of her throat.

She gagged and braced her hands against my knees, trying to push away.

"Breathe through it," I growled. "You know how."

Her frantic pulls slowed to calm, steady rhythms as she sucked my dick.

I combed through her hair with my fingers, rewarding her for taking me so well.

"That's it, kitten," I said as I let out a slow, calculated breath. "Such a pretty little slut." I stroked her cheek with the back of my knuckles. "You're by far the most beautiful woman I've ever seen, but you're the most stunning when you're in front of me on your knees."

Jo hummed in satisfaction.

The vibration of her voice skittered up my shaft, instantly setting me on a hair-trigger.

"That's enough." I grabbed her hair and pulled her head back until my shaft fell from her lips. My length bobbed mere centimeters away from her face.

"Please." She panted and gasped for breath. "Please let me make you come."

I grabbed her by the front of her shirt and hauled her up. Her eyes were dark with lust, a deep stormy slate color that reminded me of tornadoes and hurricanes.

"I think you like when I call you names," I said.

Jo grinned from ear-to-ear as she rolled on top of me. I couldn't let that go.

I flipped her onto her back and started tearing at her shirt.

"I think your efforts to get under my skin are best suited for the bedroom, Mr. Thompson," she teased.

My blood went from a simmer to an explosion. "I want you lying with your hands behind your back and your feet flat on the bed. Bring your knees up just a bit."

She moved quickly and obediently.

"Good girl," I said with a touch of sarcasm.

Jo rolled her eyes. "We both know I'm not a good girl."

I chuckled and kissed the inside of her thigh. "Maybe I'm giving you some *aspirational* praise."

She reached down and fisted the collar of my button-up. "Fuck that."

I slammed her wrists to the bed and pinned them down. "So disagreeable."

"Just fuck me already," she hissed, and dug her fingers into my wrists.

Instead of giving her what she wanted, I reared back and eased off the bed.

Jo scowled. "Vaughan—"

"Patience, kitten."

"So help me, I will disembowel you with a rusty spoon if you don't give me an orgasm right now."

I whipped my belt out of the loops, doubled it over, and snapped the layers of leather together. The sound echoed like gun fire. "I said to put your hands underneath you."

Jo clamped her mouth shut at the warning shot and scrambled to obey.

I turned away from her and unbuttoned my shirt. "That's better." The mattress creaked, and I cut my eyes to her. "Did I say you could move?"

Jo barely bit back a growl. "No."

"No *what*?"

"No, *sir*."

I smirked. "That's what I thought."

My clothes fell to the floor, and I pawed around our pile of bags from the Chicago trip until I found my box of toys. When my eyes landed on her again, the breath escaped my lungs.

She was calm, eyes closed, lying exactly as I'd commanded. There was no fear in her. Her fight hadn't been tamed, she simply trusted that I'd take care of her.

"Your cunt is dripping for me," I said in a low rasp and slid a single finger through her folds. "Such a needy pussy." I bent at the waist and let a feather-light kiss dance across her lips. "Pretty little pillow princess."

Jo snarled. "You know better than to call me that."

I offered a merciless laugh, then dipped a single finger into her cunt and traced the opening. "You know better than to talk back to me, kitten."

She thrashed and smacked her palm against the bed when I didn't give her even a moment of relief.

I pulled my finger out of her and spanked her exposed pussy. "Now get on your hands and knees."

Jo keened and scrambled to obey. She knew whatever I had in store was for her pleasure.

I readjusted the pillows, wedging them under her stomach and chest before shoving her face into the mattress.

A low moan escaped her lips. "I love you," she whispered, turning her cheek to steal a peek at the toys I was arranging.

I kissed her tenderly. "I love you, too."

She propped her ass in the air and swayed side-to-side just to tease me.

I swatted her cheek and enjoyed the needy whimper that escaped her lips as I soothed the sting away.

"If I could have you like this forever—on your knees with your ass in the air, obediently waiting for whatever I decide to give you—it wouldn't be long enough." I smoothed my hand up her spine and felt her shudder beneath me.

My cocked ached to sink into her softness and warmth. I had always been a fan of delayed gratification for myself. But for Jo? *Hell no.*

I slid two fingers into her wet pussy and stroked, feeling her flex and clench around me. With my other hand, I rubbed her back in soothing circles and murmured to myself my adoration.

The plug and bottle of lube sitting in the box caught my eye. Jo's arousal had gone from critical to explosive when I'd used it on her in Chicago.

I stole a peek of her face as I pawed around in the box. Her features were completely serene.

"Who does this pussy belong to?" I said in a low, calculated tone as I steadily pumped my fingers in and out.

"You," she whispered, panting in desperation. She widened her knees, silently begging for more stimulation.

"That's right, kitten," I said as I rolled her clit between my fingers.

Her knees buckled and she buried her face in the pillow to muffle her whimper. My cock pressed against her entrance, barely dipping inside. Still, it was enough to have her pleading for me.

I lubed up the plug and pressed it against her hole. Jo shuddered.

"And who does this ass belong to?"

"You," she said, completely breathless.

I shoved it inside of her, and her body immediately closed around the flared base. I slid my fingers back into her pussy, curling up to stroke her tightened walls. Her arousal flooded my fingers.

I yanked the pillows out from under her and flipped her onto her back. "You are so beautiful, Joelle," I murmured, peppering kisses all over her body. My dick was notched in her entrance, but I didn't move any further. *No need to rush.*

I palmed her breasts, teasing and toying with her nipples as she writhed beneath me.

My lips lingered on the scar that streaked across her face like a bolt of lightning as I teased her with the tip of my dick.

Jo squirmed beneath me. Sharp nails left scarlet claw marks on my shoulders and arms as she grappled, trying to get a little more satisfaction and relief. Her fingers dug into my thighs and she opened her legs further.

"Patience, love," I murmured as I kissed up her neck. "Is that toy in your ass making you needy?"

"Yes!" she cried. "Please."

I chuckled as I sat back on my haunches and cupped her cheek, giving it a gentle caress with my thumb. "You poor thing," I said as I rolled my hips, grinding circles against her clit with the base of my shaft. "All hot and bothered. Maybe I should leave you like this. Maybe—" I leaned down and grazed my lips against the shell of her ear "—maybe I should tie you down, lay a vibrator against your clit, and leave you like that while I go on a walk."

"No!" she squeaked and shut her eyes.

I reached between her legs, finding the smooth silicone base peeking out of her cheeks. "Don't worry, kitten. No way would I leave you like this. Not when you look so pretty begging for me."

"Please fuck me, Vaughan," she pleaded.

Slowly, I pressed my dick into her cunt. It slid into her slick heat inch by glorious inch.

Jo's raven hair spilled across the pillows as her head lolled from side to side. Incoherent profanities skipped off her tongue as she dug her claws into my hips and tried to pull me all the way in.

I slid into her and settled, surrounded by pure heaven. "Fuck, baby," I groaned and rocked inside of her, then pulled out and pushed back in. "Your body is a luxury."

I wrapped my hand behind her thigh and drew it up, pressing her knee to her chest before pumping in her again.

The change of angle made Jo cry out. Her chest heaved as she adjusted to the tightness.

"You okay, love?" I said between grunts as I thrust into her over and over.

Jo nodded, but that wasn't good enough.

I paused, buried deep inside of her. "I need you to *say* that you're okay."

"I'm okay," she said in a near panic. "Please don't stop. Give me what I want."

Usually, I would have flipped her over my knee and turned her ass bright red for making such demands. She knew damn well I would satisfy her beyond what she wanted.

But not tonight. Not this time.

"What do you want, kitten?"

"You," she choked out. "You all over me. I want you to know that every piece of me is yours."

Her request was my undoing.

I grabbed the vibrator out of the box and flipped it on, keeping the pressure light against her clit as I drove into her again and again. The headboard cracked against the wood-paneled wall.

Her tits bounced and bobbed with each thrust, and I was

certain she would draw blood from how deep her nails were buried in my skin.

I didn't give a shit.

Jo exploded at the seams in an instant, and I wasn't far behind.

My release flooded her cunt.

"Fuck!" I sputtered.

She squeezed the living daylights out of my cock with her pussy.

I growled and nipped at her breast. "You are so fucking hot." My release dripped from her pussy as I withdrew. "You look beautiful like this," I murmured, my lips pressed against her glistening skin.

"Vaughan, what are you—"

"I don't give a fuck about the sheets getting messy." I pulled her nipple between my teeth and shoved two fingers into her pussy, trapping my release and pushing it deeper inside of her. "But you make me a possessive bastard. I will never be satisfied with anything less than all of you for the rest of our lives."

Jo was still catching her breath. I gave her a moment to descend from the high before reaching between her legs to remove the plug. I gave it a quick tug and drew a moan from her lips.

"Vaughan..." Her hips were grinding into the mattress.

I kissed up her stomach and across her cleavage. "You need another orgasm, Tiger?"

She nodded and whimpered as I tugged on the toy again. My attempt to remove it for her turned into steady, shallow pumps.

"You like that?" I asked.

She nodded.

"Don't make me teach you a lesson for not using your words."

"Yes," she whispered.

I pulled it out a little further than before and let the bulb stretch her.

Jo's eyes rolled back, and the noise that escaped her mouth could only be described as animalistic. My dick thickened instantly at the sound, even though I'd already finished. I repeated the motion, pumping in and out of her ass with the plug, stretching her ring a little more each time.

Her lips moved, but no sound came out.

"Vaughan?"

"Yeah, beautiful?"

"Take me."

It took everything in me to even feign self-control. "You sure?"

Her eyes flashed pale cerulean like spears of ice. "Do I really need to repeat myself? Take me like a fucking snowstorm. I want six to eight inches and I don't want to be able to walk anywhere in the morning."

I grabbed her hips and flipped her onto her stomach, ready to fuck that attitude right out of her. "Hands and knees."

She positioned her body exactly how I wanted her, her legs still trembling from the first orgasm.

I smoothed my palm up her thigh and over her ass, giving her a moment to breathe. I flipped open the lube and gave the plug in her ass a little tug, drizzling the liquid onto the tapered end of the bulb and letting it slide back into her. I repeated it four more times, slowly pulling the plug out more and more with each pump.

When she was stretched and slick, I positioned myself behind her.

"You ready?" I asked.

"Yes," she said in a threadbare voice.

"If you need me to stop, just say so."

Jo nodded. "I trust you."

She mewled as I removed the plug and set it aside.

I lined up behind her and pressed the head of my cock into her hole. My release from the first orgasm trailed down her thigh. It was the most erotic scene I could have imagined.

I grabbed the vibrator and turned it onto the lowest setting before pressing it to her clit. I pushed in a little further, feeling her tight muscle stretch around the thickness of my shaft.

Jo's knuckles were white as she fisted the pillow and used it to stifle her soft grunts. "Shit—"

Her sharp reaction halted my movement, but she shook her head.

"Keep going," she panted. "Don't stop now."

I pushed in a little further. The tightness of taking her like this was excruciatingly blissful. Sweat beaded on our skin. I was almost seated in her. The roiling pleasure neared a crescendo from the entry alone.

"Vaughan," Jo gasped. "It feels ... so good."

"Breathe, kitten," I soothed and pushed all the way in. The heat and pressure were exquisite.

I turned the vibrator up and kept it nestled against her clit. The buzz mingled with our labored breathing.

"You look so fucking sexy like this," I said, and traced her stretched hole with my thumb, pulling a whine from deep in her throat. "Every part of you is heaven."

Jo turned her head, resting her cheek on the pillow. "Fuck me, baby. *Please.*"

I gave her ass a little slap. "Yes, ma'am."

She cried out at the first pull out, then moaned as I pushed back in. We fell into a rhythm of slow, intentional movements, savoring every bit of the connection.

"You are absolutely incredible, Tiger," I murmured as I admired every curve and slope of her body. "Being with you is a fucking dream."

"Pr—probably—" Her voice hitched as I pushed back into her. "Probably more of a nightmare."

"Fitting," I said as I grabbed her hips and slammed into her ass.

Jo screamed.

"Because you scare the hell out of me. You and your beauty. Your tenacity. Your fight. It scares me and entrances me all at once."

"I love you, too," she said, holding tightly to the pillow wedged under her chest.

I stroked her clit with the vibrator, waiting until she was trembling to unleash deep inside of her. She came first, her elbows and knees wobbling as she fought to hold herself up. I wrapped an arm under her stomach and braced her against my body as I came inside of her, slinging a slew of profanities as she clenched around my cock.

Jo's crash was instant. I pulled out of her and cradled her in my arms, drawing the covers over us to keep warm. We could change the sheets in a few minutes.

"Thank you," I whispered as I nibbled on her earlobe.

She nuzzled into the crook of my neck, seeking out heat and comfort. "For what? Letting you fuck my ass?"

I let out a bark of laughter. "That, among other things." I kissed her forehead. "Thank you for not shooting me. And for not cracking my head open with your baseball bat. And for not *completely* running me over with your truck. And for not crashing your plane the minute you had me in it just to spite me."

"You had a lot of near misses," she said with a quiet giggle. "I had so many more diabolical things planned if you didn't get your head out of your ass."

"I'm okay with *almosts* and *maybes*," I said.

I slid out of bed, scooped her into my arms, and carried her outside to the stock tank bathtub on the back porch. I started the flow of hot water and set her in it, then grabbed the caddy of soaps and loofahs she kept near the back door and added an abundance of body wash. We let the water run until we were both thoroughly covered in bubbles. I pulled Jo between my legs and let her recline against my chest.

"Why do you say that? About almosts and maybes?" she asked blissfully.

I sighed in contentment. "I think about all the almosts that we've had. All the near misses. There's really no explanation as to why we never met before this. But regardless of the ass-backward path that brought us together, I'm so fucking glad that it did."

41

JOELLE

"Good morning, Thompsons!" I sing-songed into the Ag Cat's radio. "This is your captain speaking. If you're not already up and at 'em, you've got five minutes to do so. Second pass is coming in fast and low."

Vaughan's voice crackled back. "Morning, Tiger. You sure you're awake enough to be flying?" I could practically hear the self-satisfied smirk behind his voice. "You only went to bed a few hours ago."

"And whose fault is that?" I clipped as I did a loop over the big house, changing my heading in the direction of the west fields. "You're the one who kept me up. You and your—"

"Ay!" That sounded like Cash. "Cool your tits, JoJo. This is an open line and that's my brother."

"Hey, those tits you're talking about belong to me," Vaughan argued.

I did another pass over the house, low enough to make it rattle. "My tits belong to me and me alone. I simply loan them out when it's convenient," I said into the radio.

"Oh for heaven's sake..." Ms. Faith had jumped on to the house's PA system that looped in with my radio. "Y'all cool it with the tit talk."

"Jesus," Ryman groaned. "I do not need to hear Mom say 'tits' ever again."

And just to spite the entire house, Ms. Faith said, "Tits, tits, tits."

It was George's turn to chime in. "Faith, honey, I'm fairly certain it's considered cruel and unusual punishment to make me think about your tits if you're not gonna let me—"

"*Hey!*" Cash, Ryman, Bristol, Vaughan, and I said in a chorus.

"Well, looks like everyone's awake!" I chirped. "See you on the ground, Thompsons!"

The big house shrunk as I climbed in altitude, heading out to the west side of the property. The dirt was freshly tilled and ready for ryegrass seed to be dropped. I'd be doing that flight tomorrow once I changed the apparatus on the belly of the plane, but today was another day of spraying fertilizer.

After the first three passes along the west field, Ryman and Cash appeared, looking like ants on the edge of the dirt. I flew as low as I could to keep from bathing them in the spray.

Farm hands were working to harvest the north field today, and I didn't want to get the fertilizer anywhere near them. The charred earth that separated the Fleming's farm from the Thompson's was still prominent. I had handed over the aerial shots I'd taken of the torched field and wished a slow and excruciatingly painful death upon the shit stains who had planned it and done it.

The lowlife who had set the fire was in the county jail.

He sang like a canary when the feds wrung him for information on who paid him to do it.

Vulkon Incorporated, obviously.

Rumor had it, it wasn't going to be long before that house of cards came crashing down.

Vaughan pulled some strings in the Texas attorney general's office and found out that Vulkon had been under investigation since descending on the state like a plague of locusts. All it took was the right people and departments talking to each other, and the hand of justice became a little more swift.

I couldn't wait to drop kick that smug look off Edward Elling-whatever-the-fuck his name was's face.

I flew north to Alto Springs and refueled before spraying down a field for a farmer getting ready to plant winter greens.

There was a distinct chill in the air that reminded me that, even though we lived in the south, winter was right around the corner.

By the time I made it back to Maren, trucks were pulling away from the fields and heading toward the silos.

Vaughan was waiting, leaning against the billboard pole as I touched down on the runway and skidded to a stop. His crisply pressed slacks, button-up, and vest were out of place on the farm, but it was so distinctly *him* that I couldn't help but find it sexy.

"Hey, you," he said when I climbed out of the cockpit. "How was your day?"

I pecked his lips and strapped on my protective gear to start on the decontamination process. "Good. Yours?"

"Better now that you're on the ground."

I jumped into my rubber boots. "I thought we talked

about the whole 'you being okay with me flying how I want to fly' thing?"

Vaughan chuckled as he leaned against the edge of my tool bench and crossed his arms. "That doesn't mean I won't worry, Tiger."

I danced through the process of purging the tanks, refueling for the morning, and filling out the flight log while Vaughan scrolled through his phone. He had just finished a call with Tamara when I stripped out of my PPE.

"You ready to go?" he asked, pocketing his phone.

I frowned. "Go where?"

"Dinner."

"You want to go out?" I asked, shoving my red rubber boots into the corner and jumping into my flip-flops.

He spun his keys around his finger. "Figured we could get something from Jay's and then go for a drive."

My stomach rumbled immediately. I had been eating in the big house nearly every night since making things more official with Vaughan. We had even spent the night together in his room once.

I still felt a little uncomfortable making my presence a permanent part of the big house, but it was getting better. Having Vaughan beside me made everything better.

I ran into the cabin and filled Bean's food dish, changed into a pair of clean jeans, then jogged out to Vaughan's car. The thing was a dream.

Vaughan shifted in the seat as he pulled out of the farm and onto the road. He was quiet and it unnerved me. There was nothing abnormal about Vaughan being quiet, but there was an undercurrent of tension that left me unsettled.

There was plenty for him to be worried about. The farm. Vulkon. The deal with the Griffith brothers. Things were tentatively good, but it felt like we were holding tight to a trapeze, not sure if the safety net was below us or not.

I reached over and slid my hand under his palm, hooking my fingers around his. "You okay over there?"

"It's all good." He offered a tight smile. "It's, uh..." He sighed and a grin broke across his face. "The Griffiths agreed to the terms I sent over."

"Holy shit!" I squealed and threw my arms around his neck.

Vaughan swerved and I quickly seated myself.

"What was that? Another armadillo?"

He laughed. "No, Tiger, that was all you."

I squeezed his arm. "Baby, that's amazing! What does your dad think about all of it?"

"He's relieved. That deal... I don't think it would have come around if we hadn't gone on that date to the Griffith ranch."

I nudged him with my elbow. "Everything happens for a reason, city boy."

Vaughan just rolled his eyes. "You say that as if you planted that armadillo in the road."

"I saw the thing," I said. "I was just smart enough to swerve."

"Smart ass," he muttered as he pulled into Jay's Gas-N-Go.

We stood in line, waiting our turn for tacos while catching up on everything that had happened while I was in the air.

Vaughan shuffled forward, resting his elbow on a rack of penny candy. "And, uh, the physical therapist gave Dad the all clear to start heading back into the fields with Cash and Ry, so he's happy about that. Can't drive the big rigs, but he's just happy to get out of the house."

"I'm sure mom's happy about that, too," I joked.

Vaughan and I had both started calling Ms. Faith "Mom." Sometimes we still reverted to 'Ms. Faith'. Old habits were hard to break. She had been mom when both of us needed it, and I loved watching her light up every time we said it.

"Yeah, she is. It's gonna be quiet when it's just her and me in the big house during the day."

"You really need a bigger office."

"One step at a time, Tiger." He kissed the top of my head. "For now, I'm just glad the farm is in the clear and the harvest is almost done."

"JoJo!" Jay hollered as he spun his ball cap backward. "Quittin' time already?"

I snatched the grease-soaked bag out of his hand while Vaughan dug out a few bills. "Yep. And it's a damn good thing because I'm starving."

He gave Vaughan a two fingered salute and a reluctant smile.

Our conversation was shattered by the newscast on the TV behind the register. Even Jay stopped chopping up the chorizo on the flat-top grill.

"Holy shit," I whispered, eyes wide as I watched the screen.

Gerald, Edward Ellington's assistant who had been a pestilence around Maren for the better part of a year, was being led away from a Houston hotel room in handcuffs. The screen split and showed a city high-rise being flooded by FBI agents. Computers and physical files were being carried away in droves. And out in the middle of the melee was Edward Ellington being led away in handcuffs.

"You did it," I said as I took it all in.

Phrases like 'arson' and 'intimidation' flashed over

Gerald's dejected face as officers led him to the back seat of a police car. The reporter recounted the months-long investigation into Vulkon's business practices.

After little farmers started standing up to the big bad wolf, Vulkon started looking outside the country for quarry sites. The newscaster rattled off a list of ways the company had violated the Foreign Corrupt Practices Act. Vulkon had made hundreds of illicit payments to high-level officials, hoping they would ignore their country's environmental practices.

The cherry on top was an SEC investigation into misreported earnings.

Decimals are tricky little fuckers.

Vaughan stared at the old-school TV for a moment before a bark of laughter escaped his mouth. He threw his head back and howled until tears formed in his eyes.

"That case wrapped up fast," I said as we exited the Gas-N-Go and headed to the car.

"Almost like someone got really *really* good at knowing the enemy and made a few phone calls." He winked and opened my door.

"Vaughan Thompson," I began, dramatically aghast. "Are you telling me that you're cheating on me with *another* mortal enemy? I'm gutted!"

He slid behind the wheel and leaned over to kiss me. "It was just a little hate-flirt that ended in a few arrests." He pecked my lips. "You're stuck with me for life, Tiger. To love and to loathe from this day forward."

I grinned against his mouth. "You know what they say about enemies."

"What's that, kitten?"

I threaded my hand into his thick, dark hair. "Gotta keep 'em close."

We made it back to the farm in record time. Probably because Vaughan wanted to get my pants off, but I was okay with that. When we hopped out of the car, he took my hand and led me through the cabin. The two of us sat on the back porch and ate brisket tacos as the sun sank below the tree line. I couldn't imagine life being any better than this. It was simple, but no one ever said that simple wasn't good.

Bean curled up beside us and stared resentfully at the empty paper bag from Jay's. I leaned over and rested my head on Vaughan's shoulder.

"Wanna take a walk?" he asked

I groaned and closed my eyes. "You fed me tacos and now you expect me to exercise?"

He snickered. "Just a short one."

Vaughan liked to walk the fields when his mind was burdened. There had been a few nights after the fire that I had woken up to him slipping out into the blackness. He always returned an hour later and cuddled me until dawn.

Maybe that's what made us who were as humans: the ability to reflect on the things that shaped us, knowing that the elements that created us, ultimately, do not define us.

A river can cut through rock, but the rock is the one who defines itself as canyon. It can assign itself a new and greater purpose than simply being a rock that couldn't withstand the water.

We are not pebbles, tossed to and fro at the whim of the waves. We are canyons, forged in pain and elevated in purpose. Tears are not the enemy, because canyons can't be scared by a little rain.

Vaughan took my hand and we started down the path that led to the hangar. It was a short walk that edged along the runway.

Bean trotted beside us for a ways before thinking better

of it. The lazy bag of bones slowly fell behind before he finally cut his losses and turned back to the cabin.

"A lot has changed," I said as we walked beside the strip of blacktop. "You sure you're ready to pack up your life in Chicago and be here full-time?" I bumped his leg with my hip. "Tamara's not gonna know what to do with herself."

He chuckled. "I'm sure she'll be busy with whoever they bring in to replace me." He kissed my head. "I guess I never realized how replaceable I was until I didn't want to be irreplaceable anymore. My ex-wife thought I was replaceable. I'm certainly replaceable to the firm. Life goes on and they don't skip a beat." He looked around at the sunset blazing like a fire over us. "Not here, though."

"We need you." I leaned into his arm. "*I need you.*"

Vaughan stopped in his tracks and faced me. "Say it again."

"I need you. And I want you." I looked down at the asphalt, studying the cracks and ridges. "I've lived most of my life trying to convince myself that I felt safe. And I never really knew what 'safe' felt like until you."

Without a word, Vaughan took my hands and lowered down to one knee. I tried to jerk away, absolutely frightened at the gesture, but he kept me anchored.

"What the hell are you doing down there?" I shrieked.

Vaughan just laughed. "Look at your billboard, Tiger."

I glanced up at the enormous monstrosity that Vaughan had paid out the nose to have erected just to piss me off. Even after we had laid down our swords, the "Fuck You, Jo" message had never changed.

Until now.

Giant red letters spelled out, *Marry Me, Jo.*

"Vaughan—"

In his hand was a small black box with a ring perched inside. The diamond glinted in the evening light.

"The beauty of us is that, not once have we ever seen each other as anything other than exactly who we are. You saw me at my worst and didn't go running. You called me on my bullshit, and didn't cower when I did the same to you."

He pulled the ring out of the box and slid it onto my finger. "Maybe we started this thing seeing the worst in each other, but I know, without a shadow of a doubt, that you see the best in me, too. Because I see the best in you. And I want it every day for the rest of my life."

I laughed as fragments of light reflected off the ring and bounced around us. "Ask me."

Vaughan frowned. "Ask you what?" He turned and studied the billboard, as if he was slightly unsure that the message was correct. "I did."

I shook my head as tears welled up in my eyes. "*Ask* me to be your wife. Don't tell me."

He laughed long and hard. "I fucking love you, Tiger." He cupped my cheeks and kissed me before taking my hands in his. "Joelle Trisha Reed, will you marry me?"

I squealed like a schoolgirl as I jumped into his arms and wrapped my limbs around him. "Yes!"

THE BIG HOUSE erupted in cheers and congratulations as soon as we walked in.

Bristol tackled me to the ground in a bear hug. Cash and Ryman did that weird man greeting where they smacked each other's backs like a half-assed Heimlich maneuver.

George's eyes welled up with tears when I showed him

the ring. In all the years I had known him, not once had I ever seen him cry.

"It was the ring I proposed to his Momma with," he said gently, holding my left hand. He pulled a blue handkerchief from his overalls and dabbed his eyes. "She woulda really liked you."

All I had to offer was a watery smile. I threw my arms around the man who had been more of a dad than my own could have ever dreamed of being.

Ms. Faith tugged me away and pulled me into a hug of her own. "You've always been one of mine, JoJo."

Vaughan tried to cut in and pull me back into his arms, but Cash wedged between us. "You get her all the time now. All I want is a hug."

I squeezed the ever-loving daylights out of him. "I love you, kid."

"Is it weird that we've seen your fiancé's boobs?" Ryman asked Vaughan.

George and Ms. Faith rolled their eyes.

"We might be brothers, but I'll put you in the ground if you talk about my fiancé's boobs again."

"Ooh!" I shrieked. "We should go to the Silver Spur and celebrate! I've got this new trick I wanna work on. It'll be a crowd pleaser for sure!"

Vaughan gave an exasperated sigh, then bent down and hoisted me ass-up over his shoulder.

I giggled and squealed. "Don't make me fight you!"

Everyone else watched in amusement as Vaughan hauled me out of the kitchen. I lifted my head and gave the Thompsons a little wave.

"Bring it on, Tiger." He slapped my ass and headed for the door. "Bring it on."

EPILOGUE
JOELLE

One Year Later

"Vaughan?" I rubbed my eyes, bleary from sleep—*or the lack thereof.* I shifted uncomfortably on the bed and felt around blindly until my hand found his shoulder. I gave him a little shake. "Wake up."

He groaned and rolled over, nuzzling deeper into his pillow. "I already told you ... you're not flying. It's too close to your due date."

Another contraction racked my body, this one more severe than the last. I winced and placed my hand on my *very* pregnant belly, breathing slowly until I could speak.

"So help me, Thompson," I hissed. "If you don't wake up and take me to the hospital right now, I'll haul my Shamu ass into the plane and fly myself there."

Vaughan snapped awake. "What?"

Pain racked my body. I could only respond with a groan.

His eyes widened. "Oh shit."

"Yep," I choked out. "Just what every woman wants to hear."

Vaughan reached over and turned on the bedside table lamp—an actual bedside table, not just a stack of books. Those now had a proper home on a bookshelf. He blinked once, then twice as he watched me go from a state of passive exhaustion to actively pained.

"You're in labor," he mumbled.

"Thank you, Captain Obvious."

"You're in labor!" he shouted as he rocketed out of bed, throwing the covers back and jumping into a pair of slacks. Because *of course* my husband had dress clothes on standby for a 3 a.m. trip to the labor and delivery ward.

I wondered just how pissed he would be when he realized that birthing babies was messy.

Before I could blink, he threw on his trousers, dress shirt, vest, and cufflinks. He had just looped his tie around his neck and fastened it in a neat Windsor knot when the mother of all contractions slammed into me like a freight train.

"Jesus, fuck!" I swore and hunched into the fetal position.

"I've got you," he said hurriedly, slipping into his Oxfords. "Breathe through it. Like the instructor showed us in class."

An involuntary laugh tore out of me. "Yeah, breathing exercises are fine and dandy until it feels like the Hulk is ripping your pelvis in half like a phone book. I'll breathe how I damn well please."

"Bags are already in the car," he said. "I'll call the big house on the way. Up you go." He lifted me with every one of those strapping muscles.

I floated in his arms as Vaughan carried me like a new bride through the dark house.

We had broken ground on our house shortly after he proposed. The cabin was still exactly where it had been. We simply added a three bed, two-bath extension to it. One of those bedrooms was about to have a new occupant.

Downstairs, Bean was curled up in his bed, completely unaffected by his humans' panic.

Dolly—a stray orange tabby cat who had wandered into the construction site and decided it was her new home—wove between Vaughan's feet as he carried me through the kitchen.

The French doors connecting the cabin to the house hung open. Vaughan had been in there, working late in anticipation of his paternity leave. We still called it the cabin, but now it served as our shared office.

The deal with the Griffith Brothers had been a godsend. With their backing, we dug ourselves out of the financial hole the farm had fallen into. Now, Vaughan was planning for next season and hoped to expand.

"Where are the fucking keys?" he grumbled, frantically searching every which way.

"Babe." I tipped my head down. "They're in your hands."

Vaughan stared blankly at them. "Oh."

And with that, he was running again. He practically threw me into the passenger's seat of the car and gunned it. My stable, calculated man had come unraveled at the seams and it was pretty damn hilarious.

The car rattled and shook as we hauled ass toward town.

I braced a hand against the center console and one on the door, trying to mitigate the shock from each bounce. "Is this road paved with *nothing but potholes?*"

Nausea overwhelmed me as my body went to war with

itself to expel the little intruder. Our honeymoon baby wasn't waiting any longer.

Vaughan sped out of Maren and made it to the hospital in record time. We screeched to a halt under the portico.

Headlights pulled up behind us. Cash and Ryman jumped out and hurried over.

"Keys," Ryman said.

Vaughan pitched the car keys to him as he took my hand and helped me out of the car.

My feet hit the asphalt and a contraction slammed into me without warning. I doubled over and nearly hurled.

"Whoa!" Ryman exclaimed, lurching to catch me. He and Vaughan each took a hand to keep me from falling over.

The automatic doors slid open, making way for a security guard as he rolled a wheelchair toward us.

"What are y'all doing here?" I croaked.

Cash shut the truck door. "Saw y'all haul ass off the farm. Figured it was time. Momma's on her way. Dad's waiting for Bristol to drive back from school."

All three of them helped lower me into the wheelchair.

I rolled my eyes and sighed. *As if I couldn't do it my damn self.* Not that I wanted to. Just because I *could* do it myself didn't mean I had to. Especially with the threat of losing last night's dinner growing more and more imminent.

"Y'all know I'm not gonna pop right here," I warned. "It's gonna be a while."

Ryman just shrugged. "It's the first grandbaby. Dad declared it an official day off."

And when George said something, it was gospel.

Ryman jumped in Vaughan's car and went in search of a parking space.

Vaughan wheeled me inside and through the hospital until we made it up to the labor and delivery ward. A whirlwind of medical staff flurried around us for what felt like hours as they poked and prodded me. *Undress. Redress. Sign this form. Initial here. Date there.*

Holy hell, I just wanted it to be over.

Vaughan took the reins on the paperwork. Lord knew I couldn't. Not with little miss fighting her way out of my nether regions.

There was a certain grief that came with finding out I was pregnant. Then there had been another wave of it when we found out it was a girl. Ms. Faith had been irreplaceable throughout my pregnancy—coaching me through the little things like warding off morning sickness and talking me down from an emotional cliff when the insane pregnancy hormones got the better of me. But Vaughan had been there for the nights that I cried over everything I couldn't put into words.

Becoming a mother made me think of my own mom in a new light. It made me wonder about the dark place she had been in to make the choice to remove herself from the world. There were nights that I was petrified that I would feel that same darkness after our baby girl was born.

But I had Vaughan.

I had a man who held me with gentle hands while I cried. I had a man who lifted me up. He didn't tear me down. I had a man who knew what I wanted in life and pushed me to reach for more.

And I knew that, to our baby girl, he would be everything my father wasn't.

The anesthesiologist soon arrived and asked me to sit up so he could place my epidural.

I hunched over the edge of the bed and waited for sweet relief as Vaughan whispered encouragement into my ear.

A maternal calm washed over my entire body. Whether

it was the drugs or something supernatural, I didn't care. The doctor slipped quietly from the room, though I barely noticed. I leaned back against the mattress and closed my eyes to rest while I could.

"You're doing great, Tiger," Vaughan said, parking a chair right next to the bed. He leaned over and kissed my forehead. "I'm so proud of you."

"I haven't even had the baby yet." I let out a deep yawn. The nurse had encouraged me to get some sleep, but part of me wanted to savor these last few hours before two became three.

Vaughan chuckled. "That's not why I'm proud of you." He brushed my hair away from my face and cupped my cheek. "I can't wait for her to be here, but don't want you to forget that we chose each other first."

Taking a nap with an epidural was quite possibly the best sleep I'd gotten in my entire life. It's what I imagined sleeping in those fancy sensory deprivation tanks felt like. Of course, the bliss ended abruptly when my obstetrician came in wearing a smile and said it was time.

"You can do this," Vaughan said as he held my hand in his. I was already sweat-soaked, and it had only been a few minutes of pushing. His other hand was wrapped around the back of my thigh, giving me something to push against.

The sheer number of people in the room was over-whelming. I knew they were there for me and for the baby, but it didn't make it any less scary.

I let my head loll to the side while I tried to catch my breath. When I opened my eyes again at the behest of the doctor telling me to try to push again, Vaughan had moved so that all I saw was him.

"I love you," he said softly. "You're such a badass."

I shook my head, not feeling anything of the sort.

"Almost there!" the doctor said. "One more big push!"

The pain and pressure were excruciating. Drugs be damned—evacuating a human out of a very small space was painful as fuck.

I squeezed my eyes shut and bore down with every ounce of energy I had left.

Oh no. "Did I just shit myself?" I groaned as infantile cries filled the room.

Vaughan didn't say a peep, but I caught a glimpse of a nurse giving him a death glare and miming zipping her lips.

"You did great, Tiger," he said with an ear-splitting grin.

One of the nurses opened the front of my hospital gown and placed a slimy little grubworm on my chest.

But my god, she was beautiful.

Tears flooded my eyes as I held our daughter. Soft grunts escaped her perfect cupid's bow lips. Vaughan's eyes were glassy. His hand was nearly twice the size of her little head. Thick black hair covered the crown.

"She looks like Bristol did," he said when words finally came to him. Vaughan's whisper was reverent. "Wow."

But then her eyes opened, a flash of powder blue like a clear Texas sky. *Mine.*

"Hi, Lo," I said, laughing through the tears. "Nice to meet you. I'm your Momma."

Vaughan tipped my chin up and kissed me, not caring that my breath could have melted a nuclear reactor.

He reluctantly let a nurse take our baby girl off my chest to clean her up and swaddle her like a little burrito, but I could see him keeping a watchful eye on her from across the room.

Keeping the rest of the Thompsons out of the delivery suite was a near impossibility. Luckily, George held them back long enough for us to make it up to the mother-baby floor and get settled.

They piled into the room, carrying flowers and balloons and two overflowing bags from Jay's.

Tacos had never smelled so good. I was famished.

"My stars," Ms. Faith gushed in a whisper, clutching her hands against her chest. Tears filled her eyes as she took in her granddaughter.

I yawned. "Do you wanna hold her?"

She didn't have to be told twice. With a motion honed by years of practice, she scooped Lo out of my arms and cradled her.

"Did y'all pick a name?" Bristol asked.

I had never been so thankful to find out it was a girl because it eliminated about fifty percent of the name choices. That still didn't make choosing one any easier.

We bickered and picked at each other for months over the topic until finally landing on one we both loved. *Two days ago.*

Talk about cutting it close.

Vaughan smiled at me, then turned to his family and nodded. "Loretta June."

"Nice," Cash said with a grin.

"Oh, sweetheart, it's perfect," Ms. Faith said as Lo wrapped five teeny fingers around her index finger.

George leaned over and kissed my head. "You did real good, JoJo. She's pretty like her Momma."

I gave him a tired smile and squeezed his hand.

Everyone hung around until a nurse brought their visit to an unceremonious close. She whisked them away, then helped me to the bathroom so I could learn how to spray down my hoo-hah with a plastic bottle and layer up the world's sexiest mesh granny panties with the human equivalent of puppy pads.

Lo's cries carried through the thick hospital walls. She wanted everyone in the building to know she had the lung capacity of a country singer.

The nurse pushed the bathroom door open to help me get back in bed, and I caught a glimpse of the most beautiful thing I'd ever seen:

Vaughan sitting shirtless on a chair in the corner of the room, gently rocking Lo skin-to-skin.

"Shhh," he soothed and swayed side-to-side while she squalled. "It's gonna be alright." His bulging biceps flexed as he snuggled her closer. "Pretty big day for you, huh? Let me tell you something, Sweet Pea." He dotted her tufts of raven hair with a kiss. "It's okay to cry about it."

BONUS EPILOGUE
VAUGHAN

Six Years Later

The noise in the arena was deafening as Jo and I made our way to our seats. Travis was strapped to my chest in a baby backpack, snoozing away without a care in the world. His little onesie read, *Have a Willie Nice Day,* complete with two screen-printed braids.

We had to make an emergency stop at Buc-ee's for a new onesie for the little man since he decided to go all Picasso in his diaper. He'd managed to turn his entire outfit into a horrifying shade of infant poop orange.

He then launched projectile spit up all over the emergency clothes Jo kept in the car.

Willie Nelson onesie it was.

Lo thought it was hilarious that her baby brother was intent on making us late. Luckily, Cash had gotten to the arena ahead of us and checked Lo in at the registration desk.

Of course, Loretta thought that, at a whopping six-years-old, she was too cool for mom and dad to chaperone her on the arena floor. Uncle Cash was her hero.

We climbed the stairs and made it to our seats just as the MC announced the Mutton Bustin' line up. The man under the white Stetson was none other than Ray Griffith—a former rodeo champion himself.

Jo, Bristol, and Momma had decked out Loretta in a brand-new pair of Wranglers, tiny boots covered in pink sparkles, and a plaid shirt that matched the one Cash had on today. She was perched up on his shoulders for a better view of the action as kid after kid tried to hang on to a woolly sheep for eight seconds as it bounded out of the gate.

Mutton Bustin' was scored similarly to the actual rodeo —a combination of the aggression of the sheep and the time the rider stays on its back. But given that all the contestants were between the ages of five and seven, it was a hell of a lot more adorable.

I draped my arm around Jo's shoulders and tucked her into my side. "You want me to take him?" she asked.

Jo and I still had the circles under our eyes that came from a newborn sleep schedule, but we were managing. Having Mom right next door was a lifesaver.

Jo hadn't stopped flying, but she had brought on a new pilot to take over while she was on maternity leave. Waking up every three hours to feed Travis was less than optimum when it came to being rested enough to safely operate an aircraft.

"Lo hasn't gone yet, has she?" Ryman asked as he dropped into the seat beside Jo.

Jo shook her head. "No, she's after that little punk in the blue western shirt." When she realized that the parents of said "little punk" were probably close by, she lowered her voice. "She's gonna kick his ass."

We sat and watched as another kid hopped onto the back of a new sheep.

"Geez!" Jo shouted, unable to hold it in. "What are they feeding that beanstalk? He's gotta be at least twelve. Someone check his birth certificate!"

The poor kid was probably just tall for his age.

"It's just for fun, Tiger," I said and put my arm around her again—tighter this time. There were things I was still learning about my wife. Like how she was *really* fucking competitive.

No wonder we got trapped in a cycle of trying to one-up each other when we first met. She couldn't stand to lose. The first Thompson family game night had also been the last after an argument between Jo and Ryman over the balance of his Monopoly money nearly turned into a brawl.

Now, they were chummy as ever.

"Gimme," Ryman grunted as he reached over Jo for Travis.

I looked down at the baby who was *finally* sound asleep. "Hell no. Rule number one: never wake a sleeping baby."

"I haven't seen him all week," Ryman argued.

"Get your own. He's mine."

Jo rolled her eyes and unstrapped the baby carrier, gently lifting Travis out. "If he starts screaming, he's your problem."

"Nah. Little man won't cry for me," Ryman said with a grin as he took Travis and cuddled him against his chest. "Cash is Lo's favorite, and I'm this guy's." He reached down and grabbed the baby-sized noise-canceling headphones from the overflowing diaper bag.

Jo snorted. "Uh, no." She pointed to her chest. "I have the boobs. I'm his favorite."

We all bobbed our heads in agreement.

"Ooh!" Jo squealed, pointing down into the area. "Lo's up!"

The three of us stood. A few rows down, mom and dad watched with Bristol and her boyfriend. Our eyes locked on the JumboTron as Cash helped Loretta get settled on top of a fluffy sheep named Blizzard.

Her favorite game as of late had been "rodeo."

After family dinners at the big house, Lo would politely demand that one of us be the bull. She'd climb on our backs and we'd try our best to buck her off.

Cash made sure her helmet was on tight and gave her a thumbs up as the assistants shuffled the ornery little sheep to the front of the gate.

Ray Griffith looked at his notes, then spoke into the microphone. "Up next, number eighteen, six-year-old Loretta Thompson from Maren, Texas!"

There was polite applause throughout the arena as the cameras showed Lo holding on to the back of that sheep like it owed her money.

The gate flew open and Blizzard took off like a bullet out of a gun. Ryman was counting the seconds while Jo screamed her head off, cheering our baby girl on.

The sheep nearly made a whole loop around the arena, whipping and whirling, before Loretta tumbled off.

"Seven-point-nine seconds!" Jo shrieked as she threw her arms in the air. "Holy shit! Did you see that?"

I laughed. "I saw it, Tiger."

"And that sheep was bouncing! She's gonna get a hella good score!"

Cash jogged out into the arena to check on Lo. He knelt beside her and exchanged a few words before helping her up. Wide smiles painted both of their faces.

"Did'ya see me, Momma?" Lo squealed as soon as we met up with her and Cash at the bottom.

Jo dropped to her knees and squeezed the ever-loving daylights out of her. "I did! You were awesome, sweet pea!"

"Uncle Cash said I'm definitely gonna win."

"Did he?" I lifted her into a bear hug and spun her around. "I'm proud of you, kiddo."

"Ya think I can do barrel racing next year?" she asked, all wide-eyed and hopeful. There was no doubt that she got her tenacity and determination from Jo.

She rarely took "no" for an answer, which made parenting ... interesting.

I had a house full of tornadoes, and I couldn't have been luckier.

The leaderboard shifted as the next two scores were calculated. Lo was in the lead.

Ryman had met up with the rest of the Thompson clan and that boy Bristol insisted on seeing, and joined us at the arena wall.

"Gramma!" Lo squeaked, bouncing up and down in her boots.

Mom pulled Lo into a hug, "You did so good!"

"Did'ya see me?"

She laughed. "I did! Me and Gramps and Aunt Bristol and her friend all watched. You were awesome!"

Ryman jumped in with a fist bump for Lo as he held Travis with one arm. "You kicked ass, Lo Lo!"

I cut my eyes to him. "Dude, you can't say 'ass' in front of kids."

Jo laughed. "Whoops."

The last of the riders did their runs and a heavy quiet fell over the crowd as the judges tabulated the scores. We waited anxiously to see if Lo's name fell from number one.

First Place - Loretta Thompson - Maren, Texas (6) flashed on the screen, and we collectively lost our shit.

The eight of us screamed at the top of our lungs as Ray Griffith announced the winning score. Cash dropped Lo onto his shoulders and held her hands up like the victor she was.

Jo shoved two fingers in her mouth and wolf whistled while Cash took her to the stage. "That's my baby!"

Motherhood looked good on her. She was fierce and protective. Loving and sacrificed more than I could have ever asked. She was fearless in letting our kids live life. Loretta begged daily to go flying, and now she'd been bitten by the rodeo bug.

These women were the reason I was going gray. Only time would tell what fresh hell Travis would put us through when he got older, but I didn't care. I'd take it in stride.

Jo slid into my side, wrapping her arm around my hips as we watched our girl get the Mutton Bustin' Championship belt buckle.

There was no way we were ever getting that thing off her. She'd probably sleep in it.

Over the last eight years, having a family had gone from the last thing on my mind to the only thing on my mind.

And it was so damn good.

AUTHOR'S NOTE TO THE READER

Dear Reader,

Ten.

Holy fuck knuckles. Ten books. I didn't go into this one thinking I would write a "big shiny book" for number ten, but by golly, I think we did.

It's been a hot minute since I wrote an enemies-to-lovers story, and I knew I didn't want to hold anything back. Their fight, their love—I wanted it to be larger than life in their small little town.

I'm a planner at heart, so when it came to writing this book, I had everything down in my outline. Everything except the dedication.

Usually, that's one of the first things I figure out. I look at each book as a love letter. A romance, sure, but a love letter to someone. I usually know who I'll dedicate the book to before I write the first sentence, but not this one.

It could have been written for a younger me who never cried. It could have been written to the woman I am now, who learned the hard way that emotion is not a lack of strength. I could've dedicated to everyone who cheered me on over the last few months as I plunked and plodded away on this project (and you'll see them mentioned in the acknowledgments).

But all those dedications failed, so I simply settled for, "Nothing held back."

Not with this book, and not in life.

XO,

—Mags—

PS. Because you're super cool, let's be friends!

Follow me on Instagram @authormaggiegates

Want to spread the love? Tell others what you thought of this book by leaving a review on Amazon and GoodReads (I'll do a literal happy dance if you do)!

ACKNOWLEDGMENTS

To Mr. Mags: I still remember us concocting this book idea over dinner at the townhouse. It feels like it's been five minutes and fifty years all at once. I'm so glad you kept telling me to "write the crop duster book." Jo and Vaughan wouldn't be here without you. I love you. Don't ever doubt it.

To Jordan Loft: Thank you for your editing eagle eyes and graphic design prowess! Austin Hale's book might be shorter, but let's be honest, I shouldn't be making any promises there.

To Sprinters R Us: You all are amazing people with dirty minds. Thanks for being the best sprinting/study/work-group! I am so grateful to you all! Thanks for cheering me on and helping me stay on track! Stay smutty, my friends.

To My ARC Team: You guys are the greatest! Your excitement and support astound me daily. You make me feel like the coolest human being alive. I'm so grateful for each one of you. Thank you for volunteering your time and plat-forms to boost my books!

To My Author Pals: You lift me up on a daily basis. Thank you for giving me a seat at the table.

To My Readers: You all are the reason I keep writing books. I'm convinced there's no greater group of people in the world than my real-life poker club. Y'all are amazing human beings! Thank you for loving these characters and getting as excited as I do about their stories! Thank you for your hype, encouragement, and excitement!

To Lindsay: This is the circle. You're in.

ALSO BY MAGGIE GATES

Standalone Novels

The Stars Above Us: A Steamy Military Romance

Nothing Less Than Everything: A Sports Romance

Cry About It: An Enemies to Lovers Romance

100 Lifetimes of Us: A Hot Bodyguard Romance

Pretty Things on Shelves: A Second Chance Romance

The Beaufort Poker Club Series

Poker Face: A Small Town Romance

Wild Card: A Second Chance Romance

Square Deal: A Playboy Romance

In Spades: A Small Town Billionaire Romance

Not in the Cards: A Best Friend's Brother Romance

Betting Man: A Friends to Lovers Romance

The Falls Creek Series

What Hurts Us: A Small Town Fake Engagement Romance

What Heals Us: An Age Gap Romance

What Saves Us: A Small Town Single Mom Romance

The Griffith Brothers Series

Dust Storm: A Single Dad Romance

Downpour: A Grumpy Sunshine Romance

Fire Line (Coming 2024 - Preorder Now!)

ABOUT THE AUTHOR

Maggie Gates writes raw, relatable romance novels full of heat and humor. Maggie calls North Carolina home. In her spare time, she enjoys daydreaming about her characters, jamming to country music, and eating all the BBQ and tacos she can find! Her Kindle is always within reach due to a love of small-town romances that borders on obsession.

For future book updates, follow Maggie on social media.

facebook.com/AuthorMaggieGates

instagram.com/authormaggiegates

tiktok.com/@authormaggiegates

Made in the USA
Coppell, TX
27 September 2024

37765469R00270